BEFORE
THE
DAWN

East End Series:

East End Trouble
East End Diamond
East End Retribution

Harper Grant Mystery Series:

A Witchy Business
A Witchy Mystery
A Witchy Christmas
A Witchy Valentine
Harper Grant and the Poisoned Pumpkin Pie
A Witchy Bake-off

BEFORE THE THE DAWN

DETECTIVE KAREN HART SERIES

D.S. BUTLER

THOMAS & MERCER

Text copyright © 2024 by D. S. Butler
All rights reserved.

Published by Thomas & Mercer, Seattle

www.apub.com

Amazon, the Amazon logo, and Thomas & Mercer are trademarks of Amazon.com, Inc., or its affiliates.

ISBN-13: 9781662512247
eISBN: 9781662512254

Cover design by @blacksheep-uk.com

Cover image: ©Matilda Delves / Arcangel; ©Tim Parker / Getty Images

Printed in the United States of America

For Fuzz, a dear friend.

Prologue

As DC Sophie Jones drove to the meeting place, a catchy Bruno Mars song played on the radio. Sophie was too caught up in her thoughts to sing along as she usually did. She'd cancelled dinner plans with Harinder tonight, but it would be worth it.

She allowed herself a small smile as she turned on to Kesteven Street.

It was eight p.m. and the area was quiet. The small shops were shut, and the lights were off.

Sophie felt the first pang of nerves. She turned off the music and slowed the car to a crawl.

She must have taken this route over a hundred times for her weekly shop at the Tesco store, but this time, instead of turning right, she continued to the traffic lights and took the next turn on to Great Northern Terrace. Today she had something more important planned than food shopping. Something that would make people sit up and take notice. At least she hoped so.

Sophie frowned as doubts dampened some of her excitement. She hadn't told Harinder why she'd had to cancel their date. Perhaps she should have explained and told him where she was going. But no, he would have tried to talk her out of it, and she couldn't let that happen. She needed this.

Sophie was the most junior detective on her team, something she was reminded of at every opportunity. Usually, she tried to shrug off any comments or jokes, but this week at work had been particularly hard. In the middle of a team meeting, DC Rick Cooper had called one of her ideas naive. He hadn't meant to hurt her feelings. But that hadn't made his words hurt any less. He clearly thought she was inexperienced, even after they'd been working together all this time. He didn't really see her as an equal. None of them did.

Except Karen. The detective sergeant did try to be supportive, but even she had looked at Sophie as though she'd grown two heads when Sophie had enthusiastically proposed introducing a new digital filing system. But Sophie had persevered and eventually convinced the team. The new set-up functioned flawlessly. But no one appreciated the effort Sophie had put in. They just took her hard work for granted.

Detective Inspector Morgan always seemed to look for the nearest escape route whenever Sophie tried to tell him about a recent book or article she'd read on criminology. And as for DCI Churchill . . . Sophie had given up approaching him with her ideas about increasing efficiency in the department.

Sophie sighed. Her career trajectory was not going as planned. She loved her job and had been involved in some exciting and dramatic cases. And unlike most of the other people in the department, she loved paperwork. Filing systems, coding, organisation. She couldn't get enough of it.

Most of the time, she was assigned the extra paperwork – which she didn't mind – and the boring, trivial cases – which she did.

Today she'd been sent out to investigate a spat on social media. The team had dealt with nasty incidents of harassment and stalking in the past, so Sophie understood why the complaint needed to be investigated. But, as she had feared, the incident turned out to be a couple of daft keyboard warriors calling each other names. In the end, it had been like listening to a playground argument between two seven-year-olds demanding to use the police as a referee.

Sophie considered social media fights to be like road rage. Get people behind a screen or a wheel, and they thought the rules didn't apply to them anymore. They believed they were entitled to say anything they wanted to.

She knew the small cases were part of her job. She just wished there weren't so many of them. But tonight . . . tonight held promise, despite the fact she was working off the books. She'd stumbled across something very interesting. Potentially a huge case. Even though it wasn't official yet.

She smiled, imagining Churchill's face when she brought the information to him. He loved getting kudos for his team, and this could potentially be bigger than anything they'd worked on before.

They'd all be so impressed, she thought as she drove over the level crossing. She wondered what Karen would say. Karen always made time for Sophie's theories and ideas, even if she didn't agree with them. And she didn't look at Sophie like she was stark raving mad. At least, not very often.

The streetlights were further apart, making the road ahead even darker. For the second time, Sophie felt a pinch of doubt. Her confidence, brought on by the excitement of unearthing a massive case, suddenly gave way to nerves.

Karen would tell Sophie this was a silly plan.

She wouldn't approve of Sophie meeting someone she knew next to nothing about in an isolated area like this, especially without informing anyone else of what she was doing.

Sophie parked in front of a row of units. She'd been so determined to carry this out by herself. But now, sitting here in the quiet, she felt unsure. Was she really experienced enough to tackle this alone? Worry began to gnaw at her confidence, leaving her with an uncomfortable sense that she might be in over her head.

The headlights illuminated two shopfronts. Directly ahead was a store displaying party costumes. A clown mask leered at her from the window. She shuddered. Clowns gave her the creeps.

Despite her anxiety, she turned off the engine, plunging the area into near-total darkness. She hesitated, reluctant to leave the warmth and safety of the car.

She checked her phone had signal, slipped it back in her pocket, and then slowly got out of the car, her heart thudding. She couldn't shake the feeling that something was watching her, waiting to pounce. The clown mask wasn't helping.

She glanced around nervously, taking in her surroundings. The shops were closed and there were no other cars in the parking area. She attempted to breathe deeply and calm her racing thoughts, but a sense of unease settled over her like a cold shadow.

Sophie gave herself a mental shake. She had come this far; there was no point backing out now. She'd be fine. Hadn't she been in more dangerous situations than this and come away unscathed? She patted her pocket again, making sure she had her phone.

It was a cold night, and the wind had picked up, sending dry leaves swirling across the tarmac. To her right, behind a metal fence, was the train line. The meeting place was in the unit closest to the track.

She walked away from her car, past a couple of half-filled skips, her breath misting in front of her, and wished she was safely inside a cheerful, cosy restaurant with Harinder instead of this cold, deserted car park.

There was no sign of the person she was supposed to be meeting. She walked past the party supplies shop and the printing business next to it. Both were closed.

She made her way towards a large mechanic's workshop with a green roller shutter door. Above it was a white and green sign:

Tony's Workshop. There were two small windows either side of the entrance. No lights were on, and the door had been padlocked.

She checked the time. It was after eight now. They should be here at any moment. She stomped her feet, trying to get warm.

Sophie wasn't dressed for the November night. The cold air made her cheeks tingle and her nose run. She sniffed. It would be worth it. If she got the information she needed tonight, then tomorrow, she could present it to the team and bask in their admiration.

She tried to fight the wave of trepidation that threatened to overwhelm her. She had been so eager to investigate, to prove to her colleagues that she could handle something like this alone, but now she was regretting her decision. She looked around again, her eyes adjusting to the darkness. The only sound was the distant hum of traffic from the A1434 and the wind whistling around the buildings.

Where was her contact? Had they been held up, or changed their mind about the meeting?

She hunched her shoulders against the cold and stepped forward, her footsteps echoing in the stillness of the night. The low rumbling of an approaching train startled Sophie. She turned to see it clatter along the tracks. The light from the passenger cars made the shadows around her seem even darker.

She watched until it disappeared from view, then spent the next few minutes pacing, trying to keep warm. She gritted her teeth.

If they didn't show up soon, she'd head home. It was infuriating to think she'd passed up dinner with Harinder for this. She hadn't told him what she'd been planning, because he would have told her to take it to Karen. He didn't understand. How could he? Harinder worked in the tech lab, and everyone thought he was a marvel. He already had their admiration.

People at work sometimes called him Harry – as in Potter – in awe of his wizard-like skills in the lab. He could extract data from damaged equipment, recover pixelated images, and answer practically any scientific question that anyone asked. He didn't know what it was like to not be valued by his colleagues.

He'd earned their respect long ago. Sophie intended to do the same now. She deserved it.

Hearing a scraping nose, she spun around.

'Hello? Who's there?'

But there was no reply, only a rattle as the wind buffeted the roller door of the mechanic's workshop.

She tensed, noticing again how dark and isolated the area was.

Why had she thought it was a good idea to tackle this alone?

Rick had been right – she was naive. Sophie's cheeks burned. She'd been so looking forward to lording it over Rick when she brought the discovery to the team, that she'd overlooked the basics.

What had Karen told her last week? *Being a police officer is about being part of a team. It's not about getting individual praise or awards; it's about working together to achieve a common goal . . .*

A fierce gust of wind made the workshop door rattle again. Instinctively, Sophie stepped back.

Coming here had been a mistake.

She fumbled in her pocket for her mobile, intending to call Karen.

She knew exactly what Karen would say.

Don't put yourself at risk.

But before she raised the phone to her ear, there was another sound. Footsteps this time.

She spun around, her breath quickening in fear as she looked desperately for the source of the noise. But she was looking in the wrong direction.

She didn't see the figure dressed in black emerge from the darkness.

But she felt the strike.

Something solid slammed into the back of her head with a thud. The impact sent her lurching forward, and she sank to her hands and knees.

Before she could react, another blow sent an explosion of pain through her skull. Her vision blurred and her head throbbed. Sophie wanted to scream but couldn't draw enough breath. Her attacker towered above her, arm lifted as if ready to strike again.

She was powerless.

She was going to die. And no one knew she was here.

Sophie scrambled forward, trying desperately to escape her attacker. The third hit knocked her sideways, and she collapsed, her face scraping the cold tarmac. As darkness threatened to envelope her, she struggled against it, tried to speak. But it was no use.

Sophie's assailant stood over her, watching until she stopped moving altogether.

Chapter One

Karen sat at the small dining room table beside Mike and tried to think of something to say to break the awkward silence. She'd never been great at small talk.

Mike and his stepfather, James, didn't seem bothered by the lapse in conversation. They were concentrating on the food: chicken and leek pie, mashed potatoes, and peas.

Mike's mother, Lorraine, on the other hand, had barely touched her dinner, instead preferring to subject Karen to rapid-fire questions: *How long have you been in the police? Do you intend to retire early? Do you own your house or rent? Did you grow up in the area?* Karen expected to be asked her shoe size next, but Lorraine paused and watched Karen instead, as though gauging her reaction. Karen shifted uncomfortably, realising this was how it felt to be on the other side of the interview table.

It was the first time the two women had met, and the meeting wasn't going as well as Karen had hoped.

Lorraine's eyes were cool and appraising.

Karen swallowed a mouthful of food and returned her gaze. 'The pie is lovely.'

Lorraine gave a tight smile. 'Chicken and leek *is* Mike's favourite.' She sipped her wine then said, 'Could you pass the potatoes?'

'Of course.' But as Karen reached for the dish of potatoes, her fork slipped and hit her plate with a clatter, and then she accidently nudged the serving spoon in the bowl of peas, sending a few rogue peas shooting across the embroidered tablecloth. She muttered a curse, drawing a disapproving look from Lorraine.

'Sorry.'

'It's only a few peas,' James said with a smile, before shovelling in another mouthful of potatoes.

'I'm not sure why you still use this tablecloth, Mum,' Mike said. 'It's not very practical.'

'I happen to like it.'

'It is very pretty,' Karen said, hoping to make amends. She was making a real effort tonight because Mike spoke fondly of his mother. For many years, Lorraine had brought Mike up alone, so they were understandably close.

Without asking, Lorraine leaned over to put more peas on James and Mike's plates. She then did the same with the potatoes, and said to Karen, 'I take it you don't want any more? Us ladies have to watch our weight, don't we?'

Karen clamped her mouth shut to prevent a sharply worded retort.

What a cheek! All right, so maybe her trousers *were* a little tight at the waist. Too many dinners out with Mike and perhaps too many glasses of wine were responsible. That was part of the reason she wasn't drinking tonight. That, and she wanted to keep a clear head for work tomorrow.

Karen was very tempted to reach over and take a huge scoop of mashed potatoes, but she didn't want to rock the boat. Mike wanted her to get along with his mother. Karen was starting to think that would not be easy.

Lorraine's eyes gleamed, and Karen suspected she was trying to provoke her, trying to get a reaction.

Perhaps Lorraine was very protective. Maybe she didn't consider Karen good enough for Mike, and if that was the case, it was unlikely to be anything personal. There probably wasn't a woman alive she'd consider good enough for her precious son. In the circumstances, Karen decided to take the high road and ignore the jibe.

'What do you do, James?' Karen asked, eager to move the conversation on.

'I work in logistics for an electronics firm. I make sure things get where they're supposed to.'

'UK-based?'

'Well, actually,' James began, putting his knife and fork together on one side of his now-empty plate.

But Lorraine cut in. 'Really, no one wants to hear about your job, James.'

'Well, Karen did ask—'

'She's merely being polite.'

'No, really, I'm interested,' Karen insisted, earning a glare from Lorraine.

James explained the set-up of his company and the recent international expansion, and Karen smiled politely and asked questions at the appropriate points.

As Lorraine looked extremely miffed, Karen attempted to draw her into the conversation. 'What do you do, Lorraine?'

'I'm retired now. I worked long enough. I had to put in long hours and make lots of sacrifices bringing Mike up alone. It wasn't easy. I've earned my retirement.'

'I can imagine.'

'I'm not sure you can.' Lorraine smiled, perhaps to soften her words. 'It's impossible to know what it was like unless you've been through it. Mike told me you had a child.'

Karen held her breath. Whenever anyone mentioned Tilly, she felt a hollow sensation accompanied by a tight pain in her chest. Karen's daughter and husband had been killed in a car accident caused by a member of a criminal gang, and the true cause of the crash had been covered up by corrupt police officers. Although a few years had passed since she lost them, the pain hadn't eased.

The raging anger had lessened, but the hurt was still fresh and raw. She now realised it would always be there. Therapy had helped her accept it, but there was nothing she could do to take away the pain of losing the two most important people in her life. Acceptance meant she could live an ordinary life, but the loss would always be with her.

Mike had lost a child, too. His son had drowned. The tragedies they'd experienced gave them a bond. An understanding. He knew what it was like to survive such a devastating, life-altering blow. Somehow, they both managed to carry on. One day at a time, creating a routine and a new life together.

Karen's mouth was dry. She wouldn't be able to reply without her voice cracking. She reached for her glass of water, forcing herself to swallow past the lump in her throat.

But Lorraine wasn't waiting for a response from Karen. She continued, 'But you had a husband. It's really not the same as trying to bring a child up alone.'

'No.' Karen had suddenly lost her appetite. She put her knife and fork together.

'It was hard, but it was worth it,' Lorraine said. 'Look how my darling boy has turned out.'

Mike grimaced. 'Mum, don't—'

'Nonsense. I'm proud of my son. I'm allowed to be proud, aren't I, Karen?'

'Yes.' Karen gave an awkward smile and took another gulp of water.

'This is lovely wine,' Mike said, raising his glass.

'I got it from Waitrose,' James said. 'It's called Apothic, I think. I don't know much about wine, except that I like it.' He gave Karen a wink and chuckled.

'Honestly, James,' Lorraine muttered.

'You chose well,' Karen said. 'We've had that before. We prefer red wine.'

Lorraine looked at her sharply. 'Oh, really. I thought you preferred beer, Mike?'

'I like both,' he said with a shrug. He nodded at the empty plates. 'Shall I clear the table?'

'No, I'll do it,' Lorraine said, picking up her plate and then looking meaningfully at James.

He got the message and scrambled to his feet. 'Oh, yes. I'll help.'

'It's going well, isn't it?' Mike asked as soon as his mother and stepfather had left the room.

'It's been interesting getting to know them,' Karen said, thinking that if this was Mike's idea of going well, she'd hate to know what going badly was like.

Before they'd arrived, Mike had warned Karen his mother could be a little difficult. At the time, Karen hadn't really understood what he meant, but now she had a much better idea. His mother was hard work.

'Don't you look at me with those puppy-dog eyes!' Lorraine's voice carried from the kitchen.

Karen's eyes widened with surprise, thinking she was talking to James, before remembering that Sandy, Mike's dog, was in the kitchen.

'I'd better make sure Sandy isn't getting under their feet,' Mike said, getting up.

Left alone, Karen took the opportunity to check the time on her mobile phone. Almost eight thirty. They'd booked a taxi for nine thirty, so she only had one more hour to get through.

Lorraine came back into the room, and her face fell at the sight of Karen's mobile.

'We don't usually use our phones at the table.'

'Sorry,' Karen said, slipping the device into her pocket.

Mike and James came back into the room.

'Ta-da!' James said, putting a bowl of sticky toffee pudding with vanilla ice cream in front of Karen. 'Mike said you'd like some.'

'Absolutely,' Karen said. 'Thank you. It smells delicious.'

'I wasn't sure if you were on a diet,' Lorraine said. 'I'm trying to avoid sugar.'

'Good for you, but I can't resist sticky toffee pudding,' Karen replied.

'So I see,' Lorraine said slowly.

Karen ignored the implied judgement and got stuck into the dessert. It was as delicious as it looked.

'Smashing,' James said after he'd finished, leaning back in his chair and patting his stomach, earning him a chastising look from Lorraine.

'That was absolutely gorgeous,' Karen agreed. 'Did you make it yourself?'

'No,' James said. 'Supermarket.'

'I would've made one from scratch,' Lorraine said quickly. 'I usually like to, but you didn't give me much notice about tonight.'

'Well, it tasted as good as home-made to me,' Karen said. 'And why waste time in the kitchen if you don't have to?'

'I don't consider cooking food from scratch to be a waste of time. I just didn't have enough prior warning.' It seemed nothing Karen said tonight would be taken without offence.

'We didn't have to get together tonight, Mum,' Mike said. 'In fact, it was you who suggested dinner today.'

Lorraine started to protest, but Karen's mobile interrupted her, ringing with a shrill chirping tone. Lorraine shook her head disapprovingly.

'Sorry,' Karen muttered as she pulled the phone from her pocket.

'Do you need to take the call?' Mike asked. 'Is it work?'

'I'm not on duty tonight.' She didn't recognise the number. Probably an unwanted sales call. She switched the phone to silent and apologised again.

'That was a fantastic dinner. Thank you both,' Mike said, standing up. 'We'd better make a move.'

Karen frowned. The taxi wasn't due for at least another half an hour, but she wasn't about to argue.

Lorraine hadn't warmed to her, and if Karen was honest, she didn't much like the older woman either. Still, it was early days. Perhaps Lorraine was just out of her comfort zone.

Mike collected Sandy from the kitchen, and they said their goodbyes. Outside, Mike waited until they were walking along the street before asking, 'So, how do you think it went?'

'Well,' Karen began carefully, 'I suppose it could've been worse. I could've spilled the gravy rather than the peas.'

Mike laughed. 'She's not normally like that. So fussy, I mean. I think she was trying to impress you. She was nervous, too.'

Karen shot him a sceptical look, but kept her thoughts on Lorraine to herself. 'I think James liked me.'

'Yes, he's a good bloke. Been like a father to me.'

'You don't call him Dad, though?'

'No.'

'What about your real dad? You never mention him.'

The shutters came down. Mike looked away. 'I don't remember him. According to Mum, I've not seen him since I was three years old.'

'You don't remember him at all?'

'No.'

'Do you know anything about him? Where he might be now?'

Mike shook his head. 'I'd better give Gary a ring.' Gary was a local chap who ran a one-man taxi business from his home. 'I'll let him know to pick us up at the pub instead of Mum's house.' He pointed to the White Hart, just ahead of them.

As Mike dialled, Karen pulled out her own phone and noticed that the person who'd called earlier had left a message.

She checked her voicemail.

'Karen, it's Harinder.'

That was odd.

She got on well with Harinder, but he only ever called her about work. And she wasn't on duty.

As the message continued, Karen suddenly stopped walking. Blood froze in her veins.

'That's sorted,' Mike said, turning around, noticing Karen had stopped moving. 'Gary will pick us up in ten minutes from outside the White Hart. Are you all right? You look pale.'

Karen shook her head. 'It's Sophie. She's been attacked.'

Chapter Two

Karen had asked the taxi driver to take her directly to the hospital. Though Mike had wanted to go with her, she'd asked him to go home. Sophie was in ITU. Her parents and Harinder were both at the hospital already. They wouldn't want too many people there at a time like this.

'If you're sure,' Mike had said doubtfully.

'I am,' Karen had replied. 'I'll update you as soon as I hear anything new.'

She dashed across the car park, the air cold and stinging her cheeks. The thudding in her chest hadn't let up since she'd listened to Harinder's voicemail.

She went through the main entrance, which was far quieter than A&E, and walked the long and sterile corridors toward ITU. Near the security door that led into the intensive therapy unit, she spotted Harinder.

He was leaning against the wall and staring at the floor dejectedly.

'Is there any more news?' Karen asked as she got closer.

He looked up, his face tense and etched with worry. 'Karen, thank you for coming. I feel like I'm in a nightmare. Do you know what she was doing there? Was it work? The officer on duty said he had no idea.'

Harinder's eyes were misted with tears. He was trying to make sense of it, trying to use his high IQ to solve the puzzle, but perhaps for the first time, his brilliant mind wasn't giving him the answers he needed.

Beyond Harinder, Karen could see Sophie's dad sitting on a moulded chair that had been bolted to the floor. He was leaning forward, resting his elbows on his thighs with his head in his hands. She guessed Sophie's mother was at her daughter's bedside.

'No, I don't know why Sophie was there. She didn't mention anything to you?'

Harinder shook his head, then explained that when Sophie hadn't answered her mother's call earlier, and Harinder said he hadn't heard from her for a few hours either, Sophie's parents had used a tracking app linked to her phone and discovered the phone was at Great Northern Terrace. When the signal had remained there and there was no movement, Sophie's dad had decided to go and check it out.

He'd found her car. Then seen his daughter lying bleeding on the tarmac.

'Sophie told me she couldn't make dinner tonight. She said she was studying for her criminal psychology course at home.' Harinder ran a hand through his hair in exasperation. 'It doesn't add up.'

'Have you got her phone?' Karen asked.

'No. DI Goodridge took it. He's the duty SIO. Look, Karen, I'm sure he's good at his job, but he doesn't know Sophie like you.'

Karen understood what he was getting at. She put a hand on his arm. 'I'll look into it. Sophie is part of our team. Everyone is going to feel this personally. We'll get whoever did this.'

Harinder blinked and looked away. 'Her mum and dad are distraught.' He lowered his voice, and looking at Sophie's father, he said, 'I'm trying to support them. But I think they're taking care of me more than I am of them.' He turned back to Karen. 'You'll look into it personally? You won't leave it to DI Goodridge?'

'I promise, Harinder.' As soon as Karen said the words, she regretted them. She'd do her best, but DCI Churchill would likely decide she was too close to Sophie to view the case objectively.

But no matter what DCI Churchill said, Karen would fight tooth and nail to get to the bottom of this, whether officially or by other means.

'Has there been an update on her condition?'

'She's been unconscious since they brought her in. They've sedated her now. They said they saw swelling on her brain during the scan. The swelling could go down on its own, but they won't know until they do another scan tomorrow.'

'She's stable?'

Harinder bit his lip, pausing before saying, 'She's on a ventilator. She needs a machine to breathe for her, so that's not a good sign, but she's as stable as she can be.' He took a deep breath. 'The doctor said she had to be honest with us. There's a chance we could lose her.'

Karen wanted to say something comforting. But words failed her. Her throat was tight and her mouth too dry. It was hard to imagine Sophie, usually so chatty, enthusiastic and full of life, in a hospital bed hooked up to machines.

'She's strong, though,' Harinder said, his tone clearly trying to convince himself as much as Karen. 'She's going to make it.'

'Yes, and she's in the best possible place.'

He looked past her along the corridor. 'I need to get a coffee. I think the vending machines are the only thing open. Would you like one?'

'No, thank you. I'd better have a word with Sophie's dad.'

They both looked at Geoff Jones. He seemed smaller than Karen remembered from the few times they'd met when he'd come to meet Sophie at the station. He hadn't moved since she'd arrived. Head bent over, shoulders slumped, he looked defeated.

'Geoff?' Sophie's dad looked up as Karen approached. He had light brown hair, flecked with grey. His eyes showed his worry. He had the same dimples as Sophie when he smiled, but he wasn't smiling today. 'Mind if I sit down?' She pointed to the empty seat next to him.

'Karen.' He half rose and then slumped back. 'I can't believe this is happening. Who would do such a thing?'

'It's awful. I'm so sorry. You found her?'

His eyes were glassy. 'Yes, she was so cold. Bleeding . . . Whoever did this . . . they just left her there to die. Pure evil.' He clenched his fists. 'When you catch the person who did this, I'm going to . . .' His sentence ended with a sob. 'I feel so useless just sitting here.'

'Harinder told me it was thanks to you that Sophie was found so quickly. Your actions saved her life, Geoff.'

'We don't know if she'll pull through yet. The doctors don't sound optimistic.'

'We might get good news after the next scan.'

'I hope so.'

'What was the app you used to track Sophie's phone?'

'We've all got it,' Geoff explained, pulling his own mobile out of his coat pocket. He tapped the screen and brought up a map with red, blue and green dots for each phone. 'Sophie's phone is in green, I'm red and Clara's is blue.'

Sophie's phone had been taken as evidence, so that explained why it was in Nettleham, according to the map. Both Geoff and Clara's phones were shown to be at the hospital.

'And you checked the app because you couldn't get in touch with her?'

'Yes, Clara had tried to ring her. She even sent a couple of messages. Sophie doesn't always reply straightaway, so Clara didn't think anything of it. She just assumed Sophie's phone was on silent, or she'd gone out to dinner and didn't want to be disturbed. It was Sophie's idea to have the app installed. She worries about us. Because of her job. Because . . .' He met Karen's gaze and continued softly. 'Because of incidents involving officers' families in the past.'

Karen knew what he was driving at, although he was attempting to tiptoe around it. She was touched that even at a time like this he was sensitive of her feelings. After what had happened to Karen's husband and daughter, it was no wonder Sophie was extra cautious when it came to protecting her own family.

'That was a good decision on Sophie's part. Does the app give more details? It would be helpful to know what time she got to Great Northern Terrace, or where she was before travelling there.'

He nodded, and gave Karen his phone, explaining how the app worked. It was like a handful of other tracking apps Karen was familiar with. There were locations listed, along with times. According to the app, Sophie had been at Nettleham station until seven forty, and then she'd headed straight to Great Northern Terrace.

Why? There wasn't much there – at least nowhere Karen could think of that would be open at eight p.m. Had Sophie been on her way to the supermarket and seen something that made her go to Great Northern Terrace instead? If she'd witnessed suspicious behaviour, surely she would have called it in rather than try to tackle it herself?

But it was possible Sophie had seen something she believed to be an emergency and decided to intervene.

Sophie had always been keen. Right from the start, she'd been eager to please and do the right thing. If she saw a crime in progress

21

and thought she could help, it would be just like her to act quickly, perhaps not considering the danger.

Karen would need to talk to DI Goodridge. She was sure he'd already be tracking down any witnesses or relevant CCTV in the vicinity. Harinder had asked if Sophie had been working a case, but as Sophie's direct line manager, Karen knew everything Sophie was working on at the moment and nothing should have required a visit to Great Northern Terrace, and definitely not without checking in with a colleague first.

'You saw her phone had been at the same location for a while, and that's why you decided to go and look for her?' Karen asked.

'That's right. Clara said the app was probably on the blink. Or it was confused somehow. But I thought it couldn't hurt to check, just to be safe.'

'Thank goodness you did.'

'I saw . . . her car.' He stared down at his hands. 'Even then, I didn't think the worst. I thought her car had broken down. I parked up and walked over, and then . . .' He broke off, lost in the horror of finding his daughter battered and bleeding.

'You called an ambulance?'

'Yes, straightaway. And the police came out too.'

'Was there anybody else around when you got there?'

'Not that I saw.'

'Any other cars or vehicles parked in the area?'

He hesitated. 'I'm not sure. After seeing Sophie like that I wasn't really paying attention to anything else. I acted on autopilot, calling the ambulance, and then I held her hand and kept talking to her until the paramedics arrived.'

'Has Sophie been acting any differently lately? Anything worrying her?'

'You'd probably know that better than me, Karen. You see more of her than I do these days. We're lucky to see her once a week, with

22

her job, her studies, and Harinder.' Geoff smiled. 'He's a good lad. She's been so happy.' Then his smile disappeared, and he banged his fist against his leg. 'I don't understand why someone would do this. You have to make sure they pay.'

'I intend to. I'm going to speak to the senior investigating officer now, and then I'll start looking into it myself. There's not much I can do here.' She didn't want to get in the way. Sophie felt like family to Karen, but she had her parents and Harinder to help her here at the hospital. The most useful thing Karen could do was start looking for the perpetrator.

'All right, Karen. Keep us updated, won't you?'

'I will, and please tell Clara I'm thinking of you all.'

Karen found Harinder before she left. He promised to let her know if there was any change in Sophie's condition.

She walked away, no closer to understanding what had happened. Why had Sophie been in such a deserted area of Lincoln on her own? Why had she told Harinder she was revising at home? Had they been having problems? Why else would she lie to him?

Perhaps Karen had missed the signs. Sophie certainly hadn't confided in her. Relationships were difficult, particularly when a couple worked together. There was a possibility things had gone sour between Harinder and Sophie, and Sophie hadn't wanted to draw attention to it. But Harinder hadn't given any indication they were having problems, either.

Karen thought back, trying to recall whether Sophie had changed her behaviour over the last few days, but she drew a blank.

Sophie had been cheerful and mostly upbeat, except in one meeting when Rick had poured cold water on one of her ideas and called her naive.

Rick and Sophie were close, but often argued like brother and sister. They were competitive, but deep down there was a mutual respect.

Karen managed to grab a taxi that had just dropped a passenger at A&E.

The usually short drive back to Branston seemed to go on forever.

Karen tried to call DI Goodridge, but his line was engaged. She then performed the difficult task of calling each member of the team to let them know what had happened.

Rick was horrified, wanting to join the investigation immediately, but Karen told him to stay home. DI Morgan was equally shocked, and Arnie, who Karen called last, went silent for so long that Karen thought she'd lost the connection.

Eventually, he let loose a string of curse words, expressing exactly how angry and upset he felt. Karen let him vent as the fields rushed past the window.

She was almost home by the time she finished the call with Arnie. As the taxi pulled into her driveway, she sent a quick text to Mike, letting him know Sophie's condition and that she'd probably be working late for the next few days.

'That'll be £10.50, duck,' the taxi driver said, turning around.

Karen handed him the cash. 'Thanks.'

'Sorry to hear about your friend,' he said. 'I didn't mean to eavesdrop, but I couldn't help overhearing.'

'Thank you,' Karen said quietly, reaching for the door.

'It's dangerous out there these days,' he said. 'The police don't help. They don't catch them half of the time. I hope they pull their finger out for once and find out who did this to your friend.'

Karen didn't reply.

Chapter Three

Karen didn't bother entering the house. Instead, she got straight into her car and drove back towards Lincoln. She intended to visit the crime scene. With any luck, DI Goodridge would still be there, and Karen could offer her help.

The traffic was light, and it took her only minutes to arrive at Great Northern Terrace.

As her car rounded the corner, Karen saw the crime scene illuminated with powerful portable lights. Crime scene tape was stretched across a section of the parking area. A uniformed officer stood shivering beside it. SOCOs clad in white suits were still busy working. One crime scene van and two other police vehicles were parked on the road.

Karen pulled up beside the kerb and got out of the car.

Her presence was immediately noticed. The uniformed officer standing beside the tape called out, 'Can I help you?'

Karen walked towards him, holding up her ID. 'Is DI Goodridge still here?'

The officer shook his head. 'You just missed him. Is the victim a colleague of yours?'

'She is,' Karen confirmed.

The sound of someone calling her name made her turn. Tim Farthing. His white SOCO suit rustled with each step, and his face was a squashed red circle beneath the white hood.

Tim had joined the SOCO team about a year ago. Originally from London, when he'd first arrived he had looked down on the work they did in Lincolnshire, seeing it as somehow beneath him. He was a difficult man, and they had clashed at the start. Everything Karen said had seemed to annoy him, and the feeling had been mutual. Over time, they'd been forced to get along. Karen thought he'd mellowed, but he could still be an irritating so-and-so.

'Tim,' Karen said. 'Anything you can tell me?'

'Are you working the case?' he asked.

'DC Sophie Jones was the victim.' Karen thought that was all that needed to be said.

'I know. Absolutely awful. Have you got any idea what she was doing out here?'

Usually, Tim liked to stick to the evidence side of things. His job was to bag and tag. He left the theories and motives to the detectives. But it wasn't surprising he was interested now. No matter what he thought of Karen, he was part of the same police family, and Sophie was one of their own.

'No,' Karen admitted. 'I've been trying to understand what Sophie was doing here alone.'

Tim gave a knowing nod. 'I see.'

Karen frowned. 'What exactly do you see?'

'Well, I don't like to speculate, especially when she's in hospital . . .'

Then don't, thought Karen. But she needed to hear his ideas and theories even if they were outlandish or hurtful.

'Go on.'

'This area. It's notorious for drug pickups.'

That wasn't strictly true. Karen knew the area well. A few years ago, dealers had been taking advantage of the lack of car and foot traffic at night to meet up and hand over packages. It wasn't used for big supply deals, but a few drug runners had hung around, farming the gear out to their customers.

A year or two ago, there had been a clampdown, which had sent them running to new areas.

And even if the drug runners had returned, Karen couldn't see Sophie taking drugs. Sophie liked to play by the rules. She was the epitome of the school swot. She would never risk her job doing something so stupid.

'Sophie isn't on drugs,' Karen said confidently.

Tim raised his hands. 'Just thought I'd mention the possibility. She's been studying a lot recently, burning the candle at both ends, maybe she needed a little boost?'

How did he know so much about Sophie? Karen hadn't realised she'd taken up another course. 'Do you speak to her often?'

'Now and again at work. She's a nice kid. She certainly didn't deserve this. Is there any news from the hospital?'

'Nothing new yet, but she's stable, for now,' Karen said. 'Have you found anything at the scene? Anything to give us an idea why she was here, other than drugs?'

'No, but I think DI Goodridge is looking into the CCTV now.' He nodded at the cameras on the front of the commercial units.

Karen focused on one of the shopfronts. 'What on earth is that?'

Tim turned to where Karen was pointing. 'Oh, the mask? It's creepy, isn't it?'

'Why would they put that on display?' she wondered aloud, staring at the clown mask in the window of the party supplies shop and thinking it probably scared off more customers than it attracted.

She shivered and looked around, taking in the other two units. There was a huge one at the end near the rail track – Tony's Workshop. The other one was smaller. Unfortunately, they were all probably closed when Sophie was here. But the security cameras might give them something.

'There's no one in any of the units now?' Karen asked.

'No, there's been no one since I got here. Signs say they shut at five.'

'What do you think happened?'

'You know I don't like to speculate, but if you're forcing me—'

'I am.'

'All right. I think she parked up here.' He pointed to Sophie's small car. 'We're going to have a closer look at her car back at the depot. She got out. Maybe to meet someone. Perhaps the meeting turned nasty. Paramedics said she'd been hit on the back of the head.' He pointed to an area of tarmac near Sophie's car. 'She was lying there. Bleeding.' He took a deep breath and shook his head. 'She was so close to her car. So close to getting away or just being able to call for backup.'

'Did you find the weapon?'

'A Roughneck tyre lever was dropped a few feet away. It's made from hardened steel alloy. It's heavy. With enough force, it could have caused Sophie's injuries. It's got a powder coating, which might make getting prints difficult, but there was blood and hair along one edge, so we can be confident it was used in the attack.'

Karen hated to do it, but she forced herself to imagine how the situation might have played out. Had Sophie panicked and tried to run? She'd still had her phone on her, so why hadn't she tried to call for help? Perhaps things had happened too quickly. She may have been caught off guard.

The tyre lever could have come from the workshop. Maybe someone was working late, or it might have been stolen by the attacker to use as a weapon.

'Did she have any other injuries?'

Tim understood what Karen was getting at. 'Her clothes were intact. No sign of a sexual assault, so at least it's unlikely to have been a sexually motivated attack.' When Karen didn't respond, Tim shifted from foot to foot, looking uncomfortable. 'Sorry. I know how close you are. Perhaps it's better that DI Goodridge is heading the case.'

'Thanks for your help, Tim.'

'Sure, take care of yourself.'

Tim walked away, and Karen took the opportunity to take a closer look at the area. She tightened her coat around her as the cold wind picked up.

A train clattered past, and she wondered if one had passed near the time when Sophie was attacked. It was worth checking, to see if any passengers had seen anything.

If Sophie had come here, it might have something to do with the units. The party shop. The printing service. Or the mechanic's workshop. Was she meeting someone who worked at one of them?

Or was it just a coincidence she stopped here? Had Sophie been following a vehicle and ended up here? Or had she arranged to meet someone? If she had, then it seemed likely they'd picked this remote spot intentionally.

But why? What did Sophie have to hide?

Karen shivered. First thing tomorrow, she'd come back and speak to the employees and owners of these units. It shouldn't take long to track them down.

It was hard to accept this had happened to the open, enthusiastic young woman Karen knew. At times Sophie could be frustratingly eager to please, and Karen had to admit that her patience was tested at times, but Sophie's heart was always in the right place.

Karen had believed they shared a close relationship. Sophie looked up to her, and usually confided in her. So what had gone wrong?

Had she been unable to come to Karen? Was she involved in something so terrible she couldn't confide in a colleague? They were more than co-workers; Karen had a taken a motherly role in mentoring the younger officer. They'd been through some tough times together, so it was hard to accept Sophie felt unwilling to ask Karen for help.

Karen got back into her car, turned the heaters up high, and sat motionless behind the wheel, thinking.

She hated not knowing. Her curiosity was one of the things that meant she was suited to this job. Unearthing the truth. Unravelling secrets. But as hard as it was to accept, she had to acknowledge that if this wasn't a random attack, Sophie may have been keeping secrets. But why? And what could they possibly be that someone would have done something like this to her?

Chapter Four

The following morning, Karen woke early. It was still dark, but she knew there was no way she'd get back to sleep. So rather than just lie there, tossing and turning, she decided to get up and get in to work.

Mike hadn't stayed over last night, and the house seemed strangely quiet without him and Sandy.

Her route to work took her past the crematorium, and her eyes, as always, were magnetically drawn towards the final resting place of her husband and daughter. She experienced a twinge of shame. It had been some time since her last visit. Her life was evolving. But it was a struggle to shove away the feeling she was forgetting Josh and Tilly to move forward. Meeting Mike's mother and stepfather had been another brick in the wall of their relationship. They'd even recently discussed moving in together.

Josh would not have expected her to put her life on hold forever. Feeling guilty wasn't logical, but then feelings rarely were.

Her eyes felt gritty through lack of sleep. She'd need a serious amount of coffee to get going this morning.

As she drove by Buildbase, she made the decision to revisit the crime scene. It was still early, but she thought there might be someone at one of the units.

She couldn't turn right, due to traffic regulations, so she drove on, turning left on to Portland Street before looping around and going under the A1434 and then taking the link road towards Great Northern Terrace.

There were no lights on as she cruised past the buildings and industrial units.

She parked close to where Sophie had been found last night and got out of the car. Karen shivered, a chill penetrating her bones. She couldn't tell if it was due to the cold morning air or being back in the place where Sophie had suffered such a horrific attack.

The area was quiet. The crime scene tape had been removed. There was nothing to show that a crime had been committed last night.

She approached the party shop first. Her distorted reflection in the glass window stared back at her. The grotesque clown mask hung menacingly, taunting her. Its wide, sinister smile seemed to stretch out into a knowing grin, and its eyes seemed to follow her as she moved. An icy tingle raced down her spine. *It's just a stupid mask.*

No one responded to her knock, so she moved on to the print service, and having no luck there either, finally began to walk towards the workshop.

It was so quiet. So isolated. It must have been the same when Sophie had been attacked. She turned in a slow circle, making sure she was alone.

Karen paused, cocking her head to one side, and listened. A gentle squeaking sound seemed to be coming from inside the workshop. She banged on the huge roller door, but no one answered. The noise stopped. Had she imagined it?

At the top of the door was a black security camera. Was someone watching her now?

She walked around the perimeter, peering in through the dirty windows. Nothing stirred. Empty cars were parked up in a line behind the workshop. There was a second uPVC door around the back. She tried the handle, but it was locked.

The squeaking began again as she walked back to the front, and the squeak was followed by a rattle as the wind picked up.

The noise was the door moving and squeaking in the wind.

She muttered a curse. The noise continued, seeming to mock her, laughing at her suspicions.

Of course, there was no one here this early. She'd have to come back later when the units were open.

She could achieve more at the station. For a start, she could find out what progress DI Goodridge had made.

Her phone chirped with an incoming message.

Harinder.

No change in Sophie's condition overnight. The scan is scheduled for 10am. H.

Karen tapped out a reply and headed back to her car.

All they could do was cross their fingers and hope Sophie's scan showed improvement.

The office was very quiet when Karen arrived, with only a couple of heads bent over desks. As she got closer to her own workstation, she caught sight of Arnie, hunched over his computer screen.

He'd come to Nettleham as part of DCI Churchill's original team, and it had taken a while for Arnie and Churchill to fit in.

Arnie seemed to take pride in his slovenly appearance. It was part of his character. His thinning hair was tousled. He always wore trousers that looked at least two sizes too big, with a wrinkled shirt that was never tucked in properly. She'd not seen him at work without his patterned ties, quite often with the addition of food stains.

Arnie's appearance may have been dishevelled, but Karen regarded him fondly. He looked tired, she noticed. He was taking Sophie's attack hard.

He was content and comfortable in himself, and usually had a twinkle in his eye and a joke to tell. Karen liked him. He was a hard worker; although she had never seen him get to work this early before.

She guessed he'd had trouble sleeping too.

'Arnie, you're here early,' she said as she reached his desk.

He looked up sharply. 'Any news on Sophie?'

She told him what Harinder had said about the scan.

Arnie sighed, leaned back in his chair and stretched.

'What time did you get in?' Karen asked.

Arnie shrugged. 'A couple of hours ago. I was lying in bed staring at the ceiling, so I decided I might as well be here doing something useful.'

'Same,' Karen said. 'I had trouble sleeping, too. Coffee?'

Arnie picked up the cup on his desk. 'Go on, then.'

He walked with her to the coffee station. 'Have you heard anything about the investigation? You know they used a tyre lever to batter the back of her head?' He swore. 'Evil. Absolutely despicable.'

Karen agreed. 'I spoke to Tim Farthing at the scene. Has DI Goodridge gone off duty yet?'

Arnie shook his head. 'Not yet, no. I think he's going to lead this one.'

Karen had expected as much, but she was still disappointed. She'd hoped Churchill would ask to be involved. Karen wanted to work the investigation. Sophie was her teammate. And her friend.

'Goodridge is a decent DI,' Arnie said, picking up on Karen's feelings. 'And he understands we want to be part of this.'

'Does Churchill?' Karen asked.

Arnie smirked. 'I've not asked him. What he doesn't know won't hurt him. Besides, it's not even clocking-on time yet, so I can do this in my own time.'

'You've spoken to Goodridge?' Karen asked.

'Yes. He's not had much from the CCTV so far. The council ones anyway. They've only captured Sophie's car stopping at the last set of traffic lights before she parked. That lines up with the timing from the phone tracking app, and there's still a chance we might get something more from private cameras.'

'I saw some security cameras near to where Sophie was attacked,' Karen said. 'There's one at the front of the workshop that could be useful, and I noticed another camera on the front of the party supplies place.'

Arnie regarded the coffee machine suspiciously before putting his mug on the stainless-steel holder. 'Fingers crossed. I've been looking into the places near to where Sophie was found. I've got all the details here.' He tapped the notebook in his back pocket.

The coffee machine began to make a high screeching noise, and steam plumed from the top. Arnie looked at it in disgust. 'I'm telling you, this machine has it in for me.'

Karen removed the full cup and handed it to him, before programming the machine again.

'Ta,' Arnie said. 'Goodridge is happy for us to go and talk to the staff at the units this morning, if you're up for it?'

'Absolutely,' Karen said.

After the machine stopped pumping out coffee, she ignored the whirring noise it was making and grabbed her cup.

She blew over the top of the steaming coffee. 'Anything suspicious come up when you did the searches into the premises?'

Arnie shook his head. 'No. I've not gone very deep yet, so there might be something to unearth, but so far they look very boring.'

Karen took a sip of her scalding coffee, then asked, 'All right, when do you want to go?'

'Let's give it half an hour,' Arnie said. 'We want to make sure they're open when we arrive. The workshop opens at eight o'clock. The party supplies and the print shop open at eight thirty.'

◆　◆　◆

The sun was shining, but it was still bitterly cold when Karen and Arnie arrived at Great Northern Terrace. The workshop's green roller door was open, and the sound of pop music flowed out of the premises mixed with the clang of metal tools being moved around.

Arnie announced their presence loudly.

At the rear of the workshop was a pit for car inspections where an old Ford Fiesta had been raised up. A man in grubby overalls crouched underneath. Another man stood beside a metal work-bench. The two men didn't move.

The third person in Tony's Workshop was a woman. She was the one who made her way towards them, smiling uncertainly. She had a stocky build and blonde hair scooped back in a long ponytail. She wore no make-up, and her cheeks were ruddy. Karen guessed she was probably in her early fifties.

The sleeves of her overalls were rolled up and her forearms were smeared with grease. She wiped them with a rag before holding out her hand.

'Hello,' she said. 'Car trouble?'

'No, nothing like that,' Karen said, as she and Arnie held up their warrant cards.

The woman's eyebrows lifted. 'Police? What can we do to help?' She looked over her shoulder, perhaps hoping for backup from her colleagues, who suddenly found themselves very busy and avoided eye contact.

'What's your name?' Karen asked.

'Valerie Anderson,' the woman said after a moment's hesitation.

'There was an incident last night. A young woman was attacked very close to this workshop,' Karen said. 'Did you see or hear anything?'

'No, I locked up last night. I left about six,' Valerie said. 'What time did it happen?'

'We believe around eight o'clock. I noticed you've got a security camera out the front. Do you mind if we take a look at the footage?'

Valerie had an open and friendly face. She hadn't immediately panicked when they introduced themselves as the police, so Karen didn't think the staff were doing anything dodgy like repurposing stolen cars. She'd expected Valerie to offer the security camera footage without complaint, and so she was surprised when Valerie shook her head.

'I'm sorry,' Valerie said, 'I can't do that without the owner's permission.'

'That's disappointing,' Arnie said, with a frown.

'I'm sorry . . . I'd like to help . . . but . . .' She looked to her colleagues for assistance, but they kept their heads down. 'I need to check with the owner first.'

'The owner is Tony Withers?' Arnie asked.

'That's right.'

'Well, why don't you call him while we wait?'

'Now?' Valerie looked horrified.

'Yes, please,' Arnie said.

They waited as she walked over to the telephone and placed the call. In less than a minute she'd hung up, looking relieved. 'No answer.'

'How long have you been working here, Valerie?' Karen asked.

'About eighteen months now,' Valerie said. 'I moved down from Yorkshire. I can't lose this job. Mr Withers is . . . very particular.'

Karen and Arnie exchanged a look. They had been working together long enough now to interpret each other's silent signals. Arnie nodded, then went off to talk to the man working on the Ford.

'Don't suppose I could trouble you for a cup of tea?' Karen asked.

'Yes, of course,' Valerie said. 'I was just about to make one anyway.'

Karen followed her through a door at the side of the workshop, into a tiny kitchenette.

'It's not much,' Valerie said with an apologetic smile. 'The toilet is on the other side. Sadly, I have to share that with the lads. And let me say before you ask, yes, they do forget to put the toilet seat down.' She smiled nervously. She was babbling. Was this her normal behaviour or was she on edge?

Valerie switched the kettle on, arranged some mugs and asked Karen how she and Arnie took their tea. After Karen told her, Valerie asked, 'What happened last night? It's worrying. It's usually so quiet around here.'

Normally Karen would veer on the side of caution, not giving out any more information than she had to, but she wanted to put Valerie at ease. Often, people were more likely to help when they knew the full story.

'The young woman was a colleague of mine,' Karen said. 'Someone hit her over the back of the head with a tyre lever and left her bleeding only a few feet from the front of the workshop.'

Valerie raised a hand to her mouth. 'Oh, that's awful. How old is she?'

'Mid-twenties,' Karen said, feeling a lump in her throat. She hadn't realized it would be so hard to talk about. She steeled herself. 'I don't suppose the workshop is missing a tyre lever?'

Valerie's eyes widened, and she said hurriedly, 'No, nothing is missing.'

Karen wondered if she could really be so sure. There had to be a lot of tools around. 'Perhaps you could double-check later and let me know if you notice anything missing.'

'All right.'

'You left at six, and were the last to leave?'

'That's right. I didn't see anything suspicious. Although it was dark when I left.'

'Were there any vehicles parked nearby?'

Valerie paused, thinking, then said, 'Not that I remember.'

'And neither you nor any of your colleagues returned to the workshop at any point last night?'

Valerie shook her head. 'No, not last night. I took the keys home with me.'

'Has anyone else got a set of keys to the workshop?'

'Um, yes. Mr Withers,' Valerie said. 'But he never opens up or locks up at night. Me and the lads take it in turns. It was my turn last night and so I opened up first thing this morning.'

The kettle came to the boil, and Valerie poured hot water into a huge brown teapot. 'Will your colleague be all right?'

'She's very badly injured. We're hoping she pulls through.' Karen took out her mobile to show Valerie a headshot of Sophie. 'Do you recognise her?'

Valerie stared at the phone screen, eyes wide. A few seconds passed, then her eyes filled with tears, and she said, 'No . . . Sorry, just the thought of her being attacked like that.' She grabbed a kitchen roll from the counter and used a sheet to dab her eyes. 'You must think I'm an idiot.'

'Not at all,' Karen said. 'It's a horrible thing to happen and it's worrying if you're last to leave after locking up. It might be an idea to get one of the lads to do it for the next few days, just until we know what happened.'

Valerie nodded. 'I will. I wasn't thinking about myself though.'

'No?' Karen prompted.

She shook her head. 'I have a daughter . . . just a couple of years younger than your colleague, and if anything like that was to happen to her, I . . .'

'I understand.'

Valerie dabbed at her eyes again. Then finished off making the tea. 'I don't even know where my daughter is,' she said, a note of panic threading its way into her voice. 'We had a row, and she stormed out. I've not seen her since.'

Karen frowned. 'So, she's missing?'

But suddenly, Valerie clammed up. 'It was just a silly argument,' she said dismissively, shaking her head. 'I'm overreacting.' She passed Karen a mug of tea.

Karen thanked her before gently suggesting, 'If you're concerned, you could come into the station—'

'Thank you, but there's nothing you can do,' Valerie said abruptly, cutting Karen off, and she put the other mugs on a tray.

'I'm sorry; I didn't mean to upset you.'

'You didn't.' Valerie gave her a watery smile. 'I'm still a bit emotional about it.'

Arnie wandered over to the other two mechanics. Both men kept their heads down, like students hoping not to be called on by the teacher. They were out of luck.

'All right, lads?' Arnie stopped beside the Ford.

One of them grunted. The other kept his back to Arnie as he leaned over the workbench.

The friendly approach wouldn't work with these two. 'Names?' Arnie barked.

Both men turned, watching him warily.

'Brian Sully,' the bloke by the Ford said.

'Mark McArthur,' the other said.

Sully had a receding hairline and blond hair, which was cut so close to his scalp that he looked bald from a distance. The overhead light shone on his large forehead. Arnie judged him to still be in his thirties.

McArthur looked younger. His dark hair was too long and scraggly. It fell forward, covering one eye. Both looked shifty and wore guarded expressions that Arnie associated with unhelpful small-time criminals. Even if they'd seen or heard something, Arnie guessed they'd keep it to themselves. Unless it was pried out of them using force or devious means. Arnie wasn't above using unorthodox methods, but he'd try the conventional option first.

'What time did you leave the workshop yesterday?'

The men exchanged a glance. 'Around five thirty.'

'You see anyone hanging around?'

They shook their heads in unison.

'Who locked up?'

'Val,' Sully said, dropping a spanner into a metal toolbox on the floor.

'Does she usually lock up?'

'We take it in turns,' McArthur said, then sniffed and wiped his nose on the sleeve of his overalls.

Arnie selected a photograph of Sophie on his phone. 'Do you recognise her?'

Both men reluctantly peered at the screen for a few seconds then shook their heads.

'Really? Take a closer look. Maybe you worked on her car?'

Sully sighed and took another look, but McArthur stared petulantly at his boots.

'We ain't seen her before,' Sully said.

'Is the workshop missing a tyre lever?' Arnie asked.

'What? No.' McArthur turned to Sully.

Sully squinted with suspicion. 'Are you accusing us of something?'

'I'm asking if the workshop is missing a tyre lever,' Arnie said, speaking slowly and deliberately, enunciating his words as though he was talking to five-year-olds rather than grown men. He was being condescending, deliberately trying to rile them. He knew from experience that Sully and McArthur weren't the kind of men to spend time chatting and inadvertently reveal too much. But they might get angry and blurt out whatever it was they were attempting to hide. Arnie had been working this job long enough to know they were nervous. They didn't want him here asking questions.

'Nothing is missing,' Sully said.

'How long have you both worked for Tony?' Arnie asked.

'Over fifteen years,' Sully replied.

'About five.' McArthur wedged his hands in the pockets of his overalls and avoided eye contact.

'You like it?'

Sully shrugged. 'It's a job.'

'What's your boss like?'

Both men tensed, but neither said a word.

Give me strength, Arnie thought. He hoped Karen was having more luck.

Karen and Valerie went back into the main workshop. Valerie held up the tray. 'Tea's up,' she called to the lads and Arnie.

'Can you give us all the contact details you have for Tony Withers?' Karen asked.

'Absolutely,' Valerie said, reaching for a notebook on the shelf above the telephone. She grabbed a pen and scribbled down a number on a piece of notepaper then handed it to Karen.

'Thanks,' Karen said. 'We'll get on to him to request access to the footage. In the meantime, could you make sure it's not recorded over?'

'It's stored on the cloud for a month. It won't be wiped. Don't worry.'

'Appreciate it.'

Arnie wandered over and picked up his mug. 'Now this is a proper cup of tea,' he said, with his most winning smile. 'Perfect colour.'

Valerie beamed. 'I do like a good cup of tea.'

'I can tell you're an expert. Can't beat a nice strong brew.' Arnie looked at Karen and sighed. 'I suppose we'd better get back and break the news to the DCI that we've been denied access to the security footage. He's not going to be happy.'

'Oh,' Valerie said. 'I'd like to show you now, but it's just . . . Mr Withers can be . . . well, he can be difficult.'

Karen noticed her hands were trembling. 'Are you all right, Valerie?'

'It's just . . . well, he's quite an exacting boss, and I don't want to do anything to annoy him. I've only been here eighteen months. I don't want to lose this job.'

'I understand, but we really need to look at that footage,' Arnie said, persuasively. 'You could access the cloud now, couldn't you? He doesn't need to know.'

Karen was desperate to see the footage, too. But they needed a clear chain of evidence when it came to a future prosecution. Eagerness now could lead to a ruined case later. Plus, Valerie was concerned she might lose her job, and Karen didn't want to get her in trouble.

'What do you say?' Arnie prompted. 'Just a quick look. Where's the harm in that?'

'No, I really can't.' Valerie trembled and her voice quivered with fear.

She was petrified, Karen thought. Valerie was more than just concerned about keeping her job; she was terrified of her boss, the mysterious Tony Withers.

Chapter Five

After finishing off their tea, Arnie and Karen left the workshop. Before they got far, Arnie crouched down. Karen thought he was tying a shoelace but noticed his shoes were slip-ons.

'What—?'

Arnie put a finger to his lips then pointed to the window. Raised voices came from inside the workshop.

A male voice snarled, 'What did you tell them?'

'Nothing! Honestly, I told them I'd never seen the young woman before, and I hadn't noticed anything out of the ordinary.' Karen recognised Valerie's voice.

'You'd better be telling the truth. We don't need them sniffing around!'

'I promise, Sully. I didn't say anything.'

Then the radio was turned up, drowning out the voices.

'I knew it,' Arnie said. 'Definitely hiding something.'

'Do you think it's related to Sophie?'

'I don't know, but we'll find out.'

'I think Valerie's scared of her boss, Tony Withers. I'm curious to know where he was last night at eight o'clock.'

Arnie stood up and looked over his shoulder towards the workshop door. 'The other two were as much use as a chocolate teapot. I wouldn't be surprised if they're all intimidated by their boss.'

'It sounds like he keeps them on a short leash. He's always checking in, never warning them before he arrives.'

They walked towards the other two units. 'So, which one first?' Karen asked. 'Party Fun or Print World?'

'Do you want to split up and do one each?' Arnie suggested.

Karen considered it. 'No, I think it's better if we do it together. If there's more than one member of staff, we can split them between us.'

'All right, then. It's party time,' Arnie said, pointing at Party Fun.

Karen averted her gaze from the creepy clown mask in the window, though it didn't look half as scary in the daylight.

The door squeaked open, and they were met by an explosion of colour. Packets of balloons, streamers and banners were crammed into baskets. Hanging on the walls were all sorts of costumes: frilly princess dresses, Spider-Man costumes, and witches' hats. They walked along an aisle stacked with paper plates, cups and napkins in pink, yellow and gold on one side, and the section for practical jokes, including whoopee cushions and exploding candy, on the other.

The young woman behind the counter looked up. She was dressed in the goth style, with long black hair, a diamond nose piercing, and dark eyeliner around her eyes. Completing the look, she wore black lipstick. Karen thought she looked about twelve. Her phone was on the counter in front of her. It looked like she'd been using it to play a fantasy-style game with dragons when they'd walked in.

'Can I help you?' she asked politely.

'I hope so,' Karen said, and they both showed their ID.

The young woman's eyes widened. 'My boss isn't here today. It's just me.'

'That's fine,' Karen said. 'We just need to ask you a few general questions. What's your name?'

'Mel. Melinda Cartwright.'

Karen introduced herself and Arnie formally and tried to put Mel at ease, then said, 'It's about an incident that occurred in the parking area out front.' Karen gestured towards the spot where Sophie had been found. 'A young woman was attacked there at about eight p.m. last night.'

'Attacked?' Mel repeated. 'Is she okay?'

'No, she's in a serious condition in hospital,' Arnie said. 'How long have you been working here, Mel?'

'Only six months. I don't mind it. The lady I work for, Tara, is nice and she leaves me alone most of the time . . . but you've got me worried now. I'm alone here a lot.'

Arnie gave her a reassuring smile. 'We're doing our best to find out what happened last night. There are other people close by during the day when you're working – at the print shop next door and at the workshop. You're not usually here alone at night?'

Mel shook her head. 'Do you have any idea who did it – who attacked her, I mean?'

'Not yet,' Karen said. 'We were hoping to look at your security footage.'

'Oh, you won't have much luck there I'm afraid,' Mel said.

'Why not?' Arnie asked.

'Because it's just a dummy camera.'

'It looks real enough,' he said.

'That's because it's technically a real camera, but it's not wired up to anything. It doesn't record.'

'Great,' Arnie said. 'No other security footage?'

'No, sorry. We never leave money on the premises, and my boss thinks people aren't likely to break in to steal clown costumes.'

'What time did you leave here last night, Mel?' Karen asked.

'Five,' Mel said. 'But actually I did pop back briefly.'

'What time was that?'

'Seven thirty,' she said. 'I forgot my mobile. I couldn't cope without my phone all night, so I came back to get it.'

'And did you see anything unusual?'

'Nothing out of the ordinary,' she said. 'I was only here a few minutes. I just grabbed my phone and locked up again.'

'Were there any cars parked outside?'

'I think so.' She bit her lower lip. 'But I can't remember for sure. I'm sorry; I wasn't paying much attention. I didn't know it would be important.'

'Are vehicles usually left in the parking area?' Arnie asked.

'Not overnight. If they've got more vehicles at the workshop than they can fit inside, they usually park around the back.'

Arnie placed his notebook on the counter, opened it at the appropriate page and asked, 'This is your boss's name and contact details, correct?'

Mel scanned the page. 'Yes, that's right.'

'All right. We'll get in touch with her as well, in case she saw anything.'

'She wasn't here.'

'Right, but we'll talk to her directly just in case,' Arnie said.

Karen asked, 'You haven't noticed anyone hanging around? Anyone out of place? Not necessarily last night, but at any time?'

'No. It's been quiet. It always is. We tend to get customers who have ordered stuff online and come to pick it up, or they know where we are from a friend recommending us. We don't get much passing trade here.'

'And how do you get on with all the people in the other units?' Arnie asked.

'Who do you mean?'

'Well, there's a print shop next to you. What are they like?'

'Oh, I don't know really. Nice enough. We say hello now and again. I don't really know them, though. It's run by two brothers, I think.'

'And what about Tony's Workshop? Have you ever met Tony?'

Mel shook her head. 'I haven't met him, but there is a bloke who turns up in a silver Jag every now and then, quite old, a bit . . .' She used her hands to mime a substantial stomach area. 'I thought that might be Tony, but I don't know for sure.'

'And the people that work there?'

Mel shrugged her shoulders in response. 'I don't know them. I keep to myself really.'

Karen suspected Mel spent most of her time playing games on her phone, and not paying attention to much else.

They thanked Mel for her time and headed back outside into the sunshine. Karen shivered and zipped up her coat. A second strike on the security footage, she thought as she looked across to the print shop. She only had the faintest hope they had cameras that had caught the attack on Sophie, because she couldn't see any at the front of the unit.

They were running into too many dead ends. They desperately needed that footage. She would have to find some way to get her hands on it. They could get a warrant, but that took time.

Arnie looked at Karen. 'We need the security tapes from the workshop. It's looking like they are the only ones in the area that might have caught the attack. You want me to call Rick? Get a start on a warrant in case Tony Withers decides not to play ball?'

'Yes.' Going by Valerie's body language and the jumpiness of the other two mechanics, Karen guessed Tony Withers might be the type of man who would make things difficult just because he could. They needed the footage, and they didn't have time to waste.

Valerie had said the recordings were stored on the cloud, but Karen didn't want to risk the footage being 'accidently' deleted. Not when it might be their only chance to track down Sophie's attacker.

The print shop was the smallest of the three premises. As they entered, Karen noted the sharp, chemical smell of hot ink. A machine hummed in the background. The walls were white and decorated with brightly coloured, glossy posters. A man stood behind the counter, tapping at a computer, and didn't look up straightaway. On the counter was a pile of yellow flyers that listed the prices for various printing options.

The man finally looked up from the computer screen, stood up, and gave them a wide smile. Behind him were white bookshelves stacked with reams of paper.

'How can I help?' he asked.

'We'd like to ask you a few questions, please,' Arnie said, and they both showed their warrant cards, introducing themselves and asking his name.

'Vishal Mishra,' he said, deflating as he leaned across the counter to take a closer look at their ID. 'I thought you were here to place an order and save my business from going under.'

Karen felt a twinge of sympathy for him. 'Sorry to hear business isn't doing well.'

He smiled sadly. 'It's the location. We're stuck out here in the middle of nowhere. We get repeat customers, but we just don't grow. No one sees us. And don't even talk to me about online advertising. All I ever do is lose money when I try that.'

'Were you working here last night?' Karen asked, directing the conversation away from his business troubles.

'I was, actually. I was here until seven doing the accounts. Trying to rustle up money out of thin air,' he said with a sigh. 'I didn't have much luck.'

'And you left at seven o'clock?'

'That's right.'

'Did you come back?'

'No, I went home for dinner.'

50

'What about your brother?'

Vishal's eyes narrowed. 'Wait a minute. How do you know about my brother? What's all this about?'

'Mel, at the party shop next door, told us you run this place with your brother.'

'Oh, right, yeah. I do. But it's mostly me these days. Amit's got . . . well, we don't really know what he's got, but he's not been well. The after-effects of a virus we think. He's barely able to get out of bed some days.'

'Sorry to hear that.'

'Yeah, well, everyone's got a sob story, haven't they?' he said, now looking thoroughly depressed. 'Anyway, why are you so interested in me and what I was doing last night?'

'A young woman was attacked near your premises, about eight o'clock.'

He was silent for a moment. 'That's shocking,' he said. 'How is she?'

'Not too good,' Arnie replied.

'I'm sorry to hear that. Will she pull through?'

There was another silence before Karen said, 'We hope so.'

'I wish I could help, but I didn't see anything. I wasn't here when it happened.'

'Any security cameras?' Arnie asked.

'No, we can't afford anything like that. We've not even got an alarm. Stupid really. Some of our equipment costs an arm and a leg.' Vishal shook his head. 'I'm probably going to have to sell it all. I won't get back what I paid for it, of course. Another business down the drain.' He sat on the stool behind the counter. 'I have to say I'm impressed that you're doing the legwork. Coming out here, talking to people, trying to find out what happened.'

'That's our job,' Arnie said, with more than a hint of impatience.

'Yeah, but it's good to see you covering all the bases, isn't it? I was mugged a few months back and the police weren't too impressive. Don't think they spent much time on it. Never charged anyone. But you guys are doing this one by the book.'

'I'm sorry to hear that you were mugged,' Karen said. 'Where did it happen?'

'Town centre, Lucy Tower Street car park, quite late at night. I reported it straightaway. Fat lot of good it did me.'

'I'm sorry we weren't able to catch the mugger.'

There was a bang at the door as a man barrelled in, struggling under the weight of a huge box.

'Don't just stand there, Vishal. Give me a hand. I've got ten of these in the van.' He heaved the box on to the counter.

'Not right now, Jared,' Vishal said, frowning. 'I'm busy. Talking to customers.'

Jared frowned and wiped his forehead. He was red and sweaty despite the freezing temperature outside. He looked Karen and Arnie up and down. 'They're not customers.'

'They could be customers for all you know.' Vishal folded his arms over his chest.

'They're not though, are they?' Jared said, smirking.

'How do you know?'

'Because they're coppers. It's obvious. Just look at them.'

'Yeah, well, they're here to ask about a terrible incident that happened last night. A young woman got attacked.'

'Yeah, I heard about it,' Jared said.

Karen listened to their conversation unfold in disbelief. They were carrying on as though she and Arnie weren't there.

'Well then, you can see they need my help,' Vishal said, puffing himself up with self-importance. 'So, if you don't mind, Jared, perhaps you could just wait outside until I'm ready to take the delivery.'

'You didn't see anything, did you?'

'Well, no.'

'Then just tell them that. Job done.'

Vishal pursed his lips. 'It's not got anything to do with you, Jared.' He waved his hands. 'They want to talk to me. And I'll have you know they're doing a good job, really trying to get to the bottom of it.'

'Well, of course they are,' Jared said. 'It's one of their own, isn't it?'

'Is that true?' Vishal looked at Karen.

'Yes, a member of our team,' she said.

'Oh, well, that explains why you're working so hard then.'

Karen placed her hands flat on the counter. 'No, it doesn't. We don't pick and choose the crimes we want to solve. I'm sure the officers you dealt with wanted to find out who mugged you, but it's not always easy without witnesses or evidence.'

'Yeah, right,' Vishal said.

Karen was fuming as they left the print shop. She understood the frustration people felt when the crimes they reported weren't solved and no one was brought to justice. She felt frustrated too. But it wasn't like the officers were trying to get no results. The regulations they had to abide by often made detectives feel as though they had their hands tied behind their backs.

When Vishal implied that if a different woman had been attacked, they wouldn't be here doing their jobs, Karen's blood had boiled. Because she did care. Every victim mattered. Whether they wore the uniform or not.

'Don't let them get to you,' Arnie said as they walked back to the car.

'It's so unfair, though, Arnie. We can't win. If we make a quick arrest without being completely prepared, the CPS can't get a conviction, and we get the blame. Take too long, and the press crucify us.'

'Tell me about it,' he said. 'Some things never change.'

Chapter Six

When Karen and Arnie got back to the station, they had just enough time to get some coffee before the briefing began.

Karen grabbed two cups from the machine and handed one to Arnie.

'It's frustrating we can't access the security footage from Tony's Workshop,' she said.

'Suspicious, if you ask me,' he replied. 'What are they hiding?'

'The woman who works there did seem nervous about something.'

'Could be a chop shop,' Arnie said.

Karen mulled that over as they quickly made their way to the briefing room. Chop shops were often linked to car-theft rings and organised crime. It would explain why Valerie had been so reluctant to give them access to the footage.

'Have you seen Superintendent Murray?' Karen asked, wondering if the super would be there for the briefing. She didn't usually, but as this case was such a personal one for the officers, Karen thought she might come down to show support.

'She's on medical leave,' Arnie said, as he pushed open the door. 'Off work for an operation.'

The briefing room was a sombre place today. The walls were painted a dull shade of grey. The fluorescent lights overhead flickered occasionally above the desks and chairs arranged in neat rows.

The room was packed with detectives and civilian support staff, and Karen and Arnie only just managed to squeeze in. They stood with their backs to the filing cabinets.

Usually before a briefing the room would be full of chatter, but today there was a solemn silence. The atmosphere was tense with anticipation, as everyone waited for details of what had happened to Sophie.

Karen felt a heavy weight in her chest as she looked around the room, feeling Sophie's absence keenly.

Usually, Sophie would be sitting at the front, bright and eager, and ready to ask questions. She would have volunteered to hand out the briefing notes, but today they were left in a pile on top of a desk for people to help themselves.

Arnie stood silently beside Karen, tense and still, his head bowed. Rick was sitting at the front, his gaze fixed on the whiteboards at the front of the room, which had details of the investigation scribbled across them in red marker and were dotted with photographs of the crime scene, though thankfully there were none of Sophie's injuries. Karen knew Rick was taking this attack hard, and she felt a wave of sadness for him.

DI Morgan caught her eye from across the room and mouthed, *Are you all right?*

Karen nodded and took a sip of her coffee. It tasted bitter, and she put it down on top of the metal filing cabinet behind her.

It was hot and airless in the briefing room, with the heating blasting out. The room smelled of stale coffee and was so quiet Karen could hear the ticking of the clock behind her.

DC Farzana Shah squeezed past a couple of the support staff to reach Karen. Her eyes were red, and she was clutching a tissue. She usually wore her long dark hair in a braid for work, but this morning, her hair hung loose.

'How are you doing?' Karen asked, though it was clear from Farzana's expression she was taking the news badly.

'I can't believe this happened to Sophie,' she said. 'She is such a kind person. We were studying for our online criminal psychology course together at the station last night. She shared her notes with me.' Farzana's lower lip wobbled. 'It's hard to believe that just an hour later, she was attacked.'

Karen put her arm around Farzana's shoulders and squeezed. 'We'll get the person who did this.'

DI Goodridge stepped forward, his mouth set in a grim line. He was tall and broad-shouldered, with short, cropped hair and sharp features. His navy-blue suit was rumpled from working all night. He surveyed the room before beginning to speak in a low, authoritative voice. 'I know that you're all aware of what happened to our colleague, DC Sophie Jones, last night. She was attacked in Great Northern Terrace, at approximately eight p.m., most likely hit over the head with a tyre lever, which was discovered at the scene. She is currently in hospital with a head injury and her condition remains serious.'

The room was silent as the detectives processed the news.

Rick sat silently in the front row, his gaze fixed on the DI. He looked as though he was barely holding it together, his hands clenched into fists. Karen knew how close Rick and Sophie were, despite them bickering like children at times; it had to be tearing him apart.

Some of the detectives shifted and fidgeted in their seats, while others were still as statues, their eyes downcast, as Goodridge continued. 'We've been analysing Sophie's timeline. She left Nettleham station at seven forty p.m. and drove to Great Northern Terrace. We don't yet know the purpose of her trip.' He looked around the room. 'Did Sophie share her plans with anyone yesterday?'

There were murmurs, but no one volunteered any information.

Goodridge leaned on the desk in front of him. He was silent for a moment, his gaze flitting around the room. 'Did Sophie share anything with any of you yesterday that might help our investigation?' Goodridge turned his gaze on Rick, who remained silent.

'She told me she was going home to make dinner and do some more studying,' Farzana said. 'I spoke to her just before she left the station.'

Goodridge frowned. 'She either wasn't telling you the truth or changed her mind en route because we know she didn't go home. She went to Great Northern Terrace.'

'Does Sophie have any connection to Great Northern Terrace?' Morgan asked from his spot at the back of the room.

'I was hoping you could tell us that,' Goodridge said. 'What has she been working on? Was Sophie's visit connected to an active investigation?'

'Not a present investigation,' Morgan said. 'She'd been following up complaints of social media harassment and hate speech, but there is no connection with Great Northern Terrace as far as I'm aware.'

'It's worth double-checking.'

Morgan nodded. 'Of course.' But Karen knew Morgan. He would have already checked. He was painstakingly methodical in his work, so would probably have checked the paperwork a dozen or more times to be thorough.

'Any recent threats that haven't been reported?' Goodridge looked at Karen. 'To your team, or Sophie personally?'

Karen was aware of everyone's eyes on her. 'No threats, but Sophie has been involved in building the case against Quentin Chapman.'

'Has Chapman issued any direct threats?'

Karen shook her head. 'No.'

'Do you think Sophie's attack is related to the Chapman case?'

'It's hardly a case,' someone at the front muttered. 'We've nothing concrete against him.'

Karen hesitated. That was true. Chapman was like a snake, slippery and venomous. He'd walked away from his encounter with Karen notably less wealthy but still a free man, much to her disgust. She hadn't let it go, though. Every spare moment she spent looking into his background and dodgy dealings, determined to one day topple his criminal enterprise.

'I've no evidence to link Sophie's attack to Chapman,' Karen said. 'It's just as likely to be a random attack.'

'Okay, let's move on to relationships,' Goodridge said, and then sighed. This was hard. Sophie was a friend and colleague, but they had to delve into her personal life just as they would for any victim. 'I'm aware Sophie has been dating Harinder Singh from tech for a few months now. Relationships can be complicated. Were they having problems?'

Rick put down his pen. 'You're not suggesting Harinder had anything to do with this?'

Goodridge met Rick's gaze. 'We need to look at all Sophie's personal relationships. They could be problematic.'

'I think they've been getting on great,' Karen said. 'Sophie hasn't mentioned any problems or arguments.'

Goodridge nodded. 'Her parents?'

'They adore her,' Karen said.

Goodridge looked at Rick. 'How about Sophie's previous romantic relationships? Any aggrieved exes we should be aware of?'

Rick grimaced. 'She didn't really talk to me about stuff like that. But I'm sure she would have mentioned it if someone from her past was making her feel unsafe.'

'We need to find out if Sophie had a connection with anyone at Great Northern Terrace,' Morgan said, moving the focus away from Sophie's personal life. 'If she wasn't there for work, perhaps she knew one of the owners of the units there.'

Karen shook her head. 'She didn't mention it to me if she did. Have we been able to find out if there were any vehicles following her?'

Rick replied, 'I've been looking through the traffic camera footage. There's potentially one vehicle – a white Citroën, which turns off the main road a few seconds after Sophie. I'm looking into that now.'

Goodridge nodded. 'Good. And what about Sophie's phone? Did we get anything from it?'

Farzana said, 'I've been through her recent messages and phone calls, but there's nothing immediately apparent. I've now given the phone to the tech lab and applied to the phone company to access her call logs.'

Rick said, 'I've checked her emails too. Both her work account and her personal email account on her phone. It'll take me a while to go through them thoroughly, but there's no mention of a meeting at Great Northern Terrace, or that Sophie was in danger.'

Karen spoke up, her mind on a potential link with Quentin Chapman. 'What about Sophie's recent searches on the police databases? I can look into that.'

'That's okay, Karen,' DI Goodridge replied gently. 'My team is already working on it.'

Karen immediately saw he wanted to keep her away from the Chapman angle, which made sense looking at it objectively. She was working the same case, gathering information against Chapman, and so was as much a risk as Sophie from the gangster. But this was personal, and it was hard to be objective.

Goodridge continued the briefing, his voice hard and brittle as he read out the details of Sophie's injuries. It was hard to listen to.

Some of the detectives winced or looked away as he spoke, unable to bear the thought of their colleague being violently attacked.

'The blows were to the back of her head and base of her skull, so it's likely the attacker struck when her back was turned. Like a coward,' Rick said, his voice filled with anger.

Arnie nodded in agreement. His face was grim as he said, 'Anyone attacking a woman like that is an utter scumbag in my book.'

Goodridge warned them to try to keep their distance emotionally. 'I know it's not easy, but we need to stay focused and keep our feelings out of this.'

He went on to ask Rick about the tyre lever found at the scene.

'We're getting the blood matched at the lab and hoping to get DNA or prints off it too,' Rick said.

'Right, let's turn our attention to the premises close to where Sophie was found. Farzana, what have you found out so far?'

Farzana sniffed and shoved her tissue into the pocket of her trousers. 'There are no residential properties in the immediate vicinity. The parking area, where Sophie was found, is next to the railway tracks, which are fenced off. There are several businesses and storage facilities in the area. Next to the rail line is Tony's Workshop. There's also a party supplies shop, called Party Fun, and a printing shop called Print World. I've identified the owners but haven't made contact with them yet.'

'That should be a priority, and let's keep our focus wide. We need to speak to the owners of all the units in the area, not just the three closest ones,' Goodridge said. 'That's too much for one person. Perhaps Karen and Arnie . . .' He turned to them. 'Could you follow up on that too?'

'Yes,' Karen said. 'We've already spoken to one of the owners of Print World, and the employees of the workshop and Party Fun this morning.'

'Did they see anything or anyone suspicious?' asked Goodridge.

'Unfortunately not. The workshop has a security camera, but they were reluctant to hand over the footage without speaking to the owner, Tony Withers, first.'

Goodridge frowned. 'You'll need to contact him. We need that footage.'

'I'll follow up,' Karen assured him.

Goodridge continued the briefing. He asked if anyone had been to see Quentin Chapman.

'I can do that, too,' Karen volunteered. She knew more about the gangster than anyone else on the team. He'd walked away unpunished after Karen's last big case; she wasn't about to let that happen again. She wanted to look into his eyes when she asked him about Sophie.

'I'm not sure that's a good idea. Chapman might—'

'I can handle it.'

Goodridge looked over at DCI Churchill. 'What do you think?'

Churchill looked back, his eyes steely. 'Karen's more likely to get something from Chapman than anyone else.'

Goodridge turned back to Karen. 'Be careful.'

'Thank you.'

'I want someone with you.'

'I'll go with her,' Rick volunteered.

'All right,' Goodridge agreed, before moving on and assigning new tasks.

Karen thought it unlikely Sophie's attack was related to her personal life. Which left two main options.

Option one was that what had happened was linked to her work – a previous case, a criminal out for revenge. Karen had experienced something similar herself after a run-in with a criminal gang. If that was the case, Karen's money was on Chapman.

Or there was still the possibility that Sophie had simply been in the wrong place at the wrong time, and this had been a random assault.

Goodridge summarised the rest of their early findings before adding, 'I want you all to know that we will do whatever it takes to find out who did this. We will get justice for our colleague.' He paused for a moment, looking around the room. Some of the staff were visibly upset. 'If any of you need to talk, counselling services are available. This is a shock to all of us, but none more so than the officers in the same team as Sophie. DCI Churchill would like to add a few words.'

Churchill stepped forward and adjusted his tie, his eyes scanning the room. He was as composed as ever and immaculately dressed. Standing beside Goodridge in his rumpled suit, Churchill made a stark contrast. His charcoal suit fit perfectly.

'This is a difficult time for all of us, but I want you to know that I am personally overseeing this investigation, and my team will be involved,' he said.

Karen felt a rush of relief to know Churchill wouldn't be blocking their participation in the case due to the team's personal connection with Sophie.

'We will find who did this and they will be held to account. Sophie is a bright, ambitious officer and is a great asset to our team.' Churchill raised his chin and looked around the room. 'This is hard for all of us, but by working together, we'll do her proud.'

The room was silent as he finished, and Karen found she had a lump in her throat. She'd had a few clashes with the DCI since he'd arrived at Nettleham, but right now she welcomed his quiet confidence and determination.

Chapter Seven

After the briefing, Karen decided to talk to Rick. She was worried about how he was handling the situation. He'd lost his mum not long ago, and Sophie had helped him through his grief. She'd been like a mother hen, fussing over him, helping him with the paperwork involved, making sure he wasn't subsisting on takeaways and that he always had someone to talk to.

Their relationship had its ups and downs, but they had a unique bond. Though fiercely protective of one another, they could argue over the most trivial things. Usually because Rick would say something tactless, and Sophie would get in a huff. They were competitive at work too. But their fallouts never lasted more than a couple of days, and then they'd be as close as ever. Until the next spat. They acted like squabbling siblings at times.

Rick was sitting at his desk, head in his hands. Karen walked over and stood in front of him.

'I know this is hard, Rick. I'm here if you need to talk.'

He looked up, guilt written all over his face. 'I feel terrible,' he said. 'The last thing I said to Sophie . . . it was that meeting, where I said she was naive.'

'I'm sure she knows you didn't mean it,' Karen said.

'I was irritated,' Rick said. 'She can be so prim and self-righteous sometimes. Like when she refuses to accept she could be wrong—' He broke off. 'I know that's a horrible thing to say.'

'Forget it,' Karen said. 'You were frustrated. You said something you didn't mean.'

Rick shook his head. 'But what if Sophie got some crazy idea in her head to prove me wrong?'

'What do you mean?'

'What if she was trying to prove she isn't naive and can handle an investigation on her own?'

'Did she say anything?'

'No, but I know what she's like. It's just the sort of thing she would do.'

'Do you think it's something to do with that social media row she's been sorting out?'

'I don't think so. She told me she'd wrapped that case up.'

'Then what?'

'Another investigation? Something new?' Rick put his head in his hands again. 'If she did, it's my fault.'

Karen put a hand on his shoulder. 'Rick, listen to me. It's not your fault. Sophie is responsible for her own actions. If there is another investigation she decided to tackle alone, we need to find out what it is. You don't have time to sit around feeling guilty.'

'How?'

'You can start by looking through her desk – see if she made any notes. You know she loves using those notebooks. The details might not be on her computer, but she might have scribbled something down.'

'I'll check,' Rick agreed as he rose to his feet. He smiled. 'Thanks, boss.'

Karen walked back to her own desk, thinking over what Rick had said. It was a plausible theory. Sophie was a high achiever. She worked hard, but her weakness was always trying to be top of the class. She was competitive and attracted to exciting cases. Rick's suggestion made sense.

Karen logged on to the system and accessed Tony Withers's details. They needed to get hold of the security footage from his workshop as soon as possible.

She dialled the landline number. A female voice answered. 'Tony Withers's office.'

'Can I speak to Mr Withers, please?'

'I'm afraid he's not here at the moment. Can I take a message?'

'This is Detective Sergeant Hart of the Lincolnshire Police. I need to meet with Mr Withers urgently. Can you get him to call me?' Karen gave out her direct line and her mobile number.

It wasn't long before the phone on Karen's desk rang. She snatched it up, expecting it to be Withers. But it was his secretary again.

'DS Hart. Mr Withers sends his apologies. He's unable to take calls today and instead asked me to call you. He'd like to meet you tomorrow morning at eleven if that's convenient.'

No, it isn't. Karen inwardly raged. 'Why can't he take calls?'

Maybe she should give him the benefit of the doubt. He might be sitting at a dying relative's bedside or—

'He's playing golf.'

Withers's secretary didn't even try to hide the disapproval in her voice. Karen was beginning to feel sorry for her for having a boss like Withers. She asked for the name of the golf course and the secretary gave it to her.

'It can't wait until tomorrow. Please, let him know I'll see him at the golf course.'

'Oh, er . . . I don't think he'll like that.'

'I'm sure he'll cope,' Karen said and hung up.

◆ ◆ ◆

Karen and Rick pulled into the gravel car park at the golf club, their car splashing through icy puddles. The cold air hit them like a slap as they stepped out of the vehicle. Karen's breath froze the moment it left her mouth. She quickly zipped up her heavy winter coat, her fingertips already numb from the cold. Rick wrapped a thick scarf around his neck. The sky was an unrelenting grey, and dead leaves skittered across their path as a glacial wind danced around them.

They walked up the sloping drive. Karen had heard about this new and exclusive golf course. The clubhouse was a white single-storey building with large tinted windows, surrounded by landscaped gardens containing recently planted evergreen shrubs.

The clubhouse had a luxurious interior with dark hardwood floors and high ceilings with crystal light fittings. There were chairs and sofas covered in teal velvet. There was a bar and Karen spotted a sign to the restaurant. The staff were dressed in identical uniforms – black trousers and teal polo shirts with the club's insignia.

'Bet it costs a pretty packet to become a member,' Rick muttered. 'Tony Withers isn't short of a few quid.'

A helpful attendant directed them towards the putting green. Tony Withers was there. He was a thickset man of average height. He wore blue pleated trousers and a patterned electric-blue wool jumper, with a yellow polo shirt, the collar just visible around his neck, topped off with a tweed flat cap.

It was an ugly outfit, but Karen recognised the expensive brand names.

There was a taller, much thinner man standing beside Withers. His arms hung limply at his sides, and his head was bowed. It looked like Withers was barking orders at him, though it was impossible to hear what he was saying.

'Do you know who that is with Mr Withers?' Karen asked the young woman who'd directed them.

'I've not seen him before. He's not a member. Mr Withers probably invited him. Members are permitted to bring a guest four times a month.'

Karen and Rick nodded and thanked her before setting off towards the two men.

'Good morning, gentlemen,' Karen said as she and Rick held up their IDs.

Tony Withers's eyes narrowed. He had a ruddy complexion, and thick strawberry-blonde hair poked out from beneath his flat cap.

'Good morning.' Tony spoke with a strong East London accent.

'Your secretary told you to expect us?' Karen asked.

'She did.'

'Perhaps we'd be more comfortable talking inside?' Rick suggested.

'No, I'm perfectly comfortable here,' Tony said, slapping his hands together. 'I find this weather bracing.'

The tall man beside him shivered violently.

Karen held out her hand to him and said, 'DS Hart of the Lincolnshire Police. This is my colleague DC Rick Cooper. And you are?'

'Emmett Jenkins,' he said, switching the golf club he was holding to his left hand so he could shake Karen's.

Tony gave an irritated sigh. 'He's just my accountant. What is it you want from me, detectives?'

'Are you sure you don't want to go inside?' Rick asked again, watching Emmett shivering.

'Too many ears in there. I don't want people hearing my business. Now, what is it you want?'

Rick shoved his hands in his pockets, something he did whenever he was feeling tense. 'We need to take a look at the security tapes from your workshop on Great Northern Terrace,' he explained. 'Our colleague was attacked nearby at around eight p.m. last night, and we want to review the footage to see if it caught anything.'

'How awful!' Emmett burst out.

Tony silenced him with a look.

'It was a vicious attack, and she's in a serious condition in hospital,' Rick said.

'I'm sorry to hear that. What happened?' Tony asked.

'That's what we're trying to find out, and your security footage should help us with that,' Karen said.

'All right.'

'You'll give us access to the recordings?'

'Of course. I'll tell Valerie to hand them over. She's the one you should speak to. She's only been working for me for a year or so, but she runs rings around the blokes.' Tony balanced a club in his hand, feeling the weight of it.

'Thank you. We appreciate it,' Karen said.

That had been easier than she'd expected. Maybe Arnie's theory about Withers's business being a chop shop was wrong.

'Just one more thing, could you tell me where you were at eight p.m. last night?'

'I . . . I was at home,' Emmett stammered.

'Thank you,' Karen said with a nod, 'but I was asking about Mr Withers's whereabouts.'

Tony Withers smirked. 'I was having dinner with friends at the Bronze Pig in Lincoln. Lots of people can verify.' He reeled off some names. Karen recognised one of them as a local councillor. 'I even paid the bill with my credit card.'

'Thank you for your cooperation,' Karen said after Rick jotted down the names.

'No problem. Happy to help. Now, if that's all, Emmett and I have some putting practice to get back to.'

Emmett was shivering so violently now that Karen thought he'd barely be able to hold the golf club, let alone putt the ball. She didn't understand the attraction of golf – all that time wasted trying to get a tiny white ball into a hole in the ground. What was the point? Mike enjoyed it though, and often played with friends at the local course.

'Enjoy your game, gentlemen,' Rick said as he and Karen turned to leave.

'Wait a minute,' Tony called after them.

They turned back.

'Tell me your names again.'

'DS Hart and DC Cooper,' Karen said.

A wide smile stretched across Tony's mouth.

The smile gave Karen the creeps.

'I've heard of you, DS Hart,' Tony said, a knowing chuckle accompanying his words. 'A business associate of mine had a run-in with you.'

'Who?' Karen tried not to react but felt her stomach clench as she waited for his answer.

'Quentin Chapman.'

'You know Chapman?' Her voice was barely a whisper.

'Don't get upset,' Tony said, with a grin. 'He only said nice things.' He paused for effect before continuing. 'I gather he was quite impressed. Even if you did cost him a hefty whack.'

'How do you know him?' Karen demanded.

'We go back a long way.'

'You said he was a business associate?' Karen's tone was hard. She was fighting to keep calm, trying to make sense of this new information.

Sophie had been assaulted outside the workshop belonging to a man connected to Quentin Chapman. This had to be linked somehow. It was a coincidence too far.

Chapman was one of the most powerful men in Lincolnshire. Corrupt and cruel, he'd gained his wealth and importance through threats and violence. Just months ago, Karen had been close to finally exposing his criminal empire and taking him down once and for all, but like a snake he'd managed to slither away.

He wasn't above using intimidation tactics, and had used his heavies to try to scare Karen off. It hadn't worked, and she was more dedicated than ever to seeing him behind bars.

Chapman was notorious for using his influence to worm his way into positions of authority in various businesses around the city. Suspected of being involved in illegal imports and money laundering, he'd been on their watch list for years.

Had Sophie tried to take on Chapman herself? Attempted to bring the gangster to account?

Surely, she wouldn't be that stupid. Quentin Chapman was dangerous. Sophie knew that.

'We are in business together, yes.' Tony was still smirking.

'What sort of business?'

'My workshop, of course. What else could it be?'

She wanted to wipe the smirk off his face.

'Although we do enjoy a game of cards on occasion. Lovely man.'

There were many things Karen would call Quentin Chapman, but *lovely man* wasn't one of them.

'Are you thinking what I'm thinking, boss?' Rick asked as they walked back to the car.

'No, Sophie wouldn't do that,' Karen said, knowing exactly what Rick was getting at. 'She knows what Quentin Chapman is like. He's managed to wriggle out of charges time and time again. She wouldn't take him on alone.'

'I don't know. I think it's exactly something she'd do to prove herself, trying to impress everyone.'

Karen didn't reply. She didn't want to believe it. But she knew Rick could be right. Sophie was desperate to impress, eager to climb the ranks.

'The fact no one else has been able to pin anything on him would only make her more eager to be the first,' Rick said.

Karen sighed. 'You could be right. We need to update the team and trace all the connections between Withers and Chapman. I doubt it's just a workshop that links them.'

'It won't be easy,' Rick replied. 'Chapman oversees multiple companies. Not all of them are in his name.'

'Nothing is ever easy when it comes to Quentin Chapman.'

Karen stopped and turned to see Tony Withers still watching them, a mobile phone clamped to his ear. So much for not taking calls, Karen thought. He was probably talking to Chapman now, telling him about their visit.

'You can tell a lot about people by the way they treat their staff, don't you think?' Rick said, a hint of disapproval in his voice as he looked back at Emmett, who was still standing hunched over beside Withers.

Karen agreed. 'Valerie seemed scared of him too. That tells me Tony Withers is a nasty piece of work.'

Rick folded his arms across his chest as they carried on walking. 'Do you think he had anything to do with the attack on Sophie?'

It was a sensible question, driven by logic, but his voice was tense and bitter.

'I doubt he'd be directly involved,' Karen replied. 'Tony Withers seems like the kind of man to get others to do his dirty work.'

'Yeah, a real lowlife. But at least he's handing over the security footage.'

'Let's get over to the workshop and get it before he changes his mind,' Karen said.

She was keen to see the recording. It could be their only opportunity to discover what had happened to Sophie last night.

Chapter Eight

Valerie was waiting for them at the entrance to the workshop. 'Tony called,' she said as soon as they got out of the car. 'He told me to expect you and asked me to get last night's recording ready.'

'Great,' Karen said, and they followed Valerie inside.

The smell of oil, grease and solvents hung heavy in the air. Pop music tinkled out of the speakers as Valerie pressed the button to lower the roller door. 'It's so cold today we're shutting the door to try and keep some heat inside.'

The other two mechanics studiously ignored Karen and Rick, and the banging and clattering of their tools echoed off the walls.

Valerie motioned for Karen and Rick to follow her and led them through the workshop. The lighting was uneven, bright in spots but so dim it was hard to see in other areas. The space was filled with tools and parts from old cars.

Valerie walked ahead of them, weaving her way between stacks of spare parts, heading to a desk in the far corner. It was covered with paperwork and old Haynes car manuals, the covers marked by smudged black grease. A battered laptop computer sat on top of a pile of papers.

Valerie gestured to the computer before turning to face Karen and Rick. 'You have options. I can copy the footage to a DVD for you, but my burner is temperamental so it might not work.'

She paused before continuing. 'Alternatively, I've set up a temporary password for accessing our cloud storage service, so you could download the footage yourselves. Or I could log on now, and you can watch it here.'

Karen shuddered at the thought of watching the recording at the workshop. Watching it here, in the presence of strangers, would only make it more painful. Even back at the station, with her colleagues and in familiar surroundings, it would be traumatic to see the assault on her friend. 'We'll take the login details and the password,' she said.

'And if you don't mind,' Rick said, rummaging through his pockets and coming up with sweet wrappers and a set of keys. 'Could you download a copy on to this?' He held up a USB stick attached to his keyring.

'Absolutely,' Valerie said.

Rick removed the memory stick from the keyring and handed it to her.

Karen asked, 'Have you watched the recording from last night?'

Valerie shook her head, her eyes clouded with worry. 'No, I didn't want to. The newspapers are filled with stories about women being attacked. That's bad enough, but this happened so close, and your colleague is similar in age to my daughter . . . It would give me nightmares.'

It took a few minutes to transfer the video files, and Valerie filled the time jotting down the website address and temporary password so they could still log on to the cloud and access the recordings there if they needed to.

◆ ◆ ◆

Karen and Rick were quiet on the journey back to the station. Both knew that when they arrived, they would have to view something unspeakable: footage of a vicious attack on Sophie, their friend and colleague. Karen had to watch the recording in order to identify Sophie's attacker, but she was dreading it.

Rather than watch the security footage in the open-plan office, they booked a viewing room. Rick set things up, while Karen went to get them both a cup of coffee.

She entered the viewing room, which was filled with large screens and various bits of electronic equipment that hummed and displayed tiny flashing lights. Karen had no idea what half the gadgets did. She nudged the door closed with her foot and handed one of the cups to Rick.

He looked pale.

Karen guessed immediately he'd seen the attack already. 'The camera caught something?'

Rick put down the cup and ran his hands through his dark hair. He looked younger and more vulnerable than usual.

'I jumped forward to the time we had from the app on Sophie's phone. The camera captured the attack.'

Karen suddenly no longer wanted her coffee either. She pulled out a chair and sat down. 'You can go and get some air if you need a break. I can do this.'

But Rick set his mouth in a grim line, took a deep breath, then sat next to Karen. 'No, I can handle it.'

Rick tapped a key on the keyboard and the recording started to play.

It was very dark, but they could see Sophie's car pull up and park. A minute passed before Sophie got out of the car. She stood alone at first, pacing back and forth, walking past the units and right up to the workshop.

'What's she doing?' Karen muttered. 'Is she waiting for someone?'

Sophie pulled out her mobile phone; the screen lit up, but she didn't make a call.

Suddenly Sophie spun around and then stood rigid in one spot.

'Did she hear something?' Karen wondered aloud.

Her heart was racing. This had already happened. There was nothing she could do to change the outcome, but her body's flight-or-fight response was acting on instinct. She wanted to shout a warning. Tell Sophie to get out of there.

They saw the shadowy figure before Sophie did.

Rick took a sharp intake of breath as the attacker lifted an arm and slammed the tyre lever into Sophie's head.

Karen tried to keep in touch with the logical, analytical part of her brain. She needed to view this as a police officer investigating a crime, not a woman witnessing a brutal attack on a friend.

The attacker was right-handed. Wearing a black hat, coat, scarf and gloves. Karen mentally listed the things that could be important. But all the while, her mind was screaming at her to look away, to turn it off.

They watched the rest of the footage in silence. When the attack was over, and the assailant walked back into the shadows, Rick said, 'I'll try to increase the exposure and contrast. Let's see if we can get a better look at him.'

Karen noted Rick's assumption the attacker was male. It was possible, even likely, but they couldn't be sure from the footage.

She stood up. 'I'll be back in a minute.'

Karen yanked open the door and strode down the corridor to the ladies' toilets, her fists clenched at her sides. Rushing into a stall, she bent over just in time as her stomach heaved. The multiple cups of coffee she'd drunk that morning came up in waves, mixed with bile, burning her throat.

Afterwards, she stumbled to a sink and rinsed the taste away, splashing water on her burning cheeks. Her face was a blotchy mess. She used a paper towel to dry her face, and then kicked the bin because it had the audacity to be a few inches out of place. It wobbled across the tiles, falling on its side. She let out a string of expletives as she righted the bin and picked up the spilled paper towels.

A couple of minutes later, she'd composed herself and was back beside Rick in the viewing room. They went back through the footage, watching it on 4x speed until they reached the point where Sophie's dad arrived at the scene. They saw him frantically rush to his daughter as she lay unconscious on the tarmac. It was heart-wrenching. Karen watched in stunned silence, while Rick muttered curse words and vividly described the revenge he'd like to take on the person who'd hurt Sophie.

Karen felt numb as they discussed the footage. It showed the attack, but there was little on the recording that would help them identify Sophie's assailant. The clothing was generic and the resolution of the camera didn't give much detail. The camera's angle, and the fact the attacker had worn a hat pulled down low, meant most of their face was obscured. And there was no other vehicle visible in the area besides Sophie's.

'I can take a look at the cameras on the main road. See if we can pick the scumbag up from there and follow the route he took,' Rick suggested.

'Good idea.' Karen stood up, feeling light-headed. 'I'll update Morgan and Churchill.'

◆ ◆ ◆

Karen rapped her knuckles on the glass door of DI Morgan's office, and entered when he waved her in.

He frowned when she got closer. 'Are you okay? You look out of sorts.'

Karen sank into a chair in front of his desk and took a deep breath. 'Not really. Rick and I just watched the footage of Sophie's attack.'

Morgan's expression shifted from shock to sympathy. 'It's never easy, but when it's someone you know . . .'

He trailed off, and Karen nodded.

'It was brutal, Morgan. Sophie didn't even see it coming.'

Morgan's face was grim as Karen recounted the details from the recording. She was shaking with anger by the time she'd finished. 'They can't get away with this.'

Morgan's voice was steely. 'They won't.' He glanced at his computer. 'I'm not sure you'll want to hear this—'

'What?'

'I've been looking through Sophie's recent database searches, and one stood out. She'd been looking for businesses with connections to Quentin Chapman.'

Karen felt her stomach drop as Morgan's words sunk in. She recalled the smirk on Tony Withers's face when he'd told her about his business connection to the gangster. The news hadn't come as a complete surprise, but it was still a shock to hear Morgan confirm it now.

'I can't believe Sophie would go after Chapman alone,' Karen said after she'd told Morgan what Tony Withers had said at the golf course. 'It's reckless. Stupid. If she found something incriminating, why didn't she tell one of us?' Karen balled her fists. 'Do you think Chapman is behind this?'

'We can't ignore the possibility.'

'Then I'd better speak to him.'

'It might be better if someone else—'

Karen raised a hand and cut him off. 'Goodridge and Churchill are okay with me going. Besides, I know more about him than anyone else. He remembers me.'

'That's what I'm worried about,' Morgan muttered as Karen got to her feet and stretched.

'Where is DI Goodridge anyway? Gone home?'

'Yes, to get a few hours' sleep. He's still heading up the operation, though.'

'Have you heard anything from the hospital? Sophie should have had her scan by now. It was supposed to be at ten a.m.'

'I haven't, but you know what hospitals are like. There are always delays.'

Karen nodded. 'I'm going to head to Chapman's place and find out where he was at eight last night.'

'He won't have done the deed himself.'

'No, but at least he'll know we're on to him. Make him sweat. I'll find out where his grunt men were last night too.'

'Want me to come?'

'No, I'll be fine.'

'Then at least take Arnie or Rick with you.'

'I don't—'

It was Morgan's turn to cut Karen off. 'No arguments. You just suggested Sophie would have been reckless to meet Chapman on her own.'

Morgan was right. Annoying. But right. 'Fine. I'll see if one of them is free.'

She turned to leave.

'Karen?'

She paused by the door. 'Yes?'

'Don't let your guard down.'

Chapter Nine

It was almost lunchtime, and the traffic was heavy, which meant travelling to Burton Waters took longer than usual.

Karen drove up Chapman's sweeping driveway, shaking her head at the obnoxiously huge fountain, complete with life-size stone statues.

'Good grief. The size of the place,' Rick said in awe as Karen pulled up to the front of the house. It didn't look much different to the last time she'd visited. Although, the Georgian-style sash windows, white pillars, and the portico around the front door looked brighter. Perhaps a recent paint job. The bay trees that had been in stone pots beside the front door were gone. There were no other cars on the drive, but it was possible they were parked in the huge garage.

They both got out of the car and walked up the stone path. Karen pressed the doorbell, listening to the chimes echoing from inside and waiting for Chapman, or more likely one of his lackeys, to answer.

Karen shivered, rubbing her arms. Finally, the door opened.

A tall, thin man Karen had seen on a previous visit stared down at her. 'Yes?'

They held up their ID, and Karen asked to see Chapman.

'He's not home,' the man said, preparing to close the door.

Rick put a hand out to stop him. 'When's he due back?'

'I have no idea.'

Karen fumed as he shut the door on them. 'I'll call Chapman directly. If he doesn't answer I'm going to put a trace on his car.'

She started to walk back to the car, pulling her mobile from her coat pocket, but before she could place the call her phone rang.

It was Mike. 'I don't want to worry you . . .' he began.

She didn't like the sound of that. 'What is it?'

'I recognised his car. The black Range Rover from a few months back. Didn't one of his heavies have a ponytail?'

Karen's blood ran cold. 'You can see Chapman's car? Where is it?'

'Near my flat. They followed me on my way home for lunch, all the way back to Lincoln.'

'Are you inside?'

'Yes.'

'Stay there. We're on our way.'

◆　◆　◆

Karen's stomach had twisted into knots on the drive to Mike's place. She felt a mixture of relief and love wash over her when the door opened and she saw him safe and unharmed.

She was so glad to see his familiar face. She gave him a hug and then followed him into the living room and sank down into the sofa. Her legs were shaking.

Mike crossed his arms and frowned down at her. His dark good looks were familiar and comforting. 'Karen, it's fine. Nothing happened. They're probably just trying to spook you, but I thought you should know.'

'Did you actually see Chapman?' Rick asked.

'No, just the bloke with the ponytail,' Mike said.

Karen shuddered at the thought of Chapman's menacing foot solider, Jamie Goode, trailing Mike. A few months ago, she'd caught him outside Mike's apartment. He had been waiting for her, his eyes never straying from the entrance. He'd wanted to unnerve her. No charges brought against him had ever stuck, but he was violent, and it wasn't difficult to imagine what he could do if she crossed his boss. He would do anything on Chapman's orders.

'Might not have been Chapman's car,' Rick said with a shrug.

'Of course it was,' Karen said, more harshly than she intended. 'He's trying to get to all of us. First Sophie—'

'Sophie was attacked by Chapman?' Mike stared at Karen, then Rick.

'It's a working theory,' Rick explained.

Rick and Mike might both believe Karen was overreacting, but Karen's family had been targeted before, and she didn't want history to repeat itself.

'Any update on Sophie's condition?' Mike asked.

'No,' Karen said. 'She was supposed to have a scan this morning, but I haven't heard anything.'

'No news is good news,' Rick said, but even he didn't look like he believed it.

Karen shuffled forward on the sofa. 'Look, Mike, why don't you stay with your mum for a few days. Just until things cool down a bit.'

'No.'

'I don't like Chapman knowing where you live.'

'If Quentin Chapman is a danger to me, then there's no way I'm going to stay with Mum and James and put them at risk.'

'He's got a point,' Rick said.

Karen shot him a look. 'You're not helping.' She turned back to Mike. 'Maybe stay with a friend, out of the area. What about your old boss . . . Stephen, isn't it?'

Mike sat down beside Karen on the sofa, put his arm around her shoulders and squeezed. 'I'm not going anywhere. I know you're scared, but—'

She shifted away, irritated. 'I'm not scared. I'm being sensible.' It was a lie. She was terrified. She couldn't get the image of the attacker smashing the back of Sophie's skull with a tyre lever out of her mind. She couldn't let that happen to anyone else.

He sighed. 'All right. I know you're being *sensible*. But I can look after myself. I'm staying put.'

He could handle himself. He'd been in the service for years. She looked at his leg, the one he'd injured in a suicide attempt after his son had died. He still walked with a limp. On days when the pain was really bad, he used a cane.

His frown deepened. 'My leg isn't going to stop me throwing a punch.'

Mike didn't seem to understand. With criminals like Quentin Chapman, it was never a fair fight. Like cowards, they crept up behind you and hit you from behind, or they forced your car off the road when your little girl was in the back seat.

Karen swallowed the lump in her throat. 'All right.' She stood up and gave Mike the same advice Morgan had given her. 'Don't let your guard down.'

◆　◆　◆

Rick drove the car through the busy streets as they headed out of central Lincoln. Karen was quiet, her gaze fixed on the passing buildings and occasional pedestrians.

'He's a tough guy. He'll be fine,' Rick said, giving her a sideways glance. When she didn't answer, he asked, 'Everything all right between you two?'

'Yes, pretty good. I met his mum and stepdad for the first time yesterday.'

'You did?' Rick's eyes widened with curiosity. 'What are they like?'
Karen grimaced.

'That bad?' Rick laughed.

'Let's just say I didn't make a good first impression. The evening was a disaster. I spilled peas all over his mum's fancy tablecloth. I couldn't seem to say a single word right.' She groaned. 'I'm pretty sure she hates me.'

'How could she? I remember when we first met Mike. He's a different man now. Even she must have to admit you make him happy.'

'Hmmm.' Karen wasn't convinced.

'Did you really spill the peas?' Rick grinned.

'I knocked the serving spoon, and they flew across the table. A few probably made it to the floor. She'll be cursing my name every time they find a rogue pea for the next few days.'

Rick laughed again and Karen smiled and shook her head, relieved to hear laughter and forget – at least for a moment – all the bad stuff going on.

◆ ◆ ◆

When Rick and Karen arrived back at the station, she remembered to ask him if he'd found anything while looking through Sophie's notebooks.

As they walked into the open-plan office, Rick said, 'I skimmed through the ones I found in her desk, but nothing stood out. I'll go through them more carefully this afternoon.' He rubbed his stomach. 'I'm famished. Want to grab something to eat?'

Karen shrugged off her coat and draped it over the back of her chair. 'No, I'm fine.' Her stomach was still tied in knots from earlier and she didn't feel like eating.

Rick walked off to the canteen, and Karen pulled a water bottle from her bag and took a sip, then put it on her desk and went to find Arnie.

She found him at his workstation, staring intently at his screen.

Karen peered at Arnie's desk, wondering how he managed to work like that. Stacks of paper teetered precariously around his computer. A mug – printed with the words *World's Best Detective* – was stuffed with pens, pencils and highlighters, memory sticks, as well as a couple of reusable drinking straws.

He had three other cups on his desk and only one of them contained fresh coffee. The others had only the dregs left and were encircled with stains. Karen guessed they were probably from yesterday.

'How do you keep track of everything in this mess?' Karen asked as she tried to make sense of the disorder.

Arnie grinned. 'There's a method to my madness. I know exactly where everything is. It's intricate.'

'I'm not sure *intricate* is the right word.'

Arnie shrugged. 'Maybe not. Any news from the hospital?'

'No, not yet.' The lack of updates was making Karen nervous. Sophie was supposed to have had her scan by now. She didn't want to hassle Harinder or Sophie's parents with demands for news, but surely a quick text to Harinder wouldn't hurt. At least he'd know she was thinking of them.

She tapped out a message as Arnie said, 'It's looking more likely Quentin Chapman is involved.'

'I know. Mike thinks Chapman's Range Rover followed him home at lunchtime.'

'What? Was it Chapman himself?'

'Mike didn't see him. Just one of his goons – the one with the ponytail – Jamie Goode.'

'What was he following Mike for?'

'The usual scare tactics I suppose. They did the same to me earlier this year. That ponytailed thug was waiting for me outside Mike's flat on one occasion. I really don't like the fact they know where Mike lives.'

Arnie shuddered. 'Be careful, Karen. He's a nasty piece of work. After the team's last interaction with Quentin Chapman, it's no surprise Sophie was looking into him.'

'It came as a surprise to me,' Karen said. 'If she found something during her digging into his background, why didn't she come to me . . . or Morgan?'

'You know why.'

Karen frowned. 'No, I really don't.'

He sighed. 'You know Sophie better than me. What's her top priority? What's her goal in life?'

Karen didn't know what he was getting at. 'Improving our admin system?'

Arnie looked disappointed. 'She's an organiser, sure, but she's also a people pleaser. She's so desperate to be admired, praised by her bosses, it's painful.'

He had a point, but it felt very wrong to be discussing Sophie's character flaws while she lay in a hospital bed.

Arnie must have sensed her discomfort because he added, 'Don't get me wrong. She's a good worker. I like her a lot, but she's needy. It's a weakness.'

Karen sighed and wheeled a chair from an empty desk to sit beside Arnie. 'All right, Freud, give me your best analysis.'

'It's not about any of that pretentious psychology stuff. It's about understanding people. Sophie wants to impress you. And what better way to do that than clinching the evidence that would lead to Chapman's downfall.'

'So, you think if Sophie was attempting to bring down Chapman alone – and we don't know that for sure yet – it's because she wanted to impress me. It's my fault?'

'No. Don't take it personally. I'm saying she wanted to amaze everyone. She wanted to save the day. Get the applause. The accolades. She's close to you, so getting your approval would mean a lot to her. That doesn't mean it's your fault.'

Karen didn't respond.

'We'd all like to see that crook behind bars. Maybe Sophie uncovered evidence that implicated him in something big. Something that could finally bring him down.'

'Even if she was looking into Chapman in her own time, he might not be behind the attack.'

Arnie looked incredulous. 'And it's just a coincidence the attack happened outside Tony's Workshop in which Chapman owns a stake?'

'Could be,' Karen said, playing devil's advocate, though she didn't really believe it.

'Pah,' Arnie said with a grunt of disapproval. 'I don't believe in coincidence. Besides—'

'Karen?' someone behind them said.

They both turned. It was Goodridge. His suit was even more rumpled, and his eyes were red-rimmed with exhaustion. His broad shoulders were slumped, hands in his pockets. His light blue tie was askew, his collar undone. He looked shattered.

'I thought you'd gone home,' Karen said.

'I'm about to, but I need to talk to you about something delicate.'

Arnie pushed his chair back and quirked an eyebrow. 'Need me to leave?'

Goodridge put a hand on the back of Arnie's chair. 'No, you can stay.'

'What is it?' Karen asked, wheeling another chair over for Goodridge.

He slumped into it wearily. 'It's Harinder. I sent a couple of my officers to talk to him at the hospital. He's being difficult.'

Karen frowned. 'What sort of questions did they ask?'

'You can't honestly think Harinder would hurt Sophie,' Arnie said. 'He's a good lad.'

Goodridge blew out an exasperated breath. 'It doesn't matter what I think. It doesn't matter what either of you think.' His tone was sharp. 'You know as well as I do, the number one suspect when something like this happens is the partner or boyfriend.'

'Maybe in a domestic setting,' Karen said. 'But this doesn't have the hallmarks of that sort of case.' She chose her words carefully. Goodridge wasn't trying to target Harinder. He wanted to do his job by the book, and after being up all night, he was understandably tetchy and irritated.

'I'm not trying to be unreasonable,' Goodridge said. 'I like Harinder. But we need to know what he was doing last night. Investigations follow procedure. We don't ignore the rules just because he's our buddy.'

'No, of course not,' Karen agreed. 'You want me to talk to him?'

Goodridge nodded. 'Be diplomatic but find out what he was doing when Sophie was attacked. See if you can find out if they've been having problems.'

Digging into Harinder and Sophie's private business wouldn't be pleasant, but if it had to be done, at least Karen could try to handle it sensitively, without causing offence. She was close to them both. Harinder would trust her and be more likely to open up.

'And talk to her parents as well,' Goodridge added, his expression hard.

'You want their alibi too?' Karen asked.

Goodridge's gaze was unwavering. 'I want to know if they had concerns about Harinder.'

Karen felt a chill. Goodridge's eyes were cold. Despite all his talk of procedure and rules, it was clear he suspected Harinder of something sinister.

Chapter Ten

Karen strode across the station car park in the light drizzle, her mood as dreary as the heavy grey sky above. She wasn't looking forward to the task Goodridge had assigned her. She didn't want to pick over the details of Harinder and Sophie's relationship like it was a puzzle to solve. It felt rude and invasive. Yes, it was part of her job as a detective, but she knew these people. She cared about them both, and that made it so much worse.

It felt like a betrayal. How would she feel in Harinder's shoes? She'd be hurt and angry. The timing couldn't be worse. A catastrophe had rocked his personal life, and he needed support from his colleagues. Instead, he was going to get an interrogation.

A gentle, diplomatic interrogation, but it would be cruel and prying no matter how careful Karen was with her word choices.

Her phone chirped with a text message as she reached her car. It was Harinder.

She read the message, the knot in her stomach tightening. Sophie's condition remained the same and the scan had been delayed due to a backlog of patients and staffing issues.

Karen got in the car and slammed the door shut. Guilt nagged at her, but she pushed it away. No matter how much she hated it, she had a job to do.

By the time she reached the hospital, the light drizzle had turned into a torrential downpour. She parked and sprinted along the pavement, dodging puddles, as she headed for the hospital entrance. Sad-eyed patients in dressing gowns stood outside, under the plastic awning that sheltered them from the rain.

Once inside, Karen headed to the intensive therapy unit.

Harinder was standing beside the sign for ITU, staring at the floor. He looked up when he heard her approach. 'Karen! Hi. Sorry I didn't message earlier. But there was no news. No change. Sophie's dad is in with her now. Her mum went home to try and get a couple of hours' sleep. Do you want me to ask her dad to step out so you can see her?'

'No,' Karen said quickly, the guilt now gnawing at her stomach. 'I just came to see how you're all holding up.' The lie tasted sour on her tongue.

He ran a hand through his hair and exhaled. 'Feels like we're in limbo, just waiting for answers.'

'Do you want to go and get a drink or something to eat?'

'Sure. There's a family room here. It's kitted out with armchairs, a tea and coffee station . . . but it's small and it makes me feel . . .' He paused. 'Claustrophobic, I suppose. There are no windows.'

'The canteen then?' Karen suggested.

They went upstairs to the canteen. It was quiet, the lunch rush long gone. Karen thought she should try to eat something but couldn't face anything too heavy. She grabbed a tray and a packet of ready-salted crisps.

Harinder picked a mozzarella and pesto baguette. Karen opted for tea rather than coffee, thinking it would be better for her stomach.

Harinder stood by the tall fridge filled with various drinks, his body language tense and his lips drawn into a tight line. He grabbed a Coke Zero and said, 'You know they don't sell full-sugar Coke here anymore?'

'I suppose it's not very healthy.'

'When my dad was in here with cancer, he was wasting away, but had no appetite. I went to the hospital shop, looking for a drink with sugar to give him some energy, but it was all water or diet drinks.'

'Being here must bring back bad memories.'

He nodded glumly. 'I suppose hospitals are like that for a lot of people.'

After Karen paid, they chose a table by one of the windows.

'Goodridge said he sent a couple of his officers to talk to you,' Karen said, keeping her tone light, while opening the bag of crisps.

'Yeah,' Harinder said, his expression making his disgust clear. 'Can you believe it? They were really pushy, too. Insinuating I had something to do with what happened to Sophie.' His jaw clenched as he shook his head. He unwrapped his baguette and continued. 'They wanted to know where I was when Sophie was attacked.'

Karen put the bag of crisps on the table. 'They're just doing their jobs, Harinder. They need to ask. You know it's routine to look at partners and family members first.'

His eyes narrowed and a sudden realisation dawned in his eyes. 'That's why you're here, isn't it? You're not here to see how I'm doing, or Sophie's parents. You want to know where I was at eight o'clock last night?'

He pushed the baguette away, seething with anger. 'I never expected you of all people would think that of me.'

Karen reached out, but he pulled away.

She had to take control of the conversation before it got out of hand. Harinder felt betrayed and was understandably emotional, but she needed him to believe she was still on his side.

'I know you both,' Karen insisted. 'I don't believe for one second that you would hurt Sophie, but the questions still need to be asked. You know that, Harinder. But you also know how an investigation works.'

He took a deep breath, clearly trying to rein in his anger.

'These are just routine questions,' Karen said. 'Don't make this more difficult than it needs to be. Let's get them out of the way, so we can focus on catching who did this to Sophie, and you can focus on being here for her when she wakes up.'

'Do you think she will wake up?' Harinder's anger evaporated, and he looked vulnerable and scared.

Karen's chest was tight. She had to break eye contact and swallow the lump in her throat. 'Sophie's been through so much, and she always pulls through.'

He took a shaky breath, trying to compose himself. 'Yes, you're right.'

'So, where were you last night?'

'At home.'

'Can anybody vouch for your whereabouts?'

He thought for a moment. 'There are security cameras outside my apartment building. You'll be able to see I got home at six twenty. I called Sophie to confirm our dinner plans, but she told me she was busy and needed to revise. So, I put a frozen lasagne in the oven and then played an online game on my PC. You can check that too since they log who's online. I was still playing when I got the call from Sophie's dad, telling me . . .' He shivered as he remembered.

'All right.' Karen smiled. 'We'll check that, then draw a line under it and move on. I'm sorry I had to ask.'

But Harinder didn't return her smile.

Karen tried to quash her doubts, but one wormed its way into her head. Harinder had the technical knowhow to use online gaming to invent an alibi if he needed one. He certainly had the knowledge and technical resources to do so.

After all, it was Harinder's department that investigated things like this. If he needed to cover his tracks, he knew exactly what to do. Karen pushed the thought away, but it persisted like a stubborn weed.

She sipped her tea, picked up the crisps again and offered the bag to Harinder. He shook his head, ripped his baguette in half and took a bite.

Years of working for the police had given Karen a heavy dose of suspicion. Which was a good thing when it came to her work as a detective. But when it came to personal relationships, it made things complicated. She didn't want to entertain doubts about a long-term colleague and friend like Harinder.

They'd worked so many cases together. She trusted him implicitly. Didn't she?

Harinder looked up, and his gaze met hers. His eyes were full of pain. Of course he wasn't lying, she told herself. He was worried about Sophie. There was no way he'd hurt her.

'So where are you at with the investigation?' he asked. 'I take it it's not going well if I'm your number one suspect.'

Karen winced. 'You're not,' she assured him. 'We just need to check everyone close to Sophie. It's not unusual for the partner to be involved, so if these questions don't get asked, and it's not all recorded correctly in the logbook, it's Goodridge's backside on the line. He's just making sure everything is actioned correctly.' She waved a hand dismissively. 'You know how it is.'

Harinder didn't look convinced.

'Do you know why she went to Great Northern Terrace? Did she have a connection with any of the businesses or staff there?'

Harinder shook his head.

'She'd never been to the workshop?' Out of the three premises in the immediate vicinity of where Sophie had been attacked, Karen thought the workshop seemed the most likely place for there to be a connection. Perhaps Sophie had taken her car there. The tyre lever used as a weapon was likely from there too. When Harinder didn't answer immediately, Karen added, 'Have you ever been there?'

Harinder hesitated before crossing his arms. 'No.'

His hesitation prompted Karen to say, 'You're sure?'

'Of course I'm sure.'

He was upset and clearly fed up with her questions, but Karen wasn't finished yet.

'I wanted to ask you again if Sophie mentioned anything she was looking into? Perhaps outside of her normal work?' Karen asked.

She felt a pang of sympathy as he sadly shook his head.

'No, nothing out of the ordinary. She said she was revising for her online course in criminal psychology last night, but she wasn't. She'd gone to Great Northern Terrace. For some reason, she didn't want me to know that.' He looked down at the table. 'I don't understand why she lied to me.'

'She may not have lied,' Karen said. 'Perhaps she intended to revise, but something came up. Maybe someone asked her to meet them—'

'Who?'

'I wish I knew,' Karen said.

He drummed his fingers on the table. 'I thought you would have had something by now. Is there any CCTV footage? Did Sophie tell anyone where she was going?'

Karen understood why he was impatient. She didn't want to go into detail about the security footage they had showing the brutal attack on Sophie. He was too fragile, and it hadn't been much help anyway.

She decided against telling him about Quentin Chapman's potential involvement too. They had no solid evidence yet, and the last thing they needed was Harinder trying to track down Chapman and confronting the gangster himself.

'Do you want me to stay for a while, so you can go home and get some rest?' Karen offered.

'No, I want to stick around in case they do the scan.'

'I understand,' Karen said. 'I could come back tonight and give you a bit of a break?'

'That's kind of you.' His voice was stiff and formal. He was keeping distance between them now, and Karen couldn't blame him. She'd come here asking questions, making him feel like a suspect.

Harinder swallowed another mouthful of baguette. 'Rick has offered to come by tonight, so I can get a couple of hours' rest. I can always take a quick nap in the family room.'

Karen knew she was pushing it, but she had to ask. 'Have you and Sophie been getting on all right recently?'

Harinder's eyes blazed, and he clenched his fists on the table. 'Yes, Karen,' he said bitingly. 'Sophie and I have been getting on just fine, and no, I didn't lure her out to Great Northern Terrace to attack her.'

At the sound of Harinder's raised voice, one of the catering staff glanced over.

Karen spoke quickly, her tone apologetic. 'I know. I'm sorry. I understand your relationship should be private, but I had to ask.'

'Did you really, though?' he asked coldly, his gaze filled with contempt.

Karen felt her cheeks burn.

Harinder tossed the rest of his baguette on to the tray and rose from his seat.

'I've lost my appetite,' he said, his voice sharp and bitter.

He shoved the tray into the rack, and walked out of the canteen without looking back, leaving Karen with a half-eaten packet of crisps and a cup of tea that had gone cold.

Chapter Eleven

Karen felt like the world's most despicable person when she left the canteen. She'd hurt Harinder. He was furious with her, and understandably so. She wanted to give him space to cool off but had promised Goodridge she'd speak to Sophie's parents while she was at the hospital.

She found Sophie's dad in the ITU family room.

Holding her breath, she pushed the door open slowly, praying Harinder wasn't in there. She breathed a sigh of relief when she saw the room was empty except for Geoff Jones. He sat in an armchair, his coat thrown over him like a blanket.

He blinked and opened his eyes when Karen walked in.

'Sorry,' he said, pushing away the coat and sitting up properly. 'I didn't realise you were here.'

'I didn't mean to disturb you, are you trying to get some rest? I popped by to see how Sophie is,' Karen said.

'It's fine. I can't sleep anyway,' he said. 'There's no change unfortunately. The nurse is just doing some tests, so I came in here. Clara's gone home for a few hours to get some rest. We've organised it so one of us is always here for when Sophie wakes up.'

'Any news on the scan?' Karen asked.

He shook his head angrily. 'No, it's ridiculous. I keep asking, but they tell me there's another priority. An urgent case. I don't see how anyone could be more urgent than Sophie. She's comatose! Her brain . . .' He gripped the arms of the chair. 'It's infuriating. I know they work hard, but we need better resources.'

Karen sat beside him. 'I'm sorry. The waiting must be agony.'

'Have you made any progress?' he asked. 'Any idea who did this?'

'We've got some early leads,' Karen said, 'but nothing concrete. Nothing I can share at the moment, I'm afraid.'

He sighed. 'I understand. I just hope you catch them.'

'How was Sophie before this happened?' Karen asked tentatively. 'Has she been happy? Upset about anything?'

Geoff rubbed his eyes, smothering a yawn. 'She's been doing great. Last week she told us that everything's going really well at work. She mentioned how you complimented her on a presentation.' He smiled fondly, folding his coat on his lap. 'She thinks a lot of you. She's always talking about how you help her and support her career.' He gave a tight smile and reached across to pat Karen's hand. 'I thought you should know that.'

'I think a lot of her too. She's such a crucial part of our team. We're all missing her very much.'

'There's tea and coffee if you want to help yourself,' Geoff said, settling back in the armchair and nodding over to a counter, where there was a kettle and a filter coffee machine, along with the fixings and individual packets of biscuits.

'Thanks, but I'm fine,' Karen said. 'How's Sophie been getting on with Harinder?' She kept her tone light. She really didn't want to cause any disruption in their family dynamic. The last thing she wanted was to feed unnecessary suspicions to Geoff's mind. But Goodridge had assigned her the task of finding out if Sophie's parents had any worries over their daughter's relationship.

'They've been getting along great. She's so happy with him,' Geoff said. 'And he's very sharp, isn't he? I got into a discussion about computer graphics with him last week. He'd lost me by the second sentence.'

'Don't worry. I often feel the same way,' Karen said, with a smile. 'It must be extremely difficult for him too.'

'He's a good lad. Sophie's mad about him. I just wish she'd wake up, even if she needs rehabilitation, or we have to look after her . . .' He trailed off. He sniffed and looked up to the ceiling. 'I really need my little girl to wake up.'

◆ ◆ ◆

Goodridge had gone home by the time Karen returned to the station, so she gave her update to Churchill. She then spent the rest of the afternoon driving around, visiting establishments that had ties to Chapman and his known associates, but he was nowhere to be found. He'd vanished into thin air after the brutal attack on Sophie.

Karen had put out an alert on his vehicle, but there had been no hits since lunchtime.

Rick and Arnie were hard at work digging up any leads they could find that might reveal where Chapman was hiding out. While they were working on that, Karen decided to revisit the workshop before it closed for the day. Valerie's reaction when she'd spoken about her boss made Karen think she might have some dirt on him. If Karen could persuade her to talk, Valerie might be able to provide information on Tony Withers and Chapman's current business dealings.

It was dark by the time Karen got to the workshop. The roller door was open, and the radio was playing an annoying advert about second-hand cars.

She couldn't see any of the staff. Stepping into the dimly lit space, she quickly took in the wall of tools. Hammers, sockets, different-sized spanners and some kind of drill, all hanging from hooks. Is this where Sophie's attacker got the tyre lever from?

The sound of the blaring radio raised the hairs on the back of her neck. It seemed to smother every other sound, disturbing Karen's senses. It would be hard to hear if anyone was close enough to creep up behind her.

Valerie stepped out from behind the old Ford Fiesta, and gasped when she spotted Karen. She pressed a hand to her chest. 'You scared me!'

'Where are the other mechanics?' Karen felt a spark of anger. Had the men left her here alone when they knew there'd been a violent attack against a woman last night?

Valerie gave her a resigned smile. 'They've gone. It's just me locking up again.'

'You couldn't get one of the lads to cover it tonight?'

Valerie rolled her eyes. 'I did ask. Apparently, they had prior commitments that couldn't be cancelled.'

That was out of order, Karen thought.

'I was just doing a few last bits on the Ford, so it'll be ready when the owner comes to pick it up tomorrow.' She began gathering the tools on the ground and deftly putting them in the appropriate spot in the metal toolbox beside her. 'How can I help?'

'I hoped you'd have time for a chat.'

'Sure.' Valerie walked across to a large metal sink, scooped out a dollop of Swarfega and began lathering up her hands and forearms. 'I'll just get this grease off,' she said. 'I won't keep you a minute.'

'No problem,' Karen said, taking a moment to look around.

There were various machine parts disassembled on the bench closest to her, but Karen didn't know what they were for. Underneath the bench was a hydraulic lift, and up top, a set of tiny drawers containing nuts and screws. Tools of all shapes and sizes hung above this bench too. Some nasty-looking ones. Karen's gaze lingered on a long, sharp, metal chisel.

Valerie dried her arms. 'Fancy a cuppa?'

'I don't want to keep you,' Karen said. 'I only have a couple of questions.'

'It's fine,' Valerie said, tucking a loose strand of hair behind her ear. 'It's just me at home these days, so I've got no reason to rush back. I think that's the main reason I get left to lock up. The others have got families, you see.'

Karen frowned. She still didn't think it was fair.

'I've been thinking about your colleague all day. Is there any news?'

'No, she's still critical.'

Valerie fell silent for a few moments, lost in thought. Then she looked up, straight into Karen's eyes. 'I mentioned my daughter before . . .'

Karen nodded and waited for her to continue.

'Her name's Claudia.' Valerie's voice was thick with sadness, and a single tear ran down her cheek as she continued. 'The row wasn't recent. It was over two years ago now. She stormed out, and I haven't seen her since.'

The weight of her sorrow seemed to hang between them.

'I'm sorry, that must be really difficult,' Karen said.

'I reported her missing to the police up in Yorkshire. They were as helpful as they could be in the circumstances. They put me in touch with a few charities that try to reconnect families, but I've not heard anything. She hasn't used her bank cards – not that there was ever much in her account – and she left her passport behind. I can't stop thinking about her, wondering where she is and if she's safe.'

Tears welled up again in Valerie's eyes, and Karen's heart broke for her. She understood some of the pain Valerie was feeling. Her own daughter had been taken from her too soon. Tilly had been just five years old. The thought of all the experiences and milestones they'd been denied left Karen feeling hollow and broken. No matter how much time passed, Karen would always desperately want her daughter back.

She placed a comforting hand on Valerie's arm. 'I'm so sorry.' It was difficult to know what else to say.

'I'll always keep looking, but . . .' Valerie shrugged. 'One of her friends mentioned she might have come to Lincolnshire.'

'That's why you moved here?' Karen asked.

'Yes, and then I got this job and, well, I stayed.'

Valerie busied herself making the tea. They chatted about the history of the workshop for a while and the two men Valerie worked with.

It was only when Valerie passed Karen a mug of tea that she decided now was the right time to broach the subject of Tony. 'Valerie, I need your help. I'll be honest with you, we're looking closely at Tony Withers.'

Valerie didn't turn around, but she stopped stirring her tea. 'Tony? For the attack on your colleague?'

'I don't have any evidence to connect him to that yet,' Karen said. 'But my instincts tell me he's a bad sort.'

Valerie's hands trembled as she laid down the teaspoon and slowly turned to face Karen.

She took a deep breath before answering. 'I've heard stories about his past. Nothing solid, only rumours.'

'What sort of rumours?'

'I've heard Tony runs a poker club. Members only. But it's not just cards the members are interested in . . .'

'Meaning?'

'I don't have any evidence.'

'Just tell me what you've heard. Let me worry about the evidence.'

'I don't think he has much respect for women. He doesn't pay me any attention. I'm past it in his eyes. But there was a young woman here last week. Pretty, tall, looked like a model. She wanted to talk to Tony, but he wasn't here. I'm not sure why she wanted to see him, but something didn't feel right. I suspect the poker club is a cover for something more sinister – involving young women. I think Tony is exploiting the women. I think he's . . . a pimp.'

Karen leaned forward. 'Did you get the name of this young woman?'

Valerie's gaze broke away as she wrung her hands. 'No, I was trying to keep my head down. I don't want to cross Tony.'

'I can understand that. He's quite a domineering man.'

Valerie nodded. 'That's one way to put it.'

'Do you know anything about Tony's connection to Quentin Chapman?'

'No, I've never met Chapman.'

'Do you know the club's location?'

'No, but the members are powerful people who'd do anything to keep things quiet.'

Just then a male voice called out, causing both women to jump.

Valerie leaned out of the kitchenette. 'Oh, it's all right,' she said. 'It's just Emmett.'

Tony's accountant, Emmett Jenkins, appeared in the doorway, looking sheepish. His fluffy brown hair was messily styled, and his cheeks were pink from the cold. He wore a yellow checked scarf that was more suited to Rupert Bear than a financial wizard.

'Sorry, I didn't think anyone would still be here.' He held up a set of keys. 'I just needed to pick up some paperwork. Is it okay if I grab it and go?'

Valerie gave him a warm smile. 'Of course, but stay, have a cup of tea with us. I've just made a pot.'

Emmett looked like that was the last thing he wanted to do. 'Oh, no, I don't want to disturb you. I—'

'Don't be daft,' Valerie said, ignoring him and reaching for a mug. As she poured tea for Emmett, Karen took the chance to study him.

He pushed his glasses up the bridge of his nose. He avoided looking at Karen directly as he loosened his scarf.

'Emmett's a good sort,' Valerie said to Karen. 'I'm sure he'd be happy to answer any questions you'd like to ask him about Tony.'

Emmett seemed uncomfortable. 'I can try to help, but . . . I don't really know much about him.'

Valerie raised her eyebrows. 'Emmett's Tony's accountant. He knows a great deal about him.'

Emmett shook his head and looked like he wished the ground would swallow him up. 'Well, not really.'

'Do you mind if I ask you both why you keep working for him? He sounds like a difficult boss.'

Valerie's expression hardened. 'I need the job,' she said. 'It's not as if I'm inundated with offers.'

'He's not so bad,' Emmett said quietly. 'A bit overbearing at times.'

Valerie rummaged in the cupboard and found some chocolate biscuits.

'Your favourites!' she announced, beaming at Emmett.

She seemed to enjoy fussing over him. Perhaps his vulnerability and the fact he was being bullied by Tony had brought out her maternal instinct.

Emmett was clearly uncomfortable in Karen's presence, though. No doubt terrified anything he said would get back to his boss. She was willing to bet he knew many of Tony's secrets.

Emmett bolted down a chocolate biscuit and a boiling hot cup of tea in double-quick time, as he evaded Karen's questions. He reluctantly handed over one of his business cards, before excusing himself.

It was like he couldn't leave fast enough.

After he'd left the kitchenette to gather his paperwork, Karen turned to Valerie. 'Is Tony particularly hard on him?'

'Yes,' Valerie said, frowning. 'He's always shouting and putting him down. It's cruel. Emmett used to work for a big accountancy firm in London. He's incredibly bright. I have no idea how he got tangled up with Tony Withers.'

Karen felt a pang of sympathy for them both. 'Look, I know talking to me might put you and Emmett in a difficult position, but I really need to gather information on Tony and Quentin Chapman's relationship. If you find out anything that could be important, would you give me a call?' She handed Valerie her card.

Valerie stared down at it. 'I don't know. I want to help but . . .'

'I understand if you need to think of your safety first, but I have to find out what happened to Sophie—'

Valerie lifted her head. 'Is that your colleague's name? Sophie?'

Karen nodded.

Valerie shoved the card into the pocket of her overalls, a determined expression on her face. 'All right. I'll keep my ear to the ground. I'll let you know if I hear anything that could help.' She still looked nervous, but she lifted her chin. 'I'd like to think if my daughter had been hurt someone would do the same for her.'

Chapter Twelve

Before she left work for the night, Karen sent a message to Harinder asking how Sophie was.

She received a two-word text in reply: *No change*.

He was still angry with her, and she couldn't blame him.

The rain had finally stopped bucketing down by the time she arrived in her home village of Branston. Mike was having dinner with a few colleagues who helped with his training courses, so he'd be back home late. She slowed the car and yawned as she drove past the Woodview Care Home. It had been a long, stressful day and she still had no clear idea of who had attacked Sophie.

Karen's driveway was shielded by evergreen shrubs, which meant she didn't notice the unwelcome car parked in her usual spot until she'd already pulled off the road.

Her stomach tightened at the sight of the sleek black Range Rover. The silhouette of a tall bulky figure stood next to the car: one of Chapman's goons.

After a moment's hesitation, she parked alongside the Range Rover and tapped out a quick text message to Rick.

Karen turned off the engine and got out of the car slowly. Her movement triggered the security light by the front door. The face of goon number one, who Karen liked to refer to as Ponytail, was illuminated. He looked at her but kept his face expressionless.

The light glinted off his dark hair, which was slicked back with copious amounts of an oil-based styling product. His face was stony, the angles of his cheeks and chin exaggerated by the severe hairstyle.

'What are you doing here?' Karen asked.

But he ignored her and reached over to open the back passenger door of the Range Rover.

Chapman got out, wearing a long navy-blue wool coat, with a mustard-yellow cashmere scarf draped around his neck. He looked dapper, and for all the world like a kindly grandfather.

He gave her a smile that didn't reach his cold eyes. 'Lovely to see you again, DS Hart,' he said.

Karen felt a shiver run down her spine. 'I'll ask again,' she said, glaring at Ponytail and then at Chapman. 'What are you doing outside my house?'

'I've come to see you of course,' Chapman said. 'Aren't you going to invite me in?'

Karen would be mad to agree. She was alone here tonight. Mike wouldn't be back for hours. Inviting the mobster who she suspected of attacking Sophie into her house was a crazy idea.

His face was craggy and menacing under the security lights. She suppressed a shudder. He was like a vampire, needing to be invited over the threshold.

But she had to talk to him. She'd sent Rick a message, so if anything happened to her, they'd know who was responsible. Plus, his face would be captured by her doorbell camera.

She took a few seconds to think it through, then let herself in the front door, kicked off her boots and left the door ajar as she walked into the kitchen, expecting Chapman to follow.

'Wait out here,' he ordered his goon.

As he walked into the kitchen, Karen noticed he'd taken his shoes off. Seeing Chapman, one of the most powerful criminals in

Lincolnshire, standing there in his socks was an absurd sight, and she felt an inappropriate urge to laugh.

Karen turned away and opened the fridge. She took out a bottle of water and held it out to Chapman. 'Want one?'

'No, thank you.'

She twisted off the cap, brought the bottle to her lips and took a sip of the cold water, gathering her thoughts. Chapman had caught her off guard, which was exactly the sort of thing he liked to do. But now that she had the opportunity to finally get answers to her questions, she wasn't going to let him off the hook easily. She set the drink down, steeling herself as she prepared to face him.

'What do you know about the attack on DC Sophie Jones?' Karen demanded.

'Is she a colleague of yours?' Chapman asked.

'Let's not play these games, Quentin. You know she is.'

They both stood beside the kitchen table, but neither of them sat down. Karen was far too tense, and Chapman wasn't going to sit without being invited.

He spread his hands and smiled apologetically. 'I'm afraid I don't keep track of your team, DS Hart.'

'You remember me, though?' Karen said.

'Indeed, I do.' He gave a theatrical sigh. 'It's not easy to forget someone who cost me so dearly.' When Karen didn't respond, he added, 'I lost a lot of money because of you.'

'No,' Karen said, 'you lost a lot of money because you were trying to sell a diagnostic scanner that didn't work. It was a con. You deserved to lose the money.'

Chapman shrugged. 'That's one way to look at it.'

'Are you seriously telling me you had nothing to do with the attack on DC Sophie Jones?'

'Yes, that's exactly what I'm telling you,' he said. 'I don't even know who she is.'

'So it's just a coincidence she was found, unconscious and bleeding, outside a workshop owned by one of your business associates?'

Chapman frowned. 'That is concerning.'

She almost believed he was telling the truth.

'Are you talking about Tony?' he asked, stroking his chin thoughtfully.

'Yes. Tony Withers.'

'He can be a little hot-headed. I'll admit that. But he's not foolish enough to attack a police officer.'

'Well, someone was,' Karen said. 'How do you know Tony Withers?'

Chapman shrugged. 'We have some business interests in common.'

'And you play cards together?' Karen asked, her heart hammering.

The change in Chapman was dramatic. His eyes grew distant and hard, his smile cruel, and he was no longer the warm grandfather figure she had seen when he'd walked in. He looked dangerous.

Karen's mouth grew dry. She reached for her water and took another sip.

'On occasion we'll have a game of cards,' Chapman said. His smile softened, but his eyes were still cold. 'You have done your research, haven't you? You know, I could do with someone like you watching my back.' His steely gaze bored into her as a chilling smirk played at the corner of his lips.

Karen had borne the brunt of the police corruption she'd exposed. The loss had been devastating – her husband and daughter killed in the fallout. She was not the type to look away when faced with the truth. If Chapman thought she would turn a blind eye to his dealings, then he was gravely mistaken.

'I'd sooner die than be on your payroll,' Karen said bluntly.

He sighed again. 'You are determined to make things difficult for me, aren't you, DS Hart?'

'If you don't know anything about Sophie,' Karen said, 'then why are you here?'

'I saw that you'd paid me a visit earlier. My security cameras picked you up outside my house. I thought I'd save you a return trip.'

'How kind of you.'

'And . . . I wanted to ask your advice on a professional level.'

Karen frowned at the unexpected turn in the conversation. Chapman sounded uncertain. His usual confident tone had abandoned him.

'You want my advice?'

'Yes, if you'd be so kind. I have a problem.'

'What kind of problem?'

'I think my life is in danger.'

Karen folded her arms. 'And?'

'You don't seem surprised.' Chapman raised an eyebrow.

'Well, I thought it would be an occupational hazard for you.'

Chapman looked thoughtful. 'Perhaps it is, but when you get to my level, you've earned respect. If someone is targeting me, I know who it is and I . . .' He trailed off. There was no need for him to finish his sentence. Karen knew what he was going to say. Chapman would hit his enemy first. With the network he'd built up around him, he presumed he was close to untouchable.

'At this stage in my . . . career, I don't expect to fear for my life. But a friend of mine was killed last week in London. It was a professional hit.'

'Maybe you tried to con the wrong person this time,' Karen said. 'I'll give you my advice for free. Stop committing crimes. Give it all up. Retire.'

He looked incredulous. 'Why would I do that?'

'Why wouldn't you?'

'I don't have much. You know I lost my wife a few years ago. All I have left is my work.'

'Well, that's depressing,' Karen said.

'I thought you'd understand,' he said. 'Work is the most important thing in your life, too, isn't it?'

'Not the most important thing. No,' Karen said defensively.

'Ah, yes, I forgot. You have a boyfriend now, don't you? Mike, isn't it?'

She gritted her teeth. 'Is that a threat?'

'Not at all. I'm simply interested,' Chapman said.

'You can't scare us off,' Karen said. 'We won't stop looking into your dealings. One day we'll find something, and you will go to jail, Quentin.'

He gave another long sigh. 'I was afraid you'd say that. But before you dedicate all your energy to taking me down, perhaps you could find out who is trying to kill me. Someone is picking off my men, getting to them all over the country. The hit in London is just one incident.'

Karen pulled out a chair and sat down. She nodded to the one opposite. Quentin sat too.

He undid the buttons of his coat and loosened his scarf. 'I admire you, DS Hart. I know you can't be bought and that's a rare thing in this life. Believe me.'

'So why come to me? I'm never going to be on your side.'

'Because, no matter what you think of me, I know you'll do the right thing.'

'And what's that?'

'Find out who's behind the attack on my associate.'

'You said it happened in London. That's out of my jurisdiction. By a considerable margin,' Karen said.

'But you're interested. I can see it in your eyes.' Chapman smirked.

It annoyed Karen that he was right. As soon as he was gone, she would look into it. But not because she wanted to help Chapman or watch his back. Her job was stopping crime and catching criminals, no matter who the victim was.

'Maybe you could do me a favour,' Karen said.

'I'd be happy to.'

'Find out who was behind the attack on DC Sophie Jones.'

He started to shake his head.

Karen held up her hand. 'Don't tell me you can't. It happened on your turf. Eight o'clock last night.'

'I'll talk to the people at the workshop and find out what I can.'

'Thank you. Now, where did this hit happen?'

Chapman gave her the key points but kept the details vague.

'Did Sophie approach you?' Karen asked after Chapman had finished talking. 'Recently, I mean.'

'No. I know you won't believe me, but I haven't spoken to her. I don't even remember her.'

Karen met his gaze, trying to get a read on him, to work out if he was telling the truth. So many signs pointed to Chapman. Knowing her colleague as she did, it was exactly the sort of thing Sophie would try to tackle on her own, wanting to impress people. Arnie and Rick were right about that.

She pulled her mobile from her pocket, went into the photos app and selected the headshot of Sophie. Karen hesitated, looking down at Sophie's smiling face, taking in her dimples and curls, then she held the phone out to Chapman.

'That's Sophie?'

Karen nodded.

'She looks so young. Too young to be a police officer. Why was she out there alone?'

That was the million-dollar question. If she knew the answer to that, she wouldn't need Chapman.

Instead of answering him, Karen said, 'I've got another question for you.'

He inclined his head. 'Go on.'

'My partner, Mike, saw your car earlier today. You were following him.'

'No, that wasn't me,' Chapman said quickly. 'Must have been a similar car.' Though he kept his face calm with a blank smile, a small muscle beside his eye twitched.

He was lying.

Why?

Either Chapman or one of his heavies had been following Mike at lunchtime. And if Chapman wasn't trailing Mike to scare Karen off, then why was he doing it?

It was all mind games with someone like Chapman. On the surface, he'd appeared vulnerable tonight. He'd shared information about a threat to his life, appearing helpless. But it was an act. Beneath the facade, he was a master manipulator. It was a chess match between him and his adversaries.

Karen refused to be taken in by his tricks and dummy moves. She didn't trust him one bit.

Chapter Thirteen

Shortly after Chapman left, someone started hammering on Karen's door. Before answering, she checked the app on her phone to access the camera.

It was Rick. His dark hair was dishevelled, his eyes wild, and his cheeks were flushed.

When she opened the door, he asked urgently, 'Are you all right?'

She stepped back so he could come in. 'I'm fine. He's gone.'

Rick raked a hand through his hair and exhaled with relief. 'When I got your message, I thought . . .' He shook his head.

'The shock of finding Chapman here gave me quite a scare.'

'I'll bet,' Rick said.

'If anything had happened to me, I wanted someone to know he'd been here.'

'What did he want?'

'He said he knew I've been looking for him.'

'Did he threaten you?'

Karen shook her head slowly because Chapman hadn't issued any direct threats. He'd unnerved her, but even when she'd told him she intended to see him in jail, he hadn't responded with a threat.

They walked into the kitchen and sat down at the table at which Karen had just had a much more tense conversation with Quentin Chapman.

'So what did he say?' Rick asked.

'I asked him about Sophie. He point-blank denied knowing anything about the attack.' Karen leaned forward, resting her elbows on the table. 'He also told me an associate of his was killed in London, and that it looked like a professional hit. He actually sounded worried.'

'Some kind of turf war?' Rick suggested. 'Maybe someone's trying to muscle Chapman out of the way.' He frowned. 'How does that connect to the attack on Sophie?'

'If there is a link, I can't figure it out.'

'It's a bit rich – Chapman coming to us for help now, after everything he's done. He wants the police involved when it suits him.'

Karen agreed. She couldn't quite figure Chapman out. She felt as though she should have been able to tell when he was being honest, but it wasn't easy. She was sure he'd been lying about tailing Mike, but she thought he'd been telling the truth when he'd said he knew nothing about Sophie's assault. But if that was the case, then it meant everything Karen had pieced together so far was useless.

Maybe Chapman had been lying about not knowing what had happened to Sophie too. The only way to find out was to keep digging.

'He's got to be involved somehow,' Karen mused aloud. 'That's our working theory, right? Sophie was looking into Chapman on her own time. She stumbled across some information, arranged to meet somebody, perhaps to get some more evidence – likely from somebody who works at the workshop . . . only, the assailant thought she was a threat and attacked her.'

Rick shrugged off his coat. 'It sounds like the most plausible theory so far to me. It makes more sense than Goodridge's idea that Harinder is somehow behind it.'

'He's really angry with me,' Karen said quietly.

Rick looked up, surprised. 'Harinder?'

Karen nodded. 'I understand. I'd be furious in his shoes.'

'Harinder knows you don't really believe he would hurt Sophie, though. He knows you're just doing your job.' Rick waited a beat and then frowned. 'That's all it is, isn't it? You don't actually think he would hurt her.'

'I've no reason to think that he's involved, and I hated asking him those questions. He's going through an awful time, and I've made it worse.'

Rick smothered a yawn and rubbed his eyes. 'Sorry. I've been running on fumes all day and it's catching up with me.' He shifted forward so he was looking into Karen's eyes. 'There's no nice way to ask questions like that. You drew the short straw there for sure. But once this is over, once Sophie's back on her feet again, I'm sure he'll understand.'

Rick sounded so optimistic. Karen hoped he was right, and Sophie would soon be back to her normal cheerful, high-achieving self.

'Can I get you a drink?' Karen asked.

Rick checked his watch. 'No, if you're okay, I'm going to head to the hospital now. I'll stay there for a few hours so Harinder and Sophie's parents can get some rest.'

'Good idea,' Karen said.

'You'll be all right on your own?'

'I'll be fine. Mike will be back in a couple of hours.'

Rick looked doubtful. 'I could call—'

Karen cut him off. 'I'll be absolutely fine. Go to the hospital, and . . . tell Sophie we're all missing her. I mean, I know she's unconscious, but—'

It was Rick's turn to interrupt. 'They say people in comas can sometimes hear and respond to what's going on around them.' He squeezed Karen's hand. 'I'll tell her.'

◆ ◆ ◆

After Rick left, Karen couldn't relax enough to eat a full meal, so she made a round of toast, intending to eat it at the kitchen table while on her laptop.

She wanted to locate the poker club Valerie had mentioned. A club that seemed to be connected to the dark rumours of Tony's brothel. She worked at it for a while, looking at properties owned by Tony Withers or Quentin Chapman to identify possible locations. But there was nothing that stood out. And it was possible, or even likely, that Withers and Chapman would do anything they could to avoid a paper trail. The building may have been registered under another name. Another one of Chapman's many associates perhaps?

She glanced at her mobile, wondering if she should have convinced Mike not to go out tonight. She wished he was here, so she knew he was safe. She sent him a text and relaxed a little when she saw the dots indicating he was typing.

His reply came through quickly, telling her he was fine, having a good time and just eating dessert. She was glad he was enjoying himself, but she'd be on edge until she saw him in person.

Karen turned her attention to digging into the murder of Tim Fletcher in Soho. It didn't take her long to find the details. There were write-ups in the mainstream media. She skimmed the articles. This was no ordinary, messy gangland dispute, no spray of bullets from a moving vehicle. This was a hit by a professional. The police were looking for a sniper. No wonder Chapman was scared.

But it was hard to feel sorry for him.

She stretched, then rubbed the back of her head. Something felt off. Her gut told her that by looking at Chapman for Sophie's assault she was digging in the wrong direction.

He wouldn't stoop to doing the grim work himself. His goons were always willing to do his bidding. Yet there had been something about Chapman's body language and actions that told Karen he was shocked to hear what had happened to Sophie.

If Chapman had been involved in the attack on Sophie, then he had managed to lie convincingly, unconcerned, straight to Karen's face. But what if he was being honest? Had someone at the workshop acted on their own? Or maybe under Tony's instructions? Had Sophie been seeking information on Chapman's background and stumbled on something potentially damaging to Tony?

The shrill ring of her mobile made Karen jump. She glanced at the screen.

Mike's mother, Lorraine.

Karen was tempted to let it ring out. But in the end, guilt got the better of her.

She answered it, forcing some cheerfulness into her voice. 'Hello, Lorraine, how nice to hear from you.'

'Karen, I'm not disturbing you, am I?'

'No, not at all.' Karen glanced at her cold toast.

'I thought we should have a chat about Mike's birthday.'

'His birthday?' Karen glanced at the mini calendar stuck to the fridge. Mike's birthday was on Saturday. She'd forgotten. She felt a wave of shame.

'Yes, I thought we could arrange a surprise birthday meal on Saturday.'

'Oh,' Karen said. 'Do you think he'd like that?'

'Of course he will,' Lorraine said. 'But you don't sound very enthusiastic. I can organise things on my own if you like.'

'It's not that,' Karen said hurriedly. 'I've just had a long day at work.'

'Ah, I see. Mike mentioned you were a workaholic.'

'Did he?' Karen felt a flash of irritation. 'Well, I wouldn't say that exactly, but it can be draining.'

'If it's too draining, just let me know, and I'll handle everything. Trust me, I know all Mike's favourite restaurants and exactly what he likes to eat, so it's probably better if I do it anyway. I just wanted to make sure that we were on the same page, and you weren't making plans for a separate celebration.'

'That sounds really nice. I'll look forward to it.'

'I'll book somewhere and let you know. We'll keep it between us. Our little secret.'

'I won't breathe a word. I'm sure Mike will love it.'

'I thought I'd limit it to close family.'

'That sounds lovely. Mike told me he hasn't seen his father for a long time. I don't suppose he'll be coming?'

Karen regretted the question as soon as she spoke. Mike gave the impression he didn't like to talk about his father. It was none of her business. She shouldn't be prying into his past. But she was shattered. Diplomacy was not her strong point when she was tired, and it was in Karen's DNA to delve into secrets.

Lorraine seemed unconcerned. 'No, he certainly won't be,' she said brusquely. 'He walked out on me when Mike was tiny.' But she didn't offer any further information except to add, 'We did just fine without him.'

'So just the four of us?' Karen queried.

'Yes. Me, James, you and Mike. Unless there's anyone else you'd like to invite?'

'No, I think a small family get-together will be great,' Karen said.

'Right. I'll keep you updated.'

After Karen ended the call, she picked up a slice of toast, took a bite and then pulled a face. It was stone cold.

She didn't mind cold toast if it had been left to get cold intentionally and then slathered with butter. But buttered toast that had gone cold was not a pleasant experience.

She pushed the plate to one side and then got back to work on her laptop, trying to put together the pieces of the puzzle. It was like working with a one-million-piece jigsaw, but with half the pieces missing.

After a few minutes of feeling like she was going around in circles, she gave up on that too and reached again for her mobile phone. She called Morgan. She needed his calm, logical input.

He answered on the second ring.

She could hear music playing in the background. 'Sorry, are you busy?'

'No. Just listening to some music,' Morgan said. 'Trying to relax, but it's not working. Are you faring any better?'

'No, but that's no surprise because I had a visit from Chapman earlier.'

'When?'

'About an hour ago. He was waiting for me outside my house.'

'Is he still there?'

'No, he's gone.'

'Do you want me to come over?' Morgan asked.

Karen wavered. She didn't want to be alone – not just due to the fear of a return visit from Chapman, but also because she'd be left with her own racing thoughts, picking over her last conversations with Sophie and convincing herself that there was something she'd missed, and that it was her fault Sophie was in hospital.

'If you're not busy,' Karen said. 'Mike won't be home for a while and—'

'And you don't want to be alone?'

'I thought maybe we could go over some details, try and get things straight in our minds. Come up with some proper working theories about what happened to Sophie.'

'I'll be there soon,' Morgan said. 'Have you eaten?'

Karen looked again at her cold toast. 'I wasn't really hungry.'

'I'll pick up something on my way over.' The gentle warmth of his words eased some of the nervous churning in her stomach.

'Morgan?'

'Yes?'

She was immensely grateful to have Morgan's support and understanding; he never made her explain, he just knew. The whole team meant so much to her, and they were all hurting now that one of their own lay in the hospital. Having Morgan come over, even just to go through their options and test theories, was a source of comfort. But it was hard to put all those feelings into something she could say out loud, so she simply said, 'Thanks.'

Chapter Fourteen

Karen got some plates out of the cupboard as Morgan unloaded the takeaway bag. They piled their plates with fried rice and Kung Po chicken.

'Are you and Mike okay?' Morgan asked as they carried their plates to the table.

'Yeah, we're fine,' Karen replied, filling her fork with fried rice, then taking a bite of the chicken. 'This is good. I didn't realise how hungry I was.'

'I just had a chat with Goodridge about Harinder,' Morgan said.

'I was going to ask if you'd spoken with him. How seriously is he focusing on Harinder?'

Morgan stabbed a piece of chicken with his fork. 'He's still looking at him as a potential suspect.'

'I think he's barking up the wrong tree, then,' Karen said with a frown.

'Agreed,' Morgan said. 'But it's his case. He's the senior investigating officer.'

'Right, but he might listen to you if you put a good word in for Harinder.'

'You know how it works, Karen. We have to go through the motions. If Harinder had nothing to do with what happened to Sophie, then he'll be in the clear.'

'But at what cost?' Karen asked. 'His reputation will be dragged through the mud, and he's had to endure his own colleagues treating him like a suspect. It's not right.'

Morgan sighed. 'It's not a great situation,' he said, in his typical understated way. 'What do you think happened? We don't think Harinder attacked Sophie, so who are we left with? Chapman?'

Karen's stomach protested at the greasy fried rice. She put down her fork and thought back to her conversation with Chapman. 'I just can't get a handle on him,' she muttered. 'He's so slippery.'

'Chapman's a tricky character,' Morgan said, his eyes narrowing slightly. 'What did he say when you spoke to him?'

Karen recounted the conversation, and then said, 'I almost believed Chapman when he said he had nothing to do with Sophie's attack, but if he wasn't involved, then we're back at square one.'

Morgan nodded slowly. 'It's a mess, but we'll figure it out.' He thought for a moment, then said, 'It could be someone close to Chapman. Tony Withers?'

Karen nodded. 'I did wonder if Sophie had been trying to dig up dirt on Chapman and uncovered something about Tony instead. Perhaps Tony wasn't happy about that and wanted to keep Sophie quiet.'

'So, what's our next step? Bring Tony in for questioning?'

The fried rice churned in Karen's stomach. She pushed her plate away. 'I'm not sure. I think it's too soon. We don't have anything on him. I'd really like to know where his poker club is. From what Valerie told me, it sounds to me like he's running an illegal gambling ring, along with a brothel.'

'Valerie didn't have any idea where it could be?' Morgan asked.

Karen shook her head. 'She said she didn't. But maybe she's scared to say too much. One of the male mechanics might know.'

'Brian Sully and Mark McArthur?' Morgan queried. 'I can speak with them tomorrow.'

'That might be a good idea,' Karen said. 'Let's put a bit of pressure on and see if someone talks.' She looked down at her plate and shook her head. 'Although I don't think we're going to get much out of Sully and McArthur. They don't strike me as the cooperative type. I think we'd have more luck trying Valerie again, or maybe even Emmett.'

'Emmett?'

'Emmett Jenkins. He's Tony Withers's accountant. I believe he also does some work for Chapman. His background check was clean, although his employment history is vague. Rick is still digging.'

'Then I guess he'd be aware of some of their financial dealings. He might even know about the gambling and the brothel,' Morgan said.

Karen leaned forward, her mind whirring with possibilities. 'He might. Chapman and Tony obviously have something over him. Emmett doesn't seem happy working for them. We could use their hold on him to our advantage. Perhaps he's the weak spot in Chapman's armour.'

'That's how men like Chapman and Withers operate. They like to keep their minions in line with threats and intimidation.'

Karen nodded slowly, seeing the pattern of behaviour come together in her mind. 'Valerie told me Tony Withers bullies Emmett. I noticed it when Rick and I went to see Tony at the golf club. Emmett appeared truly miserable. It makes sense that they'd keep him under their control by keeping a stranglehold on him. He's probably been bullied into doing some dodgy accounting.'

Morgan looked thoughtful. 'It wouldn't be easy to stand up to men like Tony Withers and Quentin Chapman and resist their strong-arm tactics.'

He was right. It would be difficult for anyone to stand up to the likes of Chapman and Tony, and Emmett seemed the type to want to avoid trouble. If he'd been persuaded to do false accounting for them, Tony and Chapman could threaten to turn him in if he stepped out of line. That would keep Emmett under control and make him easy to manipulate.

Karen smiled. 'Maybe it's time to present Emmett with a way out.' Her gaze met Morgan's as she continued. 'Offer some kind of immunity in exchange for his cooperation.'

'You think he'd talk if he had a deal in place?'

Karen nodded. 'It could be the sweetener we need to get him to divulge what he knows. You could ask Churchill what we can offer Emmett.'

'All right. I'll speak to Churchill about it tomorrow,' Morgan said, then leaned back in his chair. 'I'm stuffed. Are you not hungry?' He nodded at the food remaining on Karen's plate.

'Sorry,' she said. 'I'm finding it hard to relax enough to eat properly.'

He gave her a sympathetic smile. 'I understand, but you need to keep your strength up. Although Chinese food probably wasn't the healthiest choice.' He grinned. 'What time will Mike get back?'

Karen picked up their plates. 'He won't be back for at least another hour or so.'

'Right then,' Morgan said as he glanced over to the pile of paperwork on the kitchen worktop. 'Let's make some headway on these files.'

◆ ◆ ◆

The night was cold and damp. Rick shivered as he pulled his coat around him and trudged towards the hospital. He was there to see Sophie and offer support to Harinder and Sophie's mum and dad, but he felt an overwhelming sense of dread as he approached the building.

He'd last been here when his mother was admitted, rushed in by ambulance after being hit by a car, and he lost her just hours later. Rick paused at the entrance. There was a taxi parked out front. The driver sat behind the wheel staring blankly ahead. A man wearing a flimsy hospital gown with a grey hoodie draped over his shoulders stood by the double doors, puffing on a cigarette, despite the multiple 'No Smoking' signs.

Rick wanted to turn on his heel, get in his car and drive home. It had been a horrible experience losing his mum. Coming here had brought memories of that day rushing back. He'd expected that to happen, but he hadn't anticipated it being so overwhelming.

He took a couple of deep breaths, inhaling the cold night air, then squared his shoulders and marched into the hospital.

The building was a maze of corridors filled with the smell of antiseptic and the low hum of machines.

Rick made his way towards ITU and found Harinder in the relatives' room.

'How's it going, mate?' Rick said, keeping his voice low and shutting the door quietly behind him.

He wasn't sure why, but he felt the need to whisper.

Harinder looked up. His face was etched with exhaustion. Rick had never seen him look so tired. His broad shoulders were slumped, and the circles under his eyes were like bruises. It was as though a decade had passed since Rick had last seen him.

Harinder stayed silent, weighing his response with a furrowed brow and a bleak expression. Rick felt a cold clutch of fear grip his stomach.

Had something happened while he was driving over here?

'Sophie?' Rick asked, his chest tight.

'No news,' Harinder said, finally breaking his silence. 'There's been no change. It's driving me mad, Rick. They can't give us any answers.'

'Has she had it yet?' Rick asked. He wasn't exactly sure what the scan was for, but he knew they'd been waiting on it.

Harinder rubbed the stubble along his jawline. 'Apparently they're going to wait a bit. There's been no change in her condition, so there's no rush for the scan.' He shrugged. 'That's what they say anyway, but I think they're just too busy, and—' He broke off, and then put his head in his hands.

'I'm sure they're doing their best for her, mate,' Rick said, moving closer and putting his hand on Harinder's shoulder. Harinder kept his head bowed but managed to nod.

Rick shrugged off his coat. It was hot and airless in the small room. It felt stifling.

At that moment, the door to the relatives' room opened and a woman Rick didn't recognise entered. Her eyes were red, and she gave them a thin smile as she moved towards the coffee maker.

Harinder nodded an acknowledgement at her, but they didn't speak. Rick watched her from the corner of his eye as she made herself a cup of coffee.

'Why don't you take a break?' Rick asked. 'Sophie's mum and dad are in there with her now, aren't they?'

'Sophie's mum is. Geoff has gone home to get a couple of hours' sleep.'

'That's sensible,' Rick said. 'Why don't you do the same. I can stay, and I'll call you if anything happens.'

Harinder dipped his head. 'I appreciate it, but I think I'd prefer to stay close. Maybe I'll just rest my eyes for half an hour in here.'

'Well, if you're sure,' Rick said doubtfully, 'but you might feel better if you go home. Even just to have a shower and something to eat.'

Harinder wasn't really paying attention to Rick; he was deep in thought. 'I don't understand how this happened. I've been trying to make sense of it, to work out why she was out there on her own.' He rubbed his forehead. 'She doesn't lie to me. We've never had that sort of relationship. I don't understand why she wouldn't tell me what she was doing. Why would Sophie tell me she was studying when she wasn't?' He looked at Rick. 'Has she been seeing someone else?'

'No,' Rick said quickly. 'I'm sure it's nothing like that. She's happy with you. I know she is.'

Harinder took a deep breath. 'It doesn't make sense. I've got nothing to do here but think, and I keep going over things in my mind, but I'm not coming up with answers.'

Rick sat down in the chair beside him. 'I know what you mean. I've been doing the same. We're working on a theory that Sophie was looking into something on the side.'

Harinder's eyes narrowed. 'Something you didn't know about?'

Rick nodded. 'Well, that's the working theory. We don't know for sure.'

'What was she looking into? Is there something I can do to help?' Harinder said. 'I could get my laptop and—'

Rick shook his head. 'No. You just focus on being here for Sophie. We'll find out what happened.'

Harinder scowled. 'Of course. You don't want me involved when I'm a suspect.'

'Don't be daft. I don't think you're a suspect.'

'Karen does.'

'No, she doesn't,' Rick said emphatically. 'We're all just trying to piece together what happened outside that workshop.'

'Do you think you'll figure it out? How close are you? It's been over twenty-four hours.'

Harinder sounded impatient. He wanted results, and that was understandable. Rick wanted them too. He hated not knowing. Almost as much as he hated knowing his colleague was lying in a hospital bed just a few feet away, unconscious and potentially brain-damaged.

'You have no idea what she was doing there? None at all?' Rick asked.

Harinder hesitated. 'No,' he said, eventually. 'I haven't got a clue.'

Rick shifted in his seat to face Harinder. 'As far as you're aware, she never went to that workshop, got them to do something on her car, or anything like that?'

Harinder looked away, gripped his hands together, and stared down at the floor. 'I . . .'

'What is it?' Rick asked.

Harinder wasn't good at hiding what he was feeling. He knew something. Rick was sure of it.

'If you know anything, mate, you need to tell me. It could be important.'

Harinder opened his mouth, yet no words came out. The woman, who had finished making her coffee, slipped out of the room as quietly as she'd entered.

Rick suspected his friend was holding something back. 'Seriously, if you have any idea why she was there, you need to tell me, now.'

Harinder crossed his arms and cleared his throat. His voice was defensive. 'I told you already. I don't know. If I did, I'd tell you.'

Rick frowned and studied Harinder intently. After all these years of working together, Rick – like the rest of the team – had come to see Harinder as a trusted colleague and friend. He was a genius in the tech lab, getting results nobody else could. And he was a great bloke to share a beer with and chat about the football.

At no point in all the years he had known Harinder had Rick ever doubted him. Until now.

He'd always admired Harinder. And Sophie, clearly, adored him.

But why was his kind-hearted, dependable, football-loving buddy avoiding Rick's gaze?

Harinder had a tell. Everyone did. But some were better at hiding it. Harinder's eyes darted from side to side when he was worried or holding something back, and he rubbed his forehead again and again, in the exact same spot above his right eyebrow. He had done both during their brief conversation.

Yes, he was under a lot of pressure. And that made people act strangely. But not like this. Rick knew Harinder well enough to know when he was lying.

And he was lying now.

But Rick was more interested in *why* he was concealing the truth. What did he have to hide?

Chapter Fifteen

Karen and Morgan spent most of the next morning trailing around Lincoln, visiting various establishments that had connections to Quentin Chapman or Tony Withers. But they didn't find anywhere that seemed a likely location for the poker club or brothel.

It wasn't even lunchtime and Mike had already sent Karen four text messages, including one about dinner plans and another concerning the whereabouts of Sandy's spare lead – things he didn't usually bother her with during working hours.

The flurry of messages was unusual, but Karen knew it was just Mike's way of checking in and making sure she was okay. He had served with the police for many years and understood the job. But he was concerned about her. More so now that Chapman was in the picture.

She wanted to reassure him, to tell him that she was all right and could handle Chapman, but all the words in the world couldn't put his mind at ease. She knew that because it worked both ways. Karen worried about him too. After he'd been followed home, her stomach had been in knots. The fear that something might happen to someone she loved was hard to deal with, but it showed how much she cared, and sometimes the stress was worth it.

'You know,' Karen said from the passenger seat as Morgan drove along the A46, 'I think I should go and talk to Emmett Jenkins now.'

'Do you want me to come with you?' Morgan asked.

'I think it might be better if I talk to him alone,' Karen said. 'He's intimidated by Tony Withers. He seems a nervous character. I've met him a couple of times now. I might be able to get him to open up if it's just me and him.'

Morgan nodded. 'Right, well, don't go offering any deals. I need to talk to Churchill first. We have to do that by the book.'

'I won't offer anything concrete, but I might hint at the possibility, just to test the waters and see if he's willing to talk.'

'Fair enough,' Morgan said, slowing the car as the traffic crawled to a halt at the roundabout. 'Do you want to go back to the station first or should I drop you there?'

'Can you drop me there?' Karen said, digging around in her bag for Emmett's business card. 'His office is just off Brayford Wharf.'

'All right. While you're doing that, I'm going to have a word with Sully and McArthur. I don't think they'll be as willing to talk as the accountant, but it can't hurt to try.'

Morgan let Karen out on the wharf, and from there she walked up a side street towards the accountancy firm.

The earlier rain had created puddles on the pavement, but the sky was now much lighter, a mix of grey and white clouds.

Karen stopped beside the building. It wasn't one of the posh premises that lined the wharf. It was a bit shabby, with a pale-yellow frontage, white shuttered windows and a glass door. There was no sign announcing the accountancy business operated from there, but there was a small intercom fixed to the wall beside the door with Emmett Jenkins's name next to one of the buttons.

Karen pressed the buzzer. The intercom crackled to life and a nervous voice that Karen thought sounded like Emmett's said, 'Yes, can I help you?'

Karen announced herself and was buzzed in. She entered the building and climbed a narrow staircase, following the signs to Emmett Jenkins Accountancy.

At the top of the stairs was another door. This one was open, and Emmett stood there, waiting for her, nervously licking his lips.

'Er . . . hello?' he said, rubbing the back of his neck. 'I wasn't expecting you . . .'

'No,' Karen said, but she didn't elaborate. She didn't always like to give prior warning. Sometimes turning up out of the blue got better results.

He invited her in. The office was small, with a large desk in the middle of the room and filing cabinets in the corner.

As far as she could tell, Emmett's Accountancy was a one-man outfit.

A sleek silver laptop sat in the centre of the desk, but it was closed. The walls were lined with shelves filled with books and papers.

'So how can I help?' Emmett said, clearing his throat.

He scooped up some papers that had been stacked on a chair and slid them on to his desk, then he pulled the chair over so Karen could sit down.

'Thank you. I wanted to ask you a few questions about your relationship with Tony Withers and Quentin Chapman.'

'Oh, I see,' Emmett said, sitting down behind his desk. He fiddled with the sheets of paper in front of him. 'There's not much I can tell you really.' He stood up again. 'Let me get you a coffee.'

Before Karen had time to tell him she didn't need a coffee, he'd stridden out of the small room.

Rather than wait for him, Karen got up and followed. She found him a short distance along the narrow corridor, in a small kitchen.

He pulled a mug, patterned with pink flowers, from the cupboard and filled it to the brim. 'Sorry, I haven't got any milk,' he said. 'But I do have sugar, if you take—'

'No, it's fine. Just like this is great,' Karen replied, taking the mug.

He poured himself a coffee too. 'Right,' he said. 'Shall we go back?' He kept attempting to smile, but the smile wouldn't stick.

They went back into his office.

He was jittery. Karen thought he seemed uneasy. It wasn't surprising that Emmett was anxious. Most people were when confronted by police officers. Was this just run-of-the-mill apprehension, or was something else going on? Something to do with his boss perhaps? She had a feeling there was more to it than just simple nervousness.

He spilled some of his coffee on to the desk as he put the mug down and used a bit of crumpled paper to mop it up.

'I'd like to help, I really would, but . . .' he said, staring down at the coffee-drenched paper.

'But you're scared?' Karen finished kindly. 'I don't blame you. They're both intimidating characters.'

Emmett leaned back in his chair and looked sadly around the room. 'It's not quite the job I expected. I got a first from Oxford, you know.' He gave her a regretful smile. 'I thought accountancy would be a safe, sensible career.'

'How did you get involved with them?'

'I met Tony at a charity function, and he introduced me to Quentin.'

'When was this?'

'Four years ago.' His hand shook slightly as he reached for his coffee. 'They won't like me talking to you.'

'They don't have to know. I won't tell them.' She smiled, but Emmett avoided looking at her directly.

'I'm sorry, I can't tell you anything. I wish I could be more help.'

'Do you know anything about the poker games Tony organises?'

Emmett shook his head firmly. 'No.'

'What about the rumours that Tony operates a brothel?' Emmett gave a small, sharp intake of breath before closing his mouth in a thin line.

A moment later the door flew open, and Tony Withers burst in. His thick strawberry-blond hair looked messy, and his face was even redder than the last time she'd seen him.

Tony glared at the accountant and then at Karen. 'I heard you'd been snooping around,' he snarled. 'Typical police. Can't you tell when you're not wanted?'

'I'm just doing my job, Mr Withers,' Karen said.

'Well, what do you want? You've been visiting all my staff putting pressure on them, hassling them. With no due cause, I might add. I gave you my alibi *and* access to my security tapes. Why don't you just speak to me? Get whatever information you're after straight from the horse's mouth.' He jerked a thumb at his chest. His eyes glinted as he whipped around to face Emmett. 'And what are you doing chatting to her anyway? Haven't you got work to be getting on with?'

'Yes,' Emmett said in a voice so low it was barely a whisper. 'But I couldn't refuse to cooperate with the police—'

'Of course you can, you spineless fool,' Tony roared.

Emmett's face flushed.

Karen thought she and Morgan might have been on the right track last night. The accountant could be the weak link. He was quiet, but she saw a small light of rebellion spark in his eyes as Tony berated him. A little pressure and Emmett might spill any information he had on Tony and Chapman.

'All right then, Mr Withers,' Karen said in a bored tone, leaning forward, taking a long, slow sip of coffee and deliberately taking her time. 'Why don't you tell me about your card games?'

'Nothing to tell,' Tony said with false nonchalance. 'A few of my associates like to get together for a civilised game of cards occasionally.'

'Sex workers?'

Tony chuckled. 'I assure you the evenings are gentlemen only.'

'Male sex workers then?'

Tony frowned. 'That's not what I meant, and you know it!'

'I've heard rumours about you running a brothel, Tony.'

He smirked. 'You shouldn't listen to gossip. Brothels aren't my cup of tea. I've never had to pay for it.' He was back to his usual cocky self. He knew she was here on a fishing expedition. She didn't have anything solid.

At least, not yet. But she would.

'Look, little lady—' Tony began, hitching up his trousers and puffing out his stomach.

'Little lady?' Karen laughed. 'We're not in the seventies, Tony.'

He looked like he might burst a blood vessel. 'Are we done here?' he snapped. 'You're disturbing my accountant. He's got work to do.'

Karen glanced at Emmett, who looked like he wanted to disappear. 'I am quite busy,' he said, keeping his gaze down and shuffling his paperwork.

It wasn't much use trying to talk to Emmett in Tony's presence anyway. She would have to come back later and try again.

'Have you seen Quentin Chapman recently?' Karen asked Tony.

'I don't see how that's any of your business,' he replied.

'I spoke to him yesterday,' Karen said.

There was a hint of curiosity in Tony's eyes. 'Oh yeah, what about?'

'He told me about the hits, said that some of his men were being taken out.'

Tony rolled his eyes. 'Oh, that. It's got nothing to do with Chapman.'

'How do you know?'

'Well, it didn't happen here, did it? One in Nottingham, one in London. The men were only loosely associated with Chapman. They were probably involved in something dodgy. Nothing to do with us.'

'Because you'd never do anything dodgy, would you, Tony?' Karen said dryly, making a mental note to look up the incident in Nottingham.

'No, DS Hart. I'm a perfect law-abiding citizen.' He smirked again and followed her out of the office and down the stairs.

When they got out on to the street, he said, 'If you want to visit any of my staff in the future, I'd appreciate it if you let me know first.'

A large silver Jaguar was parked up by the kerb.

'Is that yours?' Karen asked, making a note of the number plate.

'Yeah, and it's all above board, so no need to waste your time looking it up.'

'So kind of you to advise me on my job, Tony.'

'Just trying to save you some time, sweetheart,' he said with a wink.

'Idiot,' Karen muttered as Tony walked away and got into his Jag.

He lowered the window and waved as his car roared up the street.

She had been intending to leave and come back to talk more with Emmett later. But since Tony had already left, she figured now was as good a time as any.

She pressed the intercom again. It rang for ages, but there was no answer. There was a small camera beside the microphone. Karen imagined Emmett up in his office nervously pacing backwards and forwards, chewing his nails, trying to decide whether he should speak to the police or stay on Tony's good side.

Karen checked her watch. Morgan would be talking to Sully and McArthur by now. She hoped he was having more luck than her at generating leads. Right now, she felt like she was going round in circles.

Chapter Sixteen

Morgan's gaze hardened as he stared at the blank, petulant faces of Sully and McArthur. He hadn't expected to get much out of the mechanics, but their apathetic attitudes and monosyllabic answers were grating.

'Look, gentlemen, this would be much easier if you would just answer my questions,' Morgan said, his voice laced with ice.

'For you, maybe,' Sully muttered.

Morgan bit back a sharp retort.

The pair clearly had a deep-seated dislike of the police. Neither of the men had a record, but they'd obviously had experiences that had soured them and led to a mistrust of people like Morgan. That kind of history couldn't be undone in mere minutes, no matter how hard Morgan tried. He would have to find another way to get through to them.

He decided to go in with an easier question. 'How long have you both been working for Mr Withers? Does he employ you directly or through an agency?'

Sully shrugged. 'I've worked here for years.' He turned to his friend. 'And you started here about five years ago, right?'

McArthur nodded. 'Yeah, just over that.'

Morgan studied them closely. Both men wore guarded expressions. Sully's hair was so pale it was almost a translucent bristle against his scalp. McArthur's hair looked like it hadn't been brushed for a while and it fell in greasy clumps over his forehead.

Both men stood with their hands in the pockets of their dirty overalls, legs shoulder-width apart, chins jutted out. Defensive postures.

Morgan let out a deep breath. He was sure Sully and McArthur knew something about Tony's underground operations, but they were tight-lipped and wouldn't divulge any information. Everything he'd tried so far had failed to get them to open up. He had no evidence against them, nothing to leverage to get them to reveal what they knew.

'What is it you do here?' Morgan asked.

'Repair cars,' Sully said, trying to keep a straight face, but a nasty little smirk lifted the corners of his lips.

'Can you elaborate?' Morgan asked, not rising to the bait.

'I do bodywork stuff mainly,' McArthur said. 'Sorting out dents, scratches, that sort of thing. I do some spraying out the back as well. Sully does more of the engine stuff. Breakdowns, or MOTs. That's the bread and butter of the business.'

'Do you see Tony often?'

'No, like we told your colleague, Tony only pops in now and then,' Sully said. 'He likes to spring surprise visits on us to keep us on our toes. But sometimes weeks can go by without us seeing him.'

'Is Tony a mechanic or an engineer himself?'

'No,' Sully said with another smirk. He was presumably amused by the idea of Tony Withers working on a car.

Morgan looked around the workshop. There were three workbenches close to him, each embedded with grime and oil. Tools hung from pegboards and a collection of oily rags lay in a heap on the ground beside a grey Hyundai, which had its bonnet propped open. 'If I checked all the vehicles in this workshop, would I find anything amiss?'

Sully's eyes flashed a heated warning. 'We just work here. Customers bring their cars in, and we fix them. So, if you're looking for someone to pin something on, you should look to Tony, not us. We're only employees.'

'Do you do any stuff for Tony on the side, outside of your jobs here at the workshop?' Morgan asked.

McArthur snorted. 'You trying to nail us for cash-in-hand jobs?'

Morgan shook his head slowly. 'I'm only interested in Tony. I'm not trying to catch you out.' And he wasn't. Tony Withers was big-time. Morgan wasn't interested in McArthur's undeclared income, which probably amounted to peanuts.

'Tell me about Tony's other businesses,' Morgan said. 'Things he does on the side.'

McArthur snorted again. 'He ain't got any side businesses.'

Morgan didn't believe that for a second. 'There's a rumour he runs a poker ring.'

The two men exchanged a look. 'We don't know nothing about that,' Sully said.

'I find that really hard to believe,' Morgan replied. 'You must know something.'

Sully shifted uncomfortably, and McArthur pushed his greasy hair back from his forehead, revealing a light sheen of sweat along his brow. His hand shook slightly.

Morgan didn't think they were afraid of him. But something had them on edge. 'Do you know anything about Tony's involvement with sex workers?'

'What are you talking about?' McArthur snapped, leaning in and curling his lip. 'Are you accusing us of something?'

Morgan ignored the defensive posturing. 'I'm just trying to find out what you know.'

'Nothing! Besides, it's none of our business—' Sully began.

Morgan held up his hand. 'No, it's *my* business. And if you want to keep your nose clean and stay out of trouble, you'll both tell me what you know.'

McArthur didn't move a muscle. But Sully shifted from foot to foot, running a hand over his short bristly hair.

'Come on, tell me what you know,' Morgan cajoled. 'You're not going to get in trouble if you're honest with me.'

Sully hesitated, then gave the slightest shake of his head. 'We weren't born yesterday.'

'At least tell me where the brothel is located?' Morgan asked.

The two men both shook their heads.

'Do you know any of the sex workers? Just to talk to, I mean. I'm not bothered about anything you might have done. Anyone who might be willing to speak to me?'

The two men remained silent. Morgan knew he was pushing his luck, but he had to try.

Sully looked up, his gaze meeting Morgan's directly. 'Look, we don't know anything about it. We've never been to the brothel. We've never been inside. We have nothing to do with that stuff.'

'But you know where it is?' Morgan persisted.

Sully looked uncomfortable. 'No, Tony never told us anything about it.'

Morgan regarded them carefully, trying to work out if they were telling the truth.

He felt a prickle on the back of his neck. He slowly turned and caught Valerie watching him from the shadows of the work-shop. When their eyes connected, she quickly averted her gaze and ducked her head. Her reaction made it clear she'd been listening in on their conversation.

Morgan turned his attention back to the two men. 'I take it one of you will be locking up in the evenings for the foreseeable future. It's not a good idea for Valerie to be here alone until we figure out what happened here the other night.'

McArthur narrowed his eyes. 'Val's fine. She isn't the shrinking violet you lot seem to think she is.'

'What do you mean?'

McArthur smirked. 'You really don't do your research, do you?' He chuckled and nudged Sully with his elbow.

Morgan had no idea what he was implying. Karen had told him Valerie had moved here from Yorkshire, trying to trace the daughter she'd lost contact with after a row, but he didn't know much else.

They would be running background checks as standard protocol, as they would for everyone who worked in the vicinity and could possibly have a connection to Sophie's assault.

Morgan stared at McArthur, who quickly lost his smirk and shifted uncomfortably.

'What do I need to know about Valerie?'

'Nothing,' Sully said quickly, glaring at McArthur. 'He's just being stupid. Of course we'll lock up. We won't leave her here alone. We ain't monsters.'

◆ ◆ ◆

Karen got back to the station before Morgan. Frustrated at not getting more out of Emmett, she headed over to talk to Arnie and see how he was getting on.

Arnie looked up from his messy desk. 'Churchill's looking for you,' he said. 'And before you ask, he didn't say what it's about.'

Karen grimaced. She guessed Morgan had already had a word with Churchill about the prospect of a deal for Emmett Jenkins.

Churchill probably wanted to lecture her on the best way to approach Emmett, tell her what she could and couldn't say, and list the precise details of what would go into the potential deal. He'd then probably try to talk her out of talking to Emmett alone . . .

She sighed. Why was everything such hard work?

'All right, Arnie, thanks. I'll head up to see him now,' she said.

Karen rapped on Churchill's door and waited for him to tell her to enter. She was surprised when he opened the door himself.

'Karen,' he said, his expression serious.

As usual, he looked like he'd slept in a trouser press overnight. There was not a single crease in any of his clothes. His face was smooth as well. No laughter lines, no furrows in his brow. She wondered absently if he used Botox.

'Come in,' he said. 'Sit down.'

She took a seat in front of his desk, and he sat down behind it. She steeled herself for the lecture.

'I know what you're going to say,' Karen said.

'You do?' Churchill blinked, surprised.

'Yes, about the deal,' Karen said. 'I don't think we need to iron out the details yet. I should see if he's interested first. I know you like to be organised, but we're not sure how much he knows.'

Churchill shook his head, looking utterly confused. 'I don't know what you're talking about.' When Karen started to explain, he put up a hand to stop her. 'Listen, it's important. I've had some news from the hospital.'

Karen's breath caught in her throat.

'It's not good news, I'm afraid,' Churchill said.

Karen gripped the side of the seat.

'Sophie's had another bleed on her brain.'

Fear tightened Karen's chest. The room was suddenly too small. There wasn't enough air. 'What does that mean?'

'I don't know exactly, but it's not good.'

'She's going to make it though, isn't she?' Karen felt tears brimming in her eyes, and she bit down on her lower lip.

She wouldn't cry. Not here. Not in front of perfectly preened Churchill of all people. She stared down at her knees, trying to stop the tears.

'I'm sorry, Karen, I really am. I know you were close.'

'*Are* close!' she snapped.

'Of course,' he said quickly. 'I didn't mean . . .' He trailed off. 'I don't have the right words. Sophie is such an important part of our team, but I know that you especially must be hurting. She looks up to you.'

Those were the words that sent Karen over the edge. Traitorous tears spilled down her cheeks. She gritted her teeth.

Churchill didn't seem to know what to do with himself. He began to stand, and then sat back down, and then stood up again before saying awkwardly, 'Do you need a hug?'

Karen fully intended to snarl that no, she didn't need a hug, she was perfectly fine, thank you, but instead she found herself nodding and then burying her face in his shoulder.

Sophie had to be okay.

Churchill was right. Sophie did look up to her. So why hadn't she trusted Karen? Sophie should have been able to confide in her.

'I didn't know what she was doing. If she'd come to me, I'd have told her not to be so reckless.' Karen's words were muffled.

'I think that's probably the reason she didn't tell you about it,' Churchill said.

'But I should have known.' Karen pulled away and noticed the damp spots from her tears on his shirt. 'Sorry,' she said, sniffing and brushing away the remaining tears from her cheeks with the back of her hand.

'No problem. I have another shirt in my car,' Churchill said.

'Always prepared, huh? Never less than perfect.' She gave him a watery smile.

'You're not dealing with this alone. If it's too much, we can organise some leave. You can go to the hospital now if you want to,' Churchill offered.

'I'd be no good there,' Karen said. Her stomach knotted at the thought of visiting Sophie in the intensive care unit. 'Sophie's unconscious. She won't know if I'm there or not.'

'You never know. Recent research shows patients in comas can sometimes hear things. A recognisable voice—'

'No.' Karen cut him off, shaking her head vigorously.

She had grown to love Sophie like her own family, but there was no way she'd intrude at this delicate time. If anyone was to be at Sophie's side, it had to be her real family – not Karen.

She'd let Sophie's parents and Harinder have this moment with her instead.

Only one visitor was allowed into ITU at a time, and Karen wouldn't muscle her way in at the expense of Sophie's parents or Harinder.

Maybe when – or if – Sophie began to recover, Karen would be allowed to visit her on a different ward. Until then, all she could do was wait and hope, and track down Sophie's attacker.

They both sat back down. Karen felt a heavy weight on her chest and shoulders.

'There's something else,' Churchill said wearily. 'Goodridge is looking into Harinder.'

'I know,' Karen said. 'He needs his head examining.' Churchill smiled at Karen's blunt way of putting things. 'I'm sure it's something to do with Chapman and Tony Withers.'

'I hope you're right and it's got nothing to do with Harinder, because that really wouldn't be good for morale. Not so soon after the corruption scandal.'

'Harinder wouldn't have hurt Sophie. I know him.'

Churchill didn't reply. He merely nodded.

They chatted for a few more minutes, with Churchill sensitively trying to persuade Karen it might be a good idea to take the rest of the day off, and Karen not so sensitively refusing.

She left Churchill and walked back downstairs towards the open-plan office area. She was halfway along the corridor when she stopped dead.

In front of her were two of Goodridge's officers. They were walking either side of Harinder. He looked wrecked.

'What's going on?' Karen asked.

'We're bringing him in,' the first officer said. 'For questioning.'

'But we've already asked him questions,' Karen said.

The officer narrowed his eyes in a warning. She knew it wasn't professional behaviour. She shouldn't talk to them like this in front of a suspect.

But this wasn't just any suspect. This was Harinder, her good friend and colleague. 'Surely you don't need to do this now?'

They ignored her and carried on walking.

Harinder looked back over his shoulder at Karen as they walked past. 'I didn't do anything. I swear.'

'I know,' Karen said. 'I know you didn't. Don't worry, it's all going to be okay.'

But she could tell by the way Harinder looked at her that he didn't believe her.

Chapter Seventeen

Karen, Rick and Arnie were gathered around Arnie's desk. They were all dazed after hearing about Sophie's medical setback and then learning that Harinder had been brought in for official questioning.

Rick had been rambling on, asking Karen a lot of questions she couldn't answer, but Arnie was sitting silently, staring at the *World's Greatest Detective* mug filled with pens on his desk.

'You need to take a minute?' Karen asked gently.

Arnie looked up and then shook his head. 'No, I'm all right, it's just not what I wanted to hear. It's a pretty bleak prognosis.'

'She'll pull through,' Rick said, putting a hand on Arnie's shoulder and trying to sound confident. 'They say it's always darkest before the dawn, don't they?'

'Well, it's about bloody time the sun came up then,' Arnie muttered.

'They haven't actually arrested Harinder?' Rick asked.

'No,' Karen confirmed. 'At least I don't think so.'

Rick loosened his tie. 'This is awful.'

Karen and Arnie nodded and murmured in agreement.

'Look, don't take this the wrong way,' Rick continued. 'But last night at the hospital when I was talking to Harinder, I got the impression he was hiding something.'

Both Karen and Arnie stared at Rick.

'What do you mean?' Arnie asked.

'Just that,' Rick said. 'I was sure there was something he knew but didn't want to tell me.'

'You don't think . . .' Arnie started to say.

Rick shook his head firmly. 'No, absolutely not. I don't think he would hurt Sophie, but . . . there's something going on. I think he wanted to tell me something.'

'Why are you only just telling us about this now?' Karen demanded. 'Why didn't you get him to talk?'

'How could I do that?' Rick said. 'I didn't want to interrogate him. We were sitting in the relatives' room outside the ITU. He needed my support, not an interview.'

Karen leaned forward. 'It's all such a mess. Something must have happened for Goodridge to authorise bringing Harinder in.'

'Right,' Arnie agreed. 'But what?'

'And, more importantly, why weren't we told?' Karen said.

'I can explain that,' Arnie said with a shrug. 'We're biased, aren't we? We work closely with Harinder.'

Karen nodded slowly. 'So does most of the station.'

'But we've made it clear we don't think Harinder is a viable suspect,' Arnie said. Then his eyes widened, and he added, 'Uh-oh, don't look now.'

Naturally, both Karen and Rick turned to look.

Goodridge was striding towards them.

'DS Hart,' he said coldly when he was beside them.

'Sir,' Karen said, getting to her feet. 'What's going on with Harinder? I just saw he's been brought to the station.'

'Funnily enough, that's exactly what I wanted to talk to you about.' His eyes bored into hers.

The rest had done Goodridge some good. He wasn't looking quite as crumpled now. But tired lines were still etched on his face.

147

'I've had reports from my officers that you undermined them in front of a suspect.'

Karen inwardly winced at the rebuke. She'd expected it, but it still stung.

'I didn't exactly undermine them,' Karen started to say, although . . . technically, she supposed she had.

'It's completely unprofessional,' Goodridge said. 'And if you can't operate in a professional manner, then I'm going to have to take you off the case. Do you understand?'

She saw his point. If she wanted to remain on the case, she had to conduct herself with a certain level of professionalism.

It was no excuse, but Karen had still been reeling from the news that Sophie had suffered another bleed on the brain when she saw the officers marching Harinder along the corridor. She couldn't take it all in.

She waited a beat, looked up at Goodridge's stern face and then nodded. 'I understand, and I apologise,' she said. 'I should have saved my questions for when Harinder wasn't present.'

Goodridge gave a curt nod. 'Yes, you should,' he said, still peeved, but he sounded somewhat mollified.

'I'm curious, though,' Karen said. 'Why have we brought Harinder in? You asked me to question him. He offered an alibi and a full account of his whereabouts. Nothing seemed suspicious to me.'

Goodridge said, 'I did. And I do appreciate you asking the questions. I know it can't have been easy. That said, some new intelligence has come to light, which means we need to take a closer look at Harinder.'

'New intelligence?' Rick said, interrupting. 'Sorry,' he added when Goodridge glared at him. 'I couldn't help overhearing. What new information have we got?'

'We uncovered a connection between Harinder and an employee from Tony Withers's workshop.'

Karen frowned. 'Which one?'

'Brian Sully. He lives in the same apartment building as Harinder,' Goodridge said.

'Is that all?' Arnie scoffed. 'That doesn't even necessarily mean Harinder knew him.'

Goodridge raised an eyebrow. 'No, that in itself doesn't mean anything, but the fact that Harinder's next-door neighbour saw the two of them having a heated discussion four nights ago does.'

'They were arguing?' Karen queried.

Goodridge nodded. 'According to the witness, yes. Harinder denied knowing anyone who worked near Great Northern Terrace. He clearly lied.'

'Well, not necessarily,' Rick said. 'I mean, okay, he knew Brian Sully, but he might not have known he worked at Tony's Workshop.'

Goodridge gave Rick a look that suggested he thought the younger detective was talking nonsense. 'I think it's best if my team handle the investigation into Harinder from this point forward.'

'But we can still look into Chapman and Tony Withers?' Karen asked, 'Because I think that's where we'll find answers.' Goodridge glanced at Karen, then his gaze flicked between Arnie and Rick. 'Yes, keep working on that and see what you find. We'll have a briefing this afternoon. Three p.m.'

After Goodridge stalked away, Karen slumped into her chair. 'I can't believe this is happening.'

'I know,' Rick said. 'I'm not sure things can get much worse for Harinder. I wonder if he wanted to tell me about Brian Sully last night?'

'Why did he hide something like that?' she asked, her voice hoarse. She reached for her bottle of water and took a sip. 'It doesn't make any sense.'

'It could be a misunderstanding,' Rick suggested. 'Maybe Harinder didn't know where Brian Sully worked at first, and when he realised the connection to the workshop, he chose not to bring it up because it would distract us in our search for Sophie's attacker.'

Both Karen and Arnie gave Rick a wary look.

He sighed and ran a hand through his hair. 'Yeah, okay, so it does sound a bit far-fetched,' he admitted. 'But I just cannot believe Harinder's responsible.'

A silence fell over the group. Was their friend really a suspect? And if he'd concealed the truth from them about Sully, what other secrets was he hiding?

◆ ◆ ◆

DCI Goodridge stood at the front of the large briefing room, his arms resting on the wooden podium as he flicked through the pages of his notes with a grave expression. His jaw was set firmly, and his forehead was furrowed in deep concentration.

DCI Churchill was absent, and Morgan was nowhere to be seen either. He must have been held up talking to Brian Sully and Mark McArthur at Tony's Workshop, Karen thought.

She sat at the back of the room. Today's briefing wasn't as crowded as the last one, but nearly all the chairs were taken.

She sat beside Farzana, who leaned in close and whispered, 'Is it true what they're saying about Harinder?'

'What are they saying?'

'That they've brought him in for more questioning. But why? What's happened?'

But before Karen could reply, a hush fell over the room as Goodridge began to talk.

His voice cut through the air. Everyone in the room was silent as their eyes shifted from one colleague to the next, full of speculation.

'This has been an especially difficult case. Not only because we're investigating a brutal attack on one of our own officers, but because a recent development and fresh information has led to us bringing Harinder Singh from the technical department to the station for further questioning.'

The tension was so thick it was almost suffocating.

Farzana caught Karen's eye, her expression one of shock and disbelief.

'We must stay focused,' Goodridge said firmly, raising his voice. 'We need to focus on the basics and methodically stick to procedure.' He looked directly at Karen. 'We have to follow the evidence, no matter where it leads.'

Karen's head spun at the twist this case had taken. It was hard to believe they were seriously investigating the possibility Harinder had played a role in Sophie's assault.

Goodridge shifted the paperwork in front of him, then scrawled a name on the whiteboard.

Millie Clark.

'Millie Clark, one of Harinder's neighbours, alleges she saw him getting into a nasty altercation with Brian Sully, one of the mechanics at Tony's Workshop, four nights ago. She watched the whole thing from her bedroom window, as the two men were on the street below.'

'Altercation?' Arnie queried. 'They had a physical fight?'

'From what Millie Clarke has told us, there was pushing and shoving and shouting,' Goodridge confirmed.

'Does Harinder have an explanation for this?' Arnie asked.

Goodridge turned his attention to the two members of his team who Karen had seen bringing in Harinder. She guessed they'd overseen the interview.

The taller officer said, 'Harinder admits talking to Brian Sully, but says he's been set up.'

'There are cameras outside Harinder's apartment block,' Karen replied, remembering him telling her so himself. 'Have you looked at the footage?'

The tall officer inclined his head stiffly. 'We're looking into it. We're also looking at Harinder's computers and electronic devices, both at home and at work, with his permission. He says he has nothing to hide.'

Karen stared down at the table. This was getting out of hand. If she could just talk to Harinder . . .

'I know it's difficult,' Goodridge said, glancing at Karen and then at Rick and Arnie. 'You're close to both Sophie and Harinder. So, that's why I want to make sure you're not involved in this side of the investigation. I think it's best for all concerned.'

Karen nodded. She understood Goodridge's reasoning, but it didn't make it any easier to accept.

'Now,' Goodridge said, turning his attention to Farzana. 'Anything to report?'

Farzana straightened in her seat and nodded. 'Yes, sir. We've got some results back from the lab. The fingerprint analysis of the tyre lever we believe was used in the attack has been concluded. The test results indicate all the employees in the workshop had touched the weapon at some point. Unfortunately, no other prints were discovered. The powder coating was apparently very difficult to work with, and there's been a delay on the DNA results.'

Farzana paused as Goodridge's eyes narrowed in contemplation.

'Names of the employees?'

'Valerie Anderson, Brian Sully and Mark McArthur,' Farzana reported. 'No other prints were identified.'

'That's a pity,' Goodridge said. 'The prints don't prove much. The employees probably all had cause to use the tyre lever at work.'

'Sophie's assailant was wearing gloves,' Karen chipped in. 'We saw that on the CCTV. The chances of her attacker leaving prints were always slim.'

Goodridge sighed, his frown deepening. 'All right, thanks, Farzana. Anyone got anything else to share?'

A few people spoke up, reporting back results, but there were no major breakthroughs.

'There is one thing,' Arnie said, gruffly. He gestured towards Karen, who nodded in encouragement. 'We've been looking for properties with links to Tony Withers and Quentin Chapman. As you know, there have been rumours both men are involved in illegal gambling and possibly prostitution. We haven't been able to uncover where this is going on, but I've been able to trace one of Chapman's properties, through a convoluted trail of shell companies – one heck of a twisted path, but I've got an address.' He pulled a crumpled piece of paper from his pocket and smoothed it out on the table. 'I'd like permission to check it out.'

Goodridge thought for a moment. The room was silent except for the pattering of rain on the window. 'Do you think this has something to do with Sophie's attack?'

'It's possible Sophie was looking into this on the side,' Karen explained. 'If someone realised what she was up to, then it could have been a motive for the attack.'

Goodridge gave a firm nod. 'Check it out. It could provide useful information on Quentin Chapman, even if it isn't related to what happened to Sophie.'

Arnie cleared his throat. 'I want to talk to Brian Sully. I know you don't want me to have anything to do with the Harinder side of the investigation.' Arnie shrugged. 'And I understand your point of view, but I can keep an impartial distance.'

Goodridge squinted at him with obvious suspicion. 'I'm not sure that would be wise.'

'I can keep it professional,' Arnie said, his voice gruff but confident. 'I think I have a better than average chance of getting the truth from Brian Sully; he and I have spoken before.' He paused for a beat before adding in a softer voice, 'But if you object . . .'

'No, go ahead,' Goodridge said. 'It makes sense as you've spoken to him before. So has DI Morgan . . . but that was before we were aware of the altercation between Sully and Harinder.' Goodridge scanned the briefing room. 'Where is Morgan anyway?'

Chapter Eighteen

Geoff Jones emerged from the hospital with tears in his eyes. Most of the time he was holding it together. But the emotions came in waves. He'd had to come outside, telling his wife, Clara, he just needed some fresh air. She was being so strong, and he didn't want her to see him upset.

Rain fell softly, and he looked up at the sky and took a deep breath.

It wasn't fair. How could his daughter be lying in a hospital bed, her life hanging in the balance?

And here he was feeling hopeless, unable to do anything to help.

With every passing hour it seemed there was less chance of Sophie surviving. The doctors were being non-committal when he asked them questions, and Geoff had heard them talking in hushed tones about 'keeping her comfortable'.

He knew what that meant.

He felt wounded both inside and out. A physical pain burned in his chest. He swung from overwhelming grief to a murderous rage. But one without direction, since her attacker hadn't been caught yet. Not knowing who to blame made it worse.

All he wanted was for Sophie to get better and the person who'd hurt her brought to justice.

He needed his little girl to regain consciousness, yet all around him people were avoiding the topic, as though that wasn't an option anymore.

Clara refused to acknowledge it, but Geoff recognised they were running out of time. He had failed Sophie by not getting to her fast enough. If he'd reached her earlier, perhaps the brain injury wouldn't have been so bad.

Now though, he was powerless. All he could do was wait and keep a quiet vigil at the hospital.

He closed his eyes and muttered a prayer. Something he hadn't done in years. The cold air made his cheeks tingle and the rain mixed with his tears.

'Excuse me,' a gruff voice said.

Geoff's eyes opened.

A man stood in front of him holding out an umbrella. 'Do you need this?' He watched Geoff uncertainly, as though he suspected Geoff were a patient escaped from the psych ward.

It took Geoff a few seconds to realise the man was offering him the umbrella, and then quickly understood how stupid he was being.

He could make himself ill standing out in the rain, and he didn't have time for that. He thanked the passer-by, but refused the kind offer, and instead hurried towards his car.

Once inside, he pulled off his soggy coat and turned the heaters on, then leaned back in the seat and closed his eyes. His stomach churned as he thought back to finding Sophie bloodied and battered. The sadness was devastating, but almost immediately his mood shifted as a fire of anger ignited in his chest at the thought of Harinder, who'd been taken in for questioning.

He wanted nothing more than to take matters into his own hands and—

Geoff leaned forward and rested his head on the steering wheel. It might not mean anything. Questions were just that – questions. Harinder hadn't been charged. But why had the police carted him off to the station? They wouldn't do that if he was innocent, would they?

It was hard to imagine the Harinder he thought he knew hurting Sophie. That man was kind and generous and had never shown the slightest sign of violence. And yet, if there was even the slightest chance Harinder was responsible, Geoff couldn't let him back into the hospital ward to see Sophie.

Geoff's mind ran wild, imagining how Harinder might try to finish Sophie off while she was still unconscious, so she couldn't tell anyone who had harmed her.

He shook his head, desperate to dislodge the image he'd conjured of Harinder standing over Sophie, holding a pillow to her face. Harinder wouldn't . . . would he?

Of course, it could never happen like that. There were plenty of hospital staff in ITU. They'd stop him from acting so overtly. But Harinder was clever. Maybe he could manipulate one of the vital machines she was hooked up to?

The safest thing was to keep him away from Sophie. At least until the police got to the bottom of what happened. For now, caution would have to outweigh loyalty.

He pushed himself back in his seat and stared at the fogged-up windscreen. He was fumbling around in the glove compartment in search of something to wipe away the condensation, when his gaze landed on a green and gold notebook.

It didn't belong to him.

He stared at it, remembering that Sophie had borrowed his Honda Jazz a week ago when she was having some work done on her own car.

Slowly, Geoff took out the notebook and opened it. The first page was filled with her familiar, neat, looping handwriting. It sent him back in time to when Sophie was a little girl, learning to write. Her tiny fist clenched awkwardly around a chunky pencil as she struggled to form letters.

She hadn't given up easily. Even then she'd been an over-achiever. Concentrating and biting the tip of her tongue, she'd repeatedly tried to write her name, even though she kept drawing the 'P' backwards.

Despite his tears, Geoff found himself smiling at the memory. He continued to thumb through the notebook, treasuring the connection with Sophie. It wasn't a diary or anything personal like that. There were just random notes here and there, a list of names, and doodles of flowers and geometric shapes at the top of some pages.

He brushed away the tears from his cheeks and gently shut the notebook. He moved to place it back in the glovebox before stopping and putting it on the passenger seat.

He stared at it for a moment. Maybe it could be important. It could be something to do with work. The list contained only women's names. Perhaps they meant something.

He thought that maybe the book could provide the police with some clues as to who had attacked Sophie. Geoff scratched his chin and rubbed a finger over the embossed cover of the notebook, then reached for his mobile phone.

After they'd all filed out of the briefing room, Rick had felt despondent. They weren't making progress quickly enough for his liking.

Now they were chasing Harinder, and Rick was sure that was a wild goose chase.

Rick didn't know what had gone on between Harinder and Brian Sully, and he definitely couldn't understand why Harinder hadn't told him about it. He could only assume it had been a misunderstanding, and that Harinder was about to clear everything up with a perfectly reasonable explanation. At least, he hoped so.

Maybe Harinder and Brian Sully had got into an argument, and Sully had decided he'd take it out on Sophie.

Rick could have been leading everyone down the garden path when he'd suggested Sophie was tackling a case on her own off the books. He sighed and picked up his mug.

After he'd made a coffee and checked his messages – one was from Morgan, saying he was heading back to the station but probably wouldn't be back in time for the meeting – he headed over to Arnie's desk. 'When are you going to talk to Brian Sully?'

Arnie, who'd been rummaging through stacks of papers, looked up. 'Thought I'd wait until Morgan got back and compare notes first. Have you seen him?'

'He's on his way back to the station now.' Before he could say another word, his mobile started to ring.

He apologised, then turned away from Arnie and answered it. 'Hello?'

'Rick, it's Geoff Jones, Sophie's dad.'

Rick's stomach twisted. 'Is there any news?'

'I'm afraid not. Sophie's still the same. That's not why I'm calling. Sophie borrowed my car about a week ago. Hers needed some work.'

'Which garage did she use?' Rick asked, immediately thinking of Tony's Workshop.

'It wasn't the one on Great Northern Terrace,' Geoff said quickly. 'It was an outfit on Lincoln Road. We've been using it for years.'

'I see,' Rick said, letting go of the potential connection.

'Thing is, though, Sophie left a notebook in my glove compartment. There are only a few brief notes inside, and it's probably not important, but I thought you might want to take a look.'

'Thanks, Geoff. It could be helpful. I can pop over and pick it up. Are you at the hospital?'

'Yes, and there's something else,' Geoff said. 'Harinder isn't here. Your lot have taken him in for questioning . . .' He trailed off.

'I know,' Rick said quietly.

'Why?' Geoff asked. His voice now had a hard edge. 'Do they suspect he did something to Sophie?'

Rick spoke slowly, aware of the need to choose his words carefully. 'I'm not the one running the investigation, but I know the team will be looking into absolutely everything to find out what happened to Sophie. And if that means bringing Harinder in, then that's what they're going to do.'

Geoff sounded as though he was choking on his words. 'But . . . he wouldn't have . . .'

'No, I don't think so,' Rick said, then admitted, 'I was shocked too when I heard he'd been brought in.'

'But why do they think he's involved?' Geoff asked. 'Do they have any evidence? The police didn't tell me anything, except they needed him to come down to the station to answer some questions. Why couldn't they have just asked him the questions there?'

'I think it's easier to ask them away from the emotional environment of the hospital.' Rick tried to find the words to reassure Geoff.

'I'm sure Harinder will still be upset no matter where he is,' Geoff replied.

Rick hesitated. He wasn't sure if he should tell Geoff they'd discovered Brian Sully had been involved in an altercation with Harinder. But it might be best to tell him; maybe Geoff knew something that could help.

Rick chewed on a fingernail before saying, 'We've found out that one of the employees at the workshop near to where you found Sophie had a confrontation with Harinder a few days ago. It could be an irrelevant coincidence.'

'What's the name of this employee?'

'Brian Sully. Do you know him?'

'No,' Geoff said. 'Never heard of him before. Are you telling me Harinder had a big bust-up with somebody?'

'It may not mean anything, Geoff, but I'll keep you updated.'

'If Harinder has anything to do with what happened, then I don't want him coming back here. Not near my daughter.'

'Geoff—' Rick started to say.

But Geoff cut him off. 'No. I know it's not a kind thing to say, but it's my daughter lying in that hospital bed. If there's even an inkling that he was involved, I don't want him anywhere near her. Do you understand?'

Rick replied, 'Geoff, I'm being completely honest here; I'm telling you everything that we know. There is no evidence that Harinder hurt Sophie. You know him. He loves her.'

There was an extended silence before Geoff said, 'I have to go,' and abruptly hung up.

Rick stared down at his mobile phone. Geoff was scared and hurting. Harinder being taken to the station for questioning had put a horrible worm of suspicion in his brain.

Rick hoped Harinder would be able to answer all the questions put to him and prove his innocence quickly, because this situation had the potential to spiral out of control.

Chapter Nineteen

As Morgan pulled into Great Northern Terrace, heading for Tony's Workshop, he turned to Arnie, who was sitting in the passenger seat. 'Do you think Sully will be talkative?'

'Doubt it. What was he like when you spoke to him earlier?'

'Petulant and unhelpful.'

'Sounds like the Sully I met,' Arnie said. 'He and McArthur have a real chip on their shoulders when it comes to dealing with the police.'

Morgan had done some more digging into Chapman and Withers's backgrounds and found plenty of business and property connections between the two men. Morgan couldn't help wondering just how much power Tony held in Chapman's empire. Was he Chapman's unofficial right-hand man?

The businesses all seemed legit, but that was what Chapman wanted them to think. Tony might run many of Chapman's legal, above-board projects, but it was the illegal ones Morgan was interested in.

Morgan parked outside the workshop.

'There he is,' Arnie said, unclipping his seat belt. 'It's like he was waiting for us.'

Brian Sully stood just outside the main door of the workshop, leaning against the wall, smoking a cigarette. He wore jeans and a thick blue shirt with the sleeves rolled up, rather than the overalls he'd had on earlier.

The green roller door was raised, and music was playing in the workshop. Visible through the open door were car parts and engines in various states of disassembly.

Sully's face was hard when he caught sight of them. He pressed a button on the wall beside him to lower the door, then rubbed his free hand over his bristly scalp.

'What do you want?' he shouted as they approached.

Neither detective spoke until they reached him. Then Morgan said, 'I'm not sure you were entirely honest with me earlier, Mr Sully.'

He shrugged. 'So what. I don't owe you anything.' The words were tough, but his narrowed eyes and defensive posture told Morgan he was unsettled.

'You know,' Arnie said in a bored drawl, peering over Sully's shoulder through a dirty window, 'we're investigating a series of car thefts in the area and thought you'd be the perfect man to help us out.'

Sully said nothing, but ground out his cigarette on the wall before flicking the butt to the floor. He took his time lighting another, before finally saying, 'What makes you think I'd know anything about car thefts? Do I look like a criminal?'

Morgan decided not to answer that. He nodded at the closed roller door. 'If you've got nothing to hide, maybe we could continue this chat inside.'

Sully looked them both up and down for a few moments before finally nodding his head. He took a long drag on his cigarette, then put it out and said, 'All right, come inside.'

He hit the button and the roller door creaked and juddered into life.

Arnie and Morgan followed him into the workshop, where the smell of petrol and solvent was overwhelming. Various car parts were stacked and lined up on the workshop benches.

'You've got a lot of car parts there,' Arnie commented, walking over to inspect some of them.

'Hardly a surprise since this is a working garage.' Sully folded his arms over his chest.

'They're all legit, are they?' Morgan asked.

'Of course. We're just trying to make a living here – refurbing old parts and selling them on. There's no law against it.'

'As long as the parts aren't from stolen vehicles,' Arnie commented.

Sully's expression became increasingly hostile, but before he could respond, the back door to the workshop slammed open. Valerie came in, struggling under the weight of a large paint-splattered metal drum. She wore dirty overalls, and her hair was pulled back in a ponytail. She stopped in surprise when she saw the detectives.

'I didn't realise we had visitors,' she said breathlessly as she smiled at Arnie.

She set down the drum and hurried forward, wiping her hands on a rag she pulled from her pocket. 'Would either of you like some tea?'

Sully shook his head, scowling. 'No tea,' he growled. 'They won't be staying long.'

'Oh, right.' Valerie's smile disappeared.

'Don't just stand there. Get on with the spraying,' Sully said, jabbing a finger at her.

As Valerie silently retreated, Sully turned back to Morgan and Arnie. 'I don't know anything about any stolen vehicles. So, I guess we're done here.'

'Not quite,' Morgan said.

'What is it you want?'

'Harinder Singh. Your neighbour,' Morgan said, watching realisation dawn on Sully's face.

He curled his lip in disgust. 'Seriously? The little wimp went running to the police?'

'You had a barney the other night?' Arnie prompted.

'It was nothing.' Sully shook his head. 'I can't believe he actually reported me, the little—'

'Tell us about the altercation,' Morgan cut in.

Sully heaved a sigh. 'All right. It happened a few days ago. Harinder was trying to park in the same spot I was reversing into, and we came together. There was a little scratch on the bodywork. But it was nothing serious. My car came off worse than his. But he still threatened to call the cops on me. I told him I could fix the damage, so it looked as good as new, but he was such a moaner. Went on and on about reporting me for stuff.'

'Did it get physical?' Morgan asked.

'Nah.'

Morgan raised an eyebrow. 'There are cameras outside the apartments as well as a witness. I'd encourage you to tell the truth.'

Sully's face darkened. 'It was nothing. A bit of shoving and name-calling. That's it.'

'Did you ever see his girlfriend?'

Sully paused for a moment, and then said, 'I've seen her, yeah.' His expression softened a fraction as he added, 'Cheerful lass. Nice smile.'

Arnie stepped forward. 'Then why didn't you say you recognised her when I showed you her photograph?'

'What?' Sully looked confused. 'You didn't show me . . .' He trailed off as the confusion cleared. 'It was her? The woman who was attacked outside the workshop?'

Morgan held out his phone, showing Sully a recent headshot. 'Sophie Jones.'

Sully stared at it for a few seconds before his face drained of colour. He appeared genuinely shocked. 'Yeah, that's her. I didn't realise. I only glanced at the photo before.' He shot an accusing glare at Arnie. 'You should have given me longer to look at it.'

'I gave you plenty of time to look. You just couldn't be bothered,' Arnie growled.

Sully and Arnie scowled at each other until Morgan broke the silence. 'Did you ever see Sophie and Harinder together?'

'Yeah, sure, a few times.'

'Ever witness them arguing?'

Sully gave a mirthless laugh. 'I thought Harinder was one of your lot. You're trying to finger him for this?'

'Just answer the question,' Arnie snapped.

Sully shrugged. 'No, never saw them arguing. They seemed happy enough.'

'Did you see them often?' Morgan asked.

'No, I don't know them really, only enough to nod hello, you know?' He ran a hand over his bristly scalp. His expression softened again, and in a quiet voice, he added, 'How is she doing now? Is she still in the hospital?'

Morgan glanced at Arnie before saying, 'Yes, and she's still in a coma.'

Sully muttered under his breath and stared at the floor for a few moments, then he looked Morgan in the eye, his gaze fierce. 'You won't often find me rooting for the police, but I hope you catch the evil sod who did this.' He gritted his teeth as if to rein in his rage, then added, 'You really think Harinder is behind it?'

Morgan and Arnie didn't answer the question.

The clang of metal against concrete made all three men turn. Valerie had dropped an oil drain pan. 'Sorry,' she muttered, her face pink with embarrassment as she quickly picked it up.

Morgan hadn't noticed her coming back into the workshop. 'That's all right,' he said before turning back to Sully. 'We'll need an official statement from you about what happened the other night.'

Sully nodded slowly. He seemed less angry now. Realising the attack had been against someone he knew – even if only vaguely – had turned his temper down a notch.

Valerie finished putting away her tools without saying a word and ducked into the small kitchen at the side of the workshop.

'We'll need to talk again soon,' Morgan said to Sully. 'So, stay put.'

Sully fixed them both with a hard stare. 'Are we done?'

Arnie and Morgan exchanged glances, then Morgan said, 'I'd like a word with Valerie.'

'Why?' Sully's tone was full of suspicion.

'Just a chat. Nothing for you to worry about,' Morgan said.

Sully glanced at Arnie, who nodded in confirmation. 'Fine,' he said gruffly. 'Come on.'

He started to lead the way to the kitchenette, but Arnie said, 'We'd like to talk to her alone.'

Sully looked like he wanted to argue. His fists clenched at his sides, and his eyes narrowed. 'You want me to give you some privacy?' he sneered.

'Yes, that would be nice. We won't be long,' Arnie said firmly, his tone leaving no room for argument.

Sully grunted and turned away. He headed into the dark depths of the workshop before switching on the fluorescent lights to illuminate the area.

As he walked away, Morgan couldn't help noticing Sully appeared slightly changed since they'd last spoken just hours ago – almost as though some of the callousness had been stripped away from him. He'd never be a man to volunteer information to help the police, but with a little persuasion he might be pressured to talk.

Morgan and Arnie found Valerie in the kitchenette, staring out of the window.

'Got time for a chat?' Arnie asked gently.

Valerie jumped at the sudden sound of his voice. She quickly composed herself and tried to smile. 'Yes, of course. I'm happy to help. Would you like some tea?'

'That would be lovely,' Arnie said, and Morgan said he'd like one too.

She seemed happy to be doing something that kept her hands occupied. She busied herself boiling the kettle and preparing cups of tea.

Keeping her head down, she handed cups to Morgan and Arnie. She stole a glance towards the workshop, and Morgan followed her gaze. Sully was standing there, arms folded, scowling menacingly.

Valerie seemed frozen. A flicker of worry passed over her features, and she shuddered.

She stepped past Morgan to close the door, smiling nervously. 'Now, what did you want to talk about?'

'You told one of our colleagues a young woman visited the workshop looking for Tony Withers a while back. We're looking into your boss and—' Arnie broke off and frowned at the panic on Valerie's face. 'You're not in any trouble. We just need your help. Anything you can tell us.'

Valerie tucked a lock of hair that had slipped free from her ponytail behind her ear. 'I'm happy to tell you what I know, but I really don't know much about Tony's operations.'

'You think he's running a brothel? Exploiting women?'

'I hate considering it, but yes . . . I think he might be. I've overheard him on the phone a few times talking about *his girls*. I haven't seen any evidence myself, but something just doesn't feel right.'

Valerie sounded both frightened and embarrassed as she spoke. Her eyes flitted around nervously, as though she was worried Sully could burst in at any moment. Or perhaps she was concerned Tony might pay a surprise visit and catch her discussing him.

'I don't have any real proof,' she said reluctantly, 'but with what happened to your colleague . . . I can't help wondering if this is somehow connected.'

Valerie paused, and Morgan and Arnie waited.

After a few moments of silence, she picked up her cup of tea and continued. 'A few weeks ago, a young woman came to the workshop demanding to see Tony. I told her he wasn't here, but she didn't believe me. She stormed around, looking for him. She was really angry.' Valerie glanced up at Arnie, and then quickly lowered her gaze again. 'She told me she couldn't keep working for Tony. She was het up, but terrified at the same time.'

Arnie and Morgan exchanged meaningful glances.

'She asked me to help her,' Valerie said, clutching her cup of tea tightly between her hands, 'but I didn't know what to do . . . and then she just left.'

'Have you seen her since?'

Valerie shook her head.

'Did she give you a name?' Morgan asked.

'No. I did ask her name. I told her I'd take a message and pass it on to Tony if I saw him.' Her hand trembled as she lifted her cup to take a sip. 'I wish I'd handled it differently now, but it all happened so fast.'

Valerie spoke some more, and Morgan and Arnie listened intently as she told them about other suspicious behaviour that had gone down at the workshop over the past year. She described unusual visitors turning up at all hours to either leave or pick up bundles that Valerie suspected contained cash.

It seemed obvious now that something very sinister was going on at Tony's Workshop.

Morgan couldn't help admiring Valerie's courage. She was taking a great risk by talking to them so frankly. There could be nasty consequences if Tony discovered she'd told them anything.

She had to know she was putting herself in danger but was doing it anyway.

'Valerie,' Morgan said gently. 'We really appreciate your help with this.' He paused and glanced at Arnie before continuing. 'Do you have any idea where Tony might be running this brothel from?'

'No, I've never heard him mention a location. But the young woman who came here looking for him did mention an address . . . the street name, if that helps?'

'Yes, that would be a great help,' Arnie said.

'Old Haddington Lane.'

'Off the A46?' Morgan queried.

'I think so, yes. I'd forgotten she'd told me that. I should have mentioned it to DS Hart.'

'You've been a great help,' Morgan said. 'Thank you, we'll check it out.'

'I hope the information is useful. How is your colleague doing? Has her condition improved?'

'We're still hoping she'll pull through,' Arnie said.

'I'll keep her in my thoughts.' She gave them both a tired smile.

They thanked her again before opening the door.

As it swung open, Brian Sully toppled forwards, having been listening in on their conversation.

Valerie's hand flew to cover her mouth at the intrusion.

Sully shifted his weight and put his hand on the door to right himself. His cheeks flushed an angry red as he mumbled something about coming to get himself a drink. He was embarrassed at being caught eavesdropping.

'Didn't your mother warn you?' Arnie said with a delighted smirk. 'Eavesdroppers never hear nice things.'

Sully scowled and then stalked away without an apology.

Outside the workshop, Arnie turned to Morgan. 'Shall we go straight to Old Haddington Lane?'

Morgan unlocked the car. 'Not yet. We need a plan. Old Haddington Lane is a quiet spot and non-residential for the most part. It could be where she works. Let's go back to the station and narrow down which properties look like they could house a brothel or a gambling club. Even satellite images from Google Maps would be better than going in blind.'

'All right. You're the boss,' Arnie said. 'Although we should act fast. Sully will be squealing to Tony as we speak. He's going to know we're after him.'

Morgan got behind the wheel. 'It's a risk, but we can't just turn up and search every property along the lane. That would tip Tony off as well.'

'True,' Arnie mused. 'One way or another he's going to know we're coming for him.'

Chapter Twenty

Karen walked along the corridor, a large mug of coffee in one hand and her phone in the other. She was expecting a call back from an officer at the Metropolitan Police, but he was taking his time about it.

It was already dark outside and the muted orange of the lights in the car park glowed through the rain-speckled windows. As she entered the open-plan office, her mobile started to ring and she fumbled awkwardly, one hand still clutching her mug, trying to answer it before it went to voicemail.

The screen told her it was DS McKenzie of the Metropolitan Police.

Karen hadn't even had a chance to say hello when a gruff voice said abruptly, 'What can I do for you, DS Hart?'

Karen sat down at her desk and pulled her notebook towards her. She took a deep breath and began to explain the situation to him. As she leaned on the desk, she ran an index finger along the folder where she'd been keeping her notes. 'So that's why I'm interested in your case about the London sniper,' she said, her voice dropping to a hushed tone, even though the office wasn't busy. 'I think it could be connected to a fellow called Quentin Chapman, based in Lincoln.'

Karen was surprised by McKenzie's response. She'd expected him to be defensive or dismissive or even secretive, but instead he laughed.

'It's not a bloody sniper,' he spluttered. 'The media have taken a leak and run with it. It's sensationalist stuff. You know how it is.'

Karen did. She'd experienced her own problems with journalists. One local hack, Cindy Connor, had caused Karen a great deal of grief across several cases. Though, lately, Cindy had been helpful and less irritating than usual. Which implied maybe even hacks were capable of change.

Karen's mind was already working on the possibilities. 'What kind of weapon was used?'

'A Beretta 9000s,' the detective said. 'Whoever carried out the hit was skilled. But it wasn't a gunman on a grassy knoll with a sniper's rifle, like you'd think from reading the newspaper articles.'

Karen frowned as she processed the information. The papers had said it was one clean shot from a distance away. But she now knew it wasn't a sniper . . . The information from the police database had been limited for obvious reasons. The investigating team would keep their evidence and witnesses close to their chest rather than risk leaks or witness intimidation.

'But it was a professional hit?' she asked.

'I'd say so. It has similarities with another hit in Nottingham, and one just yesterday in Reading.'

'Yesterday?' Karen was surprised. She hadn't heard about that one yet.

'Yeah, in a public park, right in front of the Forbury Lion. That one was a statement, all right.'

'You're sure the crimes are linked?'

'Yeah, we think it was the same gun and same shooter. They were hiding in plain sight. Baseball cap and raincoat. Caught on CCTV every time, but not great pictures. All three cases, including the one in Nottingham, were carefully planned. The victim, on each occasion, was taken out on their way to work, following their usual route.' He paused for a beat, then added, 'This sort of hit isn't cheap. Someone with a lot of money hired the shooter to kill all three victims.'

'Do you have suspects?' Karen asked.

He was quiet for a moment. 'I'm not sure how much detail it's appropriate for me to give over the phone. When it comes to gang violence, which we believe this is, we tend to keep a close circle when it comes to evidence and working theories. You understand, don't you?'

'Of course,' Karen said, though it was frustrating.

'Tell me more about the connection with this man in Lincoln, Quentin Chapman.'

'He's afraid he'll be next on the list,' Karen said frankly.

'And do you believe that?'

'I don't know what to believe when it comes to Chapman,' Karen confessed.

'Well,' McKenzie said hesitantly, 'his name has been mentioned. I can tell you that much.'

Karen leaned back in her chair, thinking. She'd heard plenty of rumours about Quentin Chapman. Despite the files of information she'd collected, she hadn't linked him to the victims before Chapman himself had revealed his connection to them. But she couldn't work out exactly *how* the victims were related to him.

'The victims were all associates of his,' Karen said. 'So he tells me, but I don't know in what capacity.'

'That's what we've been trying to figure out too,' McKenzie admitted. 'We believe all the victims had ties to Chapman's business operations. So far, all signs point to a gang-related attack by a rival.'

'Do you have any idea who could be behind it?'

McKenzie exhaled heavily. 'Whoever it is, they've got some balls to carry out these hits in broad daylight. You know anyone with a vendetta against Chapman?'

Carrying out assignations in the open like that was sending a message. They weren't afraid. Some might view that as a show of strength, but Karen thought it displayed recklessness and arrogance.

She mulled it over. Perhaps a rival of Chapman's was taking out some of his men, to muscle in on his patch. Or it could be an inside job – one of Chapman's own men making a power grab. She thought of Tony Withers. Obnoxious and boastful, his confidence exceeded his common sense. Could he be behind this?

Karen explained her thoughts. 'Tony Withers is worth looking into. We've linked him to Chapman, and he's a man with far more bravado than brains in my opinion.'

McKenzie thanked her for the information and told her he'd look into Withers.

After they'd talked a little while longer, he said, 'What do you think about the possibility that Chapman himself is behind the hits and trying to pull the wool over our eyes?'

Karen's mind raced. Could Chapman himself be at the centre of this sinister web? If so, what was his end game? Was he trying to dupe them into believing he was a potential victim? She didn't want to sleepwalk into something. If Chapman had planned this devious deception, she could make Lincolnshire Police a laughing stock by getting fooled by him.

People were passing her desk, heading home. She returned Farzana's wave and then tapped her pen on her notepad.

'That's an interesting theory,' she said to McKenzie, 'and I wouldn't put it past him. It would be just like Chapman to muddy the waters and pretend he's scared, angling for the sympathy vote as he ruthlessly despatches his rivals.'

'It's certainly a possibility,' McKenzie said. 'I don't suppose you're able to get any more out of Chapman?'

'I'll try. We have an . . .' *Understanding? A relationship?* Karen didn't quite know how to put it. 'I've had dealings with him before,' she said. 'I think perhaps that's why he chose to talk to me about these hits.'

'I wouldn't believe everything he tells you.'

Karen felt a spark of indignation. She wasn't that green. 'No, I won't.'

'Sorry. I didn't mean it as an insult,' McKenzie said. 'The politics, backstabbing and manipulation that goes into some of these gangland operations . . . you wouldn't believe it. They can fool even the best of us.'

'Chapman is certainly manipulative.'

'Thanks for your help,' McKenzie said as he wrapped up their conversation, letting Karen know that it was an ongoing investigation and the Met would appreciate whatever help they could get from her and the Lincolnshire team to crack it open.

With her notebook filled with names and theories, and ideas running around in her mind, Karen thanked McKenzie for his time and hung up.

She took a sip of her coffee, and the bitter aftertaste lingered in her mouth as she reviewed her notes.

So far, they had a lot more questions than answers on this hitman case.

She looked up at the commotion as Arnie and Morgan strode into the office.

Morgan waved her over. 'Karen, come with us. We're going to have a word with DCI Churchill.'

She made her way over to them. 'All right. What's all the excitement?'

Arnie waggled his eyebrows. 'We've got a lead.'

Karen felt her heart racing as the police van sped along the A46. She sat in the back, her hands clenched tightly in her lap.

Beside her, Morgan and Arnie were both quiet, their faces etched with determination. Her stab vest seemed to be constricting her torso, a reminder of the dangerous mission they were on.

It wouldn't be long now. They'd soon reach Old Haddington Lane and the large property that Morgan had identified as the likely location of Tony Withers's brothel and illegal gambling club.

This could be the moment that brought down Tony Withers. And, with a little luck, Quentin Chapman, too.

But an odd sensation swirling in the pit of her stomach was warning her that something wasn't right. After all their hard work tracking and investigating Chapman, it seemed almost too easy.

A van filled with armed police was ahead of them. That was deemed a necessity due to the potential link between Chapman and the shootings in London, Nottingham and Reading. Arranging the armed unit and waiting for the raid to be organised had eaten up precious minutes.

'I hate to be a glass-half-empty sort,' Arnie said, even though he could usually be counted on to be pessimistic. 'But I reckon even if we catch some of Tony's girls turning tricks and spot a couple of roulette wheels spinning together with piles of cash, the CPS are going to tell us the evidence isn't good enough to pin it on Tony.'

Morgan frowned. 'Maybe so. But all we can do is execute the plan and gather the appropriate evidence. The prosecution is out of our hands.'

Despite her nerves, Karen smiled. Dependable, exacting, precise Morgan.

She glanced at Arnie, predicting an eye roll and a heavy sigh. And right on cue, Arnie obliged, then muttered, 'Tell us something we don't know.'

Karen felt she knew Morgan and Arnie so well now she could often predict their reactions, or sometimes even what they would say next, word for word. There was something comforting in that, especially as they hurtled towards a raid that had the potential to turn violent.

'We'll get the evidence,' Karen said. 'If it's not enough today, we'll keep working until the CPS are satisfied and both Tony Withers and Quentin Chapman are behind bars.'

They lapsed into silence, which suited Morgan and Karen. When they were nervous, they focused inwards and retreated into their own thoughts to cope with the situation. Arnie, on the other hand, was different. He was sweating profusely and kept adjusting his stab vest, his mouth racing to replace the silence.

He dispelled his nerves with chatter.

'Is it me or is it hot in here?' he asked with another tug on his vest.

'It's pretty warm,' Karen agreed. 'It won't be long. We must be nearly there by now.'

Morgan checked his phone. 'ETA four minutes.'

Karen's pulse sped up.

'So,' Arnie said, still determined to bury the silence. 'What did the guy from the Met say about the sniper?'

Karen hadn't had a chance to fill them in on her conversation with McKenzie yet. When Morgan and Arnie had returned to the station, all their efforts had focused on identifying properties on Old Haddington Lane that could be housing a brothel and gambling den.

Unfortunately, they hadn't been able to link any of the buildings on the lane to either Chapman or Withers. But Morgan had identified one possibility, based on its size and location.

The place Arnie had mentioned in the briefing as being connected to Chapman had ended up just being a dry-cleaners, so they were now pinning all their hopes on this new lead.

Arnie had wanted to set off for Old Haddington Lane immediately, but he'd been overruled. Safety came first.

'DS McKenzie had a theory that Chapman himself could be behind the hits,' Karen said. 'Maybe he paid a hitman to make sure he had an alibi at the times of the shootings. Coming to me with a sob story, telling me he fears for his life, could be another part of his manipulation.'

Arnie let out a low whistle. 'That would be sneaky, even for a man like Chapman. What do you think?'

'It's a possibility,' Karen said with a shrug.

The van slowed and tilted as they rounded a corner.

This was it. They'd turned off the A46 and entered Old Haddington Lane. Karen met Morgan's gaze and he gave her a reassuring smile. A few moments later, DC Farzana Shah, who was in the driver's seat, stopped the van and killed the engine.

This was all part of the plan. They were to wait a short distance from the property while the armed unit did their job and swept the building.

Farzana turned to look at them. 'You guys doing all right back there?'

'We're good,' Karen replied. 'You?'

Farzana's dark eyes showed a hint of nerves, but she nodded confidently. 'Everything is fine. We just need to wait for a signal from team A. It might be a while.'

Karen sat back and tried to relax, which was impossible with the adrenaline coursing through her system.

The time passed slowly. Even Arnie lapsed into silence as the minutes ticked by.

They got the signal twenty minutes later.

'We're clear to approach,' Farzana said, turning on the engine.

After they reached the location, Farzana got out of the van and let them out. It was dark, and the edge of the lane was filled with puddles. Arnie swore and shook his foot after he stepped in one.

The building loomed in front of them. It was an old two-storey farmhouse with a massive single-storey extension. There were multiple small windows – all obscured by curtains that allowed no view inside.

The front garden was surrounded by a low fence and was pleasantly landscaped and well maintained. Several solar lanterns lit up a path and made the area seem unexpectedly pretty and cosy.

It really didn't look how Karen had envisaged it. Had she been expecting neon lights? Signs advertising massages?

The police vans were parked in the driveway at the front of the house. Off to the side stood an old barn, its walls recently painted and with what looked like a new roof. It held an impressive collection of cars. Suggesting they'd hit the right place – if the vehicles belonged to punters.

The barn was surrounded by a small orchard of gnarled old fruit trees, the bare branches making sinister shapes. In the spring, with the blossom blooming, it would probably be a beautiful sight. But tonight, the scene was menacing and malevolent.

As Morgan and Farzana approached a member of team A for a status report, Karen and Arnie hung back.

She nodded at the massive extension. 'I can't believe they got planning permission for that. It's huge and doesn't even attempt to match the style of the original building.'

Arnie shrugged his shoulders. 'I suspect Tony Withers has connections at the council.'

After a minute, Morgan came back, his face stony.

'There's no sign of the sex workers. There are a lot of rooms back there, but it looks like they've recently been cleared out.'

Karen sighed, disappointed and angry all at once. 'I hoped we might get them this time.'

Morgan shook his head grimly, clenching his jaw as if restraining himself from saying what he truly thought.

'They must have been tipped off,' Farzana said.

'Suspected as much,' Arnie said in a low voice. 'My money's on Brian Sully.'

'Is the property completely empty?' Karen asked.

Morgan shook his head. 'No. There's a large room at the back of the main house. There were six men playing poker when team A arrived.'

'That's something at least,' Farzana said. 'Any money on the premises? Can we pin the gambling on Tony even if we don't get him for operating a brothel?'

Morgan's mouth twisted into a wry smile. 'They were playing for matchsticks apparently. They all had little piles on the table.'

'They're taking the mick,' Arnie said. 'They knew we were coming, and that little set-up was for our benefit.'

'It's a clear provocation,' Morgan agreed.

'We can take all six men to the station,' Karen said. 'Perhaps one of them can tell us something useful.'

'I doubt it,' Arnie said. 'Tony wouldn't leave anyone here that he considered a liability. They won't give him up. We'll have to accept he's won this round.'

'It's worth a try,' Morgan said, and as he argued the point with Arnie, the SOCO van arrived ready to inspect every inch of the property.

Karen looked over her shoulder at the house. A chill ran down her spine. A heavy feeling of dread settled over her.

Where had the women gone? Were they safe?

Chapter Twenty-One

After the adrenaline rush from the raid had dissipated, Karen's energy deserted her.

It was late, yet she sat at her desk, which was covered with folders and yellow sticky notes, scrolling through material she'd gathered on Quentin Chapman and Tony Withers.

They'd come close, but Tony had clearly been expecting them, and the little set-up with six of his cronies playing poker with matchsticks had been a smack in the face.

The others had left the station dejectedly, glum-faced and miserable despite Morgan's attempt to lift their spirits with a pep talk about tackling the case afresh tomorrow. Karen could tell he was just as discouraged as they were.

Goodridge's team had taken over and were questioning the six men they'd found playing poker, but Karen didn't believe they'd get anything from the diehard lackeys. They'd rather serve time than cross Tony Withers.

Karen sighed and rested her head in her hands, wondering how Sophie was doing.

She'd heard Harinder had been released after his voluntary interview, and had sent him a text message a couple of hours ago, but so far, he hadn't replied.

'Karen?'

Rick was walking towards her desk.

'I didn't realise you were still here. It's late,' she said.

'I know, but I need to show you something.' He held up a notebook. 'Geoff gave it to me. It belongs to Sophie. He found it in his car.'

Rick pulled up a chair and sat down. He opened the book, flicking through the pages.

'Have you looked through it? Anything useful?'

He rubbed his bloodshot eyes. 'Yes, but I only got it from Geoff an hour ago. There was a mix-up. He meant to leave it at the hospital for me, but he accidentally took it with him when he went home to shower. But I think it was worth the wait, though. I've found a list of names.'

'Names?' Karen leaned over to look at the familiar looping handwriting.

Sophie had jotted down a list of women's names.

'It's definitely Sophie's writing,' Karen murmured, tracing a line down the list. 'Have you checked any of these yet?'

Rick's expression was grave. 'Yes – all women reported missing over the past five years.'

Karen's eyebrows lifted. 'This must be the case she was working on without us knowing.'

A sickening sadness engulfed Karen at the thought of Sophie not trusting her enough to tell her about this. Whatever her reasons, it might have cost Sophie her life.

It was hard not to take it personally, but Karen knew there wasn't time to get into that now.

She squinted at the list of names; some had crosses beside them. 'Have you worked out what the crosses mean?'

'The ones with crosses beside them seem to be women who are no longer missing. They've been found – either dead or alive.'

'Where do these women come from?'

'All over the country,' Rick said.

Karen scanned the list again before her gaze zeroed in on one name.

'So, what do you think?' Rick prompted. 'We could speak to the families of these women . . .' His voice faded away when he caught the expression on Karen's face.

A roiling, swirling sensation swelled in the pit of her stomach – equal amounts excitement and dread.

'What is it? What's wrong?' he asked.

'This name.' Karen tapped the list with one finger. 'Claudia Anderson.'

'Do you know who that is?'

Karen slowly nodded. 'Valerie Anderson's daughter. You know, the woman who works at Tony Withers's workshop. Claudia left home after a big fight with her mother, and Valerie hasn't seen her since.'

A heavy silence hung in the air as they both mulled over the implications of this new information.

Rick's fingers moved swiftly on the keyboard as he logged into Karen's computer, pulling up a series of police reports that detailed the disappearances of young women, their ages ranging from seventeen to twenty-six, all with similar backgrounds of poverty, petty theft, drug use, domestic violence or broken homes.

Karen's fists clenched in her lap as she came to terms with the fact that Sophie had kept the investigation a secret from them.

Why hadn't Sophie trusted her? If she had, they'd be working side by side on this case, but now it seemed there was a chance the worst would happen. Sophie could die.

Karen didn't know much about brain injuries. She'd researched brain-bleed outcomes online but wished she hadn't. It was hard to contemplate Sophie's absence from her life. The idea of it made Karen feel numb. She pushed the thought out of her mind.

Sophie had been trying to trace these young, vulnerable women. Karen had to focus on that now. They had to finish what Sophie had started.

It was becoming increasingly clear that Tony Withers and possibly Chapman were likely running a brothel and exploiting these disadvantaged women.

Finally, the pieces of the puzzle began to fit together. Sophie had uncovered their scheme, and during her unofficial investigation, she'd been attacked. The location where she'd been found suddenly made sense – Sophie could have been looking for evidence or arranging to meet someone from the operation there.

Karen squeezed her eyes shut, trying to block out the unwelcome images of Sophie's attack that flooded her mind.

'Are you all right?' Rick asked gently.

Karen managed to nod. 'I wish I hadn't seen the security footage . . . I can't get it out of my head; it's stuck on a loop.'

Rick exhaled a long breath. 'It was horrific. I keep thinking about it too.'

As Rick pulled more reports from the system, Karen jotted down a few notes. Writing things by hand helped get them straight in her mind.

'There's one thing I can't figure out,' Karen said, staring at her notes.

'What's that?'

'If Claudia Anderson is involved in all this somehow, why didn't Valerie tell me her suspicions? She was up front about her daughter's disappearance, but she never mentioned a possible connection to Tony or Chapman.'

'Perhaps she didn't know,' Rick suggested.

Karen shook her head. 'Unlikely. She came down from Yorkshire to work for Tony after her daughter disappeared. That has to be because she suspected he knew Claudia.'

'I'll access the misper report. It's possible Sophie was referring to another Claudia Anderson.'

'I doubt it. The name isn't that common.'

They spent some time going through the reports together, trying to figure things out. But Karen was convinced Valerie knew a lot more about this than she'd told them.

Had Valerie come to Lincoln and got a job with Tony so she could dig for the truth or look for clues to her daughter's whereabouts?

Sophie had written Valerie's daughter's name in her notebook. Had Valerie spoken to Sophie about her daughter's disappearance? Had Sophie agreed to help her? But if so, why all the secrecy?

Karen had shown Valerie a photograph of Sophie, but the woman had denied recognising the young detective. Had they spoken over the phone rather than face to face?

She tried to think back to Valerie's reaction when they'd told her Sophie had been attacked outside the workshop.

She'd been upset but had explained that away by saying her daughter was similar in age.

One thing was for sure, Valerie knew more than she was letting on.

Rick's voice was quiet, and he sounded overwhelmed. 'So what should we do with all this information? It changes things.'

'It certainly does. For one thing, it should mean Goodridge's team diverts their attention away from Harinder. It's much more likely that the attack on Sophie was motivated by someone attempting to shut down her investigation into Tony's exploitation of sex workers.'

Rick shuffled through the thick stack of case reports he'd recently printed. 'So we're looking for someone who had a vested interest in preventing Sophie from uncovering the truth behind Tony's vile exploitation of these vulnerable women.'

'Yes,' Karen agreed. 'It's likely to be someone on Tony's payroll. He wouldn't want the seedy truth coming out.'

Rick grabbed the stapler, clipping together a report. 'But we don't think it was Tony himself who attacked Sophie?'

'Not unless he fed us a false alibi,' Karen confirmed. 'And I don't think he'd take the risk of doing it himself. Not when he has so many cronies willing to do his dirty work.'

'The order could have come from Chapman – after all, we think that's who Tony takes his orders from.'

Karen shrugged. 'It's possible.' She thought for a minute. 'We should tell Churchill about this development. I know it's late, but he'd want to know,' Karen said, searching through a pile of papers before finding her mobile. 'I'll call him.'

'Wait,' Rick said, 'let's check his office first.'

'He's probably gone home,' she said uncertainly.

'It's worth a shot.'

They walked upstairs to Churchill's office, and Karen was surprised to find the lights on. She knocked.

'Come in.'

'Hello?' Karen said, pushing open the door. 'I didn't expect you to still be here.'

Churchill looked up. His lips curved into a tired smile.

Goodridge was sitting in one of the chairs in front of Churchill's desk. His suit was crumpled. He nodded at Karen and Rick and smothered a yawn.

'We had work to finish off.' Churchill gestured to Goodridge. 'How can we help?'

Rick shuffled in behind Karen and shut the door. 'Actually, we wanted to talk to you about a development in the case.'

'Oh, yes, what is it?'

'It's about Tony Withers,' Karen said. 'The raid wasn't success-ful, but we're sure Tony operates a brothel. We believe Sophie was on to him and investigating . . . outside of work hours.'

Churchill frowned, and Goodridge spoke up. 'Why would she do something so dangerous?'

It was a good question, but Karen didn't have an answer. At least, not without delving into the psychology behind Sophie's crav-ing for approval and recognition, and she didn't feel qualified to do that.

She told them about Sophie's notebook and the list of wom-en's names. 'We think this was the motive for the assault. Sophie was attacked because someone didn't want her looking into Tony's criminal dealings.'

Goodridge sighed and rubbed a hand over the stubble on his chin. His tie was askew.

Karen turned her attention to him. 'I'm sure you'd agree this is a much more likely scenario than Harinder being behind Sophie's assault.'

Goodridge narrowed his eyes but made no comment.

Churchill leaned back in his chair, his face blank. 'I see.' Unlike Goodridge, his clothing was, as usual, pristine.

'Come on,' Karen said. 'This is a major development.' A note of desperation had entered her voice.

'I agree with Karen, sir,' Rick chipped in. 'This information sheds new light on the case. We need to start looking into who would want to stop Sophie investigating Tony's involvement in the sex trade. You need to tell the team. They can start—'

Goodridge held a hand up. 'Hold your horses.'

Rick fell silent.

'I can't just shelve the Harinder side of the investigation,' Goodridge said in a quiet but firm voice.

Karen understood his response, but she sensed Rick's anger.

'Why do you need to keep looking at him? You have no evidence—' Rick was seething.

Karen reached out, her hand lightly touching his arm.

There was an uncomfortable silence. The fact that Sophie – their colleague and friend – was fighting for her life went unspoken, but they were all feeling it. No one wanted to admit the possibility that she might not make it, but it hung heavily over them. Her plight had them all on edge and emotions were bubbling over. Rick would usually phrase his argument more tactfully, but with Sophie's condition worsening, his temper was flaring faster than it normally would.

Churchill was the first to speak. 'I'm not sure the information is enough to really change things. This new information is useful, but it doesn't give us a suspect.'

'It gives us a motive,' Rick protested.

'But no viable suspect!' Goodridge's face was tight. Karen could see he was just about keeping his annoyance in check. They were all tired. Their fear for Sophie and their emotional link to Harinder made them all more sensitive than usual.

'Then that's what we do next,' Karen said. 'We look at who benefits from keeping Tony's brothel secret. Obviously, Tony himself and—'

'He has an alibi,' Goodridge cut in coldly.

'As does Harinder,' Karen snapped back, her voice like ice. She looked at Rick for support. His face was grim as he met her gaze. 'Seriously, you've looked into Harinder's alibi?' she said, her voice steady and quiet this time. 'Does it stand up to scrutiny?'

Goodridge inclined his head stiffly. 'His alibi looks strong.'

'Then why—' Rick began, exasperated. 'Harinder has no reason to lie. He's a good bloke. I'd trust him with my life.'

Karen could relate to how Rick was feeling. She was fond of Harinder too, but she'd had her own experience of betrayal. She had been fooled by a friend and colleague in the past, someone she'd trusted and looked up to. Sometimes it was difficult to tell who was a good person and who was not. That the ones she thought she knew best could let her down in devastating ways had been a painful lesson to learn.

Despite that experience, she was still determined to believe the best about those close to her.

'Harinder remains a potential suspect,' Goodridge said stubbornly.

Rick shook his head. 'But the evidence points—'

'Enough.' Goodridge's voice was sharp. 'I don't need to hear any more. I will make the final decision.'

Rick looked as though he'd been slapped.

'You need to keep your feelings out of this if you want to remain part of this investigation,' Goodridge warned.

Rick looked away, furious.

Churchill, playing peacemaker, added, 'This is good work and almost certainly provides an important new lead.' He looked at Karen. 'What's your next step?'

She told him about the link with Valerie Anderson and her daughter. The anger and frustration over Harinder had stopped her from giving them the whole story.

'Claudia Anderson's name was in Sophie's notebook,' Karen explained. 'I don't think that's a coincidence. I'd bet on the fact Valerie and Sophie had contact of some sort.'

'And she didn't mention that?' Churchill raised a quizzical brow, waiting for confirmation.

'She did not,' Karen confirmed.

'I agree. That's more than a little suspicious,' Goodridge said.

'I think my first port of call tomorrow should be to speak to Valerie,' Karen said.

'Agreed,' Churchill said firmly. 'What was she like when you spoke to her before?'

'I thought she was nervous, scared even, but that isn't surprising with a boss like Tony Withers. I thought she was holding back but never suspected this potential connection to Sophie.'

Churchill nodded slowly and straightened his already perfectly straight tie. 'You'll have to try to gain her trust. It could be that the attack on Sophie scared her into silence.'

'I'll be sympathetic,' Karen said.

'Good.' Churchill stood up. 'I think we're done here. It's been a long day. Thank you all for your hard work.'

'Thank you, sir,' Rick and Karen both said as they left the room.

As they headed towards the stairs, they glanced at each other. They knew they wouldn't be able to clear Harinder themselves. It was a process. To fight it would only cause more stress and resistance from Goodridge.

'I suppose I'd better go home,' Rick muttered miserably.

'We'll make more progress tomorrow,' Karen said, trying to push some enthusiasm into her voice.

Rick gave her a weak smile.

As they stepped into the open-plan office, he suddenly turned to her. 'You do believe Harinder is innocent, don't you?'

Karen met his gaze, looking into his desperate eyes. He just wanted her to agree with him, to tell him she believed in Harinder without question. But she couldn't. She didn't want to believe Harinder would be involved in any way, but she had a niggling doubt. A little voice that told her no one could be trusted completely.

'I don't know what to think at the moment.'

She wanted desperately to believe in Harinder, but his withholding the truth about his link to Brian Sully was damning. That wasn't the behaviour of an innocent man, was it? She'd blindly trusted in friends and colleagues before and been betrayed. She wouldn't let that happen again.

Rick was disappointed in her, and that hurt.

'I'll do everything I can to prove his innocence,' she added quickly. 'But how well do we ever really know anyone?'

Rick's face fell. He walked away.

They collected their belongings, then headed out of the station in silence, strolling across the car park. There was a sharp chill in the air. The night sky had cleared and was spotted with stars. The moon shone brightly, competing with the orange glow of the lights beside Karen's car.

'See you tomorrow,' she said, and Rick gave a half-hearted wave.

Karen watched him leave.

'I'm sorry,' she said, even though he wasn't there to hear.

Chapter Twenty-Two

Karen arrived at the workshop just after it opened. It was a crisp, cold day. The sky was a brilliant blue, and frost clung to the patchy grass beside the railway line.

The huge roller door at the front of the workshop was closed, and so was the smaller door beside it.

Karen knocked on the smaller door and waited, her breath misting around her. She felt the morning chill, despite her coat and scarf, and shivered.

She was looking forward to getting some straight answers from Valerie, but no one was answering. She tried the handle, but the door didn't budge. Were they late opening up?

That seemed unlikely. The padlock on the bottom of the roller door was unlocked, and through the small, grimy window she could see that the lights were on.

She frowned and made her way around the back of the building, where she spotted another door. She knocked twice. Again, there was no answer. She waited a few moments, then knocked again.

Finally, she heard shuffling on the other side, and the door opened with a creak.

Brian Sully peered out, his eyes guarded. He didn't seem surprised to find Karen standing there, but he looked over her shoulder, as though he was expecting someone else as well.

'What do you want?' he grumbled when he turned his attention back to Karen.

'I'm here to see Valerie.'

'Does she know you're coming?'

Karen narrowed her eyes, a flash of irritation surging through her. 'Just let me in. It's freezing today and I'm sure Valerie will be happy to talk to me.'

Sully made a scoffing noise but moved aside to let Karen enter.

As she stepped through the doorway, she noticed the workshop wasn't that much warmer than outside, despite the oil heaters nearby.

'Val!' Sully shouted. 'Police here to see you . . . again.'

Karen shivered and shoved her hands deep into her pockets as she looked around the massive workshop. Anyone would think she wasn't welcome.

Mark McArthur was leaning over a workbench a few feet away, taking something apart, studiously ignoring her.

Sully slumped into a seat beside the computer and telephone bench and resumed eating a breakfast bap. On the computer screen was the camera feed from the front of the workshop. He'd likely been sitting there eating, watching her when she knocked.

A voice came from behind Karen. 'Hello, Detective.'

She whirled around to see Valerie standing behind her, wearing navy-blue overalls, which today were free of grease stains and oil streaks. She removed small white earbuds from her ears.

'I'm sorry,' Valerie said as she walked up to her. 'I was listening to music and didn't realise you were here.' She glanced over at McArthur, and then at Sully sitting by the computer, smirking. 'I guess the others didn't hear you either.' She shot Sully an unimpressed look before turning back to Karen. 'What can I do for you?'

'I'd like to ask you a few more questions concerning Claudia's disappearance.'

Valerie nodded slowly and gestured for Karen to follow her. 'Let's talk in here,' she said over her shoulder as she led Karen into the kitchenette and shut the door.

Once they had some privacy, Valerie offered Karen a drink. Karen turned it down and leaned back against the counter, launching straight into her questions.

'Why did you come to Lincoln?'

'I told you. Because someone mentioned they thought Claudia had come here.' Valerie spread her hands and smiled, an open friendly gesture suggesting she had nothing to hide, but Karen knew she'd not been open at all.

Karen tilted her head to the side, watching Valerie closely. 'Who told you that?'

'Um.' Valerie's gaze flitted about the small kitchen as though she might find the answer somewhere there. 'I can't remember.'

'I need you to be honest with me. It's very important.'

'I am,' Valerie said, looking hurt. 'I don't remember.'

'Your daughter is missing. You're devastated . . . but you don't remember the one person who gave you a tip-off to where she might be, Valerie? I find that incredibly hard to believe. I want to help you. You're not in trouble, but I need you to tell me the truth.'

Valerie's cheeks flushed and she wrung her hands. 'I'm not sure I can,' she whispered miserably.

'What do you mean? Are you afraid of someone?'

Valerie's mouth opened and closed as she struggled to find an answer. It was clear she was uncomfortable. Her hands fluttered at her sides, as though she couldn't keep them still.

Karen pulled out her mobile phone, tapping on the screen until Sophie's photograph appeared on the display. She held it up for Valerie to see. 'Look at this picture,' she said, gently yet firmly, trying to keep Valerie focused despite her fear. 'This time I want you to tell me the truth. Have you seen her before?'

Valerie glanced at the photo briefly before looking away again. Her face crumpled.

'Well?' Karen asked.

Valerie's eyes brimmed with tears, and she whirled around, turning her back to Karen and gripping the edge of the sink so tightly her knuckles turned white.

Her shoulders shook as she sobbed. Karen waited silently for her to regain some composure before speaking again.

She'd been devastated by the loss of her daughter, and that was something Karen could empathise with deeply. She knew what it felt like to have a daughter taken away, leaving a painful wound that would never heal.

Valerie took a deep breath and brushed away her tears with the back of her hand. She turned around and nodded. 'I didn't mean to hide the truth from you, but Sophie told me to keep quiet.'

'You met her?'

Valerie nodded. 'She came here a few weeks ago, asking questions about Tony. I told her about my daughter . . . about how I suspected she'd been working for Tony.'

'Claudia was a . . . sex worker?' Karen asked quietly.

Valerie looked up and met Karen's eye. 'I don't know for sure, but I think so. I didn't get a tip-off about her being in Lincoln. That was a lie. Claudia called me a few months after she disappeared. She'd been drinking, and she was very upset. She told me she was in Lincolnshire, working for a man called Tony Withers. She told me that she hated him. She said she was going to leave.'

'Did she tell you what sort of work she was doing for Tony?'

Valerie shook her head. 'She wasn't making much sense. She was very drunk. And I . . . I'm ashamed to say I could have handled things better. I told her to come home, but she kept telling me I wasn't listening, and then she hung up. She called from a withheld number. I thought Claudia would call back, but she never did, so I came to Lincoln. I wasn't planning on getting a job here, that was pure luck. I thought I'd have a better chance of finding out what Tony Withers was up to if I was working for him.'

'And when Sophie came to the workshop asking questions?' Karen prompted.

'I told her exactly what I told you. Sophie promised to help me find Claudia. But she told me not to tell anyone. She said it was dangerous and that I shouldn't trust anyone. And then when she was attacked . . . I didn't know what to do. I was so scared. I thought I'd be next. I wanted to run home to Yorkshire, but I couldn't go, not without my daughter.'

'I'm sure Sophie meant don't tell anyone connected to Tony. She didn't mean not to tell the police.'

Valerie looked sceptical. 'I didn't know who I could trust. I thought that if Sophie hadn't told you what she was working on, then perhaps that meant it wasn't safe for me to tell you.'

Karen flinched at Valerie's words. It was increasingly evident that Sophie hadn't trusted her and that hurt.

'Valerie, it's important that you tell me everything you know now,' Karen said in her most soothing voice. 'I'm trying to help you. I'm on your side.'

'I believe you. I'm just . . . I'm scared.'

Karen moved closer and put a comforting hand on Valerie's shoulder.

Valerie bit her lip and glanced nervously at the closed door. 'I can't talk here.'

'Come to the station.'

'Now? I can't. They'll know I've been talking to you,' she said in a whisper.

'After work then?'

'Okay.'

Karen wanted details. She needed facts and evidence strong enough to put Tony Withers away. Possibly Chapman too. She wanted to help Claudia and the other exploited women. But pushing Valerie too hard might make her clam up.

It wasn't even nine a.m., and waiting until Valerie finished work for answers seemed unbearable, but it didn't look like Karen had much choice.

◆ ◆ ◆

Karen had only made it as far as Kesteven Street when her mobile rang. She pulled off the road and picked it up. The number wasn't recognised.

She answered.

The voice on the other end of the line sent a chill down her spine. Chapman.

'DS Hart, please forgive the unsolicited phone call. I have a favour to ask.'

'I don't think you're in a position to ask me favours,' she said, her voice cold. She wondered if he'd heard of the raid on Tony Withers's premises and was calling to gloat.

'Karen, I need your help.'

She paused. His voice sounded different, strained. 'What's wrong?' she asked.

He cleared his throat. 'It's regarding our conversation the other day.'

'Yes?'

'I don't want to discuss the matter on the phone. It's very sensitive. Can you come to my house?'

'Now?'

'Yes, if that's convenient, I'd be very grateful.'

She frowned. Of course it wasn't convenient. She was at work. She had tasks to be getting on with, paperwork to file. But she had to admit she was intrigued.

She'd need to call into the station and let Morgan or Churchill know what was going on. She didn't think it was a set-up, but where Chapman was concerned, she could never be sure.

'All right. I'll head there now.'

'Thank you. You might find things a little . . . different here.'

'What do you mean?'

'I've employed extra security and installed more alarms. I'm taking precautions.' He hesitated before continuing. 'I need someone I can trust. Someone I know isn't involved in any of this.'

'And that's where I come in?' Karen asked, thinking the idea of Chapman trusting her, a police officer, was laughable.

'Exactly.'

She shook her head in disbelief. He must think she was born yesterday. 'I'll be there as soon as I can.'

'Thank you,' Chapman said, his voice full of relief. 'I was sure I could count on you. I'll see you soon.'

He hung up, and Karen was left staring at her phone. If McKenzie's theory that Quentin Chapman was really behind the hits in Nottingham, Reading and London was correct, then Chapman was quite the actor. He had sounded genuinely scared.

Before she had a chance to call the station, her phone chirped with an incoming message.

It was Harinder, finally returning the message she'd sent him yesterday.

Goodridge let me go yesterday. But Geoff refuses to let me see Sophie. He says I can't see her until I've been cleared. Can you talk to him? H.

Karen sighed, trying to imagine how Harinder must feel. He was desperately worried Sophie might not pull through, and on top of that he had to deal with his colleagues and Sophie's father suspecting him of hurting her.

She thought back, remembering Rick's expression last night when he'd asked if she believed Harinder was innocent. She pictured Rick's disappointment. He trusted Harinder. Rick was a better person than she was.

What was wrong with her?

Harinder had never given her a reason to doubt him. Not once had he done anything that would suggest he'd be capable of hurting Sophie. Why was she treating him like this? She felt thoroughly ashamed of herself.

Karen loved Sophie. She missed the young detective's nerdy, high-achieving, slightly swot-like tendencies. She missed her enthusiasm, her kindness. Karen's heart ached when she allowed herself to consider that Sophie's absence from the team might be permanent.

Karen was close to Harinder as well, but past betrayals had made her bitter and mistrustful. She'd been double-crossed in the most horrific way by a friend and colleague, and it had scarred her. But living with her guard up permanently, just in case history repeated itself, wasn't really living at all.

She didn't want to be that person anymore.

Karen cared deeply for Harinder. He deserved her support.

But what could she do? She had no authority over Sophie's father or his decisions.

She took a deep breath and typed out a reply: *I'll try to talk to Geoff later today. Hang in there, mate. K x*

Chapter Twenty-Three

As Karen turned into Chapman's drive, her jaw dropped. He hadn't been kidding about extra security measures.

Larger gates had been erected, blocking the entrance to Chapman's mock-Georgian mansion. She parked in front of them as a dozen security men all in long coats and wearing matching earpieces stared at her.

Two guard dogs strained at their leads. It was an intimidating scene.

One of the men, holding a German shepherd on a lead, approached the car. He motioned for her to lower the window. She did so.

'Name?' he asked sternly, as his eyes swept the inside of her car.

Karen introduced herself and held up her warrant card.

He peered past her, looking at her bag on the passenger seat, but finally nodded and made a gesture to the men behind him. The gates opened.

Karen slowly drove along the driveway, her gaze shifting between the men and dogs in the rear-view mirror and the imposing facade of Chapman's house.

She felt uneasy. Was this really necessary?

The front door was opened before she knocked.

Ponytail stood in the doorway, his face hard and unreadable, his eyes never leaving her as she stepped inside.

Karen nodded at him, but all she got in return was a cold, stony stare.

He shut the door then said, 'This way.' He led Karen through the entrance hall and into the huge kitchen at the rear of the property.

Chapman had his back to them, staring out at his carefully landscaped garden and the fields beyond.

'She's here, sir,' Ponytail said.

Chapman turned. 'DS Hart, good of you to come on such short notice.'

His face was tired. He looked like he carried the weight of the world on his shoulders.

Karen asked, 'Is all this security really necessary?'

Chapman nodded grimly. 'It is. You know what's happened to some of my acquaintances recently. I'm determined not to be next on the hitman's list.'

Karen glanced around the kitchen, taking in the modern appliances and sleek cabinets. Two other stone-faced security guards stood sentry in the garden. Chapman had employed a serious security presence, but surely they couldn't protect him from a professional hitman.

Private security or bodyguards in the UK were not permitted to be armed, unless under exceptional circumstances, and Chapman certainly wouldn't get an exemption from that rule.

He noticed her scrutiny. 'I know what you're thinking,' he said. 'It's extreme. But I can afford it.' He ran his fingers through his thick salt-and-pepper hair.

Karen asked, 'Who do you think is behind this?'

Chapman shrugged and walked closer to the window, gazing out at the grounds with a troubled expression. 'I don't know,' he said finally. 'All I know is that someone is after me and they won't stop until they get what they want.' He turned back to her. 'That's why I need your help.'

Karen nodded slowly. 'If you believe you're at risk, I'll speak to McKenzie at the Met. We'll need armed—'

'No.' Chapman cut her off. 'No police.'

'But I *am* police.'

'You know what I mean.'

But Karen didn't. He wasn't making any sense. If his life was in danger from a hitman, an armed unit of police officers was the only way they could protect Chapman. The grounds being full of security guards were no match for an assassin with a gun, unless . . .

'Your men aren't armed, are they?'

A smile tugged at the edge of Chapman's lips. 'That would be . . . illegal.'

'It would,' Karen confirmed. When he didn't elaborate, she asked, 'Do you have any enemies?'

'Plenty,' Chapman replied, this time with a full smile. 'There are quite a few people who would love to see me fall from grace.' He paused for a moment before continuing. 'I just hope that it's not one of my own men behind all this . . .' His voice trailed off into silence as he turned back towards the window once again, lost in thought.

Karen was having doubts about McKenzie's theory. Would Chapman go to all this effort if he wasn't in fear of his life?

'I really recommend getting the police involved. I can call my boss and—'

'That's not what I want.' His voice was firm.

'Then what do you want?'

'I want to pick your brain.' Chapman's eyes shone with bright intensity.

Karen frowned. 'How?'

'You've been digging for dirt, looking through my history, raking over my past, searching for my associates.'

Karen glared at him stubbornly. She wasn't going to deny it. She wanted to put Chapman away. He was a criminal. It was her job.

'At this point, Karen, you know me better than most of my closest confidants. It's almost as if you've already done the investigation for me. Use that information. Analyse the details you've collated . . . and find out who wants me eliminated.'

Karen stared at him. 'I don't work for you. If you want police assistance you need to go through official channels.'

Chapman gave a disappointed sigh, but his eyes were still sharp and determined. 'That's never going to happen.'

'Then you're on your own,' Karen said with a shrug.

'I don't think so,' Chapman said evenly. 'I can see you're interested. You're a problem solver. You want to find out who is behind these hits almost as much as I do.'

Karen said nothing.

'I'll leave it with you then,' he said amiably.

'While I'm here,' she said, 'I'd like to ask how much you know about Tony Withers's brothel.'

The confident smile left Chapman's face. 'What?'

'He runs a poker club linked to a brothel. We're on to him. It's only a matter of time before Tony's little empire comes crumbling down.'

'I don't know anything about a brothel. I told you, I play cards with Tony from time to time. We have other business dealings, but I am not and never have been involved in a brothel.' His steely voice carried a warning.

Karen eyed him sceptically. 'Have you ever heard the name Claudia Anderson?'

'No.'

Karen sighed and folded her arms, looking out at Chapman's garden. She had been sure that Chapman was connected to Withers's brothel, but maybe she'd been wrong.

She glanced at Chapman and saw the intensity in his gaze as he waited for her decision. He clearly wanted to find out who was behind these hits, and she had to admit she did too. Maybe she could use that to her advantage.

'You're asking me for help. I need cooperation in return. I want you to find out what you can about the brothel and Claudia Anderson's whereabouts.'

'All right,' he agreed, much to Karen's surprise.

She felt a flutter of excitement at the thought of getting closer to the answers. But she also felt a chill of apprehension at assisting Chapman. She had to find a way to get past her dislike for the mobster standing beside her. His cooperation could provide information she desperately needed. If she walked out of here now, refusing to help him, the case could fall apart. They might never find out who had attacked Sophie.

She stared at his now placid face, looking for all the world like a harmless, elderly man rather than the cold-blooded gangster he really was. Somehow, she had to find a way to get past her aversion to working with the man who over recent months had become her nemesis.

It came down to a very basic truth: her need to get justice for Sophie was bigger than her hatred of Chapman.

'Fine,' Karen said firmly. 'I'll do what I can to help you.'

Chapman's face softened with relief, and he nodded, satisfied.

'But,' she continued, pointing a finger at him, 'we need to be clear: I'm not doing this because I want to help you or because I trust you.' She paused for a moment before continuing. 'I'm doing this because it's a chance for me to get the evidence I need.'

Chapman smiled and extended his hand. Karen stared at it for a moment before reluctantly shaking it, sealing the deal.

Karen's phone vibrated in her pocket as she walked back to her car. Despite the heavy collective gaze of the security men following her, she paused and checked for messages before getting in.

There was a text from Valerie, telling Karen that Sully and McArthur had gone for an early lunch and would be away from the workshop for at least an hour if Karen wanted to talk more.

Karen thought for a moment. If she went back to the workshop now, Sully, McArthur or Tony himself would know, if they checked the security feed. Karen wasn't concerned if they found out, but Valerie was scared.

Karen had planned to visit Geoff Jones at the hospital and make him understand she didn't consider Harinder a threat to Sophie. She thought if she talked to him in person, he'd believe her and let Harinder visit his daughter.

Still, she couldn't pass up a chance to get information from Valerie earlier than expected. She would just have to talk to Geoff later.

Karen got into the car and held a hand against her forehead. Her head was banging. She rifled through her bag for painkillers but came up blank.

One of the security guards gave her a dirty look followed by what she took to be a 'hurry up' gesture. Karen held up a hand and then turned the car around. She would pick up some tablets before talking to Valerie.

Karen drove away from Burton Waters, trying to ignore her throbbing headache.

She had the uneasy feeling she was being watched. She kept her eyes on the rear-view mirror, but all she saw was regular traffic.

The attack on Sophie, the talk of hitmen, and agreeing to help Chapman had made her nervous.

After grabbing some paracetamol, a bottle of juice and a sandwich from the Tesco store, Karen sat in the car park to swallow the tablets with a mouthful of orange juice, then headed to Great Northern Terrace.

Karen parked the car and got out, glancing around. The door to Tony's Workshop was open, but there was no sign of Valerie or anyone else.

At least she wouldn't be kept waiting outside in the cold for ages this time.

She stepped inside cautiously. The bright fluorescent overhead lights made her eyes hurt.

'Hello?' Karen called out.

There were some empty wooden crates directly ahead. They hadn't been there earlier. She made her way towards them, peering inside, but they were empty. A packing slip for an exhaust lay amongst the crumpled wrapping.

'Valerie? It's Karen,' she shouted, thinking maybe Valerie had those earbuds in again.

No answer.

Karen gazed around, taking in the tools lined up against the walls and the piles of machinery stacked beside the metal workbenches.

All around her, Karen could see evidence of the mechanics' tinkering – engine parts, adjustable spanners, discarded circuit boards and soldering wire, tangled into a web that seemed it would be impossible to unravel.

Much like trying to work out who was behind the hits on Chapman's associates, Karen thought, as she shivered and walked further into the workshop.

Again, she called out for Valerie. But all that greeted her was silence and an ominous stillness that made Karen feel uneasy.

Valerie had been expecting her. So where was she?

Karen's skin prickled with goosebumps. She sensed eyes on her back. She spun around quickly but saw nothing other than shadows cast by the artificial lights.

Then suddenly she heard a noise coming from her right – a low moan . . .

Karen cautiously approached the area where the noise was coming from.

And then she saw her. In the corner, behind a large diesel generator, Valerie lay sprawled out on the floor.

Dazed and confused, she clutched her head and seemed unable to focus on Karen's face.

'Valerie, what happened?' Karen asked in alarm as she rushed over and knelt beside her.

Valerie tried to sit up, but swooned backwards, her eyes darting around as though searching for something or someone. She let out a shaky breath before saying in a hoarse voice, 'Someone attacked me . . .'

'Hold on,' Karen said, as Valerie clutched her hand. 'I'm going to call for help.'

Karen dialled for an ambulance, and then called the incident into the station. When she hung up and put her mobile back in her pocket, she asked, 'Do you know who it was?'

Valerie blinked at her. 'I heard footsteps behind me, and then I was hit from behind. I only caught a glimpse . . .'

'Did you recognise them?'

'No.'

Karen felt a wave of fear wash over her. Someone had attacked Valerie in broad daylight at Tony's Workshop just before Karen was due to talk to her. That couldn't be a coincidence.

Someone wants to shut Valerie up.

She glanced around the workshop again. Whoever had done this had likely already fled the scene, but she couldn't be too careful.

'It's all right,' Karen assured Valerie. 'We'll be able to see who did this on the security camera feed.' She squeezed Valerie's hand.

'No,' Valerie said. 'I'm sorry, I turned it off earlier.'

'Why?'

'It kept giving false alerts and was driving me crazy. So I switched it off to reset, but I forgot to turn it back on.'

'It's all right,' Karen said, trying to hide her disappointment. 'Did you notice anything about them at all?'

'They were wearing a balaclava,' Valerie said with a shudder.

Karen quickly scanned the area. The intruder probably walked in through the open door as she herself had done.

A loud slam echoed through the workshop. *The back door.* Karen tensed, but Valerie held on to her arm tightly. 'Don't leave me.'

'I won't,' Karen reassured her as she craned her neck to see if she could see somebody coming through the workshop. But there was no sign of anyone. She'd likely disturbed the attacker, but she couldn't leave Valerie alone while she went to investigate, as it could give them a chance to finish the job.

Over the next few minutes, Valerie gradually became less dazed and managed to sit up, despite Karen's protests.

When the paramedics finally arrived, Karen briefed them on what had happened, and they began to check Valerie over.

While they were doing that, Karen took the opportunity to look around the workshop, but it was as though whoever had attacked Valerie had simply vanished into thin air, leaving no trace.

Morgan and Rick arrived soon after, looking concerned. Karen filled them in as the paramedics assessed Valerie.

'We should take her to the hospital for a full check-up,' one of the paramedics declared. 'It's best practice after a head injury.'

'Yes, of course,' Karen said, thinking how similar Valerie's attack was to Sophie's. Although Sophie's had seemed more frenzied. Perhaps Karen's arrival had derailed the assault.

'Are you able to walk?' one of the paramedics asked Valerie.

Valerie nodded, wincing as she walked towards the ambulance.

Morgan said, 'I'm going to stay here until Sully and McArthur show up. We can't leave the place unattended, and I want to ask them a few questions anyway.'

'Do you think one of them could have done this?'

'That's what I intend to find out.'

'Seems a coincidence they both went to lunch at the same time,' Karen said.

'Shall I go to the hospital with Valerie?' Rick offered. 'She's understandably a bit shaken.'

'Good idea,' Karen said. 'Thanks . . . and if you have the chance when you're there could you have a quiet word with Sophie's dad? I've been meaning to go and speak to him. I want him to know we don't believe Harinder hurt Sophie. Geoff's very upset, and he's not letting Harinder see her.'

Rick frowned. 'All right. So you *do* believe Harinder's innocent? Last night, I thought—'

'Yes, I'm certain he wouldn't hurt Sophie,' Karen said confidently, and she meant it. It felt good to say it out loud. She wouldn't let past betrayals colour her judgement when it came to Harinder. She refused to be defined by hurt and bitterness.

'Excuse me!' one of the paramedics called out, gesturing for Karen. 'She's asking for you.'

Karen made her way to the ambulance.

The other paramedic was trying to get Valerie to lie down, but she was resisting. She grabbed Karen's arm as soon as she was close enough. 'Karen, I just remembered. I saw the eyes of the person that attacked me. I know who it was.'

'Who?'

Valerie's voice was confident. 'Quentin Chapman.'

Chapter Twenty-Four

The rain started to fall in big heavy drops as the paramedic closed the back doors of the ambulance.

Sully and McArthur pulled up in a blue transit van just as the ambulance was taking Valerie away.

As they got out of the van, the intensity of the rain increased. They didn't approach the workshop, but stared at Karen and Morgan, who were standing at the entrance. Then they turned to watch the ambulance leave.

McArthur's hair was plastered to his head, water trickling off the ends.

Sully watched the retreating ambulance with a scowl, ignoring the steady downpour.

Both men wore black coats and blue jeans.

'What's going on here?' Sully asked as they approached the workshop, wiping the rain from his face with his coat sleeve.

Karen and Morgan exchanged a glance before Karen spoke. 'Valerie was attacked.'

Their guarded expressions changed to shock and anger. 'Who did it?' Sully demanded.

Suddenly, thunder rumbled through the sky above them and they all looked up at the dark clouds.

'We don't know,' Karen said, deciding to keep Valerie's accusation that it was Chapman to herself for now. She'd tell Morgan as soon as they were out of earshot of Sully and McArthur.

'What do you mean?' McArthur asked incredulously. 'You must have some idea—'

'Yeah,' Sully cut in. 'I'll check the security feed.' He pushed past them, making his way into the workshop, his shoes leaving damp prints on the concrete floor.

'Valerie told me she'd turned the feed off,' Karen said.

Sully stopped and turned back. 'Why would she do that?'

'She needed to reset it but forgot to turn it back on.'

A flash of lightning momentarily brightened the workshop space and was followed by a deep crash of thunder.

Sully grunted with frustration then glared at Karen. 'So are you two going to stand around here all day or are you going to figure out who did it?'

'Yeah, we've got work to be getting on with,' McArthur chipped in.

'No, you don't,' Morgan said. 'We'll need a SOCO team to go over the workshop.'

Sully and McArthur glanced at each other again, their faces tight with worry. Were they scared that the SOCO team might find something? Evidence relating to something other than Valerie's attack?

'Do you have an alibi for the last hour?' Morgan asked.

After a tense moment of silence, McArthur finally spoke up. 'We were having lunch at the Witch and Wardrobe,' he said, referring to the well-known waterside pub. His voice was only just audible over the rain pounding against the workshop roof.

Sully nodded in agreement, his gaze still fixed on Morgan and Karen as if expecting them to challenge him on it.

'Anyone else with you?'

'No, but the staff know us. They'll tell you we were there. We go there a lot.' Sully moved to grab a small section of a toolbox sitting on the bench.

'Don't touch anything,' Karen said sharply.

McArthur sighed like a sulky teen. 'What exactly are we supposed to do then?'

Karen shrugged. 'Sit in the van and wait for the SOCO team to tell you when you can re-enter the workshop.'

Morgan turned to Karen with a silent gesture, signalling that they had what they needed from Sully and McArthur for now.

They watched Sully and McArthur trudge back to the blue van.

'Do you believe them?' Morgan asked after the van doors slammed.

'The alibi will be easy enough to check. Even if they weren't involved, it wasn't kind of them to leave Valerie alone at the workshop after Sophie's recent attack.'

Morgan nodded.

Karen turned her back to the van just in case Sully or McArthur were able to lip-read. 'Valerie said she thought it was Chapman who attacked her.'

Morgan's eyes widened then narrowed. 'That seems unlikely. From what we know of Chapman he doesn't like getting his hands dirty. He has plenty of heavies to do his bidding.'

'Yes, and I was at Chapman's house before I came here. He wouldn't have had time.'

'You came straight here?' Morgan queried.

Karen hesitated then shook her head. 'No, I stopped at Tesco's for painkillers. But I was there for less than ten minutes. There's no way he could have got here and attacked Valerie in that time.'

'Did Chapman know you were coming to the workshop?'

'No . . .' She realised what Morgan was getting at. 'It's possible he got here before me, and my arrival derailed his attack on Valerie.'

'But does that really sound like Chapman's typical behaviour to you?'

'No, it doesn't. But why would Valerie lie?'

'She only caught a glimpse of her assailant's eyes. It's hard to correctly identify someone from that. The human brain likes to fill in blanks. Sometimes incorrectly.'

Karen nodded thoughtfully.

'But we should still talk to him. As soon as the SOCOs turn up, we'll head to Chapman's house.'

Karen and Morgan were ushered into Chapman's high-end kitchen by Ponytail. Karen could tell Morgan was taken aback at the security measures, even though she had warned him about them before they arrived.

Chapman sat at the far end of the huge kitchen in a sleek, modern white armchair, a discarded newspaper lying on the floor. He looked up from his phone as they approached.

He got to his feet, put his phone in his pocket and welcomed Karen and Morgan as though they were old friends.

'I didn't expect to see you again so soon, DS Hart,' he said. 'Please, have a seat.' He gestured to two matching white armchairs opposite him.

Karen said, 'We have to ask you some questions about a disturbing incident at Tony's Workshop. Valerie Anderson, one of Tony's mechanics, was attacked just now.'

Chapman's expression changed from cordiality to suspicion. He said nothing, waiting for Karen to continue.

'Have you left the house since I spoke to you?' she asked.

'No, I haven't,' he replied firmly. 'I've been here the whole time. My security team can attest to that.' He paused and looked at Karen. 'What happened?'

She began to explain the details of the attack as Chapman listened intently, taking in and processing the information.

When Karen finished speaking, Chapman ran his hands through his greying hair before standing up and pacing back and forth in front of the bifold doors that ran the length of the kitchen. He seemed to be deep in thought.

Then he abruptly stopped moving and looked at Karen. 'Have you been able to make any progress on the subject we discussed?'

Karen felt her cheeks burn. She'd had no time to work on it, and she hadn't told Morgan about her earlier conversation with Chapman. Would Morgan understand? It wasn't as though she could just casually mention it. *Oh, and by the way, Chapman has asked me to investigate who could be targeting his men, as a personal favour.*

Karen quickly tried to change the subject by asking Chapman if he had any ideas on who could be responsible for the attack.

Morgan, to his credit, didn't show any outward sign, but Karen knew he'd picked up on it, and would want answers sooner rather than later.

'No idea,' Chapman said. 'Most likely the same person that attacked your colleague.'

'Tony Withers perhaps?' Morgan suggested.

Chapman looked amused. 'Tony? Why would *he* want to do such a thing?'

He clicked his fingers. Ponytail appeared as if from nowhere. He moved quietly for such a huge man. He towered over them, his broad frame making the seating area feel crowded, despite the ginormous size of the kitchen.

'These detectives would like to see the security footage from inside this property for the past two hours. Please get it ready to view. I don't think they're going to take my word for my whereabouts.' Chapman gave an unnerving chuckle.

Karen said nothing. Chapman could act offended if he wanted to. She didn't care about his hurt feelings.

His duplicity in the past was reason enough not to trust him. He had done terrible things. Karen was aware of the sinister stories about him: the tales of double-crossing and coercing struggling companies, and the cruel attempt to cheat a woman who had just lost her sister out of her inheritance. She was certain there were other crimes she didn't know about.

But Karen didn't believe that Chapman had sent a heavy round to attack Valerie. She certainly wasn't convinced that he had done it himself. Valerie must have been mistaken.

Karen thought it far more likely that Tony Withers was behind the attack. Perhaps Valerie had uncovered something about her daughter that Withers was desperate to keep hidden. Karen shuddered at the idea.

Karen thought back to Valerie calling her over to the ambulance and the certainty in her voice as she'd told Karen it was Chapman who attacked her.

But it couldn't be. He had the perfect alibi. He'd been with Karen just before the attack. There was no way he would have been able to get to the workshop and carry out an assault in the time it took Karen to get a few painkillers from the shop around the corner.

No, Valerie must have been mistaken. Either that, or she was lying.

Morgan got a message on his phone and took a discreet look at it while Karen continued to talk to Chapman. After a minute, he asked, 'Would you mind if I spoke to my colleague in the garden for a moment?'

Chapman inclined his head and gestured to the bifold doors. Morgan unlocked them, and they stepped outside.

Thankfully, it had stopped raining.

Morgan and Karen remained on the large patio, stopping beside a water feature constructed of smooth marble balls stacked on top of one another. Ahead of them was an outdoor chess set, which looked ridiculously expensive. Karen's eyes lingered on the pieces; she felt like a pawn in Chapman's game.

'Sorry, I know it's cold,' Morgan said, wrapping his coat around himself. 'But I thought we'd be overheard in there.'

'Good point,' Karen said. She waited for him to ask the question. What had gone down during her secret conversation with Chapman? Why had she held that back from him?

But instead, Morgan surprised her. 'This probably sounds a little off-the-wall, but do you think Valerie Anderson could have faked the attack?'

Shocked, Karen stared at him. 'Why would she?'

Morgan didn't reply, waiting as she considered the possibility some more.

'I don't know,' she said uncertainly. 'I didn't see the attacker.'

'You said she thought it was Chapman who attacked her, and yet we know that's almost impossible as you had just been talking to him at his house, *and* Valerie stopped the security camera recording.'

Karen nodded slowly. She hadn't *seen* anyone else at the workshop, though she'd heard a door slam. She'd only heard Valerie moaning and witnessed the aftermath of the attack. Had she been injured? Certainly, Valerie had seemed dazed. But there had been no blood . . .

Karen felt a chill ripple through her body.

Had Valerie been playing her?

Karen thought hard as things slotted into place, thanks to Morgan's suggestion. She then remembered Valerie previously telling her she'd never met Chapman. If that was the case, how could she identify him as the man who'd attacked her from just a glimpse of his eyes under a balaclava?

Valerie had deceived her. But why?

'It's possible,' she said. 'And if that's the case, she's trying to distract us for a reason.'

'Because?' Morgan prompted.

Karen floundered. 'Valerie came to Lincoln because she feared her daughter had fallen into Tony's clutches. She thought Claudia could be working in his brothel. Maybe Valerie wants to get Tony and Chapman arrested to force an investigation into their shady dealings?'

Karen also had to wonder if Valerie had staged the assault to avoid being questioned again.

Morgan handed Karen his phone. 'Goodridge's team just emailed me this report,' he said, with a grim expression.

The report was long, and Karen skimmed through it quickly, her heart sinking with every word. 'What does this mean?' she asked, dreading the answer.

'Valerie,' Morgan said. 'She was in the army.'

Karen was blindsided. She reached the final page and looked up, meeting Morgan's gaze. 'And she knows how to handle a gun.'

Karen's chest tightened. Suddenly Valerie's sensitive and vulnerable facade felt like an elaborate lie. Had she been playing Karen all along?

She felt her heart sink as the truth about Valerie dawned on her. She'd been so taken in by the woman's fragile act.

'Sully mentioned something to me about Valerie being able to handle herself,' Morgan said. 'I guess this is what he meant.'

'She had me fooled,' Karen muttered.

Karen had been taken in by her stories of her missing daughter, Claudia. She'd bonded with Valerie over their shared loss. Karen understood what it was like to lose a daughter.

Her insides lurched as the truth became unbearably clear – Valerie's meek persona was nothing more than a deceitful mask.

Karen suspected Valerie had done far more than just fake her attack . . .

Valerie could handle a gun. If she wanted revenge on those she held responsible for taking Claudia from her, then perhaps she was the one taking aim at Chapman's associates.

Fear and dread settled into Karen's bones as the horrifying possibility began to take shape.

What if Valerie wasn't the helpless victim, but the one exacting her own revenge?

Valerie could be the one picking off Chapman's associates one by one. The men targeted had links to Chapman, but they also had ties to Tony Withers.

If Valerie were responsible, perhaps her ultimate goal was to despatch both Chapman and Tony?

'We'd better find out where she is,' Karen said, her mind still racing. 'Rick went to the hospital with her.'

Morgan nodded. 'I'll call him now.'

Karen paced back and forth on the patio as Morgan placed the call. She could feel Chapman's eyes on her through the glass doors, but she didn't look up.

When Morgan ended the call, Karen looked at him for an answer.

He shook his head, confirming her fears. 'Rick doesn't know where she is now. Apparently, there was a long wait at A&E, and she decided she was well enough to go home.'

Karen pressed her hands to her temples. If Valerie was the shooter, then they had just let her get away . . .

She groaned. She felt so stupid. How could she not have seen it before?

Her sympathy had kept her from seeing the motive. She'd believed Valerie was a lonely woman, scared of her boss and desperately missing her daughter.

Karen had been duped.

Chapter Twenty-Five

When Karen and Morgan went back into the house, there was no sign of Chapman in the kitchen.

The armchair he'd been sitting in was empty, the newspaper still on the floor.

Heading to the hallway to find him, they stopped abruptly when Ponytail suddenly blocked their way. He said nothing, just stood there, glowering at them.

Karen waited a beat, and then asked, 'Where's Chapman?'

Ponytail shrugged but didn't move out of their way.

'We need to speak to him,' Morgan said. 'You're not helping.'

Ponytail still said nothing.

They tried to edge around him.

'Wait a minute. Stay here,' he growled. 'I'll see if he wants to speak to you.'

Karen looked at Morgan and rolled her eyes.

A moment later, he returned. He grunted and beckoned them forward. They followed him along a wide hallway, and into a study.

It was dark. The blinds had been drawn, and there were no lights on. When Ponytail withdrew and the door clicked shut behind them, it was even darker.

Chapman was sitting in a large leather office chair behind a dark wood desk. The room smelled of old books and leather, mingled with the faint hint of cigar smoke.

He removed a small earpiece and stood, turning on the desk lamp. The golden glow lit up the bookshelves behind him and the antique furniture in the room.

Large chairs sat either side of an ornate fireplace. The light from the lamp accentuated the shadows on Chapman's face, highlighting the lines. His face looked drawn and stressed. She hadn't seen him look this way before, and it unnerved her.

The room was silent.

Chapman's piercing eyes met Karen's. 'You think Valerie is the shooter,' he said without preamble.

'You were listening to us?' Karen asked.

'There are listening devices throughout the property,' Chapman said. 'I trust no one.'

'In the garden?' Morgan asked incredulously.

He nodded. 'I need eyes and ears everywhere.'

Chapman sat down again and gestured for Karen and Morgan to take seats too. Karen sank into the Chesterfield sofa, and Morgan sat in an armchair beside the fireplace.

'How much of our conversation did you hear?' Morgan asked.

Chapman shrugged. 'Most of it. You think Valerie is out for revenge. She believes my associates and I are responsible for something terrible happening to her daughter.' He paused, then added, 'What did happen to her daughter?'

'We don't know,' Karen said. 'And Valerie hasn't seen her since she left Yorkshire for Lincoln two years ago.'

At least that's what she told me, Karen thought. But they could hardly trust anything Valerie said now, so who knew if it was true?

They'd verified that Claudia had been reported missing, as Valerie had claimed. But they didn't know much more than that. Only what Valerie had told them.

Chapman steepled his fingers and looked grave. 'If you'd permit me to offer a theory . . .'

Karen and Morgan exchanged a look, and then Morgan nodded.

'Go ahead,' he said.

'You suspected I attacked Valerie because that's what she told you.' He spoke softly and watched Karen closely.

Chapman was an old hand at this. He was trying to work out what she knew from her body language.

Karen shifted on the sofa as Chapman's eyes seemed to pierce through her. The air was thick with tension.

She was uneasy sharing the information that Valerie had identified Chapman as her attacker. But he already knew that if he'd been listening in when she'd discussed the case with Morgan on the patio.

Karen felt as if she was in a battle of wits, one that she had already lost. Chapman was a master of manipulation and deception; she didn't stand a chance.

Of course she didn't. She'd already been duped by Valerie. The fact she'd been taken in so easily by the woman made Karen seriously doubt she could take this fight to Chapman and win. For all his cold charm, and requests for her help, she knew Chapman was using her. She was a means to an end. He needed her help to identify his foe.

When neither Karen nor Morgan confirmed Chapman's statement, he continued. 'I had hoped we could put all our cards on the table and work together towards a solution. Obviously, that would benefit me,' Chapman said dryly, his gaze lingering menacingly on Karen. 'However, if you're not going to be open with me, then I have to rely on my instincts.' He furrowed his brow, the lines on his forehead deepening. 'Valerie made this accusation against me for a reason. She told you that I was responsible for the attack in the hope I would be arrested. This was clearly an attempt to draw me out. She knows it wouldn't be easy to get to me in my heavily guarded home. So instead, she chose the less subtle, but quite ingenious approach of having me arrested and killed en route to the station.'

Chapman let out a hollow laugh. 'Her plan didn't work, though. I suppose Valerie didn't realise you had been with me, DS Hart. So, you knew that there was no way I could have got to the workshop fast enough. It was clear to you I couldn't have been the one behind the attack.' He gave a sinister grin. 'Her plan fell short thanks to you, DS Hart.'

He had clearly heard everything they'd discussed out on the patio. They should have gone back to the car to talk. Karen could have kicked herself for letting her guard down.

Chapman sat back in his chair, his gaze falling on Morgan. 'I believe as soon as I make the journey to the station, I'll be shot. So, I hope you're not going to go through with the ridiculous idea of arresting me, since you know DS Hart is my alibi.'

Morgan shook his head. 'I don't believe an arrest is warranted . . . yet.'

'I take it you still haven't located Valerie?' Chapman asked.

Karen felt she owed him at least that much information, and she gave a slight shake of her head.

Arnie and Rick were on their way to Valerie Anderson's house, but right now they had no idea where she was.

Chapman nodded slowly. 'You need to find her quickly because I'm sure I'm right. That is Valerie's plan. She wanted you to arrest me, and then at some point on the journey, perhaps outside my house, perhaps outside the station, I would be shot.'

Karen's mouth grew dry. What he was describing seemed plausible, but she still had doubts.

Valerie had appeared to be a gentle, motherly woman, who had trembled at the mention of Tony Withers's name and shared her pain over her missing daughter.

Karen had seen an unexpected darkness in people driven by loss before, but something about this case felt different.

The fact Sophie had been hurt and was teetering on the brink of life and death made this case personal. Was that the reason Karen had been blindsided, or was Valerie really such a good actress?

Could Valerie really be responsible for the hits on Chapman's men? And if she was behind them, what possible reason would she have to hurt Sophie, someone who'd tried to help her?

Karen had witnessed the power of grief, and the ruthlessness it had driven people to. If Sophie had been about to expose Valerie's crimes, then maybe that explained the assault . . . Karen briefly closed her eyes. There was something more here, something she couldn't quite put her finger on.

'I've ordered my men to search the grounds,' Chapman said, breaking Karen's train of thought. 'They've found nothing so far. But they'll let me know if they do.'

'I don't appreciate you listening in to a private conversation,' Morgan said, his tone clipped and his voice thick with disapproval. 'We were discussing a working theory. The fact that Valerie can handle a gun does not necessarily mean she's the one who killed your associates.'

Chapman raised an eyebrow. 'I don't cower from the truth. If someone reveals their true nature, why doubt them?'

The room seemed to close in around Karen. Its dark mahogany panelling, crowded bookshelves, closed blinds, velvet curtains and deep shadows created an ominous atmosphere.

Chapman was making a strong case, but Karen kept coming back to the moments she'd spent with Valerie. She'd seen vulnerability and fear. Could Valerie really be behind all this? The evidence pointed to yes, and Karen hated that her gut had been so wrong.

None of her instincts had warned Karen that Valerie was a killer.

She'd been worried about Sophie, terrified they might lose her. Had she let her guard down? What else had she missed?

The uncomfortable truth was that if Valerie was behind this, then Karen's judgement had truly failed her.

◆ ◆ ◆

Morgan had learned his lesson. He placed his phone call to DCI Churchill from the front seat of his car. He glanced back at Chapman's imposing house. The car was as good as Morgan could get to guaranteeing there were no listening devices earwigging on his conversation.

'DCI Churchill.'

'Sir, this is DI Morgan. I'm calling about a possible threat to the safety of Quentin Chapman.'

He felt they had to act quickly. Though he had no new tangible evidence to offer Churchill.

Their team wasn't even supposed to be working the hits on Chapman's associates. That case was being led by the Metropolitan Police with cooperation from other forces.

He explained the situation to Churchill in as few words as possible, telling the DCI his and Karen's theory about Valerie Anderson being behind the hits in Nottingham, Reading and London.

Churchill was quiet on the other end of the phone as he digested the information.

'I think we need to mobilise an armed unit,' Morgan said, underlining the seriousness of the situation.

'What other evidence do you have regarding the threat?' Churchill asked.

'Not much to be honest, sir, but I think liaising with DS McKenzie at the Met would be a good idea.'

'So we think the hits are the result of a personal vendetta for Valerie Anderson, rather than organised crime?'

'We don't know for sure yet, sir, but I think we need to move quickly. Better safe than sorry. Either way Chapman believes his life is in danger.'

'All right,' Churchill said. 'I'll speak to the acting superintendent. I'll also get in touch with McKenzie at the Met and see if they can help.'

'Thank you, sir. I'll send you over McKenzie's contact details and keep you updated.'

Morgan hung up the phone and sent a contact card via email to Churchill.

Karen opened the door on the passenger side and got in with a heavy sigh. 'It's oppressive in there,' she said, nodding back at the security milling around near the entrance to Chapman's house.

'I've spoken to Churchill about requisitioning an armed unit,' Morgan said.

Karen nodded. 'I've been trying to persuade Chapman that it would be in his best interests, but he's adamant he doesn't want police involvement.'

Morgan frowned in confusion. 'That doesn't make any sense. If his life is in danger, he needs an armed guard.'

'That's what I said. Still, we don't need his permission. The armed police can be stationed at the front of his property. If he knows what's good for him, he'll cooperate.' She pulled out her own mobile phone. 'I'm going to call McKenzie and update him.'

'I've passed his contact details on to Churchill,' Morgan said, reaching for the door handle. 'I'll go back inside. See if I can talk any sense into Chapman.'

◆ ◆ ◆

After Morgan got out of the car, Karen placed the call, and McKenzie answered with the same gruff, abrupt voice as before.

Karen filled him in, explaining their new theory about Valerie Anderson.

McKenzie was very sceptical.

'I'm not sure that adds up,' he said. 'We've been working on the assumption that these are organised crime hits. It's got all the hallmarks of a crime lord trying to muscle in on another patch. Valerie Anderson's background . . . well, it just doesn't fit.'

'I understand it's not what you were expecting,' Karen said. 'But she does have a motive: she believes that Chapman and his associates have something to do with her daughter's disappearance.'

'What do you think happened to her daughter?' McKenzie asked.

'Honestly, we don't know, but it does sound like she's become entangled with Tony Withers. We believe he's running a brothel as well as an illegal gambling ring. But we've not been able to locate either operation. Or Claudia Anderson.'

McKenzie sighed. 'It's a bit of a stretch. Does Valerie Anderson have a criminal record?'

'No.'

'So the fact she was in the army and knows how to handle a gun is your only evidence?'

Karen bristled. 'No. We think she invented an assault to blame Chapman and have him arrested.'

'Hmm.' McKenzie didn't sound convinced.

'I'm outside Chapman's house now and . . . either he's a very good actor, or he's terrified.'

'Or he's very good at manipulation,' McKenzie added pointedly. 'I appreciate your input, Karen.'

She could sense a 'but' coming.

'But we have lots of other irons in the fire at the moment.'

'So, you have a different suspect?' Karen queried.

'As I mentioned before, I don't want to discuss too much on the phone. You understand.'

Karen gave an exasperated sigh. This was all above her pay grade. She couldn't authorise the deployment of an armed unit or special protection for Chapman.

Yet even if Valerie wasn't the architect behind these hit jobs, Karen was convinced that Chapman believed he was in danger.

'I've reported it up the chain of command,' she said. 'My boss will be in touch.'

'All right. Look, if you've got access to Chapman, try to get him to open up,' McKenzie said. 'Ask him if one of his pals has double-crossed him. I think that's a more likely theory.'

Karen leaned her head against the cold car window. 'If you're right, the most logical suspect would be Tony Withers, Chapman's number two.'

McKenzie grunted. 'We did look into Tony's whereabouts. But he was nowhere near Nottingham, Reading or London at the time of the shootings, so he didn't do it himself. That's not to say he didn't hire someone, though.'

'So that's something you're looking into?'

He hesitated before saying, 'Yes, it's one of our priorities.'

'All right,' Karen said, 'but look, do me a favour, would you? I really think Chapman's afraid, and if his associates are being picked off, and he isn't behind it, then his life really could be in danger. We need an armed unit here.'

'That's not under my jurisdiction,' McKenzie said. 'You'll have to organise that with the Lincolnshire outfit.'

'Right. We've put in a request, but a word from you might help escalate it.'

He paused.

She was giving him work to do. It was outside his remit. He didn't necessarily have contacts in Lincolnshire. She was asking a lot.

Eventually, he replied, 'Get your boss to give me a call, and I'll see what I can do.'

McKenzie hung up.

Chapter Twenty-Six

A high-pitched ring pierced the stillness of Chapman's house.

Chapman looked up from behind his desk; Karen and Morgan exchanged a glance.

'What was that?' Karen asked when the noise stopped as suddenly as it had started. But Chapman didn't reply.

Like a nest of disturbed wasps, his security personnel darted into action, their voices and radio communications audible through the open study door.

Heavy footfalls sounded upstairs.

Had an intruder broken in?

Karen dashed out of the study, and Morgan followed. When they reached the large entrance hall, they rushed towards the window to see what had caused the commotion.

Ponytail stood in position by the front door, tense and alert.

Karen's eyes widened as she saw a sleek black car pull up the driveway. Her heart began to race as the car rolled to a stop.

Her stomach twisted with anxiety. 'Who is that?' she demanded, speaking to Ponytail. But as usual, he wasn't very talkative.

She held her breath as the door opened on the driver's side.

Karen exhaled as she recognised the man getting out of the car. Emmett Jenkins, the accountant. He awkwardly juggled some files in his arms, dropping one and stooping to pick it up off the gravel.

He pushed his glasses higher on the bridge of his nose, then blinked up at the house.

He shoved the car door closed with an elbow, then fumbled with the fob to lock the car. The yellow indicator lights flashed as he walked towards the front door.

Ponytail barked, 'Stand back.'

'Who is that?' Morgan asked.

'It's Emmett Jenkins,' Karen said. 'Chapman's accountant. He works for Tony Withers too. I've met him before.'

Morgan furrowed his brow. 'So, he's not a threat?'

Karen shook her head. 'No, no threat. Though it's probably not a good idea for him to be here right now.'

Ponytail opened the door and Emmett stood there with a sheepish smile.

'Ah, hello,' he said, glancing around with a curious expression. 'Seems there's been a few changes around here.'

He wiped his feet on the mat, and Ponytail stepped aside to let him in.

Ponytail grunted. 'The boss is in his study.'

Emmett adjusted the folders in his arms and moved towards Chapman's study.

'Hang on a minute,' Karen said.

He stopped and turned, waiting expectantly for her to continue.

'What are you doing here, Emmett?' she asked.

He blinked rapidly, his gaze darting around the room, taking in all the security presence. He shifted the papers cradled in his arms. 'I've just got some paperwork for Mr Chapman to sign. I wasn't quite expecting to see all these people.' He forced a smile, his gaze drifting to Morgan, an apologetic expression on his face.

He held out his free hand. 'Emmett Jenkins.'

Morgan eyed him for a moment before taking his hand. 'DI Morgan.'

'Before you go and talk to Chapman, come this way.' Karen took Emmett by the elbow and led him away.

Ponytail scowled. He didn't appreciate Karen taking control. But she ignored him.

When they entered the kitchen, she turned to Emmett and asked, 'Emmett, do you know what's going on?'

He hesitated and then shook his head. 'Not really. I only know that Mr Chapman asked me to bring some paperwork.'

'What's the paperwork for?' Karen asked, peering over Emmett's shoulder at the files. But he quickly rearranged them so she couldn't see the labels. 'Oh, it's a private matter,' he said.

'You know that some of Chapman's colleagues were shot recently?' Karen's voice was low and urgent.

Emmett nodded slowly. 'Yes, I did. Awful.'

'Well, Chapman thinks he could be next. If that's the case, then it's not a good idea for you to be here, Emmett. I think you should stay clear for a while. Do you understand?'

He looked down at the kitchen floor. 'That makes sense,' he muttered, 'but I'm not sure Mr Chapman will be very understanding.'

'I'll talk to him,' Karen said. 'Besides, I'm sure there's a lot of things you can do digitally these days, right?'

Emmett gave her a smile. 'Don't tell him I said anything, but he's not really very technologically savvy.'

For the first time since Karen had met him, she thought she saw a real smile from Emmett.

'One more thing,' she said, feeling she should warn the hapless accountant, her voice softer and more serious now, 'Chapman has listening devices all over, so be careful what you say here.'

The smile slid from the accountant's face, and he paled. He glanced around the kitchen as though expecting to spot bugs everywhere.

Karen remembered seeing Emmett interact with Valerie at the workshop. She'd mothered him, giving him his favourite biscuits and taking his side against Tony's bullying. Emmett might know where Valerie was. It was worth a try.

'How well do you know Valerie, Emmett?'

'Huh?' Emmett replied, still looking around the room, presumably for bugs.

'Valerie Anderson from Tony's Workshop?'

'Oh.' He looked at Karen. 'Not very well. Though she's always been friendly and very kind to me.'

'We can't find her. Any idea where she might be?'

He shook his head slowly, his eyes full of interest. 'No, I'm sorry. Have you tried her home address? I'm sure Tony has it. I might be able to find it in the files.'

'We already have it,' Karen told him. She thought for a moment – glancing over her shoulder to make sure that Ponytail wasn't lurking nearby – then asked, 'Did Valerie ever ask you any questions about Tony or Chapman?'

She wasn't bothered if Chapman was listening. He already knew about Valerie.

Emmett regarded Karen with a thoughtful gaze, as if deciding whether he should trust her. 'Actually, yes, she did.' He lowered his voice to a whisper. 'She was looking for her daughter. She thought she might be working for Tony.' He rubbed his chin, taking the time to think. 'Her daughter's name began with a C, I think . . . Claire.'

'Claudia,' Karen corrected.

'Yes! That was it. Why are you looking for Valerie?' Emmett queried, adjusting his glasses.

'Because they reckon Val's the one going around blasting people,' Ponytail said, with a nasty grin. Where had he sprung from? Karen wondered. How did someone that size move so quietly?

Ponytail formed his hand into the shape of a gun and pointed it at Emmett's head.

Emmett flinched. 'You can't be serious.'

'Deadly serious,' Ponytail said, chuckling at his own pun.

'We want to speak to her,' Karen said, turning her back on Ponytail. 'If you hear from her, let me know.'

Emmett nodded meekly. 'I can't believe Valerie . . .' He trailed off, shaking his head.

After Emmett went in to see Chapman, Morgan turned to Karen and asked, 'Shall we go back to the station? See if we can chase up this armed response unit. I've not heard anything from Churchill.'

'You go. I'll stay here for a while.'

'Are you sure? You don't want to get too caught up in this.'

'Yes,' Karen answered, her voice resolute. 'I'll be okay.'

She reached into her pocket and pulled out her phone, checking the screen for updates from Rick. He had gone to the hospital with Valerie after her supposed 'attack', but Karen had also asked him to speak to Sophie's dad.

She wondered if he had been able to persuade Geoff to let Harinder visit Sophie.

'No news from Rick yet,' she said as they walked towards the front door. 'I guess that means they haven't been able to locate Valerie.'

'No,' Morgan said gravely. 'I've got a bad feeling about this.'

Karen nodded. 'Me too. I'd feel a lot better if we had an armed presence here.'

◆ ◆ ◆

After Morgan left, Chapman ordered one of his security men to make coffee and then he opened a tin of biscuits from Fortnum and Mason.

How the other half live, Karen thought, helping herself to a crumbly lemon shortbread. Refined carbs were probably not the best choice, but the sugary sweetness was moreish, and after not eating much recently, she suddenly found herself very hungry.

'Come with me, Karen,' Chapman said after she'd helped herself to another two biscuits.

She wondered if he needed to talk to her privately or just wanted to stop her polishing off the whole tin.

He led the way back into his study. The blinds were still drawn. He sank into the leather chair behind his desk, while Karen settled on the Chesterfield sofa again. 'I'm glad you stayed,' he said softly. 'But you don't have to. There's no need to put yourself in danger for my sake.'

His words caught her off guard. She took a small sip of coffee to pause for thought, deciding how to word her reply. This was Chapman – nothing was ever as it seemed.

She always had to be on her guard with him, trying to analyse the subtext behind his words.

He seemed to be in a thoughtful, contemplative mood.

'I don't have to stay. But I wanted to, at least until the armed unit arrive.'

He raised an eyebrow. 'I didn't agree to that.'

'You didn't have to,' Karen said. 'We don't need your permission to have the unit outside your property.'

He frowned but didn't object. The threat must have really scared him.

His eyes held a distant look, as if his thoughts were consumed with theories. 'Tell me about Valerie Anderson and her daughter,' Chapman said, as he reached for his coffee cup.

'What do you want to know?' Karen asked.

'I'd like to know why Valerie's doing this,' Chapman said. 'I don't believe I've ever met her. But somehow she's got the idea that I'm involved in a brothel.'

Karen fixed her gaze on Chapman. 'You're not?'

His eyes blazed with anger. 'No, I'm not.'

Karen kept her suspicions to herself. Maybe Chapman wasn't involved in the brothel. But he was certainly caught up in plenty of other criminal activities. She knew he was living in fear right now, but she had to remember that he wasn't an innocent man.

'If Valerie is behind these shootings, her motive is probably her daughter, Claudia,' she said. 'From what I can tell from reading the reports, and from what Valerie told me – if we take her at face value – they had a tempestuous relationship. Lots of arguments.'

Karen paused for another sip of coffee. 'Claudia fell in with the wrong crowd after she left school,' she continued. 'There were drugs involved. And some petty theft, but Valerie always thought she'd come around eventually. But after one particularly bad row, Claudia stormed out.'

She looked up from her cup. 'Months later she had a phone call from Claudia, who told her that she was working for Tony Withers, and she wasn't happy about it.'

Chapman nodded pensively. 'Valerie never saw her again?'

'No, and the phone call was over a year ago. Since then, she's heard nothing . . .'

He leaned forward, eyebrow raised in curiosity. 'What does she think has happened to her?'

Despite recent events, Karen felt a wave of sympathy for Valerie. 'She fears the worst, as any mother would.'

He frowned, the creases deepening around his eyes. 'A sad story.'

Then he sighed heavily, his gaze settling on the photograph of his wife on the desk.

He'd once confided in Karen that he and his wife hadn't been able to have children, and had even asked about Karen's daughter, Tilly. But Karen hadn't been eager to chat about family affairs with someone like Chapman.

He continued to look wistfully at the photograph of his wife. 'I'm glad she isn't here now,' he muttered. 'I'm not sure what she'd make of this.' Then he leaned back in his chair. 'You know, I pride myself on thinking ahead and anticipating the next move, but this . . .' He shook his head. 'Valerie Anderson, a middle-aged woman, leaving me cowering in my study. Ridiculous really, when you think about it.' A sad chuckle escaped his lips.

It did seem far-fetched.

'We're trying to locate Valerie, and as soon as we do, I'll let you know,' Karen said. 'But when we do, you must stay vigilant until there is conclusive proof that Valerie was responsible for these hits; as of now she is only a suspect.'

'I always suspected I'd go out in a blaze of glory,' he said, with a half-smile. 'Better to go out with a bang than a whimper, I thought when I was younger. But now' – he drained the last of his coffee – 'going out with a whimper seems far more attractive.'

He ran a hand through his hair and sighed. 'I always thought I'd be despatched by a younger, more ambitious rival, a hungry young lion, ready to take my place as king of the pride.' He shook his head as if struggling to come to terms with the situation. 'Not a bereaved mother.'

He rasped a cold laugh, and then fell silent for a moment.

'But I forgot one crucial thing.' He lifted his head, and his lips quirked in a crooked smile. 'A lioness can be just as deadly when protecting her cub.'

Chapter Twenty-Seven

Rick and Arnie had gained entry to Valerie's rented terraced house at the end of Charles Street. There was still no sign of her, but the landlord had grudgingly allowed them into the property.

As he'd stepped into the unfamiliar house, Rick sensed an air of foreboding that seemed to envelop the rooms. The homely clutter and furnishings only increased his uneasiness.

The fragile crystal ornaments, the dainty gold-plated carriage clock and the quaint 'I've been to Grimsby' fridge magnets all felt so out of place for an assassin.

Rick and Arnie had both put on gloves to protect any evidence they stumbled on before the scenes of crime officers arrived.

The SOCOs would soon pore over every inch of the place and gather evidence. But Rick and Arnie had already stumbled on a treasure trove.

The property was only a two-bedroom place, and though the decor had seen better days, it was mostly tidy. But the spare bedroom was an alarming sight. Files were strewn about the room, some piled on the small desk, more stacked on the floor, still more on the windowsill. Photographs and notes were haphazardly affixed to the walls with Blu-Tack and Sellotape.

An ancient computer sat in the middle of the desk, its screen plastered with yellow Post-it notes.

Arnie exhaled heavily and turned in a slow circle, surveying the myriad pictures and documents strewn about the room. 'It's going to take a while to get through all this.'

Rick rummaged through the file beside the computer, his gloved fingers gliding across the documents inside. The clippings featured Tony Withers and Quentin Chapman. Valerie had been diligently gathering evidence against Withers and Chapman while she worked at Tony's Workshop, desperate to uncover any link to her missing daughter.

'No sign of the weapon,' Arnie said, opening the desk drawers. The floorboards creaked as he moved. 'Maybe she's hidden it. SOCOs might have more luck. They'll turn the place upside down.' He straightened, peering out into the hallway. 'The loft hatch is out there. Think I'll leave that to you. I'm not as young as I once was.'

'Cheers,' Rick said, but didn't look up.

'What's that?' Arnie asked as Rick moved a folder and found a small purple notebook beneath.

He lifted it, opened the cover, and his eyes quickly scanned the lines of handwritten text. 'It's a diary,' Rick said, thumbing through the pages. 'It appears Valerie has detailed all her attempts to uncover what happened to Claudia, and she mentions her meeting with Sophie.'

Arnie leaned in, his eyes widening in anticipation. 'What does she say about that?'

Rick read the words quickly. After a deep breath, he cleared his throat and related the details to Arnie.

'She met Sophie last week,' Rick began. 'Sophie turned up at the workshop asking Valerie about Tony Withers and some missing women she was looking into.'

'What did Valerie tell her?' Arnie asked.

'She told her about Claudia,' Rick said. 'Sophie promised she'd help.'

Rick swallowed. It was painful imagining Sophie rushing about, trying to help the missing women, getting in over her head with no idea of what was about to happen to her.

'What else?' Arnie asked. 'Does she mention anything about a gun? Does she say she killed Chapman's associates?'

Rick flipped through the pages, his brow furrowed in concentration. 'It's going to take a while to read all of this.'

When he reached the most recent entry, his eyes widened. 'The last thing she's written was just after Sophie's attack.'

Unlike the earlier pages that had been carefully written in neat handwriting, Valerie had scrawled the words over the final page. Rick's voice dropped to almost a whisper as he read them to Arnie: *'The police officer that was helping me has been savagely attacked. Someone smashed her over the head with a tyre lever and left her for dead. I think someone knows we're on to them. Tony stopped by earlier. He didn't say anything, but from the way he looked at me, I'm sure he knows.'*

Rick stared at the page, not seeing the words but instead remembering the recording of Sophie being viciously beaten. There had been no sound on the video, but he imagined Sophie's screams of pain and terror as in his head he replayed the moment the tyre lever came crashing down upon her.

He felt a mixture of fury and helplessness as he silently read the words again.

He glanced at Arnie.

'Is that it?' Arnie asked.

Rick nodded. 'Yeah, it stops there.'

Arnie clenched his fists. 'Unless Valerie planted that diary as evidence, she's not the one who attacked Sophie.'

'Right,' Rick confirmed. 'It still looks like Tony or one of his goons is most likely the perpetrator.' He shook his head in confusion. 'But why would Valerie fake an attack on herself?'

'Maybe she's trying to be clever?' Arnie suggested, his voice heavy with implication. 'She could be leaving false evidence here for us?'

Rick considered this. 'Maybe,' he murmured.

He flicked back through the pages. The entries went back months. It took a lot of work to plant that much false information. He wasn't convinced.

Rick looked at a photograph of Claudia stuck to the wall.

She had a heart-shaped face, with large brown eyes and dark hair in tight curls. She was beautiful.

He wondered where she was. Was she still working for Tony? Had she managed to escape his clutches or had something happened to her?

Rick felt a chill as he looked around the room again, his gaze taking in the photographs and notes covering every inch of the walls. It was the product of someone obsessed.

Valerie had clearly dedicated herself to finding Claudia, so much so it had consumed her life. The chaotic scene indicated a tormented mind.

Had Valerie's determination to find her daughter driven her to become a killer?

Rick heard the growl of a diesel engine on the street below and looked out of the bedroom window. The SOCO van had pulled up outside, stopping across the double-yellow lines.

He and Arnie had left their car further up the street, but the SOCO gang stopped near the entrance to unload equipment and avoid unnecessary contamination.

Rick sighed when he recognised Tim Farthing exiting the van. He'd be on to them in seconds, telling them they shouldn't have entered the premises without full protective gear. He was probably right, but they'd been impatient for answers, eager to finally get somewhere with this case.

Farthing looked up, squinting at the window. Rick groaned. Maybe it was his imagination, but he thought he could see the indignation in Farthing's eyes already. He called out a warning to Arnie, who joined him at the window. 'Ugh. Tim Farthing. Just our luck. We'd better meet him downstairs for our lecture.'

Rick wondered if Tim and the other scenes of crime officers would uncover a gun, or ammunition, or something that could point to Valerie being behind the shootings. Because Rick had found plenty of evidence for Valerie being a terrified mother, worried about her missing daughter. But so far nothing that unequivocally identified Valerie as a killer.

◆ ◆ ◆

Valerie surprised everyone by walking straight into the police station and asking to speak to Detective Sergeant Karen Hart. No one had anticipated her surrendering so easily, but Valerie seemed determined to have her story heard.

Morgan and Karen sat opposite Valerie in interview room two. The room was sparsely furnished, with a table in the centre. In the corner, an ever-watchful camera silently recorded the proceedings.

The air was stale and stuffy, with more heat pumping out from the radiator despite it being turned to the lowest setting.

The walls were painted in a depressing shade of grey while the floor was covered in wiry blue carpet tiles. The overhead light cast a harsh light over Valerie's blotchy face as she remained silent and still, her eyes swollen from crying.

Valerie clasped her hands together tightly and stared down at them. Her fingers were chapped, red and raw from repeatedly scrubbing the grease and oil away. Karen scrutinised Valerie, trying to comprehend how this middle-aged woman with tears in her eyes had managed to carry out such a meticulous and vengeful plan.

Valerie denied all wrongdoing with such passion and pleading, it was hard not to believe her.

Karen composed herself, taking a sip of water, and then asked the question that had been playing on her mind. 'What made you come to the station today, Valerie?'

Valerie rubbed her eyes. 'Emmett called and told me you'd been trying to track me down. He said you thought I was dangerous.' She shook her head. 'This has all been a misunderstanding. Emmett suggested I come to the station and get it sorted out.'

Valerie gave them her alibis for the dates of the shootings in Reading, Nottingham and London. Each time Valerie had claimed to be at Tony's Workshop. They would be able to confirm her story with security footage and witness testimonies from Sully, McArthur and perhaps even Tony himself.

Morgan asked her about her time in the army, and she reluctantly disclosed her proficiency with firearms. Growing up in the countryside, shooting had been a typical pastime, and she was an excellent shot. But she quickly added, her voice direct and emphatic, 'I've never taken a life. Not even in the army.'

'Let's move on to your . . . attack,' Morgan said, his voice lacing the word *attack* with scepticism. 'You said you thought Quentin Chapman was responsible?'

Valerie nodded vigorously. 'Yes, that's right. I saw his eyes. Behind the mask.'

Karen crossed her arms and leaned back in her chair. 'But you said you had no contact with Chapman before, yet you identified him only by his eyes,' she asked, disbelief tainting her voice.

Valerie blinked at Karen, then frowned and looked down at the table as she struggled for an answer. 'I . . . I've seen his picture in the paper and online. I just knew it couldn't have been Tony – he's too short,' she muttered, avoiding Karen's gaze. 'I know Tony's build, and the person who attacked me didn't have the same stature.'

'But why would you assume that it was either Chapman or Tony that attacked you?' Karen continued to press.

Valerie shifted uneasily in her chair, wringing her hands. 'Well . . . I thought maybe they found out I was digging into their background to find clues about what happened to my daughter . . .' She trailed off, her voice barely above a whisper. '. . . and your colleague was attacked in the same way.'

Karen's stomach churned with the reminder of Sophie's assault. Had that given Valerie the idea to fake her own attack? She had heard from the paramedics; they had seen a minor abrasion on the back of Valerie's neck, but it could have been self-inflicted.

Valerie seemed uncannily convincing. Genuinely believable. If she was lying, her performance was masterful – she seemed so credible.

Karen wasn't sure what to think. Was Valerie truly a victim, or had she faked her attack?

'Why didn't you tell us about Sophie visiting you and asking about your daughter, Claudia?'

'Because I was keeping my promise,' Valerie insisted. 'I told you; Sophie warned me not to trust anyone and to watch my back. And she was right. I was attacked too. This is all about my daughter. I know it is.' Valerie's voice was hoarse, the sound of desperation. Her hands trembled as she raised them to her face to push back her hair. Valerie met Karen's gaze, silently pleading for understanding. 'I promise you, I haven't killed anyone.'

Despite her determination to keep an emotional distance, Karen felt herself softening towards Valerie. DC Farzana Shah was currently hard at work, trying to validate Valerie's alibi. If she could prove she was nowhere near Reading, Nottingham or London on the days the hits took place, then they still had an assassin on the loose.

Karen hadn't yet told Chapman they'd located Valerie. She didn't work for him, and she had a feeling that if he knew Valerie was in police custody, he'd lower his guard. And although Chapman stood for everything Karen hated, she didn't want to see him shot.

'Okay,' Morgan said, giving Valerie a gentle nod. 'Can you start again at the beginning, please?'

'The beginning?' Valerie asked.

'Yes, tell us what happened the day your daughter left.'

Valerie took a deep breath and reached for her water bottle. She brought it to her lips and took a sip before beginning to talk.

'It all began two years ago when Claudia started coming home late, drunk and high on cocaine. It was horrible; her father had been a drug addict. He passed away from an overdose when she was two. So, obviously, I'm very strongly against drugs.'

Her voice tapered off. She took another drink of water and Karen and Morgan waited for her to continue.

'I decided to be firm and tell her she had to leave. If she wasn't going to give up the drugs, then she couldn't live under my roof. She called my bluff. She packed a few things in a bag and stormed out. It had happened before. We'd clashed on numerous occasions. But she'd always come back, begging for another chance, and I always gave it to her. She's my daughter. I love her. I'd never turn my back on her, but . . . I was at my wit's end. We'd tried different rehab programmes, but they never worked for long. I was sure she'd get back in touch, but she didn't. A few months passed, and I got a phone call. About one o'clock at night. I was in bed. Claudia was really upset. I could tell she'd been drinking, but I was so pleased to hear from her.'

Valerie put a shaky hand up to her mouth as her eyes brimmed with tears again. 'S . . . She was really distressed. She kept talking about Tony Withers and how cruel he was. She talked about being one of his girls in Lincoln.' Valerie looked up, her sad eyes fixed on Morgan, then Karen. 'I immediately thought she might be a sex worker, and I went off the deep end, demanding to know what she'd got herself into.' She paused and bit her lower lip, before continuing. 'Claudia hung up on me. I tried to trace the call, but it was from a withheld number.'

Valerie placed her palms down on the table and inhaled deeply. 'I kept waiting for a response, but nothing came. It was the longest Claudia had ever gone without contacting me. I'd already gone to the police, but they weren't taking it very seriously because of her history.

'I asked them for help again. They filled out more forms and connected me to an organisation that helps families in similar situations. Unfortunately, they hadn't heard anything either. On the phone, Claudia had mentioned Lincoln, so I thought, if I'm not getting anywhere with the police, I should try to find her myself.

'I told my neighbours that if Claudia returned, she could find me at the house I was renting on Charles Street. I was intending to stay there for a couple of months and see what I could find out about Tony Withers.

'When I went to the workshop, they were looking for a mechanic, so I applied, even though my experience in the army with the Royal Engineers didn't necessarily match up with the skills they needed. But I assured them that I was able to learn quickly and made up some previous job references. I don't think Tony checked.'

'What about Sully and McArthur?' Morgan asked. 'How do you get on with them?'

'All right, actually,' Valerie said. 'For the most part. We've come to an understanding . . .' Her lips curved in a weak smile. 'At first, they gave me a hard time, giving me all the menial jobs and shirking their own responsibilities. We ended up having a bit of a heart-to-heart, and I told them about my time in the army. They seemed to respect that, and from that point on, we got along a lot better.

They can still be lazy when it comes to opening and locking up, though.'

'Did you ask them about Claudia?' Morgan asked.

'I did. They warned me off. Well, Sully did. He said Tony was dangerous and not to be crossed. But he had no idea where Claudia might be. He didn't know anything about Tony's brothel.'

'And McArthur?' Morgan asked.

'The same. He told me he didn't know anything. Apparently, Tony keeps his businesses separate. They're both good mechanics and don't want to be involved in Tony's shadier operations.'

Karen wasn't sure that was true. She suspected Sully and McArthur could be selling on stolen vehicles and stolen parts, but that wasn't her priority now. Despite her suspicions, she had to remain focused on the goal of uncovering the person behind the attack on Sophie, discovering the whereabouts of Valerie's daughter, and tracking those responsible for targeting Chapman's associates. She had to keep her head in the game. They had to find the answers quickly, before it was too late.

'It couldn't have been Chapman who attacked you,' Karen said.

Valerie stared back, wide-eyed and confused.

'Just before I came to see you, I was with Chapman, talking to him.'

Valerie furrowed her brow, head shaking in disbelief. 'I must have been mistaken then . . .' She briefly glanced at Karen, then away again, her eyes filled with confusion, and muttered, 'It doesn't make sense.'

Karen had to agree. Nothing was adding up. The more she talked to Valerie, the more she thought it unlikely that this was a woman on a vengeful vendetta.

Her gaze remained steady as she moved on to a more sensitive topic. 'As you know, we've taken a DNA sample from you.'

Valerie nodded slowly. 'Yes.'

'We'll use your DNA to cross-reference any databases. It might help in our search for Claudia,' Karen said, her voice deliberate and measured.

Valerie paled, her hands trembling. 'What do you mean?'

'It's nothing to be alarmed about,' Karen said calmly. 'Claudia's been missing some time, and we're hoping this will help us find her.'

Valerie tensed as the implications of Karen's words hit home. Her voice was bitter as she said, 'I see. You mean if you don't find Claudia alive, you'll use my DNA to compare with unidentified remains.'

Chapter Twenty-Eight

Karen returned to the open-plan office, which smelled, as it always did, of coffee and hot printer ink. She and Morgan had taken a break from the interview to allow Valerie a brief respite and time to have something to eat before they resumed the questioning.

But as they'd talked to Valerie, Karen had become increasingly sure that she had nothing to do with the shootings.

Karen sighed as she sat down at her desk. She'd spoken with Tim Farthing as soon as she'd left the interview room, and he'd told her no evidence of firearms or ammunition had been found during the search on Valerie's house – there was simply no evidence tying her to the shootings or Sophie's attack.

Karen was sure that the mysterious disappearance of Valerie's daughter, Claudia, must somehow be linked to Tony's brothel. But a nagging sensation told her something far worse had befallen the young woman.

Locating his brothel was their only real hope of finding out what had happened to Claudia. It was what Sophie had been investigating too. If they could identify the brothel's location, and find the other women working for Tony, perhaps one of them would reveal some information that would identify Sophie's attacker and Claudia's whereabouts.

She had hoped the accountant Emmett Jenkins might be the key she needed to unlock the case. He was uncomfortable working for Chapman and Tony, but so far he'd been too scared to talk. He obviously had a soft spot for Valerie and hadn't turned his back on her even after she became a suspect. He'd called her to offer advice and told her to hand herself in. Time to try pushing Emmett harder, she thought. It was clear he wasn't completely bought off by the two shady characters. He was their weak point, and with luck, he'd finally give them what they needed to close the case.

'All right, Sarge?' Karen turned to see Farzana approaching. 'Do you want the good news or the bad news?'

'Um, the good news,' Karen said. 'I could do with some of that.'

'Well, to be honest, it's a mixture of both. Depends how you look at it, I suppose.' Farzana pulled over a chair and sat down.

'Go on,' Karen said.

'Well, from Valerie's point of view, it's good news. Her alibi checks out. She's in the clear. There's no way she could be the shooter.'

Karen had expected as much. But hearing Farzana say it made her realise they were back to square one.

She must have looked disappointed because Farzana gave her a reassuring smile and said, 'But that's not really our case anyway. Churchill wants us to prioritise Sophie's attack instead. Leave it to the Met to figure out who is behind the shootings – they're better equipped for this anyway.'

Karen nodded thoughtfully. 'You've seen Churchill recently?'

'Yes, a few minutes ago,' Farzana said.

'Did he mention anything about the armed response unit?'

Farzana grimaced. 'That's the bad news. Apparently, the acting superintendent isn't keen on authorising it. He's spoken to someone at the Met, and they don't think it's worth the resources.'

'Seriously?' Karen said, shaking her head in disbelief. 'There's credible evidence that Chapman could be next on the list.'

'According to Churchill, the Met say the credible evidence isn't so persuasive because it's coming from Chapman himself.'

Karen wondered if McKenzie still suspected Chapman was behind the shootings. She blew out a breath and pinched the bridge of her nose.

'Are you okay?' Farzana asked. 'It's been an awful few days, hasn't it? I just spoke to Harinder.'

'You did? Has he seen Sophie?'

Farzana nodded. 'Yes, although Sophie's dad wasn't exactly happy about it. Rick managed to persuade Geoff no further harm could come to Sophie in ICU as there is always medical staff around, so he relented. But things are still tense between Geoff and Harinder.'

'How is Sophie?'

'Much the same,' Farzana said. 'But I suppose that means she's stable. That's good, right?'

Karen nodded, though she had no idea. All she knew was that the longer Sophie stayed unconscious, the more concerned she was.

Karen said, 'I've spent ages running this case over and over in my head. I don't think Chapman is responsible for the shootings.'

Farzana shifted her weight in her seat, leaning on the back of the chair, propping her chin on her forearms. 'What makes you think that?'

'It's not so much what he said,' Karen explained, 'because I know trusting a man like Chapman is a fool's errand. But the fact that he's so scared. He's put extra security measures in place, so it's clear he's truly in fear of his life.'

Farzana considered that. 'Makes sense,' she murmured. 'Does he know who might be behind it?'

'I don't think so,' Karen replied slowly. 'He overheard a conversation between Morgan and me when we thought we were out of earshot. He latched on to that, believing Valerie was targeting him. We now know that's not the case.'

'Would he tell you if he suspected somebody else?' Farzana asked. 'He's not known for cooperating with the police. I mean, he doesn't even want the armed police guard, does he?'

Karen shook her head. 'True, but as it turns out, Chapman said something interesting,' Karen mused, remembering her conversation with him. 'He mentioned something about a young lion taking over the pride.'

Farzana raised an eyebrow. 'Like somebody aiming for the big job?'

'Precisely,' Karen replied.

'And who would that be?'

'I think the most likely candidate would be Chapman's number two, that Tony Withers chap. He's a right piece of work.' She glanced at her watch. Late again. She'd have to text Mike and let him know it was unlikely she'd make it in time for dinner.

'Should we bring Tony in for questioning?' Farzana asked.

'Let's hold off on that,' Karen said as she rose to her feet and stretched. 'We need to know more first. I'm going to go back to Chapman and see what else he can tell me. He denies any knowledge of Tony's brothel, though I'm not sure I believe him. But he must know more about Tony's other activities. If I can get him to open up about those, I'll be able to speak with other people in Tony's organisation. Hopefully one of them will lead me to the brothel and Claudia Anderson.'

Farzana asked, 'Will that help reveal who attacked Sophie?'

'I hope so. Did we get anything back from the forensic tests from the scene of the assault? Anything other than fingerprints?'

'DNA has come back, but if we take out of the equation the people at the workshop, who could have handled the tyre lever during their daily work – namely Sully, McArthur and Valerie, then we only have Sophie's DNA remaining.'

Karen shrugged on her coat and reached for her bag. 'I'm going to speak to Morgan, then head over to Chapman's.'

'What about Valerie?' Farzana asked.

'Her alibi holds up . . . which leaves us with no choice,' Karen said. 'We have to let her go.'

Karen went through the same rigmarole of getting to Chapman's house as before. The security men were as intimidating as ever, the dogs alert. Only, now that it was dark, they seemed even more ominous. Their shadowy faces were stern and unblinking, and the dogs looked ferocious, barking at her presence.

Chapman was in his study again. Karen wondered if he'd moved since the last time she'd seen him. The light was still dim, with only the desk light illuminating the room, casting shadows around the bookshelves.

'What an unexpected pleasure,' Chapman said after Ponytail had grudgingly announced her arrival. 'So many visits in one day. Have you located Valerie?'

So he didn't have ears on the inside of the police station, Karen thought. Otherwise, he'd know they'd brought Valerie in earlier. Or he could be bluffing, not wanting her to know he had a source inside.

She took a deep breath. She was overthinking it. 'I have a few more questions,' she said.

He gave her an amused look. 'But you're not going to answer mine?'

Karen frowned.

'Did you find Valerie?'

'We did.'

He lifted his eyebrows, smiling. 'Excellent news.'

'Not really. She's not the shooter,' Karen said.

'But that doesn't make sense—' Chapman began to say, but Karen cut him off.

'Trust me, it's not her. You and I need to put our heads together and work out who's doing this.'

'You almost sound eager to help me,' Chapman said.

'My colleague was attacked, and there's been three murders in the last week. I need to catch the perpetrator,' Karen said. 'You must have some idea of who shot your associates.'

He gave a weary shake of his head. 'I don't.'

'If you did, would you tell me?'

'There's one thing you learn very early in my line of work,' he said, a smile flickering across his lips, 'and that's never to be a grass.'

He was polite and well spoken, but to hear him say that was a stark reminder of who he was beneath the pleasantries – an old-fashioned gangster through and through.

'Right, but this is different. Someone out there has got a bullet with your name on it, and unless you cooperate . . .' She let the words sink in.

He leaned back in his chair and exhaled a long sigh. 'All right then. But I honestly don't know who it could be. Nobody I know would dare.'

Well, obviously one person would, Karen thought. 'Have you encountered any conflicts at work lately? Or any turf disputes?'

He smirked at her use of the term. 'No, my *turf*, as you so pleasantly put it, is well established and perfectly secure.'

'So there were no issues with deals or agreements with your . . . *associates*?'

He remained silent, evidently not willing to divulge any information.

'Very well,' Karen said. 'Since we're getting nowhere with that, let's move on. I want to know about Tony Withers.'

'Tony?' Chapman said, with a frown. 'It won't be Tony.'

'It makes sense,' Karen said. 'He's one of your men. He could be sick of taking orders. Maybe he'd like the top job for a change.'

Chapman thought for a minute, but then shook his head firmly. 'Tony is loyal. I've known him a very long time.'

'Right, but maybe he's hungry for more. More power, more money.'

'I treat him well,' Chapman said. 'I've learned that if you treat employees well, they'll work harder for you.'

'Tony isn't a normal employee. He isn't a good person. If he thought it would benefit him, wouldn't he want you out of the way?'

'Maybe you have a point,' Chapman said, plucking a book from the bookcase. *Meditations* by Marcus Aurelius. He turned it over and looked at the back cover, before opening it and flipping through the pages.

He read: '*To expect bad men not to do wrong is madness.*'

Why was he quoting passages from a book to her? This really wasn't the time.

'I'm trying to help you here, but you need to cooperate,' Karen said. 'What can you tell me about Tony's brothel?'

Chapman sighed and slowly raised his gaze until it met hers. 'I'm sorry, Karen. I don't deal with that sort of thing. I know nothing about it.'

Karen felt her frustration growing by the second. She had to do something.

'Come on, Chapman,' she said through gritted teeth. 'If you don't think it's Tony, then who? All this security isn't here for nothing. You going to all this trouble and making sure no one can get near you has to mean you think someone's out to get you. So, who is it?'

Chapman remained stubbornly silent.

Suddenly there was a piercing alarm, the same one Karen had heard earlier when Emmett arrived.

Chapman's gaze met hers, his eyes betraying a hint of fear.

'Are you expecting anyone?' Karen asked.

'No.'

'Emmett again?'

He shook his head.

Karen got up and walked out into the hall. Ponytail was at his sentry position by the front door. Two other security guards stood in the hall.

'Who is it?' she asked.

Ponytail squinted as he looked out of the window, surveying the grounds. It was dark outside, but the security lights were on.

A car was rolling up the driveway. It was a silver Jaguar. Karen had seen that car before.

Tony Withers.

Ponytail recognised the car at the same time. 'It's all right. It's only Tony.'

The alarm fell silent.

'It's not all right,' Karen said. 'Chapman wasn't expecting him. If he's coming inside, he needs to be searched first.'

'Tony?' Ponytail looked at her as though she were mad.

'Yes, Tony. In fact, everyone should be searched before they come in the house.'

'You're as paranoid as the boss,' Ponytail muttered.

A couple of the other security guards chuckled.

Karen bet they wouldn't be laughing if Chapman was in earshot. Didn't they know he had listening devices all over?

Maybe they did but were losing their fear of Chapman. Did they realise this might be the beginning of the end for their boss? It seemed that the best way to destroy his power was to undermine his control. Was this how it worked? Gradually chipping away at the foundations of a regime, weakening the respect for its leader until it crumbled?

The smile on Tony Withers's face dropped when he saw Karen. 'What's she doing here?'

He tried to walk inside, but Ponytail put a hand up and stopped him.

Tony brushed him off, furious. 'Get out of the way, you fool!' His eyes blazed a dangerous warning.

But Ponytail, to his credit, was having none of it.

He glanced at Karen.

She nodded. 'Search him.'

'What?' Tony said, his face flushed a hot red. He was apoplectic with anger. 'What are you doing? Get Chapman out here now. He'll fire you for this insubordination.'

'No, he won't,' Karen said calmly. 'Carry on.'

'Look, I just need to pat you down. Play along, mate.' Ponytail said.

Tony stood rigid at the entrance. He snarled, 'It's bloody freezing out here.'

'What's that in your pocket?' Ponytail asked.

'My wallet! Just get on with it.'

'Take your jacket off.'

Tony removed his jacket, and then held out his arms as Ponytail prepared to pat him down.

A sudden crack filled the air.

Karen knew what it was before her mind could form the thought.

Gunshot.

And then a bloom of blood appeared on the front of Tony's white shirt.

His eyes bulged. He stood there for a moment, wobbling, before finally collapsing to his knees, clutching at his chest.

Ponytail swore, hitting the alarm button by the door with the palm of his hand.

Pandemonium broke out, people rushed for shelter in all directions.

Karen yelled, lunging for Tony, grabbing him under his arms, trying to pull him back inside, where they could tend to him in safety. 'Help me!'

'Not bloody likely,' Ponytail said, stepping back inside, crouching down.

Tony weighed a ton.

Karen strained under his weight and swore at Ponytail as she tried her best to hoist Tony over the threshold. Finally, Ponytail edged forward to help, and with his assistance, it wasn't long before Tony was in the hall, lying on the floor, blood pooling on the marble beneath him.

Chapter Twenty-Nine

Ponytail kicked the front door shut. 'Stay down,' he ordered. 'And keep away from the windows.'

Karen looked up to see Chapman enter the hall and stare at Tony in horror as Karen worked to stem the bleeding.

Ponytail called one of the security men closer. 'Minchin, get over here. See what you can do.'

'You want me to take over?' Minchin said in a gruff voice, kneeling beside Tony. 'I was a field medic.'

Karen nodded and moved back, pulling out her mobile to call for backup.

If the armed response unit had been here, they would have already apprehended whoever was responsible.

But now, the culprit was likely still lurking nearby.

Would the shooter be satisfied with a hit on Tony, or were they trying to get Chapman too?

Maybe they wanted both Tony and Chapman out of the picture. What would stop them from bursting in now and finishing the job?

Karen glanced down at Tony. They wouldn't send an ambulance in until the scene was secured. With an active shooter, it wasn't safe for anyone to get close. Tony would likely die long before the paramedics got to him.

The following minutes were filled with a tense dread. With Karen's help, Minchin worked hard to stabilise Tony, but he was losing too much blood.

Despite their best efforts, life seemed to have left him already. His usually ruddy cheeks were grey. The slackness of his face told its own story – it wasn't like when someone was asleep, it was more than that. A tell-tale sign that life had departed.

'We've lost him,' Minchin said, finally accepting defeat.

Karen sat back, exhausted from the effort of trying to get Tony's heart beating again.

Chapman sat down on the bottom step of the stairs, staring at Tony's lifeless body.

He muttered, 'They won't get away with it.'

Right now, Karen wasn't worried about anyone getting away with anything. Her primary concern was that the shooter would make their way inside and finish the task they had set out to do.

Another security guard came into the hall from the kitchen. 'No sign of anyone out there yet, sir,' he said, addressing Chapman. 'But we're still looking.' He looked down at Tony's body and crossed himself.

The chime of the front doorbell made even the hardened security men flinch.

'Who is that?' Karen asked, crouching beside the window and cautiously peeking out, not wanting to make herself an obvious target. 'Is security still at the gates? Why would they let someone else in?'

Ponytail crawled over to Karen. He smelled of sweat and his breath was sour as he leaned over her shoulder.

'You see anyone?' His voice was tight with fear.

Karen was about to say no, but then a thin figure stepped back from the door and was lit up by the security lights. Emmett Jenkins.

What was he doing here again? Did he have a death wish?

Why hadn't he listened? She'd told him to stay away. Now, he'd just walked into the lion's den, risking his life.

Karen furiously wiped her bloody hands on her trousers.

'Tell him to turn around and go home,' she hissed.

Ponytail looked at her and then at Chapman, but said nothing.

Karen whirled around to face Chapman. 'What is Emmett doing here?'

'I don't know,' he said. 'I wasn't expecting him.'

Ponytail edged open the door but kept his body well clear.

'Hello?' Emmett said as he stepped inside. 'Is that blood?'

He stopped, his eyes widening as he followed the trail of blood to Tony's body.

'What are you doing here?' Karen snapped at him. 'Of all the stupid . . . I told you to stay away.'

'But I had to come,' Emmett said, unable to tear his eyes away from Tony on the floor. 'Is he going to make it?'

Karen forced herself to look at Tony, her stomach roiling at the sight of the blood pooled around him on the marble floor. It was quite clear to anyone with half a brain cell that Tony Withers was certainly not going to make it.

'What are you doing here, Emmett?' Chapman's tone was weary.

'I need to speak to you.'

'Not now,' Chapman said, waving him away, keeping his eyes on Tony.

'It's really important. I must talk to you,' Emmett said.

Chapman blinked, finally tearing his gaze away from Tony. 'Fine.' He leaned heavily on the banister as he stood up.

'Hang on,' Karen said. She motioned to the security guards who were standing by the back door in the kitchen. 'You've got to check people when they turn up.'

'But it's Emmett . . .' the taller of the two guards said.

'Just do it,' Karen said. 'And while you're checking him' – she turned to the shorter man – 'you can check the study, make sure the blinds are closed.' She narrowed her eyes and looked at Chapman. 'It would be better if you used an internal room – somewhere away from windows.'

No one spoke until Chapman said, 'I prefer my study.'

'There's an active shooter on the scene. You can't just walk around your house pretending this isn't happening.'

Chapman said, 'I appreciate your concern. I didn't realise you cared. But I'm sure security are on the case. They'll soon apprehend the killer.'

Karen shook her head in irritation.

'Security don't search everyone who turns up,' Ponytail explained in a patronising tone.

'Why not?' Karen demanded.

'There's just no need,' Ponytail replied, the corner of his mouth twitching into a smirk. 'Did they search you?'

'Well, no,' Karen answered, 'but I'm a police officer.'

'I would have thought that gave them more reason to have searched you,' Ponytail said, but his barbed comments didn't quite hit the same with Tony lying on the floor between them.

'I'm happy to be searched,' Emmett said, holding up his hands, a bewildered expression on his face.

'Okay. I'll do it.' Ponytail heaved himself to his feet, then put a hand on Minchin's shoulder. 'Are you all right, buddy?'

Minchin hadn't said a word since announcing Tony was dead. Karen guessed he'd seen traumatic deaths before as a field medic, but he looked shaken.

Minchin nodded, and Ponytail made his way over to Emmett, hands outstretched, ready to pat him down.

But when he was two feet away, Chapman said, 'Enough of this nonsense. Emmett, come on. My study.'

Ponytail dropped his hands to his sides.

'I really think—' Karen started to say, but Chapman marched off along the hallway to his study, followed by Emmett.

The blood rushed in Karen's ears. Something was off. The whole situation felt very wrong.

A memory flashed to the front of Karen's mind. When she'd seen Emmett with Valerie at the workshop, he'd had something in his hand . . .

The mental image hit her like a punch in the gut. She'd missed it. After what had happened with Valerie, she should have known better.

Her mind latched on to a half-formed theory. She rushed after them. Chapman needed protection.

Emmett turned and offered Karen a smile. 'I'm glad you're here too. It concerns you as well. I've uncovered some sensitive information regarding your colleague and what she found out about Tony's brothel.'

Karen followed them into Chapman's study. She wanted to get Chapman out of here. It wasn't safe. Her eyes darted around the room. She couldn't help wishing there weren't as many windows.

'Right,' Chapman said, striding over to his desk chair and sitting down heavily. 'Let's hear what you know.'

Instead of replying, Emmett locked the study door and pocketed the key.

'No—' Karen began to say, but the words died in her throat when Emmett drew a revolver from beneath his jacket.

'What the—' Chapman sat up sharply, leaning towards Emmett, who held a finger to his lips.

'Shhhh.'

'Emmett, what are you doing?' Karen asked, her mouth dry because she already knew the answer. 'Why have you got a gun?'

He grinned and Karen felt a fresh stab of fear. He looked so different.

As she looked into his eyes now, she saw nothing but cold calculation. Karen's stomach lurched as she realised that the man she'd believed to be a timid, shy accountant, bullied by his boss, had attacked Sophie. He was the reason she was in hospital. He'd left her for dead.

Why hadn't she remembered the keys earlier?

When she'd seen Emmett with Valerie at the workshop, he'd held up a bunch of keys, which meant he had access to the workshop. That meant he could have taken the tyre lever and attacked Sophie while wearing gloves, leaving no fingerprints or DNA evidence behind. Emmett must have attacked Valerie too.

Everything he'd said, every polite smile . . . it had all been a lie. She felt disgusted at her own naivety; he'd fooled her completely. And now here he was, pointing a gun straight at Chapman's head.

She'd been right in her earlier suspicions: someone had been keeping up an act all this time, hiding their true nature. But it hadn't been Valerie. It had been Emmett.

She'd even noticed that spark of rebellion in his eyes at his office as Tony had shouted at him. She'd seen it, thought she could use it to get Emmett to cooperate in the operation to bring Chapman and Tony down. But Emmett's rebellion went far deeper than she'd suspected.

'Give me that!' Chapman demanded, his voice a snarl.

'No.' Emmett angled the gun. 'You're not in charge anymore. I am.'

Karen couldn't speak. She couldn't even look at Emmett. All she could do was stare at the gun.

'Put your mobiles on the table,' Emmett ordered.

Silently, they complied.

After a brief silence, Chapman said, 'You killed Tony?'

'Don't look so sad. You wouldn't if you knew the whole story.'

Chapman leaned back in his chair, eyes narrowed. 'Enlighten us.'

Emmett's eyes glinted with something close to madness. 'I'd be delighted.' He stepped back towards the unlit fireplace and perched on the arm of one of the chairs, where he could observe both Chapman and Karen. He didn't lower the gun.

Karen's heart raced as she assessed the situation. She had to think of a way out. She remembered the security guards outside. Did they have any idea what was going on in the study? Even if they did, it wasn't as though they could swoop in with armed response and apprehend the killer. Not without a serious risk to her and Chapman.

A plan – a risky one, she had to admit – was bubbling up inside her head; she just had to keep Emmett talking long enough.

But then other thoughts started clamouring for attention. Thoughts about Mike, about how she'd miss his birthday because of this mess; thoughts of Morgan, who'd warned her not to go back to Chapman's until armed response were in place. She thought too of Sophie, wondering if she'd wake up. If she did, Karen probably wouldn't be there to see it. She remembered the disappointment on Rick's face when she'd told him she was uncertain about Harinder, and the hurt in Harinder's eyes as she'd questioned him.

Karen took a deep breath, pushing back the emotions crowding her mind. She couldn't give in to self-pity, not when there was a chance she might get out of this alive.

Emmett said, 'Don't get the wrong idea. Tony wasn't innocent.' He nodded at Chapman. 'He wanted to overthrow you.' He twisted to face Karen. 'Tony decided it was time to get rid of the old man, and he wanted my help. We talked about it for months before we came up with a plan. We took out the men most loyal to

265

Chapman first, men we were sure we could never turn no matter the price. We couldn't believe our luck when the police believed Valerie was responsible for the shootings. Tony said the police were gullible, but that's ridiculous.'

He threw a mocking grin in Karen's direction. She hardly recognised him. The anxious, polite figure was gone, replaced by a sinister and vindictive psychopath.

To think Karen had been *worried* about him. She'd believed Tony and Chapman had forced him into working for them, when really he'd been conspiring with Tony to take down Chapman, before then turning and double-crossing Tony. He'd played them all. Even Karen.

Emmett glanced at Chapman, then turned back to Karen with a taunting smile. 'I found it particularly amusing that you believed Chapman was behind the brothel.' Emmett gave a delighted and faintly hysterical laugh. 'He likes gambling.' Emmett gestured with the gun at Chapman. 'But he draws the line at prostitution.'

'And you don't?' Karen asked, fighting to keep her voice neutral.

He shrugged. 'It's where the money is.'

'And that's what you care about?'

'Of course.' Emmett grinned. 'I'm the money man. Chapman's too old-fashioned.'

'Do you know what happened to Claudia Anderson, Valerie's daughter?' Karen asked in a quiet voice. She didn't want to get him angry, but she wanted answers.

'You ask too many boring questions,' Emmett snapped. 'I think our little chat is over.'

'This won't work, Emmett,' Karen said. 'You'll be caught as soon as you try to leave.'

He smiled, looking pleased with himself. 'I won't. I've planned it all perfectly,' he said. 'I'm going to wipe the security footage, and then I'll tell the police that Chapman went crazy and shot' – he smiled at Karen – 'a dedicated police officer, before turning the gun on himself.'

Karen shook her head. 'That won't work. There's more security here than you think and there's an armed response unit on the way.'

He laughed. 'Detective, I believe you're bluffing.' He raised the gun, aiming at Karen's head.

'No, wait, look, first, b . . . before you . . .' she stammered. Her thoughts wouldn't connect. Her mind was blank, panicked.

He laughed again, enjoying her terror.

She finally found her voice. 'Before you shoot us, I need to know what happened to Sophie. At least you can give me that much.'

Emmett hesitated, then he lowered the gun, but only slightly. 'That was unfortunate. I wasn't carrying my gun.'

'You attacked her?'

'I needed her out of the way. She'd been sniffing around. Sophie and Valerie had been digging for information about Tony's brothel. It turned out Valerie's daughter had been caught up in it all.'

He spoke matter-of-factly, without feeling.

Karen's blood ran cold as he confirmed her suspicions. This man in front of her, who had seemed so harmless and pitiful, was responsible for the assault on Sophie. He was the one who had left her lying on the ground, barely alive. Karen felt sick. She wanted to get up, to run away from him, but she couldn't. All she could do was sit there in shock and revulsion.

Emmett sighed impatiently. 'Look, I didn't plan that part,' he said carelessly. 'It just happened.'

Karen barely heard him over the pounding of blood in her ears. She clenched her fists and forced herself to remain calm. She wanted to make him pay. But right now, staying alive was her priority.

'I'll probably have to finish her off now,' he said casually. 'Although I heard even if she regains consciousness, she'll likely be brain-damaged.' He gave a cruel, satisfied smile that made Karen want to throw something at him.

She focused on her breathing, determined not to give him the reaction he wanted. 'But why did Sophie trying to find Claudia affect you?'

'Because it was bad for business,' Emmett said coldly.

'You lured Sophie to Tony's Workshop?'

He shrugged. 'She was supposed to meet Valerie there, but I messaged Valerie pretending to be Sophie, telling her the meeting was cancelled. I went to meet Sophie instead.'

Throughout all this exchange, Chapman had been silent. Now he stood slowly, staring at Emmett.

'You'll never pull it off. People will laugh at you. This isn't how you do a takeover. If you hadn't killed Tony, you might have had a chance, but like this, no one will work with you. You're young, naive and stupid.'

What was Chapman doing? Karen had always considered him an intelligent man. Cruel, self-serving, but never stupid, so why was he deliberately winding up a man with a gun?

Emmett's cheeks flushed scarlet. He looked absolutely furious as he spat out a string of obscenities. He sprang forwards, lurching at Chapman, backhanding him, sending him sprawling over his desk.

Chapman dropped to the floor and then gripped a small cabinet beside the bookcase, pulling himself back to his feet.

A trickle of blood ran down the side of his mouth.

A banging at the door distracted Emmett. Security were trying to get in, shouting through the solid oak.

'I told you,' Karen said to him. 'There's more security, loads more. You've really underestimated this.'

For the first time since they entered the study, Emmett looked uncertain.

And the distraction had given Chapman a chance.

Suddenly, Karen realised what he'd done. He'd purposely taunted Emmett, trying to get a reaction, because he'd wanted to get to that cabinet without arousing suspicion. He wanted whatever was inside. A weapon? Another gun?

Chapman reached inside. But Emmett was too quick. He slammed the cabinet door closed on his hand.

Chapman roared in pain.

And at that moment Karen realised this might be her only opportunity. She needed to disarm Emmett.

He had turned away from her and was watching Chapman. She had a chance.

Karen took a deep breath and forced herself to focus. She knew if she went too slow, it would just make matters worse. She'd taken self-defence classes, but in the field, things were different. Her adrenaline surged as she tried to remember her training.

She moved fast, charging into Emmett, slamming him against the wall.

He was tall and strong, far stronger than her. He struggled, but she had the advantage of surprise on her side. She grasped at the gun in his hands, trying to wrench it free. The metal was cold against her skin as they grappled with each other, shifting position over the floor.

His grip on the gun was tight, and Karen battled to try to prise it out of his fingers. But Emmett was too powerful, and he regained his footing, pushing her forcefully away.

Cursing loudly, he raised the gun.

Karen backed away from him as he came closer. Her heart was thumping as she desperately tried to think of a way to disarm him before he killed both her and Chapman.

She put her hands up as Emmett pointed the gun at her chest. 'No one needs to get hurt.'

'Yes,' Emmett said, 'they do.'

And he fired.

Karen felt herself hurtling backwards, and then she hit the floor hard. She waited for the pain from the gunshot wound but felt nothing except a pain in her hip where she'd made contact with the floor.

There was banging, a loud creaking, followed by a crash. The study door broke open and two burly security guards burst in, followed by Ponytail.

Karen couldn't see Emmett.

Dazed, Karen looked around and saw Chapman crumpled beside her on the floor.

His eyes were closed. A splatter of scarlet coloured his shirt-sleeve and shoulder.

Everything had happened so quickly. Chapman must have pushed her aside and taken the bullet instead.

Karen scrambled up and tried to staunch the blood seeping from Chapman's wound.

The blinds across the open French doors rattled in the cold night air.

Emmett was escaping. But she couldn't just abandon Chapman, bleeding from the bullet he'd taken for her.

Karen worked, trying to stem the flow of blood, and all the while her mind swirled with questions. How had it come to this? Chapman had just sacrificed himself to protect her.

Chapman – the man she considered her adversary. Her nemesis, her foe, had just saved her life.

Chapter Thirty

Karen stood in the doorway, watching silently as Chapman was wheeled out on a stretcher by the paramedics. The house and its surroundings were full of chaotic activity; officers crowded in to investigate the shooting, while the study was cordoned off with tape, waiting for the scenes of crime officers to arrive.

Ponytail looked pale and gaunt as he sat beside Minchin at the kitchen table, their expressions solemn and resigned. A uniformed officer sat opposite, asking questions.

Karen stood in the middle of the busy hall, surrounded by the sound of Goodridge issuing commands and officers asking questions, feeling removed and disconnected from it all.

Goodridge started to usher officers outside, lecturing them about preserving the scene. She slowly turned, taking in the hustle and bustle. Through the window, she spotted a member of armed response, who was coordinating the unit for a sweep of the surrounding area.

A helicopter hovered close to the house, scanning the area with its powerful search light, searching for Emmett Jenkins.

She'd already recounted her version of events to Goodridge, who'd listened attentively and told her Gold Command had officially taken over, now that this was a major incident.

She felt detached and cold. So cold. Her teeth chattered.

'Hey, how are you holding up?' Morgan's familiar voice came from behind her. She was relieved to hear it; his presence brought a wave of relief from the dull, numb feeling that had surrounded her since the shooting.

'He got away,' Karen said.

'Not for long,' Morgan replied. 'Goodridge has ordered teams to search local gardens and outbuildings. We'll find him.'

'Has his car been found?'

'Not yet. Presumably he left it somewhere close by and snuck on to the property on foot, lying in wait for the opportunity to shoot Tony and Chapman. There's an alert out on his vehicle. If Emmett made it back to his car, we'll quickly pick him up.'

Karen's phone buzzed insistently in her pocket, and she saw McKenzie's name displayed on the screen.

She held it up. 'I'd better take this.' She took a deep breath before answering.

'DS Hart.'

'I've had a report of another shooting.' McKenzie's gruff voice crackled over the bad line.

Karen went outside for better reception. It was freezing.

'Yes,' she confirmed, trying to stop shivering. 'I'm at the scene. Emmett Jenkins, an accountant working for both Tony Withers and Quentin Chapman, was the shooter. He killed Tony, and Chapman was shot in the shoulder.'

She filled McKenzie in on the rest of the story.

When she'd finished, McKenzie said, 'So he's still at large? We can help. We have an insider in the network and can provide intelligence.'

Karen passed on the details for Gold Command and promised to keep McKenzie updated.

She headed back inside and made her way towards Morgan and Goodridge.

'We've located Emmett's car,' Morgan said as she approached. 'It's at the train station. We're looking into how long it's been there.'

'And Emmett?' Karen asked.

'We're not sure,' Goodridge said. 'He could still be around here. He may have left the car there earlier today. The team are going to check the station's security cameras.'

Karen thought hard. Emmett was on the back foot, but he wasn't stupid. He knew they'd be tracing his car. His first priority would be to change vehicles so he couldn't be tracked.

'Rick is working with the CCTV operators in an effort to trace him,' Morgan said. 'He can't have just disappeared.'

Karen tried to put herself in Emmett's shoes. His plan had gone horribly wrong, and he was now wanted for murder. He'd need a fresh vehicle and access to cash.

She pulled out her mobile and opened the maps app. The distance between Lincoln train station was twelve minutes' walk from Great Northern Terrace. Could Emmett have dumped his car at the station to make them think he'd caught a train, but instead gone to Tony's Workshop where he could get another vehicle – one they wouldn't be tracking?

She recalled again the time she'd seen Emmett at the workshop, when he'd held up a set of keys. His quiet and unassuming front, his nervousness – it had all been fake.

If Emmett wanted a vehicle, he'd go to the workshop.

'I think I might know where he's gone,' Karen said.

Goodridge raised an eyebrow. 'Where?'

'Tony's Workshop. It's within walking distance of the train station, and they have plenty of cars out the back. He could drive off in a vehicle that won't be on our radar.'

Karen held her breath, knowing she had to ask for permission before taking any action on her own. 'I think we should check it out,' she pressed as Goodridge frowned, looking unconvinced.

'It's a good theory,' he conceded. 'But our armed unit is spread thin searching the surrounding area; that has to be our priority.'

Karen nodded, respect for Goodridge warring with her conviction that Emmett had gone to the workshop, and that if they took too long, they'd lose the opportunity to apprehend him.

Goodridge continued, 'He could have left the car at the train station earlier today. Until we know for sure—'

'But what if he didn't?' Karen interrupted. 'What if he managed to get to his car after he shot Chapman and drove to the station, intending to send us on a wild goose chase?'

Goodridge gave a weary sigh.

'Karen and I could go to Tony's Workshop now,' Morgan suggested. He raised a hand in response to the horrified look on Goodridge's face. 'Hear me out. I know we're stretched thin. We'll only be there to observe, we'll keep our distance, and if we see any sign of Emmett, we'll call it in and wait for backup.'

It sounded so reasonable when Morgan said it. Surely Goodridge couldn't argue with that logic.

But he was still reluctant. 'He's armed. We can't risk it.'

Time was ticking away.

'Yes, he's armed, and he might be in Lincoln. Innocent people could get hurt,' Karen argued.

Goodridge rubbed his forehead and let out a deep sigh. After a long pause, he finally nodded and said, 'All right, but promise me you'll stay a safe distance away.'

He pointed a finger at each of them, emphasising the seriousness of his words. 'No heroics,' he said. 'Be careful.'

◆ ◆ ◆

The journey from Burton Waters to Great Northern Terrace seemed to take forever. Karen had sent Mike a text, letting him know she'd be late home. She hadn't mentioned the shooting. She would do that later, face to face. There was only so much you could put in a text message.

Morgan eased the car along Great Northern Terrace, the shadows of the night cloaking it in darkness. With a sharp twist of the wheel, he stopped at the edge of Party Fun, not far from Tony's Workshop.

They both peered through the windscreen, eyes searching for signs of life. But there was nothing.

There were no lights on. The doors were firmly shut. Anyone could slip around the back to access the vehicles parked there, but to get the keys, Emmett would need to go inside the workshop.

'He's not here,' Karen said after only a few seconds. 'It would have taken him twelve minutes, perhaps less if he was moving quickly, to get here on foot from the train station. We've missed him.'

'We don't know that,' Morgan said. 'Give it time. He might still turn up.' Morgan kept his eyes on the rear-view mirror, watching out for any movement.

The sky was clear and shone with stars, reminding Karen of the night that Sophie had faced her attacker. Karen shuddered at the thought of how Sophie must have felt standing outside the workshop that fateful evening, expecting to see Valerie but instead finding herself confronted by Emmett.

Had she been fooled by him too? Taken in by that vulnerable, innocent act?

Morgan's phone buzzed, snapping Karen out of her trance.

'It's Rick,' he said, answering it quickly in a hushed whisper.

Karen hoped Rick had found a lead from the CCTV, something that would direct them to Emmett, because she couldn't help feeling they'd missed their chance to catch him. He'd been too quick for them.

Suddenly, Morgan broke out into a wide smile and grabbed her hand in his. That was odd. Morgan wasn't really a demonstrative type.

'She's awake,' he mouthed, as he held the phone tightly to his ear and listened to Rick.

Karen's breath hitched in her throat. 'Sophie?' she whispered, barely able to believe it.

After he hung up, Morgan said, 'Sorry, I should have put him on speaker, but I didn't want to be too loud, just in case Emmett's lurking nearby.'

'Sophie's okay?' Karen asked.

'She regained consciousness about half an hour ago,' Morgan replied, his eyes shining. 'She can't talk yet, and she's also having trouble with the right side of her body, either due to swelling on her brain or the effects of the bleed.' He waited a beat and then added, 'It's going to be a long road to recovery, and some of her problems might be permanent.'

'Right,' Karen said, trying to take it all in. 'So, she needs extensive rehabilitation.'

'Yes,' Morgan said softly, 'but she's awake.'

Karen slumped back in her seat, her mind reeling. The past few days had been a rollercoaster. Sophie had suffered extensive trauma and the healing process would be a long one. But this was a step in the right direction.

She could only imagine the joy Harinder and Sophie's parents were feeling right now. But a wave of sadness hit Karen too. Sophie would be confused and scared, waking up in that condition. Karen couldn't help but feel protective. She wished she could be there at the hospital to reassure Sophie and tell her everything would be all right.

She waited for the news to sink in. After the long, tortuous days they'd spent waiting for updates from the hospital, almost dreading them in case they brought bad news, Sophie had made it – she'd pulled through.

Karen felt a welcome lightness in her chest as some of the worry lifted.

When the time was right, she would be able to tell Sophie about the hair-raising moments from the past few days. For now though, Karen was content to know she was safe and awake.

'Did Rick say when we could visit?'

'I didn't ask,' Morgan said. 'I expect tomorrow would be okay. She's probably feeling a bit overwhelmed right now.'

Karen nodded, staring out at the inky night.

'I think you're right,' Morgan said, gazing at the desolate street. 'Emmett's not coming, is he? I'm glad we checked it out though; it was a good theory.'

But Karen wasn't ready to give up that easily. 'We need to talk to Valerie Anderson,' she said. 'We need her help.'

'What for?'

'Well, she can check the security feed for one thing, and more importantly she'll know if a car is missing. We could walk around to the back of the workshop ourselves to check, but we won't know what's supposed to be there and what isn't.'

Morgan's mouth flattened into a thin line. 'We promised Goodridge we'd keep our distance, Karen.'

'Yes, we agreed we'd stay away from Emmett,' Karen conceded. 'But he's not even here. We can't abandon this just yet. I'm sure he came here.'

'We won't abandon the idea,' Morgan said. 'But we'll wait until appropriate resources are available.'

Karen ground her teeth. She hated it when he was so by-the-book.

'We need Valerie,' Karen stated again in a no-nonsense tone. She was quite prepared to walk to Valerie's house on Charles Street at this point if Morgan refused to help.

'Valerie won't help us. We thought she was responsible for the shootings.'

'She'll want to help,' Karen said, with certainty. 'She wants to find out where her daughter is. That's more important to her than us hurting her feelings because we suspected her of murder.'

Morgan paused, a troubled frown creasing his forehead. 'Goodridge really won't be happy with us bringing a civilian into the investigation.'

Karen's voice carried a note of urgency. 'We don't have much choice. We need Valerie to tell us which vehicle is missing because I'm positive Emmett came here.'

Morgan's frown deepened.

'Think about it,' Karen said, appealing to Morgan's logical side. 'It makes perfect sense – he needed a car, but he certainly didn't want to steal one and risk alerting the police. The workshop is the safest option. No one would notice the vehicle is missing until morning, and even if they did, Arnie suspects Sully and McArthur of selling stolen parts. So, they're unlikely to invite more police attention by reporting it. They're already sweating every time we visit.'

'We could talk to Sully or McArthur instead of Valerie?' Morgan suggested.

'Who do you think is more likely to cooperate?'

'Fair point,' Morgan said and started the engine.

They had to go under the A1434 to reach Charles Street, and even though it was a less than half a mile as the crow flies, traffic meant the journey took almost five minutes.

Karen called to let Valerie know they were on their way, and when they reached her house, she was already waiting for them on the doorstep, wearing a huge puffy coat.

She marched up to the car and climbed into the back seat without a word, securing her seat belt with a steely determination.

Morgan glanced at Karen, still not happy about having a civilian in the car while they tracked down a killer. Karen could understand that. But they needed Valerie's help.

Karen twisted around in her seat. 'You're clear about what we need you to do?' she asked.

A curt nod was Valerie's answer. 'Yes. You need me to see if any cars are missing, and check the security feed?'

'That's right, you have the keys?'

Valerie patted her bag. 'Yes, in here.'

As Morgan started the engine again and rolled away from the kerb, Valerie looked pale as she asked in an unsteady voice, 'Are you absolutely sure Emmett's responsible?'

Karen nodded. 'Yes, I am. I'm sorry. The news must have come as a shock.'

'He was always so nice to me. After what happened to DC Jones, he called in on me more than once to make sure I was okay.'

Karen suspected that Emmett's concern had been more to do with finding out about the police investigation than Valerie's welfare.

'So, he shot those three men?' she asked.

'We believe so, yes.' Karen had already gone over this briefly with Valerie on the phone, but it was a lot to take in.

'And he attacked DC Jones?'

Karen felt a surge of temper and clenched her jaw. 'Yes.'

Valerie looked at Karen with wide eyes. 'And . . . me?'

'It looks that way.'

'But why attack me?' Valerie asked, her voice trembling slightly.

'I think it was because you and Sophie were looking into Tony's brothel and Emmett was involved,' Karen explained, her anger still sharp. 'He didn't want you uncovering any secrets that could damage the business. He thought assaulting Sophie would discourage you both, but when you didn't give up—'

'He tried to murder me,' Valerie finished quietly. 'And he would have succeeded if you hadn't arrived when you did. But why didn't he just shoot me?'

Karen had thought about that. Emmett was cunning. If he'd used the same gun he'd employed to kill Chapman's associates, they would have connected the crimes faster.

'Guns are easier to link between crimes,' Karen explained.

Valerie nodded, shaken. 'I really thought it was Quentin Chapman who attacked me. I wasn't lying about that.' Karen gave her a reassuring smile. 'Do you think Emmett knows anything about Claudia?' Valerie asked.

'I don't know,' Karen said truthfully. Emmett hadn't been very helpful when she'd asked him about Valerie's daughter, but he seemed to know quite a bit about the brothel. She would have to do some more digging. 'I promise I'll find out if I can.'

Morgan pulled to a stop in front of Tony's Workshop. He turned to Valerie, who was already scanning the area. She took a deep breath and met his gaze.

'Ready?' he asked.

Valerie nodded slowly, her expression resolute. 'As I'll ever be.'

Chapter Thirty-One

Karen, Morgan and Valerie stood at the back of Tony's Workshop, their eyes trained on the lines of parked cars. They'd already been inside and checked the security feed.

Karen was right. Emmett had been there. They'd missed him by just minutes.

He'd let himself into the workshop, presumably grabbed a set of car keys, and then locked up. The camera caught a glimpse of what looked like a small white SUV leaving the premises.

Valerie scowled and bit her lip. 'It's definitely the Nissan Qashqai,' she said. 'That's the one that's missing.'

'Do you have the licence plate?' Morgan asked.

Valerie nodded. 'It's logged in the record book.'

Karen shivered and pulled out her mobile phone, getting ready to call Rick with the license plate information.

They went back inside, and Valerie opened a red, hardback book with handwritten entries.

'Don't you use the computer?' Karen said, pointing to the laptop on the next bench.

Valerie shook her head. 'It gets glitchy now and again – I find the old-fashioned ways are more reliable.' She searched through the book until she found the number plate and read it out.

Morgan tapped the number plate into his phone, and Karen placed the call to Rick.

By the time they'd thanked Valerie and dropped her back to her house on Charles Street, Rick had called back. He'd got a hit.

The white Nissan Qashqai had turned off the A46 and was heading west on Whisby Road.

Morgan stopped the car at the end of Charles Street and pulled out his mobile, taking a look at the map.

He had been looking into possible locations for Tony's brothel. The one they had previously identified had been a bust, because they'd cleared it out before the team had got there.

'Maybe they moved to one of the other properties we identified.' He switched to satellite view and then zoomed in on a large building at the end of a private road, a short distance from the garden centre. 'Here. I bet this is where it is.'

Karen leaned over and studied the map. 'He's going to the brothel to get his hands on some cash.'

Morgan had pointed out a spot which was close enough to Lincoln to be convenient, yet far enough away to avoid attracting unwanted attention.

'Perfect spot,' she said. 'Let's tell Goodridge.'

Morgan nodded and placed the call.

Karen listened as he filled Goodridge in on the details. From what she gathered listening to the one-sided conversation, the CCTV footage had just confirmed Emmett's presence at the train station about half an hour ago. Everything was falling into place. Emmett had behaved as she'd predicted. Karen felt a thrill as the puzzle pieces aligned.

She should have been pleased, but another sensation began to tug deep within her. Disappointment. She'd wanted to be present when they took Emmett down.

It didn't make her feel good to realise she wanted him to suffer for what he'd done to Sophie. Emmett had attacked an unarmed, female police officer from behind, and the thought of it filled Karen with a blinding rage.

Karen balled her fists in frustration. She was no fool. Emmett was armed, which meant there was no way Goodridge, or any more senior officers, would approve of her and Morgan attempting to apprehend him alone. And she wasn't crazy enough to press the issue. She'd already been shot at once tonight – that was enough for one evening.

Morgan ended the call and turned to Karen. 'Goodridge says we need to wait close by but stay away from the private road. An armed team is already on the way. Goodridge believes Emmett will be headed to the brothel for cash, too.'

Karen nodded, her body taut with anticipation.

The drive to Whisby Road took less than ten minutes. Morgan pulled off the main road and parked next to the entrance of the nearby quarry. The wait was torture as they wondered what was happening at the brothel and if Emmett would be caught or would slip away again.

Suddenly, Morgan's phone rang. His face was tense as he answered. His gaze locked with Karen's. It was impossible to follow the conversation with Morgan's monosyllabic replies.

When he hung up a few moments later, his expression grim, he said, 'We have permission to enter the private road. They believe Emmett is still inside and is holding two hostages.'

Karen's stomach clenched with anticipation as they raced on to the small private road.

As they rounded the corner, Morgan hit the brakes. The road had been cordoned off. Black vans were parked across the tarmac, along with police cars, their blue lights flashing.

Morgan parked up and left the car by the grass verge. DI Goodridge was waiting for them with a team of officers. He quickly filled them in. He'd had the building surrounded and instructed his officers to hold their positions until he gave the signal to move in. He believed that Emmett was still inside, but it was impossible to know how many people he may have taken hostage.

'We managed to clear most of the building.' He nodded to a group huddled by a marked police van.

Karen's gaze landed on a few scantily dressed women wrapped in silver blankets, and a big man with a thick neck, who she guessed must have acted as security for the brothel. Beside him was a tiny, birdlike woman with big hair, dressed in an electric-blue trouser suit.

Goodridge pointed at the woman, who leaned back against the van, seemingly very relaxed. 'That's Patricia Manetti. From what I can tell, she manages the women. I couldn't get much out of her. See if you have better luck.'

They walked over.

From a distance, Patricia Manetti was beautiful. She had elegant arched eyebrows, high cheekbones and perfect pouting lips. When they got closer, it was clear that the make-up was doing a lot of heavy lifting.

Her trouser suit was modest, though the colour was certainly attention-grabbing. She caught sight of them heading her way and sharpened her gaze.

'There's two women unaccounted for, and we believe they're inside with Emmett Jenkins,' Goodridge said to Karen and Morgan. 'We're keeping our distance in case he does anything stupid.'

'Mind if I speak to Patricia now?'

Goodridge nodded. 'She's pretty sharp. Almost seems unfazed by it all.'

Karen stepped forward towards Patricia Manetti, who leaned against the police van with a cigarette in one hand, her legs casually crossed. She gave off an air of nonchalance, as if she dealt with this kind of scenario every day.

Karen introduced herself. Patricia sized her up with distrustful eyes, and Karen chose her words carefully. 'When Emmett came in, what did he say to you?'

Patricia gave her a long, assessing stare before responding in a gravelly voice. 'He said Tony had told him he was to collect the cash and the books, and remove them from the premises. But I knew he was lying. His eyes were shifty.' She took a drag on the cigarette between her fingers and then exhaled, sending the smoke snaking around her head. 'I can read men,' she said with a shrug. 'In my profession you have to.'

Karen hesitated before asking her next question. 'You manage the women?'

'I'm not confessing to anything, sweetheart,' she said, blowing out another lungful of smoke.

'You've recently moved premises?'

Patricia's gaze turned razor sharp. 'Like I said, I'm not admitting anything.'

'How did you know about the previous raid?' Karen asked. 'Who tipped you off?'

Patricia smiled, though it was cold and humourless. 'No idea, sweetheart. That was all down to Tony.'

She flicked some ash from her cigarette on to the ground.

'Does Claudia Anderson work for you?' Karen asked.

Patricia kept her face expressionless, refusing to give a yes or no answer.

'I'm not looking to get you in trouble here. I just want to help Claudia. Her mother's worried about her.'

Patricia's face softened slightly, but she was looking out for her own interests first and foremost. 'Sorry, darling, can't help.'

Karen tried one last question. 'Can you at least tell me if you've seen her?'

Patricia simply shrugged in response.

Karen gave up and trudged back to talk to Goodridge and Morgan, who gave her an update on the number of armed men now surrounding the building.

It was very lucky there were no residential properties nearby. The whole place was lit by flickering blue lights.

One of the vans had a loudspeaker mounted on its roof, and they discussed strategies to contact Emmett. He had discarded his mobile phone, leaving them with no way to reach him.

They waited as Bryant, one of the female officers, attempted calling the in-house landline, but there was no reply.

'Give it one more try,' Goodridge urged.

Bryant dialled again, and this time, there was an answer. The female officer's face changed at once, her expression conveying a mix of surprise and fear. She shifted uncomfortably. 'I'm not sure that's . . . I don't know . . . I'll have to organise that . . . Give me some time.'

Abruptly, her eyes grew wide. 'He hung up on me.'

Goodridge stepped closer, a vein pulsing at his temple. 'What did he say?'

Bryant's face was pinched with worry. She looked at Karen.

'He wants to talk to Detective Karen Hart. He says he'll let one hostage go if she goes in.'

Chapter Thirty-Two

Karen's throat squeezed tight. 'I'll do it,' she said.

Morgan spun to face her. 'No.'

'Absolutely not,' Goodridge exploded, the intensity of his words slicing through the night air.

'But if—' Karen started to say.

'Not happening.' Morgan cut her off, his jaw clenching, anger radiating from him. 'Ridiculous idea. Absurd.'

'There is no way I could ever allow it.' Goodridge shook his head, raking a hand through his hair.

He looked more stressed than Karen had ever seen him.

'I need to update Gold Command,' Goodridge muttered.

Karen and Morgan stood shoulder to shoulder in the frigid night air.

'He said he'd let one of them go . . .' Karen said, her voice trailing off.

'I don't care,' Morgan snapped. 'You're not going in there. He's already come close enough to killing you once tonight.'

Karen knew it was risky, but what she didn't understand was why Emmett wanted to talk to her. What could she tell him that other people couldn't?

Did he think that if he had a police officer as a hostage, the police would be more likely to let him go? Did he really believe he could escape? She had no idea how his mind was working.

After Goodridge finished his call, he came back to them. 'Gold Command is aware of the situation,' he reported, exhaustion weighing down his words. 'It's a standoff – they've organised a specialist negotiator to come in . . .' His voice faded away, and all three fell into silence.

'What do we do in the meantime?' Karen eventually asked, her stomach knotted into a tight ball.

'We wait,' Goodridge said, eyes hard and unblinking.

Tense minutes passed and they heard nothing more from Emmett Jenkins. Bryant tried to call the landline multiple times, but he didn't answer.

'Try again,' Goodridge ordered. Clearly waiting patiently wasn't his strong suit.

This time, Emmett answered. Even over the phone line Karen could hear his voice raised in anger.

Bryant glanced nervously at Goodridge when the call finished. 'Well?'

'He's angry, sir. Demanding to know where DS Hart is. He promises to let one of the hostages go as soon as she enters the property, and he assures me he'll surrender once he's spoken to her.'

Goodridge snorted. 'I don't care if he promises me a herd of pink sparkly unicorns, none of my team are entering the property with that man.'

More stressful minutes passed.

Suddenly, there was movement at the front of the property. The head of the armed unit shouted instructions for Emmett to lay his weapon on the ground.

The piercing light atop of a police car swung around to illuminate the front door as Emmett slowly walked out of the house.

In front of him, one of the female hostages shuffled along. She was barefoot, wearing a short denim skirt and a thin camisole. Mascara had run down her cheeks.

He held another woman to his side, pressing the gun to her temple. She was wearing heels. As Emmett dragged her along the path, she stumbled. It seemed like everyone around Karen held their breath.

Emmett's voice filled the night air as he shouted out, 'Are you really going to let these women die because you're too scared to talk to me, Detective?'

He stopped in the middle of the path.

The woman in front was sobbing; the one with the gun to her head was frozen with fear.

'I just want to talk to you,' Emmett shouted. 'That's all.'

Karen's instincts told her to move forward and put an end to this madness, but Morgan's grip on her arm kept her in place. 'He doesn't just want to talk,' Morgan said in a low voice. 'He wants to kill you. In Chapman's study he told you everything. In his mind, if he gets rid of you, then there's no one who can testify against him. He thinks he can scare Tony and Chapman's men into keeping quiet. But he can't do that with you. So, he thinks he needs to get you out of the way.'

Karen's heart pounded in her chest, a suffocating mix of fear and helplessness. She wanted to do something, to take control of the situation and protect the women. But Morgan was right. Emmett wasn't planning on talking. He was planning to kill her.

But if he shot her, he wouldn't be any better off. She wouldn't be able to testify against him, but he'd be guilty of killing a police officer.

So, what was he playing at?

'Right,' Goodridge said gruffly into his mobile, his gaze trained on Karen as he ended the call. She hadn't noticed he'd been on the phone. 'Let's get you into protective clothing.'

Morgan opened his mouth to speak, but Goodridge cut him off with a look. 'Your objection is noted,' he said curtly, then turned back to Karen. 'Let's go.'

Karen followed him, her eyes straying back to Morgan, whose face was tight with anger.

They moved closer to the cordon but stayed behind the safety of the vans.

Karen found herself being manhandled into a bulletproof vest and a helmet with a visor, which made it much harder to see and harder to hear.

Someone shoved a handset into Karen's hand, the wire snaking back into the van. She guessed it was connected to the loudspeaker.

'Talk to him,' Goodridge instructed. 'Say something reassuring. Something to buy us some time.'

Karen raised the handset and said, 'Emmett, it's DS Hart.'

Her voice shook. Everyone had to be able to hear the fear in her voice.

'Come closer,' he shouted back. 'If you do, I'll let one of the girls go.'

Karen pushed aside the fear that threatened to paralyse her. She locked eyes with one of the armed officers standing opposite her – sympathy and understanding in his gaze.

'What do you want, Emmett?' Karen asked, a determined edge to her tone.

'Just talk to me,' he replied. 'If you come and talk, I'll hand myself in afterwards.' He paused before adding, 'I promise.'

Karen's stomach churned, a fierce hatred blooming for Emmett. She wanted to help the women he was using as human shields. But she didn't trust him for one second.

'Look, I'm putting my weapon down,' Emmett shouted, leaning forward, pulling one of the women down too, holding her in a headlock.

Karen strained to see over the van, and at that moment, Emmett stood back up quickly, a snarl on his face as he lifted the gun and aimed it towards where Karen was sheltering.

It was then she realised Morgan had been wrong. This was nothing about testifying against Emmett. This was about revenge.

If he shot her now, he'd be guilty of killing a police officer. It wouldn't get him off the hook. This was all about vengeance.

He hated her for ruining his plan. He must think if she hadn't been at Chapman's house, he would have been able to murder Tony and Chapman and seize power.

Morgan was right that Emmett assumed the men who'd witnessed the crimes at Chapman's house would be too scared, or too deeply entrenched in the criminal underworld, to blab to the police.

In Emmett's deluded mind, his plans for power – which had seemed so certain to succeed – had been derailed by Karen.

He clearly hated her for that, and that was why he wanted her dead.

One of the armed officers shouted a warning, but Emmett ignored it and pointed the gun, his features twisted into a snarl of hatred.

Before he got a chance to squeeze the trigger, the officer stepped forward and shot Emmett Jenkins in the chest. The force of the bullet spun him around, and he hit the ground with a thud.

The women Emmett had been using as shields quickly scattered to safety, while Karen remained rooted to the spot, allowing her mind to process what had just happened.

An officer tapped her on the shoulder. 'Are you okay?'

She managed to nod.

Other officers ran to Emmett. Dead or alive, he was incapacitated. Karen went with them. She needed to see this.

Paramedics, who'd been on standby, moved with swift efficiency. Karen stood just far enough away to allow them to do their work, but close enough to see Emmett's face.

Memories of the past and present collided in her mind.

Karen had sat alone with Emmett in the office at his accountancy firm and felt sorry for him when Tony berated him. She'd watched Valerie mother him over tea and biscuits at the workshop. She'd warned him to stay away from Chapman's house for his own safety.

Karen had been worried the gangsters were taking advantage of him, and yet all this time . . .

Part of Karen still found it hard to believe that Emmett was capable of such evil. The dramatic change in his personality had come as a huge shock. Emmett's ambition had driven him to cruel and malicious depths.

Karen had faced many sinister and harrowing cases in her career, but this was different. Staring down at Emmett Jenkins, she was sure this was as close as she'd ever come to looking at pure evil.

And she'd missed it. She'd been taken in by his deception.

He must have been orchestrating this coup for a long time. He'd likely been syphoning money away from Tony and Quentin Chapman for years, plotting his takeover. He'd wanted the power and the prestige. But when his attempt to seize control had backfired, and his vision had crumbled at the last moment, he'd blamed Karen and turned his venom towards her.

He'd wanted her dead. She'd seen it in his crazed expression just before he'd been shot.

She felt nothing for the man on the ground before her. No sympathy as he writhed in agony. Not even a flicker of sadness as he struggled for breath, frothy blood bubbling from the corner of his mouth.

He twitched and whimpered, his blood pooling around him. She felt no pity for Emmett, knowing he'd had none for Sophie.

Emmett had attacked someone Karen cared deeply about, someone she loved like a sister. Sophie was alive, but there was no guarantee she would ever recover from the trauma of the attack. Karen wanted Emmett to pay; she wanted to watch him suffer, as justice for what he had done. He should feel the same agony as his actions had caused.

Paramedics continued to work on him, trying to stem the blood loss and hook him up to fluids, but it was too late. He wouldn't recover from this.

Karen kept her eyes fixed on Emmett as she took a deep breath, trying to steady herself. Despite all that he had done, she wondered if she'd feel sorry for him in his final moments – but there was nothing except anger left inside.

Karen clenched her fists, her knuckles turning white, as his chest rose and fell for the final time.

The paramedics stood down.

Emmett Jenkins was dead.

Karen stepped back and removed her helmet, feeling the full weight of exhaustion. She closed her eyes as conflicted emotions fought in her mind. Relief flooded her body – justice had been served, but part of her wished that he could have faced a trial for his crimes.

Karen opened her eyes, taking one last look at the limp body on the ground, before turning away from the bloody remains of Emmett Jenkins.

Chapter Thirty-Three

The officers filed into the police station, herding the people who'd been at the brothel towards the canteen. One of the officers switched on a heater to take the chill from the room. They motioned for everyone to sit at the tables and chairs, providing cups of tea to everyone.

Punters who'd been caught up in the raid sat scattered, their eyes lowered and faces flushed.

The women mainly sat in groups of two or three.

No one seemed particularly talkative, which was only to be expected after the traumatic evening for all concerned.

Karen had already tried to talk to Patricia Manetti again, but the woman had stonewalled her. She'd been through the system so often that she was well versed in her legal rights. Her only goal was self-preservation, and that was no good to Karen. She desperately needed someone to talk if she was ever going to locate Claudia Anderson.

Karen took a step back and regrouped. With Emmett dead, it was time to move forward and get answers. She had to find someone who would talk. Someone who knew what had happened to Claudia.

Karen looked around the canteen, trying to identify who would be most likely to talk.

Morgan was questioning the huge security man, whose ill-fitting suit stretched tight over his shoulders. Karen took a sip of her tea and zeroed in on one of the women Emmett had held hostage – Olive Larkin. Any loyalty she had towards Emmett surely would have disappeared the moment he pressed a gun to her head.

Karen walked across the canteen, cradling a cup of tea. She sat opposite Olive, who had already shed her blanket, revealing her camisole top, short skirt and long, bare legs. The woman had declined the offer of a tracksuit and white trainers, instead choosing to keep her own clothes and heels on.

Olive chewed on a fingernail as she examined Karen with suspicion.

'What do you want?' she asked in a bitter voice.

'I'm here to help,' Karen said softly. 'You've been through an unimaginably traumatic experience. We have resources lined up for those who want to talk about it.'

Olive shrugged and muttered, 'It's no big deal. He was a bastard anyway. I'm glad he got shot.'

'You didn't like him?' Karen asked.

'Understatement of the year.' Olive's voice was cold.

Karen saw hatred burn in the young woman's eyes. Emmett hadn't kept up his innocent act around her. The women at the brothel had seen his cruelty unleashed.

'What did he do to you?' Karen asked.

Olive's expression darkened. 'What didn't he do? He was always dropping in, using one of us, without paying. He called it a perk of the job.'

'Was he violent?'

Olive's gaze hardened. Her silence spoke volumes.

'You could have saved me,' she said finally, her eyes boring into Karen. 'I did nothing wrong.'

Karen began to explain, but Olive was having none of it. 'You wound him up – all you had to do was talk to him, and he would have let me go.'

Olive shook her head and shuddered, wrapping her arms around her body protectively.

'I don't think Emmett was telling the truth,' Karen said quietly, but Olive didn't seem to hear her.

'Do you know Claudia Anderson?' Karen asked.

Olive scowled. Her voice was harsh and filled with spite. 'She wound him up too. Claudia never knew when to shut up. No wonder he . . .' Her voice trailed off, her face contorting with awareness of her own mistake.

'You saw what happened to Claudia?' Karen asked, trying to keep her voice steady. 'Did Emmett hurt her?'

She didn't reply.

'What happened, Olive?' Karen prodded gently, hoping to coax an answer out of the angry young woman.

'I didn't see anything,' she said. 'Leave me alone.'

'I'm trying to help,' Karen said.

Olive reared back and snarled, 'No, you're not. Don't try to cosy up to me now. You're not my friend. You wouldn't have cared if he shot me. He asked to talk to you. Told you he'd let me go. And you just didn't bother!'

'That's not how the situation unfolded, Olive,' Karen said evenly. 'It might have seemed that way to you, but—'

'I was there, wasn't I? I know exactly what happened,' she snapped back. 'He just wanted to talk to you.'

Karen shook her head and felt weariness tugging at her bones. 'That wasn't what he wanted,' she said softly, not wanting to get into an argument with Olive.

Karen's gut told her that Olive knew the truth about what had happened to Claudia, though the woman was tight-lipped. Their investigation relied on getting someone to talk. They needed information, and that meant finding a way to crack the stubborn silence.

Karen tried again. 'Did you see what happened to Claudia?'

Olive's expression tightened, but she remained silent.

Karen was sure now that she'd seen something. 'Did anyone else see what happened?'

Olive didn't speak, but her gaze shifted to the corner of the room, where a woman sat alone, staring into the middle distance.

'All right, Olive, thanks for your help,' Karen said, getting to her feet.

As she moved away from the table, Karen caught sight of Rick, waving to get her attention. She walked over to him.

He spoke quietly. 'We've had news from the hospital.'

Karen's stomach churned. Her mind raced to Sophie, worrying she'd had a setback since the good news earlier.

She met Rick's gaze.

Her anxiety must have been clear because Rick quickly said, 'Sophie is okay. And we've had an update on Chapman's condition. He's stable. For now.'

After Karen left Rick, she headed over to the woman sitting alone at the table.

As Karen approached, she could feel the nervous tension radiating from the young woman. Taking a quick breath, Karen smiled and positioned herself across from her. 'Hi, I'm Detective Hart. I'm one of the police officers working on this case, and I'm looking into the whereabouts of a young woman called Claudia Anderson. I hoped you might be able to tell me something.'

The woman reacted like a deer in headlights, her shoulders tensing, her gaze shifting nervously away.

'You know what happened to Claudia, don't you?'

The woman swallowed hard but didn't reply.

'What's your name?'

'Samantha Stevens,' she said in a quiet voice.

'Do you know Claudia, Samantha?'

Samantha hesitated and then nodded.

'Do you know what happened to her?'

She gave a single nod but wouldn't look up to meet Karen's gaze. After a few moments of silence, she said in a voice that was barely a whisper, 'I saw it. I saw everything.'

Samantha Stevens's eyes darted around the room, her skin pale and drawn. Karen wondered if she'd taken something. Her pupils were so dilated they seemed to swallow the rest of her eyes. She scratched at her arms.

'Can you tell me what happened?' Karen asked, leaning forward and resting her forearms on the table.

'I don't think I should,' Samantha said. 'It's not safe. He's listening.'

'Who's listening?' Karen asked, looking over her shoulder, but no one was watching them.

'Emmett,' she whispered, her eyes wide. 'He's always watching.'

Karen decided Samantha was definitely high, which meant anything she told her now had to be taken with a grain of salt.

She knew Samantha had just been through a traumatic experience, and it was clear drugs were playing a part in her current state. She needed to be comforted and supported. Karen forced herself to stay calm and meet Samantha's fearful gaze with her own reassuring one.

'You're safe here,' Karen said firmly. 'You can trust me.'

Samantha had been present when Emmett was shot. She had to know Emmett was dead, but Karen wasn't sure how Samantha would react to remembering Emmett's violent death given that she was clearly high, so she decided not to remind her of the dramatic event.

'It's fine,' Karen assured her. 'He won't hurt you ever again.'

Samantha's gaze moved around the room, never staying still. She chewed on her already bitten nails, and her tousled fringe fell forward over her eyes. 'Are you sure?'

Karen nodded. 'Absolutely. You're safe now.' She paused, then asked, 'What can you tell me about Claudia?'

'She was my friend,' Samantha said softly, her voice tinged with sadness.

Karen's stomach clenched at Samantha's use of the past tense.

The woman continued, and Karen noticed that a faint tremor shook her hands. 'I liked her a lot. We got on the first time we met – we just clicked. We had a lot in common.'

Samantha shook her head sadly, a shudder passing through her body. 'Emmett always treated us like dirt. He came around a lot, and paid Patricia money so she'd look away for a few hours.' Her voice grew low and hard. 'He treated us . . . terribly.'

Karen hesitated before asking, 'Was he violent?'

Samantha shivered and nodded. 'Yes. Any small thing could set him off. And that's what happened to Claudia. She had only been working there for six months. I'd been there two years, so I was showing her the ropes. She wasn't one to sit quietly and take orders, though. Claudia wanted to set out on her own. She didn't want other people making money off her body. I told her to keep it quiet. They wouldn't like that.'

Samantha's gaze travelled over to Patricia Manetti, who was glaring back at them.

Karen shifted subtly to shield Samantha from Patricia's gaze.

'Then what happened to Claudia?' Karen asked softly.

Samantha's gaze grew distant as if remembering a painful memory. 'It began with something so small. I'd opened a window for some fresh air. But it triggered him.'

A tremble in her voice betrayed her fear of the memory.

'Emmett went ballistic. Before I knew what was happening, his hands were around my throat.' Her fingers moved up to her neck as she remembered.

'Claudia tried to save me. She screamed at him and told him to let me go or she'd call the police. But that just set him off more. He threw me against the wall and started in on her. She fought back but . . .' Samantha shuddered, her voice cracked, and tears brimmed in her eyes. 'He strangled her.'

'You saw Emmett Jenkins strangle Claudia Anderson?' Karen said, to clarify.

'Yes . . . She was my friend,' Samantha whispered softly. 'She was trying to help me.'

Karen glanced over at the counsellor, who had just arrived and was speaking with some of the other women. They could probably all do with some help, but Samantha Stevens especially.

Karen's heart felt heavy as she thought of Valerie Anderson's long, futile search for her daughter. Claudia had been gone all this time. Such a waste of life. The loss of a child was always devastating, but this would come as a particularly brutal blow to Valerie.

Chapter Thirty-Four

The next day, after the main briefing, Churchill signalled to Karen with a subtle nod. She followed him as he marched past the desks of her colleagues, climbed the stairs, and entered his office, shutting the door behind them. He rounded his desk and sat down in his high-backed chair, his face clouded with frustration. He gestured to the seat opposite, and Karen sat down.

'Explain to me again where we are,' Churchill said.

Karen began recounting the events of the past few days. She explained how Samantha Stevens had given a statement that Emmett had removed Claudia's body from the brothel after strangling her.

Churchill nodded slowly, motioning for Karen to continue.

'I've spoken to Valerie directly and we have assigned a family liaison officer to help her with any questions she has in the coming days,' she said.

'How is she handling it?' Churchill asked.

'As expected, she's utterly devastated,' Karen replied.

'And she knows about the DNA match?' Churchill asked, referring to the sample they'd taken from Valerie.

Karen nodded. 'Yes, she does.'

An unidentified female body, matching Claudia's description, had been found along a riverbank in Sleaford eighteen months ago. Cause of death was strangulation. Churchill had authorised an expedited process for the DNA tests, and the results had just come in that morning.

Karen paused, her gaze dropping to the floor for a brief moment before continuing, 'The results give a fifty per cent match to Valerie, so the lab has concluded that the body belongs to Claudia Anderson. She hadn't been in the water too long, so when she was found swabs were taken for testing. We're still waiting on lab results from them.'

'Why?' Churchill said. 'We budgeted for an expedited test.'

Karen shrugged. 'I guess these things take time.'

Churchill's brow furrowed and his fingers drummed on the desk. 'I really don't see why they take so much time. They put them in a machine and press a button, don't they?'

'Well, I think it's a bit more complicated than that,' Karen said.

Churchill's eyes narrowed and he checked his watch. 'Chase them up,' he said. 'We know Emmett was responsible, but if we can get his DNA from her body, then it ties up the case nicely.'

Karen nodded. She had been a detective long enough to have worked many murder cases, but every time it felt fresh.

She had gone in person to tell Valerie they had found her daughter's body, and the anguish in the woman's eyes, the tears that streamed down her face, would stay with Karen. The tragedy of it all still hit her hard each time. Each of the victims had had hopes and dreams that were cruelly snatched away.

As she left Churchill's office, Karen recalled the way Valerie's eyes had searched Karen's face as though she held an answer to her grief. Karen felt a lump rise in her throat, thinking of the lives Emmett Jenkins had ruined.

The men working with Chapman, whom Emmett had shot, would not have won awards for their moral integrity, but they had families too – people who loved them. Emmett had wrecked their lives without remorse.

Karen slowly descended the stairs and saw Farzana just ahead, a bunch of files in her arms, head bowed as if in deep thought.

Karen quickened her pace and called out, 'Any news from the lab yet on the results from the swabs?'

Farzana shook her head and rolled her eyes. 'No. I tried getting hold of Tim Farthing after the briefing, but you know what he's like . . .'

'Hard to pin down?' Karen suggested.

Farzana's grimace spoke volumes. 'Yes, I thought about trying one of the other techies or SOCOs, but . . .'

Karen caught her point immediately. 'Probably not a good move. It might just set him off. I'll go talk to him and see if I can urge him to hurry.'

The main tech lab was in the basement so there were no windows. It was a big room with white walls and bright panelled lighting overhead. Although a separate office existed, the lab technicians seldom left the lab. Today, staff were busily analysing evidence at their workstations. Computers and mobile devices hummed as they examined the data. The biological tests were handled off-site at a larger laboratory. Results were then ferried back here for further review before being delivered to the investigative team. On any other day, Harinder would have been among them, working his magic – a miracle worker with a knack for unravelling technical problems and clues.

In time, as Sophie recovered, Karen hoped that she'd see them both back here again.

Karen spied Tim at the far side of the lab. He glanced over and scowled, as if he'd known she was coming.

She called out to him, but his expression stayed dour. He didn't look pleased to see her, but then he never did.

Karen squared her shoulders, adopting her most pleasant expression. 'Hi, Tim, how are you?'

He gave a dramatic sigh. 'I suppose you want something. You're not just here to wish me happy birthday, are you?'

Karen's mouth dropped open. She hadn't known it was his birthday. 'Oh . . . uh, happy birthday,' she stammered.

'Thanks,' he said, still looking miserable. 'But you didn't come down here just to say that, did you?'

'No, that's not why I'm here,' Karen admitted.

She almost mentioned it was Mike's birthday the next day before deciding against it. Tim wasn't the type for small talk, especially with her.

Karen hadn't heard anything further from Lorraine about the surprise dinner for Mike's birthday. Karen wasn't sure why it needed to be a surprise if it was only four of them, but she'd let Lorraine sort it out. After their rocky initial meeting, Karen didn't want to make things worse by questioning her decisions. She'd go along with whatever Lorraine had planned and would keep the peace for Mike's sake.

Tim was looking at her expectantly.

'Churchill asked me to chase the DNA swabs on the Anderson case. He did budget for them to be expedited, so we hoped that—'

'It takes as long as it takes,' Tim said. 'I've told you before, Karen, it's a complicated procedure. They run multiple rounds of PCR to amplify the DNA. We don't just click our fingers and get a result.'

He shook his head at the glazed look on Karen's face. 'Never mind. I'll check the computer,' he said.

With a heavy sigh, Tim clicked on a file. 'Oh, looks like we've got a result. All we need is validation.'

'Can you open it up?' Karen said.

He sighed, as though she'd asked him to lend her a million pounds, but he opened the report anyway and quickly scanned it.

He was used to reading these sorts of documents and flew through them much faster than Karen. She only saw the reports once they were in their final format.

The screen was filled with incomprehensible lists of A, T, C and Gs, and words like 'polymorphisms' that she'd heard about but always forgot what they meant.

'Hmm,' he said after studying the document for a moment. 'There was DNA collected under her fingernails.'

Karen waited expectantly.

He turned to her with a satisfied expression. 'You've got what you wanted: the DNA under her nails matches Emmett Jenkins. Looks like she fought back when he strangled her and it left his skin cells beneath her nails.'

Karen nodded slowly, trying not to imagine the violent encounter and picture Claudia's final moments.

'Thanks, Tim,' she said. 'I know it's a big ask, but can you please validate the report for me now? I need to show it to Churchill.'

Tim released a weary sigh, but Karen thought he secretly enjoyed feeling needed.

The results of the test were the final piece required to close the case. They knew Emmett Jenkins was unequivocally guilty of Claudia's murder now – Samantha Stevens's first-hand account of his attack on Claudia, his DNA beneath her fingernails, and the recovery of her body were undeniable proof.

Valerie would now be able to say a proper goodbye and hold a funeral for her daughter. Karen wished things had been different, that they could have saved Claudia, but it was too late – all that lay ahead was to see justice done for the young woman.

◆ ◆ ◆

Later that day, Karen parked up beside the bridge in Sleaford. The sun had already begun its descent, casting a golden hue over the river.

She'd arranged to meet Valerie at the location where Claudia's body had been found eighteen months earlier.

Karen's gaze drifted to the far side of the bridge, and she spotted Valerie standing there, her back turned towards Karen, her fair hair pulled back from her face in a ponytail. She stood motionless with her hands tucked in the pockets of her navy puffy coat, the coat she had been wearing when she'd helped with their search for Emmett Jenkins.

Karen walked slowly towards Valerie and paused beside her. For a moment, they both stood in silence, looking out over the river and its murky depths. Finally, Karen spoke softly.

'Hi,' she said. 'How are you doing?'

It was a question, but she didn't expect an answer. Karen knew well enough that no words could explain the emotions Valerie was experiencing at that moment.

The woman wasn't crying, but her eyes were red and swollen, evidence that tears had been shed earlier, before Karen had arrived.

'I'm not quite sure how I'm feeling,' Valerie replied in a hollow voice. 'It's good to finally have an answer, even if it's not the answer I wanted.' She paused and seemed to drift away in thought before continuing. 'I think deep down I always knew though. No matter what I told myself or what I wanted to believe, I knew . . . I always knew it would end up like this. There was no way Claudia wouldn't have contacted me for eighteen months – that wasn't like her.'

Valerie stared down at the reeds beside the riverbank and let out a sigh. 'I'm officially unemployed now,' she said, her voice heavy with resignation. 'I've decided to move back to Yorkshire.'

'Is the workshop being shut down?'

'There's talk of someone else taking over,' Valerie said, 'but I'm not interested. I only came here to look for Claudia. I have friends back in Yorkshire who will help me. It won't be easy, but it will be easier than it is here.'

Karen nodded.

'Where was she found?' Valerie asked in a whisper.

Karen pointed out a spot just before the bridge.

The river was strong and swift, often catching things and pulling them along, but Claudia's body had become trapped against the stone wall of the bridge, her lifeless form stuck, until she was discovered by a dog walker.

Valerie stared at the spot in silence for some time before turning to Karen.

'I don't think I can get through this,' she said quietly, her voice trembling with emotion. 'It feels like I have a weight on my chest and it's stopping me from breathing properly.'

Karen stepped closer and placed a comforting hand on Valerie's shoulder. 'You should talk to someone,' she suggested softly. 'A professional who can help you work through it all. I can give you contact details.'

Valerie turned and tilted her head towards Karen as she answered. 'I don't see how talking will help. This is a physical feeling.' She pressed a hand to her chest.

'Talking doesn't change what has happened or take away the pain, but it does help when you're struggling to process it all.'

Valerie looked at Karen intently. 'It helped you?'

'Yes, when I lost my daughter and my husband,' Karen said. 'It felt like the whole world had paused and all the colour had drained away. Nothing was worth the effort anymore. I'd ask myself how something so cruel could happen, why life was so unfair.'

'Did talking about it help you accept it?' Valerie looked doubtful.

'No, I don't think I'll ever really accept it.' Karen was speaking quietly now, as though she didn't even want to hear her own words. 'The injustice, the cruelty of it all will never leave me. But I've accepted that it's okay to feel that way and that I can continue with life in spite of it. Life still isn't easy, but I'm here now.' She paused, looking down at the river before continuing. 'Some days are still hard, but now I know I can manage.'

Valerie nodded. 'I'm . . . I'm glad you stopped him. At least he won't be able to hurt anyone else. That brings me a little comfort.' Her voice caught on the last words and tears filled her eyes as she added, 'When you lose someone like this, how do you ever get through it? What helped you besides talking?'

A deep sadness filled Karen as she thought back on the agonising first few months following Josh and Tilly's deaths.

'It helped knowing those responsible for it were punished. But pain never goes away. You just learn to manage it better with time. It's a cliché, but time heals. One foot after the other. Take it day by day and week by week. You'll find eventually you will be able to get through it, even if the hurt never goes away.'

Valerie looked up at Karen and gave her a sad smile. 'Thank you for meeting me here today. I couldn't have done it on my own.'

Karen returned Valerie's gaze and swallowed the lump in her throat.

Emmett Jenkins's evil had devastated Valerie and the families of the other victims. Somehow they now had to figure out how to survive in the wake of what had happened.

They both leaned against the solid stone surface of the bridge and stared down at the glimmering ripples in the water beneath them. The crimes committed by Emmett Jenkins had reverberated outwards, creating ripples and shockwaves which had changed lives forever.

Valerie reached out and took Karen's hand. She was trembling. Karen gently squeezed Valerie's fingers, silently offering her support and understanding, wishing she could do more.

Chapter Thirty-Five

Sophie awoke with a jolt, blinking her eyes open. A white ceiling with fluorescent lights stared down at her, and her head felt like it was full of bricks. She blinked several times, trying to clear her vision. She had the sensation of being underwater. Her attempt to move her right arm was useless, as if it were chained to the bed. Panic surged through her veins.

Her tongue felt thick and dry in her mouth as she tried to speak. No sound came out, so she swallowed, trying to moisten her sore throat.

She shifted slightly and pain blazed through her shoulder and the base of her skull. She hissed in a breath, letting it out again in a slow exhale between gritted teeth. Then she remembered. She was in the hospital. Fear dug its claws into her as she remembered drifting in and out of terrifying nightmares. How long had she been here?

Sophie glanced around, her vision still blurry, but she could make out shapes in the vicinity. There were other beds around her, their occupants still and silent. Machines beeped and medical staff glided around with practised movements.

Darkness lingered at the edges of the room, waiting for an opportunity to pull her back to her nightmares.

Sophie wracked her brain, desperately trying to remember how she had ended up in this hospital, but her mind was a jumble of flashbacks and confusion.

She remembered setting off for her meeting with Valerie Anderson . . . but then everything was an unsettling blur.

A chill rushed through Sophie's body as she recalled what had happened when Valerie hadn't shown up. There was a man, his face twisted with rage and fury, and the unimaginable pain of being struck with something metal and heavy.

Then she pictured the man standing over her, his face contorted with anger as he raised his arm again.

A movement outside her field of vision caught her attention, making Sophie shrink back against the pillows. She shifted her gaze, struggling to make sense of the figure taking shape.

A woman sat beside Sophie's bed. She looked familiar. Sophie's mind raced as the woman smiled and reached out, her face kind. 'Hello, Sophie. How are you feeling?'

Sophie opened her mouth to answer, but no words came out. The woman's expression changed from kindness to concern.

'Sophie, it's Karen. The doctors have said that because you've been in a coma for a few days, it may take a while for your body to get used to being awake again.'

Karen. Sophie felt a wave of guilt. She'd let Karen down. An overwhelming sense of shame made Sophie want to disappear under the thin hospital sheet and never resurface again. She'd let them all down. The whole team. They must all think she was so stupid.

Karen placed her hand on Sophie's shoulder. 'It's okay, Sophie. You're in the hospital, and you're safe now.'

Sophie tried to nod, tears stinging her eyes.

When did she wake up? Today? Yesterday? Sophie felt as if she had been in the hospital for years.

Snippets of conversations came back to her. The doctors hadn't said much about her condition, but it had been clear from the grave looks on their faces that Sophie's condition was serious.

Harinder and her parents had been on the ward on the other occasions she'd woken up.

Her parents had appeared haggard and scared. Harinder had held her hand, looking equally worried but determined to stay positive for her sake.

But it wasn't easy to stay positive when she was hooked up to machines in the intensive care unit and couldn't move her right arm or even speak properly.

Her dreams were filled with terrifying flashbacks, always ending the same way, no matter how hard she tried to get away.

She shouldn't have gone to meet Valerie Anderson alone. She was a detective and should have known better. If she hadn't been so naive, this never would have happened.

Sophie tried to explain, to tell Karen how sorry she was, but the croaking sounds that left her mouth didn't resemble words.

'You don't have to talk,' Karen said. 'I just needed to come and see you. I'm so glad you're awake.'

Carefully, she took Sophie's hand in hers, avoiding the tubes attached to her skin.

'We tracked down the man who attacked you. You don't have to worry. He won't be hurting anyone ever again. I'll tell you all about it when you're feeling stronger.' She gently squeezed Sophie's hand. 'Everything is going to be okay.'

Sophie let Karen's comforting words wash over her as she felt the tug of sleep pulling her back into the darkness.

◆ ◆ ◆

Karen arrived at Quentin Chapman's hospital room. He had managed to wrangle himself a private side room off the main ward. Sitting outside was Ponytail, guarding the entrance. He gave Karen a curt nod and gestured for her to go ahead.

She felt a strange mix of dread and guilt as she stepped through the doorway. She wanted answers, and she felt obligated to check up on the man who'd saved her from a bullet.

She'd already spoken to a nurse who'd informed her Chapman was recovering and would soon be discharged, but Karen was still surprised by how well he looked.

He sat in a high-backed chair beside the bed, his salt-and-pepper hair impeccably styled, and his navy-blue pyjamas were a stark contrast to the standard hospital-issue garments. His left arm was in a sling, and he had a newspaper open on his lap, though he was leaning back with his eyes closed. He was pale but otherwise appeared to be in good health.

Karen took a deep breath, trying to push away the sudden wave of conflicted emotions that washed over her. Chapman had saved her life, but one good deed didn't make a good person.

She stepped forward, and as she did, his eyes opened and he met her gaze.

Karen swallowed; her throat was dry. She felt oddly emotional. Perhaps it hadn't been a good idea to come here directly after seeing Sophie.

She wanted to ask why he'd risked his life for hers, but the words wouldn't come.

The silence stretched out between them, heavy and awkward. Finally, Chapman spoke.

'What brings you here, Detective?' His voice was low and raspy, but there was an edge of amusement to it.

'I came to see how you were doing. The nurse I spoke to says you're recovering well.'

'Yes, I should be discharged tomorrow,' he replied, flinching as he moved in his seat to face her. He gestured towards a small chair in the corner of the room. 'Please, sit down.'

She pulled the chair closer to him and sat. 'Thank you.'

'It's just a chair.'

'No, I mean thank you for pushing me out of the way when Emmett was about to shoot me.'

He folded the newspaper absently. 'It was nothing.'

Karen frowned. It wasn't. She had no doubt that he had risked his life to save hers when Emmett Jenkins had pulled out a gun and aimed it at her. She wanted to know why Chapman had done it, why he had put himself in harm's way to protect her. But more than that, she wanted to know if he believed she now owed him for his act of bravery, or if he thought she was now one of his puppets. If he did, then he didn't know her very well.

'I appreciate what you did, but I'd like to know why,' Karen said. Her words came out clumsily, but she forced herself to continue. 'Why did you risk your life like that for me?'

Chapman was quiet for a moment, his gaze never leaving Karen. He seemed to be studying her, evaluating her. Finally, he spoke.

'What makes you think I did it for you?' His voice was low and had a dark edge that sent a chill down Karen's spine.

'Who else would you do it for?' Karen asked, bemused.

'I didn't do it for anyone,' Chapman said dryly. 'I acted on instinct. I saw someone in danger and acted before I could think. But if you want to believe that I did it for you, go ahead.' He shifted in his seat, and Karen noticed a muscle twitch in his jaw.

She studied him, trying to decipher the truth in his words. Was he really being honest? Or was this some kind of game he was playing, a way to manipulate her for his own agenda?

As for acting on instinct, she didn't believe that for a moment. Chapman was cold and calculating. He must have had an angle, and the only one Karen could think of was that he wanted another police officer under his thumb. But that didn't really add up.

Risking his life was too high a price to pay for getting another detective in his pocket. So why?

Maybe she was being too hard on him. Just maybe, there was a part of Chapman that felt compassion after all. That feeling could be what had spurred him to take such a drastic action. But could it really be that simple?

'Well, thank you anyway,' Karen said. 'But I feel the need to point out that this changes nothing. I'm still going to do my best to see that your criminal enterprises are dismantled and that you—'

Chapman chuckled, and his lips curled up in an amused grin. 'I think I would have preferred it if you stopped at the *thank you* part.'

'I can't be bought,' Karen warned, 'not with money or with . . .' She trailed off as Chapman looked away, his expression unreadable.

She waited, the silence stretching out between them, until finally he turned back to her.

'Why did you come here really, Karen?'

Karen took a deep breath before answering. 'I need to know why you did it.'

Chapman's gaze softened slightly, and he gave a small nod. 'I didn't want you to get shot,' he said simply. 'That's why I did it.'

Still, the word *why* swirled in her mind.

Karen knew there had to be more beneath the surface – there had to be a deeper reason why Chapman had risked his own neck for hers.

He continued. 'You were just doing your job. Emmett was my enemy, not yours. Why should you be a victim?'

Karen murmured her thanks again. Her gaze stayed steady on him, searching for answers she'd likely never discover.

She said goodbye and stepped away, still uncertain about Quentin Chapman. Was there some light inside him too? A spark of humanity beneath the darkness?

Chapter Thirty-Six

Karen reluctantly stepped out of the comforting warmth of the shower. She really didn't want to face dinner with Lorraine and James. But it was Mike's birthday, and Lorraine had been excitedly arranging the dinner as a surprise for her son.

She pulled on a simple black dress and reached for her lipstick, wishing she could spend the evening relaxing with Mike on the sofa instead.

Karen had just put her shoes on when her phone buzzed. She picked it up and read the message: *Meet us at the village hall. We're already here.*

Karen sighed, realising what Lorraine must have done. They wouldn't be going to the village hall for a dinner for four. Lorraine must have expanded the guest list considerably.

So much for her hopes of a quiet evening.

She grabbed her jacket and pulled it on, before making her way downstairs.

Mike sat at the kitchen table. He looked good. His tailored shirt suited his muscular frame, and his dark hair was brushed into a casual style, still damp from the shower. He was motionless, his face taut and brooding and focused on his phone.

When they'd first got together, Karen used to think that brooding intensity meant he was unhappy, but now she knew it was his default expression.

'Are you ready?' she asked.

'I've been ready for ages,' he said, looking up from his phone. 'You look stunning.'

'We've got to make a quick stop-off on the way to dinner.'

Mike eyed her suspiciously. 'What for?'

'I just need to pick something up from one of the neighbours,' Karen said, avoiding eye contact.

'Which neighbour?' he asked, standing up.

'Um, Sue,' Karen said, plucking the first name that came to mind.

'What do you need to pick up?' Mike raised a single dark eyebrow, folding his arms and looking at her suspiciously as she searched for her keys.

Karen gave an impatient sigh. What was with all the questions? Was he the detective in the relationship now?

'A book,' she said, picking the first random object she thought of.

'But we're walking. Why do you want to carry a book to the restaurant?' he asked, his lips twitching in barely concealed amusement. 'You wouldn't be hiding anything from me, would you?'

'Can you please just get your coat?' Karen said. 'We're going to be late.'

Mike grinned, eyes sparkling with mischief.

The village hall was only a short walk along the main road from Karen's house. There were lots of cars parked at the front.

'I'll wait out here, shall I?' Mike said with an impish grin.

He knew this had something to do with his birthday and was enjoying teasing her.

'No,' Karen replied, looping her arm through his and leading him into the building.

'SURPRISE!' a chorus of voices shouted as the room filled with colourful streamers, and party poppers flew around them.

Karen looked around the hall and saw it filled with people she didn't recognise. She plastered on a smile.

Mike grinned at the sight of the decorations, the presents, and all the guests.

He leaned in close to Karen, a glint in his eye. 'All this and I didn't have a clue.' He winked.

Karen opened her mouth to tell him she hadn't put this together, but his mother swooped in and embraced him before she could get a word out.

'Darling,' Lorraine said as she hugged him tightly. 'Happy birthday!'

The hall was filled with people chatting and mingling. In small groups, they came up to Mike to wish him a happy birthday.

In a brief respite from the well-wishers, Mike asked Karen, 'Did you organise all this?'

'No, your mum arranged everything,' she said, but he barely heard her, too busy greeting another guest with a warm smile.

Karen hadn't realised Mike knew this many people. He didn't have many relatives, so she assumed most of them were friends.

Tables were covered with party food – sausage rolls, cheese and pineapple on cocktail sticks, bowls of couscous and mixed salad. The kids were ignoring the healthier options and making a beeline for the cupcakes. Karen didn't blame them.

She felt Mike's warm hand grab hers. 'C'mon, I need to introduce you to some people.'

The evening passed in a blur, with Karen attempting and failing to remember dozens of names. But it was a good night. Everyone seemed happy to see Mike and celebrate his birthday.

'It's fantastic to see him so happy,' said a woman's voice.

Karen turned. They been introduced earlier in the evening, but she'd already forgotten the woman's name.

'Yes, it's great.'

'Isn't Lorraine wonderful for laying all this on?'

'Yes, it's lovely.' Karen managed a smile that felt forced.

'It's nice to see Mike happy after . . . well, you know.' The woman trailed off, her expression suddenly full of pity. 'Is he doing okay now?'

Karen gave a single nod. Mike had lost his son in a tragic accident, and in the aftermath he'd lost his way. He'd driven his car into a wall with every intention of ending it all.

That had all happened before he met Karen, but he still carried his loss with him, just as she did hers.

'Sorry for interrupting! I just need a quick word with Karen.' It was Lorraine.

Karen let Mike's mother lead her away to a quiet corner.

'I hope you're not angry,' she said.

Karen shook her head. 'No, why would I be angry?'

Lorraine gave Karen a knowing look. 'You thought I was organising a small dinner for Mike's birthday, not this,' she said, gesturing to the party.

Karen took in a deep breath. She hadn't expected Lorraine to throw such a big bash, but it was clear she had done it out of love for Mike. Perhaps they'd got off on the wrong foot in their first encounter, and maybe Lorraine just wanted to make sure her son celebrated his birthday in style after all he'd been through.

'Mike is having a wonderful time, and that's all that matters.'

'I just wanted to do something special for him. But the word got out, and I ended up inviting more people than I'd planned. I didn't want to bother you with the details.'

Karen said, 'I'm sorry if I gave the impression I was too busy to get involved.'

'Let's start over? I'm sorry we got off to a bad start,' Lorraine said, and she surprised Karen by pulling her in for a hug. 'Mike said you found me prickly—'

'Oh, no—' Karen started to say, feeling awkward and mentally cursing Mike.

'He was right. I wasn't very welcoming, and I regret that.' Lorraine gave a rueful smile. 'Mike told me about your family – your parents and sister – and I suppose I thought you might look down on us for not having such a normal family.'

Karen frowned. 'I would never—'

'Oh, I know that now. I was just being silly. Forgive me?'

Feeling a bit blindsided, Karen said, 'Of course.'

'I want us to get on. You're clearly very important to Mike, and I just want him to be happy.'

'Me too,' Karen said, honestly.

Lorraine gave her a warm smile. 'Good. Then we can both work together to make sure that happens.'

Karen nodded, feeling relieved that the tension between her and Lorraine had been diffused.

Lorraine looped her arm through Karen's and began to present her to some of the guests. She introduced one couple as old neighbours they'd lived next door to twenty years ago. Lorraine really had invited everybody, Karen thought.

Mike was happily chatting to some of his friends from the dog training centre, laughing and joking.

Karen watched him with a smile, glad that Lorraine had organised this surprise for him and thankful that, despite their rocky start, she and Lorraine had found some common ground.

◆ ◆ ◆

The small, cosy pub was abuzz with chatter. In the back corner, Karen, Morgan, Rick and Arnie were huddled around a table, their words barely audible over the clinking of glasses and laughter of other patrons. They were deep in conversation, keeping their voices low as they discussed the Emmett Jenkins investigation.

Untangling the web of evidence had been an exhausting task, but they'd assisted the Met and had eventually succeeded in tying up the loose ends necessary to close the case. Emmett Jenkins would never go to court, but his death hadn't lessened the paperwork required.

It had been a long, tiring process, and tonight they were marking the end of it with a drink. Churchill had gathered them together to congratulate the team on a job well done. He didn't do that often, so it was something to celebrate.

Just as the conversation was beginning to lull, a draft of cold air whipped in as the door opened. Harinder stepped into the bar, bundled up in a heavy coat and wool scarf.

'Over here,' Karen called out, gesturing for him to join their table.

Rick slid from his seat and veered towards the bar. 'Usual, Harry?' he asked Harinder, who answered with a nod.

Harinder sat down, unbuttoning his coat, and allowing himself to relax. 'I've just come from visiting Sophie.'

The mood at the table shifted, and everyone waited in anticipation for him to continue.

'She's doing much better,' Harinder said. 'The doctor indicated that the neural pathways between her arm and her brain were disrupted, so her body needs to build new connections. That's going to take some time. But she's already speaking again, which is incredible.' His expression softened into a crooked grin. 'I feel like I've won the lottery.'

Karen reached out and placed a hand on his shoulder. 'I'm so glad for you both.'

'Brilliant news,' Rick said, handing Harinder his pint and then proposing a toast to Sophie's recovery.

They raised their glasses to their missing colleague and friend.

Then Morgan, Rick and Arnie began noisily debating the merits of lager versus bitter – a familiar conversation – so Karen took the opportunity to speak to Harinder.

'I'm sorry for all the questions I had to ask you during the investigation,' she apologised. 'I know they must have made things more difficult.'

Harinder waved away her words. 'No, I should have trusted you and told you everything right from the start,' he said. 'I wasn't thinking straight. I panicked.'

'I get it,' Karen said reassuringly. 'It's a difficult situation to be in.'

Harinder nodded and then smiled at her, his eyes warm and full of gratitude. 'DI Goodridge made it clear you advocated for me,' he said softly. 'And I told Sophie that.'

Karen felt guilt creep in. There had been times when she had wavered between the belief that there was no way that Harinder could have hurt Sophie and her suspicions about his involvement.

'I can't deny that I had concerns, but I wanted to prove your innocence.'

'I understand. I didn't at the time. It hurt that you didn't believe in me. I see now why it was important to examine every lead and look at every angle. And it can't have made it any easier for you to trust me when you found out Brian Sully was the neighbour I'd had an argument with just before Sophie's assault.'

'Is everything okay with you and Geoff now?'

Harinder sighed. 'It's still a bit awkward. He apologised, but . . .'

'I don't think it was personal. She's his little girl. His head must have been all over the place, and then when you were questioned—'

Harinder cut in. 'I know. I don't blame him really. It's just hard to go back to how things were knowing that he suspected me of doing something so evil. But we'll get there. We'll put it behind us, for Sophie's sake.' He smiled as Rick handed him a packet of crisps. 'Cheers, mate.' He turned back to Karen. 'I'm glad you got the scum who attacked her.' He took a sip of his pint then said, 'I hear you came close to getting shot.'

'Not an experience I want to repeat in a hurry,' Karen said.

Just then, the door opened and Mike walked in, his cheeks flushed from the cold and his dark hair dishevelled as usual. Karen smiled as he made his way over to her.

'Hey,' he said, leaning down, his lips brushing Karen's cheek, before greeting the rest of the group.

Rick clapped Mike on the back and greeted him enthusiastically. 'Any more news on peagate?' he joked, referring to Karen's mishap when she'd sent peas flying all over the floor during her first dinner with Mike's mum and stepdad.

Karen covered her face and groaned.

Mike grinned and teased, 'Yeah, about that . . . Mum did mention she found a pea under the sofa yesterday.'

'She didn't!' Karen said, her face flushing with embarrassment.

'No, I'm just kidding.'

Karen nudged him in the ribs.

Harinder chuckled. 'I hear your birthday party went well?'

Mike's face lit up. 'It did. And this wily creature kept it a complete surprise.' He nodded at Karen. 'I didn't have a clue. Not even one tiny inkling. Not so much as a—'

Karen narrowed her eyes and interrupted him. 'If you hadn't been so nosy about why I was picking up a book from the village hall, it *would* have been a surprise.'

Laughing, Mike put his arm around her shoulders. 'You did well. Seriously, Mum can be . . . a lot at times, and it means the world to me that you're getting along with her so well. Now,' he said, clapping his hands together, 'who needs a drink?'

When Mike returned with the drinks, Arnie piped up. 'Did my party invite get lost in the post then?'

'Well . . .' Mike glanced at Karen. 'I'm not sure exactly—'

'I'm only pulling your leg,' Arnie said with a grin. 'I'm glad things are going well between you two. She deserves a bit of luck.' He gave Karen an affectionate pat on the arm before turning his gaze back to Mike. 'You look after her.'

Karen rolled her eyes good-naturedly. 'You're not my dad, Arnie!' she protested, feeling oddly touched by his protectiveness.

Arnie laughed and patted her arm again before taking a sip of his pint. 'Feels like I am sometimes,' he muttered under his breath, 'surrounded by young people . . . I'm outnumbered – even Morgan here is ten years younger than me!' He gestured towards Morgan, who was lounging back in his seat and sipping his own beer.

Morgan gave Arnie a lazy smile and raised his glass in acknowledgement. 'Here's to the old men of the group.'

'With age comes experience,' Arnie replied, lifting his own glass to chink against Morgan's.

Suddenly, Rick spoke up. 'Come to think of it, Arnie, you might be the oldest detective at the station.'

Karen turned towards Arnie with a teasing smile. 'Well, well. I think Rick's right.'

The group dissolved into laughter at Arnie's expression.

'So much for respecting your elders.' He let out a fake huff of indignation and tossed a peanut at Rick, who was quick enough to snatch it out of the air.

The laughter subsided, but the atmosphere remained light and warm. Karen smiled as she watched her co-workers, grateful for their company.

She felt a glow of contentment as she watched them interact – even if most of the time they bantered and teased each other, it was obvious that they were all close friends in their own way.

Karen smiled to herself before taking another sip from her wine glass.

She longed for Sophie to be here with them. The team didn't feel complete without her. But in time, Sophie would recover, and that was something they could have only dreamed of a few days ago.

Karen sighed happily and looked around at her team – a group that was now like family to her. She met Mike's gaze and leaned into his side. Life could be cruel at times, but it could also be pretty wonderful too.

ACKNOWLEDGEMENTS

The fabulous editors who have worked on the Karen Hart series deserve a massive thank you. It's been a pleasure to work with such a talented group of people at Amazon Publishing.

Special thanks must also go to the talented Russel D. McLean for his developmental editing and invaluable attention to detail over the series.

To my family, I'm so lucky to have you – thank you for everything. And as always, special thanks to Chris for his support and general all-round awesomeness.

And finally, most importantly, thank you to the readers who have read and recommended my books. Your kind words and encouragement mean the world to me.

ABOUT THE AUTHOR

 Born in Kent, D. S. Butler grew up as an avid reader with a love for crime fiction and mysteries. She has worked as a scientific officer in a hospital pathology laboratory and as a research scientist. After obtaining a PhD in biochemistry, she worked at the University of Oxford for four years before moving to the Middle East. While living in Bahrain, she wrote her first novel and hasn't stopped writing since. She now lives in Lincolnshire with her husband.

Follow the Author on Amazon

If you enjoyed this book, follow D. S. Butler on Amazon to be notified when the author releases a new book!
To do this, please follow these instructions:

Desktop:

1) Search for the author's name on Amazon or in the Amazon App.
2) Click on the author's name to arrive on their Amazon page.
3) Click the 'Follow' button.

Mobile and Tablet:

1) Search for the author's name on Amazon or in the Amazon App.
2) Click on one of the author's books.
3) Click on the author's name to arrive on their Amazon page.
4) Click the 'Follow' button.

Kindle eReader and Kindle App:

If you enjoyed this book on a Kindle eReader or in the Kindle App, you will find the author 'Follow' button after the last page.